THE WILD SIDE

BAEN BOOKS by MARK L. VAN NAME

THE JON & LOBO NOVELS

One Jump Ahead

Slanted Jack

Overthrowing Heaven

Children No More

Jump Gate Twist (omnibus of
One Jump Ahead & *Slanted Jack*)

No Going Back (forthcoming)

Anthology

Transhuman (edited w/ T. K. F. Weisskopf)

THE WILD SIDE

EDITED BY
MARK L. VAN NAME

A Baen Books Original

Baen Publishing Enterprises
P.O. Box 1403
Riverdale, NY 10471
www.baen.com

ISBN: 978-1-4391-3456-6

Cover art by Dan Dos Santos

First printing, August 2011

Distributed by Simon & Schuster
1230 Avenue of the Americas
New York, NY 10020

Library of Congress Cataloging-in-Publication Data
      The wild side / edited by Mark L. Van Name.
        p. cm.
   ISBN 978-1-4391-3456-6 (trade pbk.)
   1. Fantasy fiction, American. 2. Noir fiction, American. I. Van Name, Mark L.
   PS648.F3W55 2011
   813'.087308--dc23
                            2011016243

10 9 8 7 6 5 4 3 2 1

Pages by Joy Freeman (www.pagesbyjoy.com)
Printed in the United States of America

For Toni Weisskopf,
Publisher, Editor, and most importantly, friend

CONTENTS

THE WILD SIDE

INTRODUCTION: TAKE A WALK ON THE WILD SIDE

MARK L. VAN NAME

When Lou Reed exhorted us to do just that in his 1972 song, he was singing about a very particular urban landscape—New York City—teeming with many different types of people. Urban fantasy writers have for some time explored a far broader range of cityscapes—and inhabitants. When I invited the authors whose tales you're about to read, I told them only that we were looking for stories that mixed urban fantasy and an erotic edge. The way each combined the ingredients was up to her.

The resulting stories cover a wide range indeed. Vampires, shape shifters, witches, demons, fallen angels, and more. Toronto, Las Vegas, San Francisco, London, New England, and other locales. Positively chaste to a tad raunchy. What they share, though, is more important than their differences: all are good stories that will take you into another world.

As a reader, I'm always curious what writers have to say about their works, so I asked these authors to provide afterwords. I think you'll find them interesting.

Enjoy.

SONGS SUNG RED

TANYA HUFF

In a few short weeks, Millennium Ten, the latest club to spring up on Queen West's transitional block between money and attitude, had become the place to be on a Friday night. It didn't seem to matter that the bouncer guarding the entrance was an arbitrary ass, that the drinks were expensive, that the dance floor was too small; people still waited for hours in line, determined to get in.

Vicki didn't like waiting.

As she made her way up the line, she let the Hunger rise. Not enough to give anything away, but enough that the people she passed knew. No one protested when the bouncer's gaze skittered off her face and he stepped aside.

The stairs down to the lower level were lit with strips of neon, mounted low on the walls. Descending patrons could see their feet clearly while their features were already wrapped in a play of light and shadow that made everyone, if not more beautiful, more mysterious.

Vicki carried mystery with her.

A cluster of young women in brightly colored, nearly there dresses—high on thighs and low over breasts—shuffled aside on spike heels when she passed, instinctively giving way before the superior predator.

Making her way slowly around the room, Vicki ignored the crowd at the bar, her eyes locked on the moving bodies that filled the dance floor. It wasn't easy, not with the combined scents of heated flesh and arousal, but she kept the Hunger damped down far enough it attracted only positive attention. Dangerous but not deadly.

No one likely to approach her would believe the danger was real.

"You here alone?"

She'd known he was there before he'd spoken. Felt his eyes on her. Felt him move up behind her, close enough she could feel his clothing brush against her shoulder blades. He'd tipped his head forward to ask the question, warm breath lapping against her ear, his voice low, as intimate as possible given the ambient noise. He was tall, he had to be to pull off that maneuver when she was in heels, and he smelled like clean sweat and fabric softener.

Stepping back just a little, just enough for her ass to accidentally brush against him, she turned and smiled. "I am."

He was in his mid-twenties, seven or eight years younger than she'd been when she changed. His eyes were a medium blue flecked with gold. His hair was the same dark blond as hers, short enough to be military, but his beard, even though it was barely more than stubble, suggested otherwise. He wore a dark blue button-down with the sleeves rolled up over muscular forearms, black jeans, black boots. Fully aware she was checking him out, his eyes crinkled at the corners when he smiled and his smile said he thought he controlled their interaction.

"Do you want to dance?" He nodded toward the dance floor as if reassuring her that he actually meant dance—although given the vertical foreplay happening out there, Vicki wasn't sure why he thought drawing her attention to it would be reassuring.

"Love to."

There were protocols for this type of hunt. As easy as it would be to lead this young man out into the alley behind the club and take what she wanted, part of the fun was allowing him to believe he was leading her.

That way, everyone was happy. And besides, no one wanted fast food every time they ate out.

The press of bodies kept them close. He kept his eyes on her face as they danced. He was good, Vicki gave him that—one Hunter to another. She had no idea what song was playing; as his heart began to beat in sync with the throbbing bass from the surrounding speakers, she danced to the pulsing of his blood. The thin fabric of his shirt began to stick to damp skin, outlining muscle, accentuating movement. As she breathed in his desire, a little more of the Hunger slipped free.

Outside, in the real world, people would have instinctively moved away. Down here, in the fantasy, they moved closer, flirting with fear, believing the same anonymity that allowed Vicki to Hunt would hide them. Like lambs to the slaughter.

Clubs like this were practically designed to become bloodbaths.

Vicki hurriedly damped it down at the look of terror on her partner's face and, rather than make her move at the end of the song, kept them dancing until he regained his confidence. It didn't take long. When she slid her leg between his, rubbing against the hard muscle of his thigh, showing him what she wanted, he closed his hands on her hips, fingers hot and strong, directing her movement.

She let him think so.

At the end of the song, the music stopped. Before a protest could rise from the dance floor, the DJ leaned into his microphone and said, "And now the voice you've all been waiting for!"

A single spotlight illuminated a tiny blonde woman standing alone on the small stage at the narrow end of club.

Vicki had no interest in even high-end karaoke, so she tucked herself up close to the young man's body, tilted her face up—barely resisting the urge to lick the salt off the tanned column of his throat—and opened her mouth to suggest they take their dance elsewhere.

And the tiny woman began to sing.

Vicki closed her mouth again.

Soaring melodies and raw emotion held the audience in thrall without the need for words. Looking around the dance floor, Vicki could see smiles and tears and want and near worship. Strong arms wrapped around her from behind. His cheek resting against the side of her head, their bodies in contact from shoulder to floor, Vicki could feel the fine tremors running under her young man's skin. He rocked his hips gently forward, in time to the music, and she knew the way no one else in the room could that neither the motion nor his arousal had anything to do with her.

That wasn't right.

At this stage in the game, that wasn't possible.

As the last note soared through blood and bone, blue-green eyes met hers for an instant.

Then the spotlight went out.

Before mortal eyes had time to adjust, Vicki had slipped through the door marked STAFF ONLY and was moving down the corridor behind the stage. Under normal circumstances, she'd have lingered long enough to tell the young man to forget he'd ever seen her but these were not normal circumstances and she very much doubted that, while he was still in thrall to the song, she needed to bother.

Light spilled into the far end of the hall through an open door. As she walked at a mortal pace toward it, her heels announcing her presence against the worn, tile floor, Vicki could hear a single heartbeat and smell...

Seawater?

The dressing room was functional rather than opulent—cinder block walls, a rack for clothes, a dressing table.

The young woman sitting in the captain's chair, combing her hair, looked better than she had any right to, given the industrial lighting. Her song had commanded all available attention while she was on stage, but here the silence paid her beauty its due. She sat facing the door, her back to the mirror. Her feet were bare. The hem of her floor length dress was...

Wet.

There was a drain in the floor, not really surprising in a basement room that had likely gone through a hundred renovations over the years, but the tiles looked dry.

As Vicki closed the door, the young woman looked up and smiled, familiar blue-green eyes crinkling slightly at the corners. "I know you," she said softly. The comb slid through the long fall of her hair. "Vampire. Nightwalker."

"I prefer Vicki, if it's all the same to you."

"Vicki?"

She frowned and Vicki had to fight the urge to run her thumb over the delicate arch of her brows. Interesting. Probably a leftover from the dance floor; she'd never been physically interested in women.

On the other hand, as Henry was fond of saying, blood had no gender.

"Victoria." Her voice slid over the syllables like she was tasting them, making them into a song. Vicki could see the tip of her tongue moving behind the parted barrier of her lips. "No, Vicki suits you better. Direct. To the point." The comb slid through her hair again. "You may call me Lorelei, if you wish."

"What are you?"

The question surprised a laugh out of her. "You're young to the night. The day is not far behind you."

"I know what I am." Vicki allowed a little more of the Hunger to show, let it ride the throb of the bass beat from the club up to the surface. Allowed it to imply she was not going to ask again.

"What am I..." Lorelei tilted her head and watched the comb stroke through her hair, the movement slow, almost languid. The comb didn't appear to be anything special; plain tortoiseshell plastic, wide teeth, and from the wear, she'd obviously had it a long time. "I am vaguely appalled by modern education. I am a stranger on these shores. I am a woman wronged." When she lifted her head, her eyes were sad and she met Vicki's gaze as though she had nothing to fear. "Tell me, has your heart always been true?"

"I don't..."

"Know what I'm talking about? Yes, you do."

Vicki couldn't remember when the other woman had started to sing, thought maybe she'd been singing throughout their conversation, although that would be...

"I give you the freedom to be yourself, Vampire."

"Looks like someone really hated these guys."

Moving carefully through the destruction, Detective Sergeant Mike Celluci glanced over at his partner and muttered a terse, "You think?" The head office of Droege Shipping had been literally ripped apart. Desks and filing cabinets had been thrown through walls and windows, doors had been ripped from their hinges, and computers had been smashed. Even the light fixtures had been ripped from the ceiling and if there was an unbroken piece of glass anywhere on the 26th floor—excluding the external windows—Mike hadn't seen it.

The management offices along the west wall had received the same attention the central cubicles had. Rank had no privileges.

He nodded toward the steel mount that had held one of the destroyed cameras and then to Detective Dave Graham, his partner. "Dave, see if they got anything."

"On it."

The two security guards had been found by the employees' lunchroom. Before it had been destroyed, the lunchroom had probably been a pleasant enough place—pale brown walls, a fridge, toaster oven, microwave, kettle and two coffee makers. There'd been—Mike paused to count the pieces—six round tables, each with half a dozen comfortable chairs.

EMTs surrounded the survivor. Male, early twenties, black, six one or two, packing impressive muscle under the ruin of his uniform. Whoever had taken him down wouldn't have had an easy time of it. He was already up on the gurney, strapped in with an IV working but his eyes were open so Mike moved to him first, hoping to get some kind of a statement before they moved him out.

He shifted his coat far enough to expose his badge. "Can you tell me what happened?"

The injured man's eyes opened a little wider, far enough for Mike to see his pupils were dilated. He rolled his head over, exposing what looked like bite marks on the side of his throat, and sighed. "So easy to fall into the darkness." Long fingers clutched at Mike's wrist. "You know?"

"Duncan Riley. Twenty-four. And you're not going to get anything coherent out of him." The EMT waited as Mike gently extricated himself from Duncan Riley's grip. "He's been babbling off and on about the seductive darkness since we got here."

He seemed to be off at the moment, staring at the ceiling, smiling at nothing. "Seductive?" Mike asked.

The EMT sighed. "That's what he says." She stepped away as one of her team checked the straps. "And the evidence points to it being literally seductive, if you catch my meaning."

Mike blinked. "He was..."

"He definitely had sex with a woman at some time after his uniform was ripped off him." She shrugged. "Professional opinion from eyeballing the equipment."

Mentally, Duncan Riley was obviously not one hundred percent. "Physical condition?"

"All things considered, not too bad. His blood pressure's way down and, given the way he reacts to touch, I'm guessing there's going to be some bruising coming up along both arms." Her tone was frankly appreciative of those arms.

"And the injury?"

"The injury? On his throat? No, it looks bad but there's no bleeding so it's got to be a couple of days old. Looks like he got into a fight with a big dog or something, doesn't it?"

It didn't actually. Mike had seen dog bites and this... wasn't.

Mike had also seen enough to know there were other things it could be.

He watched as they rolled him away.

So easy to fall into the darkness. You know?

Yeah. He did.

The other guard—Chris Adams, male, white, mid-forties—was dead.

"Not a mark on him." The coroner stood and dusted off his knees as his people moved in with the body bag. "At least not one that'd kill him. If I had to make an educated guess, I'd say heart attack. He just wasn't up to what he walked in on."

Had he walked in on Riley and the darkness?

"Why didn't he push the panic button?" Mike wondered aloud. "Call in the police?"

Dave snorted, moving into place at Mike's side. "Who calls the police because their partner's getting some?"

"Point," Mike admitted.

"Not that one woman did all this," Dave continued. "And whoever did do it, they took out the security cameras first. They all show the same thing, a blur then nothing." Dave pointed toward the camera nearest the door. "That one first. Then that one. Then this one here. This kind of total destruction looks like crazy people did it but no, they were thinking."

"A blur?"

"Yeah. Like..." Dave grinned. "Like the Flash. Like evil Flash on a rampage."

"You need to cut back on your caffeine."

"You got a better idea?"

Mike glanced around at the ruin of Droege Shipping, then down at the body bag and sighed. "No."

Over the last few years, he'd become a very good liar.

One moment she was dead to the world, the next Vicki was awake. She drew in a deep breath redolent with sex and blood and remembered.

The freedom of not holding back.

Of strength and speed and letting the Hunter run...

The sound of blood surging below the surface. The taste of salt licked from firm flesh. The feel of terror turning to desire.

She remembered seeing the security guard come through the door...

He hadn't seen her yet; she wore the darkness like a cloak and she moved too fast for him to find, easily eluding the searching flashlight beam. Stepping out into the room, he tripped over a piece of the wreckage and swore, his voice a low rumble that rubbed against her like crushed velvet. As he reached for his radio, Vicki slid between him and escape, lightly running her fingers over the muscles of his broad back.

She ducked, his swinging fist passing over her head, and when they were face to face, she smiled, caught his gaze with hers, and had the darkness hold it.

His heartbeat quickened. His pulse throbbed at wrist and throat and temple and at the meeting of his thighs. She didn't want terror, although terror had a flavor uniquely its own and it would take little effort to push his response toward it. She wanted the less primal, more personal response to her presence. She wanted to finish what she'd started in the club.

His name would make it faster to evoke a specific response but she didn't want to know.

She wanted the heat and anonymity she'd left behind.

He was taller than the first young man. Built. With beautiful dark skin and eyes. And the seams of his cheap uniform parted so easily.

She pressed her face against the warm planes of his chest and breathed deeply. Taunting herself with his scent. Keeping the Hunger reigned in until she got everything else she wanted. When she looked up, he wrapped a hand around her cheek, his skin warm against hers. She caught his gaze again, her eyes silvered, and she let her desire draw up his.

"Say yes."

He swallowed. She touched his throat, following the movement, then licked the sweat from the tips of her fingers. He exhaled, shakily, his breath smelling of mint and coffee.

"Say yes."

"Yes."

She slipped a hand behind his head as she took him to the floor, careful of her strength, careful not to damage him. His belt buckle jammed so she ripped the leather apart and threw it hard enough to sink it into the drywall.

When he bucked up under her, his rhythm gone, his fingers dimpling the flesh of her hips, she let the Hunger go. Curved her body over him, hands gripping his arms, and sank her teeth into his throat. Hot blood gushed into her mouth as he slammed up into her one final time. She drank without caring, drank her fill, drank until . . .

"What the hell is going on here?"

It was the Hunter who twisted in place to face him, lips drawn back off bloody teeth.

The second guard gasped, staggered, and fell, right hand clutching his left arm.

Vicki felt her hands curl into fists. "Son of a fucking bitch."

Rage sizzled under her skin. Rage at the singer who'd used her. Rage at herself for being used. The wooden end of the packing crate splintered against the cinder block wall as she shoved it aside. Vicki had never been the icy cold anger type. Her anger burned and she only barely managed to keep it under control as she slid through the false wall and into Mike's crawlspace.

Sunset came late enough this time of the year that he was home. Above her. In the kitchen.

She used his heartbeat—slow and steady, more familiar to her than her own—to find calm. Enough calm, at least, to allow her to get a handle on her emotions. By the time she'd showered in the basement bathroom and shrugged into the robe hanging on the back of the door, she'd managed to use the same techniques that hid the Hunter to bury the events of the night before. Bury them deeply enough that even Detective Sergeant Mike Celluci wouldn't be able to find them.

Mike worked violent crimes; if this wasn't his case, he'd have heard about it.

He'd know where the evidence pointed and at what.

Not who.

And Vicki intended to keep it that way.

He could know what vampires were capable of, he just couldn't believe it of her.

Her clothing was in the master bedroom closet with his—
because that's what normal couples did and they fought to keep
the line as close to normal as possible—but she could avoid the
kitchen on her way through and delay facing him until she was
dressed and ready.

To lie.

Hide the rage at being used. Hide the other emotions roiling
about below that.

Show time.

"Any chance there's another vampire in town?"

Vicki stopped and stared across the kitchen at Mike who
watched her over the edge of his laptop, his expression completely
police neutral. The question was a little more direct than she'd
been expecting but infinitely preferable to what were you doing
between midnight and four A.M. "Say what?"

"The offices of Droege Shipping were destroyed last night..."

"Destroyed as in blown up?"

He turned the computer around.

Vicki moved closer, frowned down at the pictures, and remembered strength and speed unchecked. "Messy. Explosives aren't
out of the question. Anyone hurt?" The logical question to ask.
Cop question.

"One security guard dead. One"—Mike reached around and
changed the screen—"used."

She remembered the heat of his flesh under her mouth. Remembered the cry he'd given, caught somewhere between pain and
pleasure. She hadn't been careful. If not for the coagulant in her
saliva, he'd have bled out when she pulled away.

"Vicki?"

She forced her lips down off her teeth and made sure she had
her anger under control before she looked up. "I can see why
you asked."

"And?"

"I'll look into it."

He had a small scar on his inner thigh where she'd gotten a
bit enthusiastic and a puckered ridge across one shoulder where
she'd shot him, accidentally, in another life. He met her gaze, not
fearlessly because Mike Celluci was no fool, but in the full and
certain knowledge that he was in no personal danger. "A man
died, Vicki, I'll be looking into it too. You share what you find."

Oh, she knew what she was going to find and she knew where to find it.

Mike sighed as the edge of the table cracked under her grip. He lifted his arm, then let it fall back, clearly reconsidering reaching out for her. "Vicki?"

"When I know something..." He wouldn't believe a smile so she didn't try one. "...you'll know something."

Mike sat at the kitchen table listening to Vicki's car pull out of the driveway, his hands curled into fists. She'd always been a terrible liar. She was better now than she used to be, but then her condition gave her plenty of opportunity to practice.

Sometimes she forgot that while he couldn't hear blood moving under the delicate skin of her wrist, he wasn't deaf. He'd heard the crash when she opened the packing case. Heard the way she moved as she showered and dressed. She'd been furious from the moment the sunset had wakened her. Furious and trying to hide it from him.

Why?

She'd have told him if she'd known there was another vampire hunting in her territory.

What else could have gotten her so angry?

Vicki could have... was capable of...

He forced his hands flat on the kitchen table.

...was physically capable of doing the damage, all the damage, Droege Shipping and its employees had suffered last night.

Millennium Ten opened at nine. At eight-forty, Vicki ripped the lock off the back door, snarled, "Forget you saw me," at the young man stacking cases of empties at the bottom of the stairs in the back hall, and made her way down the corridor to Lorelei's dressing room. She could hear a familiar heartbeat, smell the sea, and had reached nearly full speed when she charged through the open door.

Only to be stopped by a single note that hung in the air like an invisible wall.

"Why so angry, Nightwalker? Didn't you enjoy yourself?" Lorelei sat in the chair combing her hair. Same position she'd been sitting in the night before. Same comb. Same languid movements. The cuffs of her jeans were wet, the denim dark against the pale skin of her feet.

Vicki threw herself against the barrier. The seawater smell was stronger up against it. "A man died!"

"And you're surprised?" Her brows rose. "Oh, don't tell me; you're one of those good vampires. Tortured. Tormented. Misunderstood. Sparkly. You'd have given that young man in the club last night a choice."

"He'd made his choice," Vicki growled, her eyes silvering.

"Did he know what he was choosing?" She laughed, unaffected by the Hunger as Vicki struggled to get closer. "You killed because that's what you are. All I sent you to do was destroy the office."

"Of Droege Shipping."

"Yes."

"What's your connection to a shipping company?"

"It's a long story."

"I've got time."

She paused the constant motion of the comb. "I suppose you do. Well, all right then. A long, long time ago . . ."

"How long?" Vicki demanded. She knew she should just let the woman talk but anger made it hard to keep silent.

Lorelei met Vicki's gaze and Vicki found herself sinking into blue-green depths. Deeper. Deeper. This sea was confined but no less deadly for all of that. Anyone else would have drowned, but Vicki had the Hunger to pull her back to the surface.

"That long?"

"That long." Lorelei's grip tightened on the comb, her knuckles white. "Year after year after interminable year." She drew in a deep breath and let it out slowly. "I had a lover once. He betrayed me. Heartbroken, I gave myself to the river and the river changed me, tied me to it with the curse of lost love. Still grieving, I sang."

Vicki rolled her eyes. "Oh yeah, singing. Very proactive. You should've kicked his ass."

Lorelei blinked, frowned, and said, "Times change."

"Assholes are eternal."

She blinked again, then nodded. "True. The sailors who heard my song tried to get to me but the river protected me and took their ships. Took their lives."

"I know this story . . ."

"I can stop if you're bored."

The barrier between them continued to hold against her assault. "Go on."

"If you're sure." When Vicki growled, Lorelei nodded and continued. "One day, a handsome young man named Fredrick Droege braved the river for my song, for me. He told me he loved me. Why wouldn't I believe him? He'd risked drowning, risked death to hold me. He owned a shipping company and he convinced me to sing only for him."

"To sink the ships of his competition."

"So you have heard this story."

"Not that unusual," Vicki snorted. She'd have been a lot more sympathetic had she not been used the night before, had Chris Adams not died. "Let me guess. Fredrick Droege lied about loving you."

"He did. And when I tried to leave him, the curse of love betrayed, that had bound me to the river, bound me as firmly to him. When he died, I became just another asset of the company, controlled by his son and then his grandson and now his great-grandson, Albert Droege. I have given them power and power has corrupted them."

"Yadda yadda. Same old. But if there's no company there's nothing for the curse to tie you to. That's why you had me destroy the offices."

"But it wasn't enough." A graceful gesture indicated both the dressing room and the club beyond. "They give me this, an audience for the songs I choose to sing to keep me happy."

"Bird in a gilded cage."

"It's concrete."

"It's a metaphor."

"Fair enough. The point is, I'm still not free. I need you to deal with the people who run the company. Begin with Albert Droege, work your way through the board of directors, and finish in the mail room if that's what it takes."

"Deal with?" Vicki snorted and folded her arms. "Nice euphemism. I don't care how corrupt they are, you can't make me kill for you."

"Actually, I can." She drew the comb through her hair, her smile cruel. "Who was he, Nightwalker? Who did you betray?"

Vicki watched in amazement as Henry exploded out into the light, face and hair a pale blur above the moving shadow of his body. The gunman on the nearest rack got a shot off just as she knocked him into the air. Henry's howl of pain drowned out the ripe melon sound of the gunman's head making contact with the concrete floor nine meters down.

The smell of Henry's blood rose to obliterate the singed sulfur smell of the gunpowder, the hot metal smell of the spent casings, and the warm meaty smell of the men below. Henry's blood. The blood that had made her.

The Hunger ripped aside all controls.

When they were all dead, when the screaming and the running was over, when she stood with Henry in the midst of broken bodies, she drew in a deep breath of the rich, meaty, blood-scented air and laid her palm flat against his chest. Leaning forward, she licked a bit of blood from the corner of his mouth.

Henry caught her tongue between his teeth, carefully so as not to break the skin.

She moaned against his mouth, pushed a body aside with the edge of her foot, and dragged him to the ground. They managed to get most of their clothing out of the way without destroying it and then it was flesh against flesh and a strength that could answer hers. No need to hold back. No need to be careful.

So Vicki let the Hunger have its head again.

She dragged his mouth back down to hers as she slammed up to meet his thrusts. Tasted the mix of lives on his lips as he could taste them on hers. Challenged his darkness. Matched it.

Streaked with blood, his skin was slick under her hands.

Her back arced up. His teeth found her breast as hers found his shoulder.

The world went red.

When she got back to the condo, Vicki stood just inside the master bedroom and watched Mike sleep. Watched the rise and fall of his chest. Traced the curve of the arm he'd flung over his head. Listened to his heart beat.

He shifted and a curl of hair fell down onto his face.

She stepped forward, hand outstretched to brush it back but stopped as the movement pulled the saturated cuff of her sweater across her wrist, drawing a dark smear over bruises rising in the shape of Henry's fingers . . .

The only other property Droege Shipping owned in Toronto was a trendy dance club called Millennium Ten. Technically, Mike was off the clock but if this case involved—God help them all—a second vampire, he wanted it solved as quickly as possible. Nine-twenty found him pulling up outside the club, using his lights to grab one of the rare Queen Street parking spots. He was still standing by the driver's door, ignoring the traffic passing two inches from his ass when he noticed Vicki's car half a block east.

No real surprise that she'd found the same information and headed here as well.

In an effort to delay exposure to the music he could hear being pumped out the front door, Mike headed down the alley leading to the back of the club. The people he wanted to talk to wouldn't be out on the dance floor.

Rounding the ubiquitous dumpster, he paused as the rear door opened and Vicki stepped into the alley, lips pulled back off her teeth, her eyes gleaming silver. The terror was instinctive, his hindbrain momentarily taking over. A little harder to place blame for the surge of arousal but given the twisted strands of their relationship, it certainly didn't surprise him.

He fought to control both reactions, knowing that with the Hunger released Vicki would sense them. If he wanted to maintain any kind of equality in the conversation they were about to have, he couldn't...

Between one heartbeat and the next, Vicki was on the roof. And then she was gone, the not-quite-visible flicker of a vampire moving at full speed heading south toward the lake.

Forcing himself to unclench his jaw—they were definitely going to have a talk before the sun came up—he took a step toward the club and paused. Why would she be heading south? Relatively speaking, there wasn't a lot of city between Queen Street and the lake.

Vicki had emerged from the club fully vamped out.

Something or someone in a club owned by Droege Shipping, the same Droege Shipping that had been destroyed by a supernatural creature the night before, had set Vicki on the Hunt.

To the south.

Albert Droege, the man with controlling interest in Droege Shipping, was currently staying in a company-owned penthouse at Queens Quay. Mike had spoken with him briefly that afternoon and had been ripped a new one for not having already found the vandals who'd destroyed the office. Were he a betting man, Mike would have bet big bucks that the elderly CEO's temper tantrum hid something significant.

His gut told him that Vicki had gone south to find out exactly what that was and, given the mood she was in, she wouldn't give a rat's ass about following even the spirit of the law.

"Son of a fucking bitch!"

He hit the siren and forced his car out into bumper-to-bumper traffic. South on Niagara to Bathurst. South on Bathurst slowed by the fucking streetcar and an SUV driven by a fucker who wouldn't yield. Left turn onto Queens Quay West. East to Droege's condominium. He wouldn't beat her there, but God willing he wouldn't be far behind.

The concierge met him at the door, mouth open to complain about his car, not so much parked as abandoned up on the wide sidewalk. Mike flashed his badge as he pushed by, heading for the elevators. Security had just been improved, replacing decades-old locks with electronic keypads. "Can you unlock the condos from here?"

"If it's an emergency but..."

"Unlock penthouse four." If Vicki was already in there, no one would be available to let him in. Mike had no idea what the concierge saw in his expression, nor did he want to know, but as the elevator door closed he saw the man nod and run for his desk.

And thank fucking God it was only nine floors to the two-story penthouses.

The door to four was open when he got there.

The glass doors out onto the terrace were still closed. Good sign. Vicki wouldn't have taken the elevator.

A crash from the upper level. Something breakable thrown, and thrown hard.

He ran for the stairs.

Charged through the first open door and nearly had his head taken off by a flat screen monitor.

Although he was clearly terrified, Albert Droege was fighting back.

Mike would consider the implications of that later. Right now, he needed to keep the situation from escalating any further out of control.

"Vicki!"

She glanced toward him. Her lips were pulled back off too

white teeth and her eyes were as inhuman as Mike had ever seen them. He'd seen her vamped out before. Had lain in her arms while she sank her teeth into his body and taken him to edge of darkness, but there'd never been a time when he hadn't been able to see Vicki. Here and now, there was nothing in her but Hunger and words weren't going to stop her.

He felt himself responding and knew that in half a heartbeat he wouldn't be able to do anything but bare his throat. A trickle of sweat ran down his side. One step, two... By the time he hit her, he was running full out. He dropped his shoulder, wrapped both arms around her, and took her with him out the open window.

If words couldn't stop her, gravity might.

Vicki's body took the brunt of the impact. She'd managed to get her feet under her, her knees and hips acting as shock absorbers for them both, but hitting the cedar decking still hurt like hell. Mike rolled, tasted blood, swore as pain shot up his arm from his wrist, and found himself, finally, staring up at Vicki as she lunged toward him.

Mike's blood wasn't, couldn't be, enough to keep her fed but it sustained her in other ways. The familiar scent cut through the song and stopped her before her teeth broke through the skin. Mouth against his throat, she breathed him in. Home. Humanity.

She wasn't...

She couldn't...

The song filled all the spaces Mike wasn't and threatened to overwhelm her tenuous control. She skimmed a hand over his body, feeling him respond. Pain. Pleasure. Want.

She needed...

She had to...

She ran.

There were uniforms in Droege's penthouse almost before Vicki disappeared over the edge of the roof. The concierge had to have called them.

By the time Mike filled them in on the situation—"I'm guessing she was on some kind of designer drug. A two-story drop barely fazed her and if you don't stop touching my fucking wrist, I'm going to shoot you."—Droege's lawyer had arrived and Droege himself was unavailable for questioning. The lawyer issued a brief statement, the clear expectation that everyone not a billionaire CEO should just clear out of the condo. A big believer in using bad moods to his advantage, Mike threw his weight around until Droege, through his lawyer, agreed to an appointment. At the club. Ten thirty A.M.

Between filing reports and having his wrist taped, Mike wasn't home until just past three. He made coffee, sat in the dark, and tried not to think about silvered eyes. Tried not to think about pain and pleasure so entwined he couldn't tell anymore where one ended and the other began.

Tried not to watch the clock as he waited for sunrise.

The crate behind the false wall in his crawlspace remained empty. He had to believe that Vicki had made it to the safety of her downtown office. He had to believe it because he wouldn't believe the alternative.

Vicki's car was still parked just down the street from Millennium Ten. She'd been ticketed but somehow missed having been towed. Staring past his refection in the car window, Mike flipped open his phone. The call went straight to voicemail.

"Nelson Investigations. Leave your name, number, and what you need me for after the tone."

And what he needed her for? He unclenched his teeth long enough to growl, "Call me the minute you're up."

Few things looked less attractive than a dance club at ten-thirty in the morning. The harsh glare of the overhead lights illuminated every stain, every scuff, every lie. Mike flashed his badge at the bored young woman running a steamer over the carpet. She half turned and pointed toward a door tucked in to the right of the small stage.

One end of the concrete corridor led to the exit up into the alley. The other to an open door, defined by a rectangular spill of light. Odds were good Droege wasn't waiting in the alley so Mike turned toward the light.

The room he stepped into seemed to be a dressing room. Four meters square, cinder block walls painted a pale institutional green; if the tiny window high in the far wall didn't give away its basement location, the off-center drain in the floor did. It held a dressing table and mirror, aluminum rack of clothes, and the most beautiful woman Mike had ever seen sitting in an old wooden captain's chair, combing her hair. She was singing softly to herself but she looked up as he entered the room.

Her smile promised sunlight and laughter.

Mornings spent lazily in bed, warm under the covers, long legs wrapped around his as they rocked slowly against each other. Afternoons sprawled on the grass, her head on his lap, bending to lick spilled jam from warm skin. Evenings at the table surrounded by family, her eating off his plate as though she didn't have exactly the same on hers while under the table, her touch wanders up his thigh. Nights together with no surprises in the moonlight.

Mike didn't remember moving but he was standing close enough to touch. He reached out, needing to know if the curve of her cheek was as soft as it appeared.

Her smile changed. "So easy," she sighed, "for you to betray her."

Considering how the investigation to this point had turned up sweet fuck-all, Mike found it amazing that the Droege Shipping case was taking up so damned much time. An autopsy had determined that yes, the dead guard had been taken out by a heart attack. The coroner had refused to speculate on the cause although had allowed that given the state of his arteries, Chris Adams was a myocardial infarction waiting to happen. Duncan Riley, the surviving guard remained physically fine and mentally unhinged. His doctors suspected he was reliving the night over and over... "He's ejaculating every two, two and a half hours. All things considered, his recovery time is impressive."

"Way, way too much information," Mike muttered as he hung up. Rolling out his shoulders, he glanced toward the window where the sunset gilded the glass. Vicki'd be calling soon and as little as he was looking forward to the conversation, at least it would get him away from the piles of futile paperwork he'd spent the day on.

"Well"—Dave propped a thigh on the corner of Mike's desk— "what'd you turn up?"

"Big fat nothing." Mike nudged his coffee mug out of harm's way with the back of his bound wrist.

"Let me guess. Droege had no idea who could possibly be after little-old-never-cheated-anyone him."

"Yeah, well, Droege's lawyer seemed to have no idea."

"He brought his lawyer to the club? That sucks."

"To the club?"

Dave stared down at him for a long moment then shook his head. "If I've said it once, I've said it a thousand times, paperwork kills brain cells. Did Droege," he continued slowly, with heavy emphasis, "bring his lawyer to the club?"

"I don't..." Mike frowned. The lawyer had been at the condo. Hadn't allowed him to speak to Droege. The club was on Queen Street West. It was...there was...he didn't... "I don't remember."

"Interesting."

"Why?"

"Because lately, my friend, all your memory lapses tend to lead back to Vicki."

"Vicki has nothing to do with this!" When Dave reared back, both hands up, he realized he'd been a little overly vehement. Dave hadn't known what the bite marks on Duncan Riley meant. Hadn't know it was Vicki that Mike had chased out of Albert Droege's condo.

"Dude, chill. I didn't say she did. I was thinking maybe you were distracted by a little afternoon delight, not that she's been ripping people apart. Not that it would matter if it did. You got it so bad you'd never give her up."

Mike rubbed his head wondering who the hell had the music playing so loud in the squad room. "Give her up...?"

"Rat her out," Dave expanded, rolling his eyes. "Squeal on her. Turn her in. Betray her trust."

So easy for you to betray her.

Memory returned as the music faded.

"Mike! Hello! Where the hell are you off to?"

"Back to the club." He shook off Dave's grip and pushed past him toward the door. "There's a loose end I need to tie up." But he'd have to beat the sunset to do it.

The second evening in a row, Vicki woke to a flood of memory.

The look on Mike's face, equal parts fear and arousal, as she bent toward his throat.

Remembered the effort of moving against the music as she turned the Hunger back into the city.

Remembered the feel of flesh compacting under her grip as she dragged the dealer into an alley, his customers scattering.

Remembered the hot splash of his blood. The dark taste of his terror.

It was easier as she fed to fight the music.

Easy enough to finally throw the first body aside and Hunt for another. One appetite fulfilled, others still needing to be.

So many people on the streets. Unaware.

An arm broken in passing, caught on the upswing between one blow and the next. So far beyond when he collapsed to the ground that the screams of his companion were nearly lost in the sounds of the city.

Blue eyes and broad shoulders and hair long enough for her to grip. His pulse pounding. Hips rising to meet hers. His blood tasted of desire. He was weak when she stopped but alive.

The look on Mike's face...

Vicki ripped the back door of the club off its hinges and threw it across the alley. Before it landed, she was running into the dressing room at the end of the corridor, ready for Lorelei's song when it hit her, "When the Levee Breaks" pounding into her ears at about a hundred decibels. She'd got her hand around fistful of hair when a bullet whistled past her cheek and smashed the mirror.

Lorelei's comb caught the wires as Vicki turned, pulling the earbuds free. The song changed. Caught her.

On the other side of the room, his back pressed up against the clothing on the rack, Mike lowered his weapon, his movements as much beyond his control as hers were.

"Kill him," Lorelei sang. "Kill him."

Vicki could feel the Hunger rising along the notes of the song. "Mike, run!"

"The hell I will!"

She heard his heart pounding. Inhaled the scent of his fear. Her tongue swept over his throat, tasting...Fuck! She didn't remember moving. The hard ridge of his gun dug into her hip and she managed to find enough control to grunt, "Shoot me!"

"Not going to happen."

"Do it!"

"No!"

He titled his head to the side, giving himself to her. Trusting her. Vicki's teeth broke the skin and she froze in place, fighting the music with everything she had. Fighting the need to rend and tear. Fighting what she was. She licked at the blood welling slowly to the surface...

Home.

Humanity.

...and used the strength it gave her to turn, shards of the mirror grinding into the tile under her shoes.

Mike's hand caught her elbow as she swayed, suddenly free of the song.

On the other side of the room, Lorelei stood and stared at them like she'd never seen a cop and a vampire hold each other up before.

Vicki was pretty sure she still had every intention of breaking the singer's neck but Mike's grip on her arm held her in place.

"In spite of everything, you'd rather die—both of you would rather die than live with the pain of killing the other."

"Because of everything," Vicki growled.

To her surprise, Lorelei smiled, suddenly looking young and hopeful and...

Translucent.

Vicki stepped back, pushing Mike with her, as a vaguely Lorelei-shaped puddle of water ran down through the drain.

"Is she...?"

"An apparently undereducated guess says she's gone. Free." Vicki bent and picked up the comb. "Albert Droege is going to be pissed." The plastic sounded like a distant gunshot when it snapped. "Can't say that I care."

Chris Adams' grave had one of the bronze memorial markers set into a granite base, the whole thing flush with the ground. Easier for groundskeepers but Vicki preferred the old slab markers. As much as it bordered on cliché, she liked cemeteries to look like cemeteries.

She'd gone to the hospital and pulled Duncan Riley up out of the darkness. Gave him back his life. Unfortunately, death's embrace was a little more final. A lot more final.

"You weren't responsible."

"Reading minds now?"

Behind her, Mike huffed out a half laugh. "I know how you think. And you weren't responsible."

"For the condition of his arteries? No. For his heart giving out when it did..."

"Vicki, she was controlling you."

Pushing back against Mike's body, centering herself in the circle of his arms, grounding herself on the beat of his heart, Vicki remembered.

I give you the freedom to be yourself, Vampire.

But that truth was a line Mike couldn't cross so she smiled, touched the comb in her pocket, and said, "I know."

TANYA HUFF lives and writes in rural Ontario with eight cats—as of this writing—two dogs, and her partner, Fiona Patton. She has a degree in Radio and Television Arts from back in the days of physically cutting audio tape. Her latest book from DAW is *Truth of Valor* (September 2010), the fifth Gunnery Sergeant Torin Kerr novel. She's currently working on a sequel to *The Enchantment Emporium* for 2011. No title as yet, although there've been a few doozies tossed around. When she's not writing, she gardens and practices the guitar—although not at the same time.

When I requested an afterword, she supplied the following:

Way back in 2007, the Vicki Nelson books were made into a television show called Blood Ties. *FInally using my RTA degree, I wrote an episode for season one called "Stone Cold" and had a verbal agreement to write two episodes for season two. Unfortunately, there wasn't a season two, but there were half a dozen pitches I'd already put together. The sirens pitch had been written with a specific guest star in mind (nope, can't tell you), and while there were obviously things about it that couldn't translate from the TV-verse to the bookverse—Henry, by way of Kyle Schmid such an amazing presence in the show, isn't in the bookverse at this point—the story had a strong core and an interesting look at the relationship between Mike and Vicki that I didn't want to lose. This version is definitely a little sexier than would be allowed on at 8 o'clock but it's basically the same story.*

CARELESS OF THE NIGHT

GINA MASSEL-CASTATER

"I'm calling 911. Whoever is back there had better leave now!" Liz yelled as soon as she heard the alley door bang open and the scuffling sounds from the rear of the photography studio. She picked up the wireless handset and grabbed her purse, rooting around for her pistol, but also making fast tracks for the front door. No reason to confront trouble if you can avoid it. She kicked off her sexy four-inch-heeled sandals behind the curved reception desk. They would just slow her down if she had to move out in a hurry.

Stilling her panic breathing, she could hear the argument coming from the back room and tiptoed over to the curtain dividing the spaces.

"I told you all to back off." Liz was sure it was Armando, but his voice was oddly low and gravelly. Each word was clipped and terse.

"Hey, man, we're just the first wave. You have to get your guys in line, or there's going to be some very big trouble on your doorstep," he threatened.

Liz didn't want to move the curtain, but she needed to see what was happening. She found a small hole in the drape and plastered her eye to it.

Armando stood in that alert-relaxed stance she'd seen in movies, the look of someone ready to fight. Shifting, she saw two young

27

punks near the back door. They wore the usual Goth-looking clothes, but their heavily muscled frames belied the wan look of the costume.

"Well, just tell your leader to stay out of my business. It's not his territory, it's mine," Armando said, raising his voice on the last word as he moved forward, forcing the guys to back up. "Get out."

"He's not gonna like this. You know it isn't over," the guy on the right said.

"It's done for now. Leave, and I won't run you down the next time I see you," he said as he opened the door to force them out.

Liz backed away from the curtain and ran to the front door. She didn't want Armando to know what she'd seen, so she repeated her warning about calling 911.

Just as she made it to the door, Armando stuck his head through the dividing curtains. Liz caught a quick glimpse of bloody scratches on his face as he yelled, "No, don't call. It's all right." Liz pulled her empty hand out of her purse, but clutched the phone like a hand grenade.

She stared hard at Armando. "Are you okay?"

"Wow, you look stunning," he replied, taking in the incredible difference in her appearance. "You don't normally dress in low-cut blouses and short skirts and how I've missed it, do you?"

He was used to her slightly mousy receptionist outfits, and this was anything but. Her simple black dress embraced her curves, emphasizing a small waist, curvy hips, and normally hidden deep, full cleavage, framed by the stark plunging neckline. He had thought her hair was a mousy gray, but with it down and in full bloom, the curls glowed like a sexy silver halo around her face, tendrils framing her eyes.

"You are one of the keenest observers of people I know, so no, you haven't had a sudden failure of vision. It's just that we usually work the opposite shifts, so you never see me when I'm going out for the night. And thank you for the compliment, but are you okay?" Liz was startled and flattered, but more, she was really worried about the amount of blood she could see. Armando still had the curtains clutched in his hands, coyly hiding behind the drapery.

"Yes, just a few scratches. I really need to be careful back here," he said. "Now, it's obvious you have a date, so get out of here. I'll be fine." He paused, "You didn't actually dial 911, did you?"

"No, I was about to push the last 1 when you spoke. Nice save."

"Well, get out of here, and have fun," he said, reminding her of a parent sending her out for the evening.

Liz's natural mom-to-the-world instincts kicked in.

"No, I want to make sure you're okay. Let me get the first aid kit and tend to those scratches. You won't even know what's bad until it's cleaned up," she said as she made her way back to the desk to return the phone and get the kit.

"No," he said a bit forcefully, "don't come back here. I can take care of myself."

Liz stopped. She didn't buy it, but she didn't really have a choice. With Armando watching her every move, she slipped back into her shoes, gathered her tote bag of work clothes, flung the garnet-red Pashmina shawl over her shoulders, and walked to the front door.

Liz was surprised at how awkward she felt to have caught his attention as anything more than a fellow professional. She had that stumbling teenage moment of idiotic blathering.

"Yeah, well, I'll be in again tomorrow at three. Remember my new schedule keeps me on three to nine for the season. I think the later hour is really bringing in the business," she replied, mentally kicking herself for the odd response.

She was conscious of his eyes on her every movement as she left. She felt that deep flutter in her center. He had noticed her; that might be enough for now.

Despite her worry, Liz kept to her original plan for the night and strolled into the lobby of the Bellagio, the piercing, vibrant, dancing colors of the Dale Chihuly glass ceiling somehow soothing in its wild excess of color and light. No matter how many times she walked through, she paid silent homage to the folks willing to spend their money so that she could have this vibrant vision as part of her world.

Tonight she had a strong hunger for a well-made martini and some forks. She'd been saving up her calories all day for the indulgence. And she needed some time to think about Armando's reaction. She turned right from the lobby and began the sometimes endless stroll towards Fix, her favorite night spot. She paused to salivate over the crystal-encrusted evening purses in the storefront, attracted and repulsed by the truly senseless beauty and expense.

The low grumble of her tummy set her back on track. If she ordered carefully, she could sit for a bit and catch the swirl of the night... and almost always, someone who would follow her home. At that thought, an unconsciously evil grin flitted over her face, causing the two men who caught the look as they walked by to nearly trip over their own feet. They stared after her, momentarily besotted by the sway of her hips and the bouncy energy of her walk. Liz had only recently come to notice her effect; in this gambler's world driven by the hunger for money and youth and style, she'd felt invisible for over a decade, since the day she turned forty.

As she walked, she glanced at the various game tables, sometimes startled by the men in such down-and-out clothes; she wondered at their willingness to hand over large amounts of cash for a few hours of entertainment. By living in Vegas for years, she had absorbed the rules of the games in all the casinos, but she had decided a long time ago that when she handed someone cash, she wanted a blouse or better, a pair of shoes, in exchange. The real entertainment value to her was in watching the people. Perhaps on the way out, she would find a table of gamblers to silently giggle over. The intensity and focus some of them brought to the table, she reserved for observing people and taking pictures. But they made a lovely study and she could count on no one noticing her in her pursuit as long as she sat very still.

"Jill, I'm so glad to see you," Liz said as she approached the hostess stand at the restaurant, startling the petite redhead into dropping her pen. Although Jill tried to cover her freckles, they gave her a sweet look slightly out of place in Vegas.

"Liz, haven't seen you in a bit. What's up?" she asked, recovering nicely.

"Oh, not much. I just had a mad craving for forks and a fine martini. Any chance I can hang out over at the bar?" she asked.

"Yeah, sure. I don't see a problem tonight, although I expect it will get busy later." Jill pointed Liz over to the high stool on the long side of the bar.

"Hey, Jasmine, good to see you tonight," Liz said to the bartender as she settled on her perch and arranged the flippy black skirt to drape over her knees. She took the shawl off her shoulders, wrapped it around the front of her neck, and let the rest hang down her back.

"I know that's a uniform, but you do look fine," she said.

Jasmine had on a very short skirt, sheer, glittery black hose, and a complicated shirt combo that suggested either her tits would escape or her straps would slip off at any moment. Liz watched Jasmine and the other bartenders move at a fast, focused, and furious pace, amazed that the uniforms of the all-female team didn't fall off or expose the women completely.

"What can I get you tonight? I'm guessing a vodka martini?" Jasmine asked, laying a cocktail napkin and utensils on the bar.

"Hmmm, surprise me on the martini, but I want two orders of the forks tonight. I've been craving them all week," she replied.

Liz watched the dance of the bartenders as they made sweet, sour, and colorful concoctions, each tall girl with some magical radar that stopped them from tripping over each other. It reminded her of the same tango she and Sam had in their kitchen as they prepared for parties. She missed that brisk movement combined with mild panic as multiple and varied dishes flew to the table for friends and family. Liz let the pleasant memory wash over her, longing still for the sense of being truly known, truly seen.

As she watched the swirling dance, she considered the tantalizing problem of Armando. She had applied for the receptionist job at the studio for two reasons: his reputation as a world-class photographer, and her need to have access to some heavy-duty photographic processing equipment. She hadn't counted on him being so mysteriously attractive. She couldn't nail down his age, his accent, or even his sexual persuasion. But after tonight, it was definitely clear that he was interested in women, well, more specifically, in her.

She hadn't counted on finding her boss to be so very hot... and assuredly too young for her. Would it cost her the job if she pursued him? She was thinking it would be worth finding a new job just to find out what he would be like as a lover.

"Okay, here's your mystery martini," Jasmine said. "Let me know what you think and what's in it, and if you guess right, I'll spot you the next one," as she placed the elegant martini glass in front of her. "Your forks should be up soon."

Liz slyly glanced left and right to see if anyone was watching her, and dipped her tongue into the drink rather than sipping; small flavors need small tastes. She closed her eyes. Vodka, a citrus note, and something way different. She opened her eyes and caught the guy to the left of her staring at her mouth. She stopped licking her lip and boldly returned his gaze.

"So, do you like the drink?" he asked. He studied her, letting his nearly black eyes openly roam over her cleavage.

"Yes, but give me a minute. There's a sweet, warm flavor that I just can't figure out. Would you like a sip?" She offered him the stem, savoring his obviously sexual attention.

He surprised her by taking the glass. He appeared a bit younger than the guys she usually attracted here, about thirty-five, his hair still dark with no gray, but that would suit her for tonight.

"I taste Stoli, lime, and the sweet you mention, but there's also a wood note. How very odd," he said as he handed back her drink. He made a point of touching her hand in the exchange. "My name's Bobby."

Liz swiveled on her stool to face him and arched her brow. "Nice to meet you, Bobby. I'm Liz. I really enjoy the way you've been studying me, but I'm wondering why?" she asked directly.

He flustered for a moment and decided to be equally direct.

"I was admiring your work," he said. She tilted her head in puzzlement.

He grinned wickedly and said, "My interest is purely professional. I'm here for the American Academy of Cosmetic Surgery annual meeting. This city is a total tribute to our skills, maybe even more so than Hollywood. But your look is so very rare... and excellently done."

"Uh, thank you...I think?" she said. "I wanted to be true to myself. There were so many possible choices. I didn't want to conceal my years, but rather look the best for my age. Do you like a dare?"

"What do you mean?"

"Guess what I had done," she challenged.

"No, no really, not a good idea," he demurred.

She giggled at him and said, "Chicken."

Surprising her, he reached out and brushed his fingers over her cleavage. "Breast implants," he whispered and caressed her cheek, "facial filler, laser resurfacing, and a little Botox," he said as he touched her lower lip. "And the overall effect is very nice."

Heated by his hands, she retreated behind a brief verbal wall. "Why thank you, darlin'," she said, affecting a quick Southern drawl as self-defense against his words and actions, and stared off across the room. "Before my Sam died, he called me his li'l trophy wife, even though we'd been married forever. I wanted to hold him, so I kept myself in good shape. When he died, I went into a bad spiral for a year, turned into a slug, and made friends with Ben and Jerry."

"So obviously something changed," he said kindly.

"My kids staged an intervention and dragged me out on one of our traditional family hiking and hunting trips. They forced me to see the error of my ways," she said, looking back at him.

"Oh, dear, way too serious, right? Anyway, I snapped out of it, worked hard to get back into my fighting shape. Even one year meant some things were beyond self-help. My kids didn't want me to look like an alien—forgive, please, their opinion of your craft. I did my research, found the best surgeon I could afford, and had all the procedures you mentioned. That meant I spent a long time thinking about what and who I am. I wanted to look good, but I wanted to respect their opinion, too."

"Well, that explains your moderation, but you have to know: Before I noticed your body, your hair was like a bright beacon. Your choice of what you had done was excellent, but I'm happy to see you left your hair alone. Although our culture doesn't value such an obvious symbol of aging, your glowing silver hair is sexy as hell," he said as he reached up to twist a bright shiny curl around his finger. "It's the perfect choice."

Jasmine interrupted and placed in front of Liz a small forest of silver forks topped with salmon, crème fraiche, and caviar. "Did you figure out the martini yet?" she asked with a warm smile.

"No, but whatever it is, it's my new favorite," Liz replied.

"Wait," Bobby interrupted. "Could the secret ingredient be sake?"

"Wow, you're good," replied Jasmine. She winked at him broadly, wiped the counter, and hustled on.

Liz held in her amusement as he watched Jasmine for a bit. Jasmine was a lovely piece of work, and to Liz's thinking, much more to Bobby's style. She lifted one of the forks out of the specially designed tray, closed her eyes, and slid the bite-sized morsel into her mouth, artlessly sighing with the pleasure.

"You had best stop that, or I might be tempted to throw you down right here on the bar," he said, surprising her. She snapped her eyes open and had to refocus: He was about two inches from her nose.

She leaned back, grinned, and handed him one of the forks. "They're the second best thing to suck down your throat. You can't judge until you've tried one of these," she purred in response. She offered to feed him and watched with pleasure as he got it. Sometimes simple foods were just perfect.

Liz shared a few more with him as they ate and chatted. She'd reeled him in; what should she do with him? He'd have a room, and he'd be fun. The more she pushed her horny self in that direction, though, the more the lingering look Armando gave her kept popping up.

Sighing, she abandoned the idea of rolling around hot and sweaty with doctor-boy. She would just be thinking of Armando.

She needed to clear her head. She needed to get out into the night.

She'd rediscovered her love of the night as she'd recovered from Sam's death. Even in this crazy nightlife town, she had no fear of being in the dark. She often felt like she had a guardian angel watching over her. No one ever bothered her or harassed her. Unlike feeling invisible in any upscale department store, this was a welcome gift, letting her roam with her cameras, catching the calling power of the moon.

Liz did a quick change in the back seat of her car behind the studio, ditching the heels, dress, and shawl for her emergency night clothes: black cargo pants, gray T-shirt, and running shoes. Reminding herself about the recent articles about strange animals in the city, she put her pistol and permit in her right thigh pocket. She slung her camera pack onto her shoulders and plopped a knit cap over her evening curls. She'd thought about going into the studio to change, but she didn't want to run into Armando, not until she'd figured out her response to him.

She sighed and stared up at the bright Klieg lights of the new construction across the back parking lot from the studio. She'd come to accept the constant reconstruction of the Strip, thankful at least that they rebuilt on the same land here instead of destroying new acreage. She did love the geometry of construction, the complex angles, the smoky dust, and the contrast of soft human shapes against the rigid lines of steel and concrete. After working on a series of conventional shots, she had recently added thermographic images to the collection. The camera had set her back a bit, but she relished her new tool. That's why she needed access to the studio for the special processing the images required.

She found the mark she'd left in the parking lot last week, set up the tripod on the same spot, and tried to keep the sequence of shots all from the same angle, hoping to capture the process of change over time. She pondered Armando as her hands automatically followed the nearly ritualistic habits of setting up her gear. She loved the hunter's thrill of capturing the attention of a new guy, but she had limits, ones she consciously chose when she decided to be alive and have fun again. Armando looked way too young for her. She felt a certain wild power knowing she'd reeled in Bobby tonight; she didn't usually want anyone that young. It was such a bother to explain stuff to the younger ones. But she gave herself a pat on the back: She could have had him, no doubt.

Did that apply to Armando, too? She wasn't sure. The way he'd looked at her tonight made her juicy and jumpy, ready to run, but in which direction? If she pursued him, wouldn't she have to leave her job? Sam's will and investments had left her with enough money to be basically comfortable, so she didn't need the income, but she did want access to all that photo-processing gear and large-format printers.

Her hormones gave her ever-practical mind a slap-down. Her lust for him was more powerful than her usual attractions, as if some extra sexual gear was engaged in her juicy bits. Shivers raced up and down her arms.

She sighed and swatted the idea away, bringing herself and the image back into focus.

She took long, steady breaths as she lined up her shots. Although the digital SLR meant she had to use the viewfinder, she had practiced stepping back to get the steadiest image. In a point-and shoot world, she'd had to develop the discipline of slow, steady shutter pressure to get the exposures she wanted. The thermal camera was more subject to shake than her others, so she'd learned to be still and silent. It paid off in sharply focused weird colors. She gently released the shutter and studied the image.

She turned at the voices far behind her and was startled that anyone had gotten within fifty feet of her without her noticing them sooner. Maybe she'd better pay more heed to the recent chatter about desert animals coming into town.

Two guys were squaring off in the alley near the studio. She couldn't see their faces. By instinct, she grabbed the long zoom lens and camera from her bag and quickly changed the lens on the thermal camera, swiveling it towards the two. She recognized Armando, but who was this other guy?

"I told you I would handle this," Armando said, his voice a harsh growl. "I'm the law for this region. You will wait for me to finish."

Liz pressed the extended trigger from the tripod.

"The new guys are literally pissing all over our turf," the other man said, "leaving their mark to shake us up. They need to go away or get with the program." Only a bit shorter than Armando, he had a bulldog build, thick around the neck and shoulders, bringing to mind a wrestler or body builder, muscles used to weight and action. Even his hair reminded Liz of a pit bull, trimmed almost to nothing on the sides, fading up to a slight thatch of silvery white over the top. He chested into Armando's space.

"Back. Off. Now." Armando said, verbally poking the man with each word. "I spoke to the council. I have a week to do it my way. If I find your spoor anywhere nearby, then I'll take out you and your punk pack."

Armando turned his back and took a step away, making it clear he expected the guy to back down. Clearly full of fight, the guy lowered his stance and prepared to leap, muscled legs flexed to spring.

Armando was hurt already, and Liz was getting scared for him. She needed to see more, so she squatted to reach for the regular lens, grappling, head down in the bag at her feet. Even through the viewfinder at fifty feet, the long lens cut out too much light.

She heard only growls and a scrambling, then scratching on the pavement. When she brought the camera back up, she couldn't locate the men. Where the hell did they go? She quickly pirouetted.

A wolf and a cougar rushed toward her, the wolf in the lead and running from the cougar. She crouched on the ground. They ran past her without stopping.

Liz was more grateful than ever to be invisible in the night.

Liz's workout was arms and shoulders, which meant the gym instead of the hills. As she worked through each set, she enjoyed the easy banter with the guys in the weight room. They'd come to respect her dedication to form and often gave her good advice on improving her lifting. That they were all hunky guys lifted her. The eye candy was worth the sweaty price of admission.

Today though, she was off balance, waiting for perhaps the pure focus of lifting to replace the persistently strange feeling about what she had witnessed last night. What had she seen? She ended up rushing her routine to get home to work on the images she had taken. She'd used the gym to procrastinate and she needed to see what was on the camera.

She plopped down in her home studio and started the download of the thermal camera. She didn't have a clear memory of what she shot last night, but she trusted the images would tell her what happened when things went weird. It had been a few nights since she had downloaded, and the process seemed agonizingly slow.

She opened Photoshop Elements and began to study the images. The first were too blurry and useless for her portfolio. The tenth image caught her eye. She had indeed clicked the shutter after she swung the camera to look at Armando and the mystery man. The two men faced each other, but she must have messed up the settings, because instead of being the usual red to yellow to green pattern of all her previous shots, each of these men was totally red, totally and evenly red. How could two humans have no variance in temperature from core to fingertips? She transferred the image to her flash drive so she could print a full-size version on the Kromekote paper at the studio; she also printed one on a regular sheet of 8½ by 11 paper for reference.

She could see they needed more work, but that would take hours, and she had to get to her job.

Liz had debated dressing up today, but decided to keep things as normal as possible; she wore her usual loose dress and flats, afraid of being too obvious in her confusion over Armando's response last night.

"There's a lot you don't know about me," she said, having a conversation inside her head.

"I do want to know more," Armando said, coming around the desk into her space.

Liz started and resisted the temptation to back away.

"How about having dinner with me tonight? We close at six on Sundays, so eight?" he continued.

"Oh, damn, did I use my outside voice?" she said, appalled that he heard her. "Hey, what are you doing here so early?" ignoring his question.

"I wanted to get some stuff caught up—and you didn't answer me," he said.

"So is dinner out with the boss a usual perk around here?" she asked.

"No, it's not about work. This is about, well the way you looked last night," he said, "and the way you look now. Maybe the way you've always looked—and I was just too dumb or busy or something to see."

Liz stared hard at him for a moment, unsure of what she thought was the right answer. She took in the amazing amber of his eyes, golden sparks around the slightly dilated pupils. There was something ferally hungry in his look, and it stirred a matching desire in her.

"Yes," she said, nodding.

"How about the open terrace at the Social House? I hear they have some inventive sushi, and I've been wanting to try it," he asked.

"Sounds good. I'll meet you there at eight," she said.

He looked down at her dowdy office attire and back up into her deep blue eyes. "Would you be offended if I asked to see the same outfit you wore last night? I know there must be some chick rule about no repeats, but, damn, you looked so very fine and so very different."

Liz's stomach dropped—and hot smoke filled her further south. How a few mundane words could stir her.

"Oh, I think you'll have to trust me. I can do you better than that," she purred in a low, breathy voice.

Liz dashed into her house, threw off her work clothes, and ran for her bedroom. Although she could get ready for a party in mere minutes, she wanted to prepare herself with a bit more care. She checked the temperature of the small hot tub in the atrium and eased down into the steamy water. She silently thanked Sam for planning the house around this oasis. It was always private, but open to the sky. Over the years, this had been her garden and meditation space, cool during the day in the shadow of the house, and protected at night from the chilling winds. She was far enough from the tall hotels to avoid their noise, but the glow of the eternal city lights bathed the space in soft, perpetual light.

She left the tub a practiced two minutes before her fingers pruneated. Skin flushed and rosy, she pampered herself, imagining that it was Armando smoothing scent and fine skin butters over her arms and thighs.

She applied concealer under her eyes, a light foundation, eyeliner, mascara, and blush, keeping it simple and minimal. She let the wild curls have their own way; they would eventually, no matter what. She checked the mirror, hoping Armando would drool. She reversed her colors of the evening before with a deep, garnet-red dress and black wrap. She ran her finger up the plunge of the neckline, lifting and nudging, making sure her nipples, excited about the possibilities, aimed forward beneath the clinging knit. She twirled, and the knee-length skirt floated out and then settled in soft folds that gave the impression of a small breeze as she walked.

She was ready.

Hoping for a ride home, Liz took a cab and asked the cabbie to drop her close to the terrace area, an oddly dim space on the overly bright Strip. They'd agreed to meet at the outside entrance rather than hustle through the hotel crowd. She stood a bit in shadow, intentionally early, wanting to calm down before she saw him again. No one bothered her as she watched the comings and goings, the overly perfected women on the expensive arms of much older men. She admired the working women and ruefully wondered about role reversals; she could get the same service, but why pay? She shrugged. She didn't like to dip as low in the age pool as men her same age routinely did.

Armando walked up, and her body took over before her mind could react. She flushed despite the cool evening air and went liquid at her core. Damn, he looked good in the night. Most men clean up pretty, but his energy was unusual, watchful and untamed, and it pulled her to him. She stood rooted to the shadow, breathing hard and waiting for him to turn and see her.

Liz was puzzled but not surprised at being able to hide in the shadow. With each day that had passed since Sam's death, she had become less noticed, but it hadn't been this pronounced before. She had expected Armando to be able to see her now that she had escaped her dowdy working exterior.

She stepped closer and touched his arm.

"Shall we go in?" she asked.

He jerked slightly, plainly startled at her sudden appearance and touch.

"I'm sorry; I must have been lost in thought. Did you just get here?" he asked.

"I've been staring at you for about two minutes," she said. "I was enjoying the show so much that I hesitated to interrupt. It's fun to watch men as they watch women," she smiled at him.

"I'm not used to being surprised," he said.

"Neither am I," she replied honestly.

"Let's go in," Armando said, recovering. "I called Jake for a table, so we shouldn't have to wait long," he said.

"Cool. I didn't think they took reservations on anything less than two days out," she said.

"Jake and I run with the same pack," he said with a grin, "so he makes allowances for me."

Liz threaded their way to the table, giving it her best walk, hips swaying, back straight, willing ownership of the path in front of her. She enjoyed the game of pretending that the other men noticed her, however recent experience had taught her otherwise. But she was sure she could keep Armando's eyes on her.

As if in answer to her thought, Armando placed his hand on her back; she felt claimed.

They settled in a back corner of the terrace and composed their order: ikura sashimi, toro and saba pieces, a complicated house roll, tomago, eel, and a salmon hand roll. It was obvious they shared a rampant craving and passion for raw fish.

They discussed the indulgent excesses of the space, even to the staff uniforms matching the interior, the women in very short, but somehow formal kimonos, and the men in black satin jackets. To Liz's way of thinking, it was unfair that the men wore long trousers; men usually have great legs.

Liz sipped her martini and ran her tongue slowly over her lips. She'd decided she wanted him—now.

"I'm not entirely sure that this is wise," she said. He started to interrupt. "No, hear me out. I know where I want this to go but I also want to keep working at the studio. So tell me now that you can be cool with this."

"I can't be sure I'll ever again be so completely indifferent to you at work," he said. "I can tell you that I'm good at keeping my personal and work lives quite separate."

"I hope you won't hold our age differences against me," she said.

He almost gagged on a sip of scotch. "You have no idea how little that matters to me," he said heatedly.

He waved over the waiter.

"When our order is ready, would you please pack it to go?" He handed the man his credit card.

"Let's go to my house," Liz responded. "The hot tub is ready." Under her breath, so quietly she doubted he could hear it, she added, "and so am I."

Liz's need for him threatened to overwhelm her. In his car, she tightly clenched the bag of food and her purse to resist distracting him as he sped through the streets, his urgency evident in his race-car-like driving. Their only words were her driving directions.

He leapt out of the car to open her door, but she was faster and pushed the bag into his hands as she dug through her purse for the house key. They made it inside the house, but just barely. Liz dropped everything and pushed him against the door. She slid her hands under his jacket and yanked it off his shoulders, savoring the width and power of him. He shrugged out of the jacket, let it fall, moved his hands down her back to her thighs, and lifted her, surprising her with his strength as he cradled her ass in his hands and spread her legs around him.

Liz took advantage of the higher position to nuzzle his neck and inhale his scent. She leaned away from him slightly and stared into his incredible eyes, bright amber with his need. She moved in to kiss him, pulled back in hesitation, and gave in, suddenly slow, softening her approach to his full lips, darting her tongue out to taste him before he took control and thrust his tongue into her mouth.

The molten fire inside her made her crazy for him, a small observing part of her bewildered by the uncontrollable lust. Time peeled back to her teens when only this, only this touch and tangle mattered.

With her thighs wrapped around him, she ground her mound into him, delighted to find he was ready, too. She was this close, this very close to coming.

She squirmed down his body and dragged him down the hall to her bedroom. He didn't resist.

She went straight for his buckle and fly.

Before she could touch his shaft, he bent and grabbed the hem of her dress, then pulled the slinky knit over her head. Liz laughed and posed for a moment, the dim light from the table lamp in the corner casting her in black and white silhouette against the colors of the room.

Her bountiful breasts slightly overflowed her demi-bra and set off the amazing curves from her small waist to full hips, a classic Vashti temple guardian come to life.

She turned her back to him, stepped out of her thong, and undid her bra. Impatient, driven, he grabbed her hips and rocked against her, the fabric of his shirttails still in the way. Liz pushed back against him, undulating like a cat in heat, then arched up to stand, reaching over her head to catch his neck and pull him closer.

"We can do slow later," she whispered, afraid to speak her desire.

Armando growled deep in his chest and lifted her into his arms. Liz was again startled by his strength, and felt light and girlish in his arms. He set her on the edge of the bed and stepped back to his pants to root in the pockets.

"Condoms are in the top drawer, there," she said, pointing. To her delight, he grabbed a few, put them on the nightstand, tore open one, and started to put it on.

"Let me. I haven't even seen you yet," she said, and took it from him.

Liz loved this moment, when she took control, got to see a man up close and oh so very personal. The weight and feel and velvet-rigid power of a man could drive her almost over the edge before she even had him in her. Tonight was the most powerful urge in years.

She peeled the wrapper down him, then she pulled him over her as she leaned back on the bed. She held onto him with one hand and used the other to spread herself for him, her juices evident even in the soft light.

Armando grabbed her and thrust all the way into her in a single motion. Liz wrapped her legs behind his back and pushed up even harder, begging for more.

Armando obliged, using all the power of his standing position to fill her tight, wet tunnel. He opened her wider still, digging hard into her muscles to hold her in place against him.

Liz tried to wait, she really did, but it was time, and if he came along with her, so much the sweeter. She grabbed his forearms and before he realized what was going on, she went rigid against him, screaming out her pleasure. He watched in amazement as she flushed from face to breast. He pulled back, then thrust again—and she came again, still panting hard.

He was beyond reason now and lifted her off the bed entirely, forcing all her weight down on him and came along with her third, howling with the intensity of it.

Liz held onto his neck, staring up at him, afraid he might drop her as he relaxed after coming. He returned to this world and opened his eyes. He grinned like a fool.

They both started to giggle. The giggle turned to a belly laugh, and they collapsed onto the bed.

"Damn," Liz said. "Why did I wait so long to ask you out?" She sighed happily as they lay back under the covers, resting up for round two, she hoped.

"Hey, I asked you out," he protested. "Why did it take you so long to reveal your true colors? You've worked for us for six months, and last week was the first time I could even tell you had a female shape."

"Yeah, I tend to wear stuff left over from my chubbier time during the day. I just didn't see a need to invest in a new wardrobe for this part-time job," she replied, "and I didn't want to distract from the business focus on the clients, not me."

"Well, now that I know what's really under all that wrapping, I would like it if you'd keep yourself under cover to keep the hoi polloi away," he said. "Hmm, or maybe we should dress you up to attract more clients."

"Not in this town, where youth and beauty are part of the holy trinity with money. When I walk around during the day, I swear I could shoplift for all that anyone sees me. And at night, it's even worse," she complained.

"What do you mean?" he asked.

"I noticed it when I came out of my mourning for Sam. Other things had happened to me during that period, too, like the big down-shift in hormones and the changes that accompany that. Still, the last time I remember being this, well, invisible, was in my early teens," she said, lost in the emotional memory. "I could go for a walk at night and never fear anyone bothering me. I didn't question it then. I just assumed it meant I wasn't worth noticing. And now I feel that way again. But only outside, in the night."

She paused. "Put me in a casino in a fancy dress though, and I'll get a few looks. So I work with the light spectrum given to me; visible indoors and not outside."

"I can't imagine not seeing you," he said. "And your scent and fragrance are quite potent."

She punched him lightly in the arm. "Hey, are you saying I need a bath?" She giggled.

"No, not at all. When I was waiting for you to arrive at the restaurant, I kept remembering your scent," he said, nuzzling her neck to emphasize his point.

"See! Even you didn't see me standing there, did you?" she said.

"What? I was there ahead of you, right?"

"No. I wasn't kidding when I said I beat you there. I watched you for at least two minutes before I stepped out of the shadow and touched your arm. I was about six feet from you the whole time." She smiled sadly. "See what I mean? In the night I'm invisible even when you're looking for me.

"Hey, wait a minute here," she said and flipped back the covers. There were no scratches on his chest.

She froze as two images merged in her mind.

She propped herself up and leaned over him. "You've healed completely. How is that possible?"

He shrugged. "I've always healed quickly."

She didn't buy it. "Wait here." She dashed out of the room and returned less than a minute later with a plain paper print of a photo.

"How do you explain this?" she asked, handing him the thermographic shot she had taken some nights ago. Careless of her nakedness, she sat next to him on the bed as he studied the paper.

"I was out working on my study of the new construction behind the studio when I saw two guys face off. When I realized it was you, I snapped some pictures, but only this one from the thermographic camera came out."

Liz watched his reaction and knew he was searching for a palatable lie. She reached to touch him, and his hand was cold, a sure reaction of fear. But why would he fear her?

"Armando, I can see you're formulating a story to throw me off. Please don't do that," she said, stroking his cool fingertips.

"How much do you know about thermographic images?"

"Just tell me what this means," she said. "I've never seen a person so totally saturated with heat."

"And from that your conclusion is...?"

"My first reaction was that you two were so angry at one another that you raised your total body temperature, but that can't be the whole answer. Just tell me," she said, her irritation growing.

Armando stared at the photo to avoid her eyes.

"What did you hear of our conversation?" he asked.

"Oh, I'm horrible at remembering words," she said. "But I'm sure he was threatening you, and you said," she paused, "you said something about being the law. Hey, are you an undercover cop?"

He sighed. "I'm a probation officer for some special cases and, uh, gangs," he said.

Liz narrowed her eyes and stared at him, trying to figure the magnitude of the lie.

"No, that's not right," she said sarcastically, "not right at all." She jerked back from him and stormed across the room. She planted her feet and stared him down. "The truth, please. Now."

She watched him and saw him decide.

"Well, you're invisible at night and I'm a shape shifter," he said, studying her face.

"So you're a werewolf? Damn, I knew all my late-night reading would come in handy one day." She laughed loudly as she bounced back onto the bed. It hurt that he wasn't going to answer her truthfully.

"No, no, I'm not a werewolf. I'm the Portal Guardian for the various packs because I'm not in their packs. I'm too different," he replied with some formality. "But if you weren't prepared to believe me, then why did you ask the question?" Some anger showed in his tone.

Liz realized her inane reaction wasn't helping. She took a deep breath and regained control. She took a few more deep breaths, letting the new information circulate in her imagination. Armando was studying her, and though she liked it when his eyes drifted to her breasts, something else held his gaze.

The animals. She suddenly remembered the animals that had raced past her.

"So that's why a cougar and a wolf ran right in front of me in the parking lot?" she said. "At least I can lay to rest my worries of hallucinations." She collapsed on the bed, her head next to his, and stared at the ceiling.

"If you were there, that close, how come I didn't see you?" He leaned up on his elbow to examine her reaction.

"I think you were too preoccupied with that thug."

"Liz, aren't you afraid to be out taking pictures at night? Las Vegas, especially back from the Strip, is not the safest place to wander after dark."

Liz did the long-distance stare before she turned to meet his eyes.

"It's like I told you," she said. "I'm always comfortable in the dark. Just the other day, I was thinking about how I used to sneak out of my house late at night when I was a teenager. I could walk anywhere, and as long as I stayed quiet, no one bothered me... ever. For safety I carry my pistol, the one Sam trained me to shoot, but I've never needed it."

Armando kept staring at her.

It made her edgy.

She deflected his next question with one of her own. "How are you different from the packs? You've come this far; tell me the whole story." She softened the request by rolling to him and stroking his back. She was equal parts curious and, despite everything he'd said, ready to fuck again.

He paused, enjoying her caresses, then sighed. "You won't believe me, but here goes," he said finally.

"A Sioux shaman turned me about a hundred years ago as part of my initiation ceremony. My dream self was a cougar, and in my soul journey, I was a cougar. What I didn't know was what my father kept hidden from me: He was a werewolf. He came to America to escape a death sentence from one of the Austrian packs for turning someone without permission. Away from the influence of the others, he was able to pass as human. He married a human and had children. Something in the shaman's magic screwed up all that. Now I change to cougar each month. I can also change to my father's form, but it takes planning and meditation, or extreme provocation."

Liz watched him in slack-jawed amazement. Her eyes darted over his features, looking for all the usual tells of the lie, the story made up to entertain or confuse.

But the truth was in his voice. She could hear the frustration, bitterness, and sadness in his confession. He must always feel alone, a fate all the more so damning for being at least in part a pack animal. Not sure whether she should offer comfort or distraction, or if she should run away, she lay still. How much *strange* could she accept in one night?

"I promised you a hot tub," she finally said, "and I could use it now myself. Let's go." She paused and arched a wiseass smile at him. "Do cougars like to get wet?"

He didn't answer her, but after a moment he followed her, naked, into the night.

Liz stepped back into the house to grab robes and towels, while Armando opened the hot tub and moved aside its lid. As she approached the open door of the patio off her bedroom, she stopped cold. A rather large wolf, cast in silhouette, crouched on the low roof of the shed.

Armando was setting the lid on the grass and seemed unaware of the intruder, but he spun suddenly when the wolf jumped into the courtyard. It changed to human form in midflight, and landed, naked, on two feet.

"Damn it to hell, Armando, why are you with a human like this?" the intruder said. "How can you expect respect from any pack anywhere if you can't keep away from the humans? Every time you veer away from our rules, you know you get further from being allowed to join a pack."

"Your pack doesn't belong here, Georg, so you matter not to me," he replied, stepping closer to the man form.

Distracted by his body, it took Liz a moment to recognize the powerful threat rolling off this guy. She dropped the towels quietly and padded over to her dresser. She slowly pulled the pistol from its holster in the bottom drawer.

She stood in the doorway, quiet and ready to move. For no good reason, she believed Armando could handle himself, but a little backup couldn't hurt.

"I told your punks to tell you to leave town. Didn't they give you the message?" Armando said.

Liz appreciated that he was steering the conversation away from her.

"Yeah, they told me, and I took them down for failing to deliver my message," Georg snarled. "I'm taking over this region, and your lame coalition of packs needs to just get over it."

"Look, if we changed pack structure every time some lame-ass traveling troupe from Europe came through this town, we'd have moon-rage every month," Armando explained, clearly exasperated. "Just pack up and move on." With apparent disdain, he turned his back on the man.

Liz was surprised at his move and clutched the pistol. She released the safety.

Georg turned at the metallic snap and stared into the house.

"You think your human play-pet will keep you safe?" Georg said, keeping an eye on the doorway. "You keep polluting the pack with them, and they let you get away with it for reasons beyond my comprehension. That's why this region needs me. You forget the old ways, the important lessons we all must heed."

Liz kept to the shadow but did not drop her aim.

"Georg, just leave it," Armando sighed, clearly trying to sound placating and lower the tension. "I've already spoken to the council, but I couldn't endorse you. Your old-world style won't play here in Vegas. I mean really, letting your pups run through the city at night? What kind of leadership is that in a town flush with security cameras every hundred yards or so. You haven't adapted, have you?"

Stiff with pride, Georg said, "We have survived, have we not? What better proof of our ways than that?"

"Then why do they keep sending you out of Europe? Could it be that your lack of adjusting isn't safe in a crowded continent," Armando countered. "But enough. Pack up your troupe, and leave us alone. When your show closes, I want you all gone."

"This isn't over, not at all. But I leave you to your human," Georg said. And in a blink, he was wolf again. In one bound, he was back on the roof and gone.

Liz shook herself: She was sure the immediate danger had passed, and now she needed to stop ogling the lovely, naked man in her garden.

Liz stepped out into the atrium, her pistol down, safety back on.

"I watched the whole thing, from a wolf jumping off my shed to two very naked men talking. Do you have any idea how weird that is in our culture, two straight guys who can hold a comfortable conversation in the buff?" she babbled.

"You are one unusual woman, Ms. Liz," he laughed with relief. "You see a transformation and focus on the nudity. Wow!" He paused to stroke her shoulder and calm her shivers. "Why couldn't either of us see you?"

She shrugged. "I told you; it's the night."

She glanced out into the garden. "The big, bad wolf is gone. I really need to soak—with you—in the hot tub. Will you join me?"

Armando picked up the forgotten towels and took her hand.

With the warm, bubbling water relaxing her, Armando pulled her into the cradle of his lap, his arms holding her, offering comfort.

"So here we sit, a shape shifter and the invisible woman," he said. She turned her head to look him in the face and laughed out loud.

"Yes, I guess that sums up the discovery," she said with a shiver. "But you left out the really worrying part: There's some kind of trouble brewing." She paused and stared at him. "I'm clearly part of it now, so I want to help."

She kissed him before he could respond.

Her plan was simple. Armando hated it.

"Look," she said as they headed to the studio, "we already discussed it. If Georg knows where my house is, how long before he comes back? I'm involved now, and I can help, so get over yourself and your overbearing loner-guy pose."

Armando shook his head but finally gave up arguing with her. He dropped her at the front of the studio.

She let herself in, disarmed the alarm, and headed to the rear. She quietly went to the door and checked the peephole. She jumped back at the sight of an amber eyeball completely filling the view. She stood back.

"Liz, open the door," Armando said.

"Don't play games," she scolded in a low whisper.

"Sorry," he said.

Before he could continue, his ears pulled back, and he shoved her into the dark doorway. He turned to face the silhouetted figure coming down the alleyway.

"Working late tonight?" the man sneered. He kept coming. "I'm done talking to you. It's time your packs accepted our leadership."

"Georg, you can't really expect seven fully autonomous packs to suddenly accept your rule." Armando stood his ground, planted like a tree.

Georg shook his head. "I can't believe the continued insolence of you curs." He sighed loudly, as if in mourning for a time gone by. "Do those weak pups appreciate that you will die for them tonight? Would they even care?" He dropped his overcoat casually over a garbage barrel. He motioned to someone down the alley.

Liz wondered how bad the trash talk would hit Armando, but she remained still. As they glared at each other, she slowly pulled her pistol from her pocket. In their planning argument, Armando warned her off bringing the weapon, but lacking wolf claws and jaws, she was determined to protect him as best she could.

Raging howls stopped her cold. Tricked by the shadows, she took a moment to focus on the sudden swirl of dust and fog that resolved into two huge wolves staring each other down. Matched in size, they differed only in color, one solid gray in the dim light, and the other darker with an odd white tip on his ears.

Liz's heart raced. Armando had not transformed into the cougar. How the hell was she supposed to know which wolf was him?

The animals circled one another, snarling, teeth bared, each looking for the other to back down.

Her heart pounded and she struggled to stay still as their circling stopped. White-tip leapt at the throat of the gray. It faked high, then dove low and grabbed the exposed flesh below the jaw. It lost its grip as Gray shook his head and rolled at the same time, forcing White-tip onto his back. Before White-tip could get up, Gray clamped its jaws on the exposed throat of White-tip, growled, and increased the pressure.

Liz was nearly paralyzed in confusion. She had to break up the fight enough to figure out which wolf was Armando. She dropped her gun back into her pocket and grabbed the broom from inside the doorway. As Gray shook his head, she planted her feet behind him and swung for all she was worth with her improvised bat. She bounced from the impact and fell back into the shadow.

The gray wolf released his opponent and fell back, more shocked than hurt by her blow. It spun, looking for its attacker. Liz froze and held her breath, wishing frantically that it would move before she passed out.

White-tip stood and faced her. She saw the glowing amber eyes. She clung to the wall, hoping the harsh breathing of the two wolves covered her sudden gasp.

Gray backed to the opposite wall and swiveled between Armando and her location. The broom lay on the pavement. Gray clearly couldn't see her.

White-tip faced her direction still, sniffing deeply.

Without warning, Gray leapt over Armando and grabbed his neck from behind. It buried his teeth in the flesh behind Armando's head and shook its whole body, ripping into Armando. Armando struggled to roll or swing his head to throw off Gray, whimpering in rage and pain. Gray forced Armando down, stood on him, and raised its head in a triumphant howl. It bent and opened its jaws wide to bite Armando another time—maybe, Liz realized, for the last time.

With more calm than she thought she possessed, Liz pulled the pistol from her pocket. She aimed for the biggest target, its chest, and calmly squeezed the trigger. She prayed the gray did not have amber eyes, too.

The impact of the close-range shot blew the gray wolf off Armando and tossed him on the pavement in a tangled heap. Armando jumped up and over him, nuzzling into the wound, assessing the damage.

As if the pain forced a change, the gray returned to his human shape. Its body slowly extended, stretched, and changed color. Jaw dropping, Liz watched as fur slowly became flesh. The gaping hole in the shoulder of the wolf now was a wound in a man's right shoulder trickling blood. The man panted, but his eyes were alert.

Liz ran into the studio and grabbed a wad of towels. She ran into Armando, naked and himself, as she charged back out.

"What are you doing?" he growled, his voice raspy and deep.

"Oh, get the hell out of the way," she yelled back. "I hurt him, and he's bleeding. I just want to staunch the blood." She shouldered past him and stopped when she realized the other man was gone.

"Where is he?" she said.

"Why would he stay?" Armando said. "Georg doesn't know exactly how, but he lost. And he won't be back." His words carried a tone of finality. "His pups saw him lose to me."

Liz looked around as Armando picked up his clothes and realized Georg's clothes were also gone.

"We get a boost in recovery from the transition," he explained as he dressed. "He'll be fine in a few hours, but his pack will know I beat him." He paused. "It'll be interesting to see how the situation plays out. Maybe we should go see their show tomorrow night."

"More importantly, I won," he grinned down at her, "because I had you, my secret weapon."

Liz backed away from his intense gaze and disappeared into the dark, then reappeared to grab his hand.

"No," she said. "We won, and *I* have you." She grabbed the back of his neck and pulled him in for a kiss. "Before we go to any show, though, you still owe me a slow, slow time in the tub."

GINA MASSEL-CASTATER works at a marketing and technology assessment company in the Research Triangle Park area of North Carolina. She is a mother and grandmother who has come late to the discipline of actually writing, instead of talking about writing.

She responded to my request for an afterword with the following:

Liz is a reaction to one of the oddities of aging: becoming slowly invisible in a youth-driven culture. I noticed that I could walk through a department store without causing a stir or even a "May I help you, ma'am," from a salesclerk. On various trips to Las Vegas for business and pleasure, I noticed the effect was even more pronounced.

I wanted to see what would happen if the invisibility became an asset rather than a brutal rite of passage into the second half of life. Liz learns to embrace the power she has been granted.

I look forward to revealing more about Liz.

FOR A GOOD TIME, CALL . . .

TONI L.P. KELNER

Witch's Haven had been customer-free for most of the day when the phone rang. It was the middle of November, so the yahoos who thought Salem would be the perfect place to spend Halloween had taken their SUVs back to whatever suburban nightmare they'd come from, and I'd already packed up all the tacky souvenir crap they would have wanted to buy. The local practitioners and practitioner-wannabes who kept the store going the rest of the year knew that my family—grandmother, mother, aunts, sister, cousins and all—were all off on their post-Halloween vacation. Excuse me, their Renewal Retreat.

That left me alone with a stack of paperback westerns, and I'd have been just as happy if the status had stayed quo, but the phone rang a second time. Since I was theoretically there to serve our customers, I reached for the green glass spray bottle my sister Ennis had left for me. She'd thoughtfully written out a label, in calligraphy, with the instructions.

For Maura:
Apply to both hands before using phone.
Do not let phone come into contact with bare skin.

"Because of course I'd forget how to use the stuff if she didn't write it down," I muttered as I spritzed first one hand and then

53

the other. It even smelled nice. After a second of waving to make sure the potion had dried, I gingerly picked up the phone and put it to my ear. "Witch's Haven."

"Maura, that's great," Ennis chirped. "Your voice isn't breaking up at all. I knew that potion would help. Now if I can just teach you more control..."

"I have plenty of control," I said between clenched teeth. It might have been more convincing if there hadn't been a loud snap at that moment.

"Control, Maura. Just keep repeating that chant I taught you."

I took a deep breath, and managed to stop the feedback on the line. "I can't chant and talk on the phone at the same time."

"You can mentally chant while you speak—it's really not that hard if—"

"What's up, Ennis? Is something wrong?"

"No, of course not. What could go wrong with this many of the Kith in one place?" She giggled at the very thought. "The retreat has been just wonderful, Maura. I really wish you'd change your mind. Close up the shop and join us." I might have been touched by her invitation if she hadn't added, "Even you'd be able to sense the richness of the vibrations."

"I don't want to let our customers down," I said, managing to cause only a couple of pops. "In fact, I can't talk long—the store is so busy today." Fortunately, Ennis couldn't smell a lie over the phone.

"Well, if you're there anyway, you can take care of that herb delivery from Rodric."

"He hasn't brought them yet."

"Well, duh! He can't come to the shop—he'd have to cross ley lines, and that would diminish his powers for a week! You have to go pick them up and get instructions for storage."

Slight crackles. "You said he'd call when he had the order ready. He hasn't called."

"Bother! He said it would be this week."

Since it was only Wednesday, it was hardly reason for concern, especially since Ennis was going to be gone for another week and a half. "Anything else?"

"Don't forget that we're setting up the circle tonight, which means we'll shut off our cell phones and—"

"I know what happens in a circle," I said. Just because I had no power to add to the ritual didn't mean I hadn't seen plenty. I'd even enjoyed them—it was the rest of the retreat that I dreaded, when people talked about techniques and methods that were meaningless to me or, even worse, stopped talking about them whenever I came near. Of course, even that was better than when I was a teenager, when the Elder Sisters of the Kith took turns trying to coax an Affinity, any Affinity at all, out of me.

"Of course you do," Ennis said in that soothing tone that made me want to pull every hair out of my head or, far more satisfying, hers. "I just wanted to remind you that you won't be able to get in touch with us by mundane means, and since you can't use magical methods, I don't know what you'll do in an emergency."

"I think the Salem Police, the Massachusetts State Police, the National Guard, the Coast Guard, and the Girl Scouts will be able to take care of anything that arises," I said.

There was a pause as she tried to figure out if I was joking. "Well, I suppose you could send somebody to find us, but that would disrupt our—"

"I'll be fine." Despite my best efforts, there was a particularly loud pair of pops. "I better let you get to the circle."

"One other thing. Aunt Hester asked me to give you a message. She had a premonition, something about a man wanting your help."

"Seriously?"

"I know." Ennis giggled again. "Her record isn't very good when it comes to you, is it? But you know Aunt Hester—she insisted that you needed to be told."

The phone line crackled ominously. As far as I knew, the only one of Aunt Hester's predictions that had ever failed to come true was the one about my Affinity. She still insisted that I was destined for great power some day. Not even my mother believed her anymore.

Ennis went on. "Anyway, she said you should do your best for him. Which is silly. Even if somebody did ask for anything important, you'd know better than to get involved. I mean, what could you do?"

"Bite me, plant girl," I muttered, wincing at the resulting sound effects from the phone.

"What? There's a lot of interference."

"Just trying a new chant. Anything else?"

"No, that's it. But if anybody does ask for help, just take his info and tell him somebody like me will be in touch after the retreat. You stay out of it, okay?"

The phone crackled so loudly I had to pull it from my ear, and I said, "Gotta go. There's a customer waiting." Then I slammed the handset down before it started sparking. If we ended up needing a new cordless phone, Ennis could pay for it. Did she have to be so freaking superior? Sure she had one of the most power-ful Affinities of our generation. Hell, she could make plants do anything for her short of dancing the lambada whereas my only talent seemed to be destroying telephones, modems, and anything connected to them. Did that really make her better than me? I decided against answering that question.

I managed to get through the next couple of hours without having to use the phone, and the only customer was a bus-trip refugee looking for "real witches." The herbs that make up most of our stock didn't hold her attention for long, and Aunt Phoebe's anti-theft spell meant that I didn't have to keep an eye out for shoplifting, so I ignored her until she got bored and left.

Around four, the phone rang again, and as I reached for it, I managed to knock the spray bottle off the shelf. It promptly fell onto the floor and shattered into a ridiculous number of pieces. Ennis's potion spread over the floor, which would now be imper-vious to my phone-destroying powers until the end of time.

"Shit!" I could ignore the phone and let it go to the answer-ing machine, except I'd probably short out both machines when I tried to retrieve the message, and it might be important. Or I could dip my hands in the pool of potion in the floor, and get cut by the glass shards. Or I could answer the phone like a normal person and hope for the best. But what I did was to pull down the arm of my long-sleeved Witch's Haven T-shirt so that my hand was covered, and use the makeshift glove to hold the phone in the general vicinity of my ear.

"Witch's Haven. Can I help you?"

I had no idea if the person on the other end understood me. I mostly got pops and snaps and ominous crackles, but just enough syllables crept in to confuse me. "I'm sorry, we have a bad con-nection," I said. There were more noises and garbled words but eventually I heard "herb," which was good enough to convince me that my caller was Rodric, Ennis's herb supplier. "Fine, can you give me the address?" I held the phone as far away from my ear as possible, and actually heard the address clearly. I scribbled it down on a pad, and said, "I'll be there as soon as I can."

I'd been planning to shut down early anyway, so after I cleaned up the spilled potion and broken bottle, I made a quick sweep to make sure everything was locked, put up the CLOSED sign Ennis had made—in calligraphy, of course—and headed for my car. Thankfully, my non-Affinity had no effect on cars, but of course any kind of GPS system was right out. Instead I had an actual paper map of Salem, and it didn't take long for me to figure out how to get to Rodric's house.

When I got there, I was sure I'd heard the address wrong after all. I was expecting enough land for a garden and a greenhouse or two, but I was in a suburban neighborhood and the address was a double-decker house in the midst of a forest of double-deckers, all of them so close together that I could nearly have stood between any two and stretched my arms far enough to touch both.

Well, it couldn't hurt to check. The door opened as soon as I rang the bell, which was a good sign, and a man looked at me expectantly. He was a couple of years older than I was, and not bad looking, though nothing special: medium height, with medium-brown hair, and a medium build. It would have been funny if he'd also been a medium, but I didn't sense even a little bit of magic from him.

"Hi, I'm Maura Allaway from Witch's Haven. I'm looking for—"

"Come on in," the man said. "There isn't much time. My mother will be home soon."

I didn't know what his mother had to do with it, but stepped inside. Like most double-deckers, the building was split into two apartments. The first door in the foyer apparently led to the downstairs home, while the one the guy opened led to a flight of stairs. He started up in a hurry, and I followed as fast as I could. Even when we got into the apartment proper, he kept leading the way down a short hall, through the kitchen, and toward the back of the place.

I was accustomed to odd manners from the practitioner community, so I wasn't too surprised until the moment he opened a door and practically pushed me into a bedroom.

I backed out into the hall. "Slow down, tiger! Aren't you going to at least buy me dinner first?"

"But this is where it happened," he said, his brow furrowed in confusion.

"I'm sure it is, but it's not going to be happening there today. Look, Rodric, Ennis said there'd be special instructions for the stuff she ordered, but this is going a bit beyond the pale."

"Who's Ennis? And why are you calling me Rodric?"

Shit! Was I in the wrong house? "Didn't you call Witch's Haven?"

"Yeah."

"And you gave me this address?"

"Yes."

"So I could pick up a batch of herbs?"

"I don't know anything about herbs."

"But you said—"

"I said my name is Herberto, Herberto Rocha, and that I need your help. That connection was really bad."

"Yeah, we've been having problems. Let's start over, Herberto."

"Everybody calls me Rocha."

"Okay, Rocha. What kind of help do you need?" I still wasn't thrilled by the proximity of the bedroom.

"I've been asking around town, and the word is that you people—you people at the store, I mean—are, you know . . . real."

Okay, maybe he wasn't after my body. "As opposed to imaginary?"

"Real witches. You can do real magic."

"Says who?"

"The Goodwins. They said you were able to help them when nobody else could."

I sniffed the air delicately, but there was no falsehood in his words. The Goodwins were trustworthy, and would never purposely send anyone to the Kith who wasn't in true need, but anybody can be fooled. So I phrased my questions carefully. "Do you mean me harm? Do you mean harm to any of the Allaway Kith?"

"What? No! Of course not."

He was still telling the truth, which was a relief. Over the years, we'd encountered some nutcase fundamentalists out to burn witches—or even to follow Salem tradition and hang them—and I didn't like the idea of facing somebody like that on my own. "Good. So what kind of help do you want?"

He took a deep breath. "Two weeks ago—two weeks yesterday— my niece was found dead in her bedroom."

"And that's her bedroom?"

He nodded.

Now I was even less inclined to go in. "What happened to her?"

"We don't know. Nothing showed on the autopsy—no injury, no illness, no nothing. She just... died. She was only fifteen years old, Miss Allaway—"

"Maura."

"Maura. Her name was Carmen, and she was only fifteen years old, and now she's dead." He looked down, and it didn't take my special senses to know that he was fighting back tears. "She was my goddaughter. I don't know if you have anything like godparents in your, um, religion, but—"

"We have godmothers," I said. Mine was Aunt Hester, a flake even by Allaway standards, but I knew she'd do anything for me.

"Then maybe you understand how important Carmen was to me. I need to know how she died."

"The cops must have some idea. What did they put on the death certificate?"

" 'Heart failure due to an undetected defect,' but I don't believe it. She was as healthy as a horse. Besides..." He hesitated. "Something else was going on. The last few weeks Carmen hadn't been herself."

"How so?"

"Distracted, not paying attention in school, forgetting her chores, not interested in spending time with her friends."

"Sounds like drugs."

I could tell he didn't like me saying that, but he kept his temper. "The cops thought that, too, but there were no drugs in her system—not so much as a Tylenol. No sign of booze, either."

"So what do you think happened?"

He rubbed his hand over his face, and I noticed he hadn't shaved that day. From the look of the bags under his eyes, he wasn't sleeping well, either. "I don't know. Maybe the cops are hiding something. Maybe the medical examiner botched something in the lab, missed some kind of poison."

"Or maybe it was an evil spell?"

"Yeah, no offense. I mean, that makes as much sense as anything else. All I know is that Carmen is gone, and I need to know why. The cops think I'm some kind of nut, and the medical examiner threatened to take out a restraining order if I didn't stop calling him. I don't know who else to ask for help."

Since most people who come to the Kith do so as a last resort,

I had a canned answer ready. "Look, I can't guarantee anything. My family will try to find whatever answers we can, but you've got to realize that nothing we learn would ever stand up in court. It might enable you to get better evidence; then again, it might not."

He nodded.

"That doesn't mean that you can use what we tell you to try for payback. We're big into the Law of Return. Do you know what that is?"

"It's like karma, right?"

"More or less. Whatever we send out, positive or negative, comes back to us. So before the Kith even thinks about investigating, you've got to promise not to do anything stupid."

"I promise."

My sister Ennis would have insisted that Rocha swear on a Bible or whatever book he held holy, but I could tell he meant it. "Okay, then I'll get somebody from the Kith to talk to you as soon as possible."

"Why not you?"

"We all have our specialties," I hedged, not wanting to tell him that my specialty was random destruction. "Somebody else will be able to help you more."

"Is there somebody you can call right away? My mother is due home in an hour, and I don't want her to know what we're doing."

"Here's the thing. I'm the only one of the Kith who's currently available. The rest are at a retreat, and they won't be back until the end of next week."

"I can't wait that long. My mother—you see my sister took off after Carmen was born, so Ma is raising her. Was raising..." He stopped to take a breath. "Ma is going to clear out Carmen's room this weekend—she says it's morbid to leave it this way. Don't you need the room intact to do whatever it is you do?"

"It usually helps."

"Then I need somebody now. Is there somebody else I can call?"

"There are other practitioners," I said, "but honestly, there's nobody else I would recommend. Maybe a regular PI?"

"I talked to a couple. They talked to the cops, and now they think I'm nuts, too."

"I'm sorry but—"

"Come on, you're here. Can't you at least look around Carmen's room? Maybe you'll be able to, um, See or Sense something."

I could tell the poor guy was capitalizing words, trying to describe something he'd probably never even considered believing in before this. It made me feel awful, and I was about to make more excuses and get the hell out of there. Then I remembered the call from Ennis. Aunt Hester had predicted that somebody would ask me for help, and she thought I should help him. Of course, Ennis would disapprove. So did I want to follow Aunt Hester's advice or Ennis's? When I looked at it that way, it was a no-brainer.

"I guess it wouldn't hurt for me to try," I said, and stepped inside. I should have realized before that it wasn't Rocha's bedroom. The Taylor Swift poster and pink-and-purple striped curtains were dead giveaways. "Where was she found?"

"On the bed," Rocha said. "Ma got home from work and went to tell Carmen she was back. She knocked, but Carmen didn't answer, so Ma went in and found her lying there. She could tell Carmen was... gone, but she called 911 and they tried to revive her. It was too late."

I stood still and opened myself up. Though I'd been short-changed in the Affinity department, I did have the usual senses of the Kith: I could smell deception, I could sense vibrations from places and sometimes people, and I could detect magic. It took a moment, but when the sensations from the room hit me, I shuddered.

"Did Carmen have a boyfriend?" I asked. "Or a girlfriend? Anybody she would have been sexually active with?"

Rocha's face turned pink, and I was still open enough to tell it was from a combination of anger and embarrassment. "Not that I know of."

"Did anybody else use this room?"

"Just Carmen. I mean, Ma came in, but she wouldn't... Why are you asking?"

"I'm sensing erotic emotion in this room."

"What does that mean?"

So much for subtlety. "Sex. Somebody had a lot of sex in here."

"Carmen? No way. Ma kept a tight leash on her—maybe too tight—but she didn't want her ending up like my sister. Besides, I live in the apartment downstairs, so it would have been hard for Carmen to sneak somebody in."

"Hard, not impossible."

"No, but—I just don't see it. And even if she had, what did that have to do with her dying?"

"I don't know. The impression is so strong it's masking everything else. I would expect to get more from the actual death, but all I'm getting is sex." I shrugged. "I told you I'm not the best choice."

"Not the best choice for what?" a voice demanded.

An older woman with the same coloring as Rocha was standing at the door, her hands on her hips. We'd been so distracted—me by what I was sensing and Rocha by what I was saying—that we hadn't heard her coming in.

She said, "Herberto, what are you doing now? Did you find another detective to waste your money on? How many people do you need to tell you that Carmen is dead?"

"Ma—"

"What gives you the right to bring a stranger into my house, into my granddaughter's room? Why do you do this to me?"

"It's not about you!" Rocha said. "It's about Carmen."

"No, it's about you. You think my heart isn't bleeding for Carmen? It will always bleed, but I have let her go. Now you must let her go!" She crossed over to him, and put a hand on his shoulder. "Please, Herberto. I cannot lose my son, too."

For a moment, I thought he was going to relent and abandon whatever it was he wanted me to find out, but he stepped away. "I can't, Ma. Not yet. I have to know." He turned, and I heard him going down the steps.

Leaving me alone with his mother. She was angry, and I was way out of my depth.

"I'm sorry," I said. "I should go."

"What are you? A detective?"

"Not exactly."

"Don't tell me. A psychic?" She rolled her eyes.

"Something like that," I said. For some reason, people are more willing to accept practitioners if we veil ourselves in pseudoscience. "Your son wanted me to see if I sensed anything about your granddaughter's death."

"What is there to sense? I get home from work, and come to check on her. She's on the bed, a schoolbook across her chest. I think she's fallen asleep while studying, but when I go to touch her, I know. I know she's—"

The scent of falsehood filled the room. "You're lying," I blurted.

"What are you saying?"

"What you just said was a lie."

"How can you—I would never—"

I waited until she sputtered to a stop, then asked, "Did you lie to your son, too?"

She looked toward the doorway, as if afraid Rocha had returned, but said nothing.

"No wonder he's making himself crazy. Don't you think he can tell that you're hiding something?"

"I did not want him to know," she said, not meeting my eyes. "Carmen would not want him to know."

Again, I waited her out.

"When I found Carmen, her clothes were open. Her hand was— I could tell what she'd been doing. I called 911—don't think I wasted any time. But while I waited for them, I covered her so nobody would know she had sinned."

"Sinned? Then she was having sex?"

If looks could kill, I'd have died that instant. "I said she sinned, not that she was a whore!"

That's when I realized what Mrs. Rocha was talking about. "She was touching herself?" That could explain what I'd picked up from the room. A girl's early experiences with masturbation could be even more intense than actual sex.

"It was nothing to do with her death. I spoke to a doctor privately and she told me Carmen's heart just stopped." Then she looked at me. "Will you tell Herberto?"

"Why didn't you tell him yourself? Maybe you think it's a sin, but—"

"The Church says it is an offense against chastity!"

No smell of deception there—she believed it. "Okay, but doesn't your Church say we're all sinners? Do you think it would make any difference in how he felt about her?"

"It would make a difference in how he feels about himself! It was his fault." She picked up the purple cell phone that was on top of Carmen's dresser and waved it at me. "I tried to protect her, but he gave her this for her birthday. He said all the kids had them and that she should, too."

"What does that have to do—?"

"It was in her other hand. Do you understand? She was playing with herself while talking to some boy. She died sinning

because of this thing." She flung it to the floor. Then, as if she'd
spent all her emotion, she walked away as calmly as if nothing
had happened.

Ennis had been right—I should have stayed out of it. I hadn't
helped. In fact, I'd probably made things worse, and I'd definitely
heard things I had no business hearing.

I had to get away from that house. I started out of Carmen's
bedroom, leaning down almost automatically to pick up her phone
and put it back on the dresser. And nearly dropped it again. I
could feel a residue of magic that had flowed through it, power
so strong I expected to see scorch marks on the plastic.

Looking up to make sure Mrs. Rocha was gone, I dropped the
phone into my purse. Then I hurried out of the room, down the
stairs, and outside to the street.

Rocha was waiting by my car. "I'm sorry," he said. "Ma got off
work early or something. I didn't mean for you to get mixed up
in all that. And maybe she's right. Maybe—"

"I found something!"

"What?"

"Carmen's phone has been used for magic. I don't know if it
had anything to do with her death, but since it was found in
her hand—"

"It was in her hand?"

"We need to talk." I realized he was looking over my shoulder,
and turned to see his mother watching us from the front porch.
"Why don't you follow me back to the store?"

"Yeah, that would be better."

After I'd made sure he knew where Witch's Haven was, I took
off, getting to the store enough ahead of him to get the lights
switched on and a pot of coffee started. I didn't know about
Rocha, but I needed a good dose of caffeine. When he tapped
at the door, I let him in, but kept the CLOSED sign up and the
window blinds down as I locked the door behind him. Then I
led the way to the nook, which is what Ennis calls the room in
the back of the store where the Kith holds consultations. It's as
twee as hell, with a foursome of overstuffed chairs surrounding
a coffee table covered with an embroidered tablecloth. The coffee
maker is on a small end table, with cups, napkins and such on
the shelf underneath, and when my mother is in town there are
usually fresh cookies, too.

Rocha accepted the coffee I offered and said, "What's this about Carmen's phone?"

"There are some circumstances your mother has been keeping to herself. When she found Carmen, it was pretty clear that she'd been...pleasuring herself."

I was afraid I'd been too circumspect, because it took a moment for him to get it. Then he blinked, and found an urgent need to look directly at his coffee cup.

"Anyway," I hurried on, "she had her phone in her hand, as if she'd been talking to somebody. And when I touched the phone I felt power. Magical power."

"In her phone?"

"Not everybody uses a wand or a crystal ball. My aunt Kristi's Affinity is for cars. She can fix them, make them run when nobody else can, and knows where they've been and who's been in them."

"Her Affinity?"

"Everybody in the Allaway Kith has some basic abilities—that's how I could sense the sex in Carmen's room and the magic on the phone. But we also have specialties, our Affinities. Each one is a little different, and they vary widely in strength, too." I went on before he could ask what mine was. "The point is, magic can manifest in just about anything, including a phone." I was reluctant to touch Carmen's phone again, both because of how it had been used and because I didn't want to destroy it. So I got a cloth napkin and used that to pull the phone from my purse and lay it on the table.

"Is it dangerous to use?" Rocha asked.

"I don't know," I said. "Your mother held it, and it didn't affect her. How long had Carmen had it?"

"Since the summer. Her birthday was in June."

"Then I don't think it's dangerous that way. If it was, Carmen would have died a long time ago."

He didn't say anything as he picked it up, but I could tell he was relieved—he hadn't bought his niece a cursed phone. "The battery is dead. I guess Ma didn't bother to plug it in. Do you have a charger I can use?"

"Sorry, no cell phone."

He looked surprised. "I thought everybody had a cell phone. That's what I told Ma when she didn't want me to get one for Carmen. All her friends had them, and I didn't want her feeling left out."

"I guess I'm just left out," I said, "but my mother and sister have phones, and I think they keep spare cords in the back." I went to the back office and rummaged around until I found a trio of cords from various phones. Rocha picked one, attached it to Carmen's phone, and plugged it in next to the coffee maker.

"We should wait a little while," he said.

We both drank coffee without speaking until the silence got to me and I floundered around for a topic. "Rocha... is that Puerto Rican?"

"No, Portuguese."

"We're Irish. And witches, of course."

"You all work here in the shop?"

"No, this is my mother's place. I work here, and so does my sister. How about you? What do you do?"

"I'm an electrician."

I nodded. Had Rocha not known it before, it would have been clear that small talk was not my Affinity. But in my defense, it was an unusual situation.

Ten minutes was all either of us could stand before Rocha announced there should be enough juice for us to check the phone. "Now what?" he asked.

"You can tell who the last person who called Carmen was, right? Or who she called?"

"Sure, easy," he said, looking at me as if I were an idiot. Was it my fault that all I knew about cell phones was from TV commercials? Nobody in the Kith would let me touch theirs, for obvious reasons.

He pushed a few buttons, and then aimed the tiny screen in my direction. "It says the last call was to somebody named Alejandro."

"Do you know who he is?"

"Carmen never mentioned an Alejandro to me. There's no address—just the phone number."

"Can't you look up an address from the phone number?"

"Sure. You got a PC?"

"There's one in the back, but I don't know how it works."

"You don't use a computer, either?"

I just shook my head.

"Even Ma knows how to use a computer."

We left the phone to charge more, and I showed Rocha to my mother's office, staying safely out of range as he did whatever was required.

"No address listed," he said. "Must be a cell phone."

We went back to the nook. "How come you don't use a computer or a cell phone?" Rocha asked. "Other witches can, right? Or you wouldn't have them here."

I sighed. I'd dodged as long as I could. "The thing is, I'm not a good witch."

He blanched. "But the Goodwins said you guys used white magic."

"I don't mean like 'Are you a good witch or a bad witch?' More like, 'Do you have enough magic to light a freaking match?' Which I don't."

"But you sensed things in Carmen's room. And the magic in the phone. You weren't just making it up, were you?"

"No, it's like I said. We're all born with that stuff. But that's all I got. Most of us get an Affinity by puberty. My sister's came when she was six. But me? Puberty came and went, but the Affinity fairy never came calling. That's what I mean about being a bad witch."

"Wait a minute. You can smell lies, and sense magic, and tell when things have happened. And you say that's being a bad witch?"

"It is compared to the rest of the Kith."

"Compared to the rest of the world, it's pretty damned good."

"Yeah? I never thought of it that way."

"Then maybe you need to hang around some regular people sometimes."

That sounded suspiciously like an invitation, but I put it aside for the moment. "Anyway," I said, "it would have been bad enough to just not have a Affinity. There have been others in the Kith who didn't get one, or got one so useless as to be meaningless. But what I got instead is a special sensitivity to phones. Most of the time when I use one, I screw it up, which is why our connection was so bad earlier. I don't use computers because of the internet tying in with phone lines."

"What about wi-fi?"

"Funny thing. Once you've ruined three computers as a kid, you're not tempted to risk another every time the technology improves."

"That's rough."

"I would love to go online," I admitted, "but not having a cell phone isn't that big a deal. Half the people I hear on theirs are just telling their friends how bored they are. Anyway, I'd probably fry Carmen's phone if I tried to use it."

"No problem. I'll do it. You think we should call this Alejandro?"

"Definitely."

Rocha dialed the number, then said, "I'll put it on speaker."

After only one ring, a voice answered. "This is Alejandro," he purred, and I felt my pulse quicken. "Is that you, Carmen? I've missed you."

The guy had, without a doubt, the sexiest voice I'd ever heard, with just a hint of some exotic accent.

Rocha did not seem affected. "Who is this?" he demanded.

"Give the phone to Carmen," Alejandro ordered. "I don't do boys."

"Listen to me, you son of a—"

There was a click as Alejandro hung up.

Rocha reached for the phone again.

"Let me talk this time," I said. I thought I could speak loudly enough to be heard on the speaker without coming close enough to hurt the phone.

Rocha pushed redial.

Again, Alejandro answered after the first ring. "Carmen?"

"No, this is a friend of Carmen's," I said. "She can't talk right now."

"But she's sharing you with me," he said with obscene insinuation. "What's your name, Carmen's friend?"

"Maura."

He breathed deeply. "What a lovely name. And I can tell you're just as lovely. Tell me what you look like, Maura."

It was so unexpected I didn't have time to come up with a lie. "I've got dark red hair—"

"Long and luxurious, or short and sassy?"

"Um, about halfway down my back. My eyes are green, and I'm five foot seven." I shrugged at Rocha, not knowing what else to say.

"What are you wearing?"

"Jeans and a black T-shirt." The shirt had the Witch's Haven logo on it, but I didn't want to broadcast that.

"I'm starting to get the picture, and it's a beautiful picture indeed. Do you want to know what I look like?"

"Sure."

"I look like a man with no interest in the world but you."

It was so cornball, but I shivered again—his words were affecting me like nothing I'd ever felt before.

He went on to tell me what he'd like to do to me, which involved an outrageous amount of licking, plunging, and straddling, all of which sounded wonderful, even the parts I wasn't sure were physically possible. I was beyond aroused. I forgot Carmen, I forgot why I'd called Alejandro, and I forgot that Rocha was in the room with me. Until he disconnected the call.

The shock was as sudden as if he'd thrown a bucket of ice-cold water over my head. I was so angry I actually slapped his shoulder. "You asshole!"

He jerked away, taking the phone with him. "What's the matter with you?"

"You're the one who—" I stopped, and swallowed hard. "What the hell was that?" I looked at Rocha, who was staying out of reach. "I am so sorry. I don't know what—I never hit people!"

"Could have fooled me," he said, but he was giving me half a smile.

"It was Alejandro's voice. Have you ever heard anything like that?"

"You really need to get out with normal people, Maura. Haven't you ever had an obscene phone call?"

"Oh, come on. This was way beyond some heavy breather humping his hand over the phone." But Rocha was looking at me as if I were crazy. "You didn't feel it?"

"It was just some guy talking dirty."

"No, it was more than that," I said slowly. "This guy was magic. Real magic."

"Then why didn't it affect me?"

"He said he doesn't do boys. Maybe there's a reason for that. Hang on." I had an idea, but wanted to verify a vague memory first, so I headed for the shelves where my mother keeps her reference books. I grabbed the biggest, then brought it back to the nook. It only took a few minutes to find the page I was looking for, and another moment to read the section. "Have you ever heard of an incubus? Not the band, the demon."

"A demon?"

"Don't freak out on me now, Rocha. If you can handle witches, you can handle demons. There are lots of legends and myths about incubi, but one of the Kith encountered one a couple of hundred years ago. She wrote that incubi seduce women, with a preference for the chaste and innocent. With every encounter, they drain a woman's vitality, bit by bit. Eventually the women die."

"You're saying that guy on the phone was a demon?"

"If my aunt can charm her 1975 Mustang, why can't a demon use a cell phone?"

"But how did he find Carmen?"

"I can think of a dozen ways. He could have a spy at a cell phone company, or he could make random calls until he gets a target. He could even have snuck into Carmen's school and written 'For a good time, call this number' on the bathroom wall. However it happened, once he made contact with Carmen, it would be awfully hard for an innocent girl to resist." I couldn't, and I wasn't particularly innocent.

"And that's what killed her. A demon."

"Yeah, I think so."

He ran his fingers through his hair. "I wanted to know, but I thought I'd be able to do something about it. What can we do to a demon?"

Carmen's phone rang, and I actually reached for it, which was hardly normal from someone who'd ruined dozens of phones in her life. Fortunately, after a quick look at the screen, Rocha put it behind his back.

"It's him," he said. "I don't think we should answer it. Especially not you."

"You're probably right," I said, but resisting the temptation to try to grab the phone from Rocha got harder with each subsequent ring. After a dozen rings, it stopped.

"Did he leave a message?" I asked.

He checked the screen again. "No."

I didn't know if I was relieved or disappointed. Then it rang again.

"I'm turning the ringer off," Rocha said. "Now what are we going to do about him?"

"My ancestor managed to kill the one she encountered, but she had an Affinity for demon fighting. Without that, she said the best thing was to stay away from them."

The phone rang.

"I thought you turned the ringer off," I said.

"I did."

"Shit!" More magic.

"This time I'm shutting it off completely," he said, and did so.

I picked up the book again. "According to this, once an incubus gets a taste of a woman's essence, he tends to go back to her over and over again." The phone rang again. I didn't even know how much power it would take to use a phone that had been turned off. "I think he got a taste of me."

"Jesus, Maura, what have I gotten you into? I'm going to take a hammer to this thing!"

"No! If you do, we'll never be able to find him."

He looked at me. "Do you want to find him because of what he did to Carmen, or because of what you want him to do to you?"

"Neither. I want him stopped from doing this to some other girl. I'm not saying he didn't get a hook into me, but he didn't get me that badly." I sincerely hoped I was telling the truth—unfortunately witches can't smell their own lies.

Rocha shoved the phone into his pants pocket. "So how do we get him?"

"I don't have a clue." The phone rang again. "I vote for more research."

While I went back to the Kith reference library, Rocha borrowed the computer and hit the web. By mutual agreement, we did our best to ignore the phone, which kept on ringing. An hour later, we had a selection of facts and theories about getting rid of incubi, and we ran down the list together.

"There's exorcism," Rocha said.

"Does the Church still do those? And even if they do, how would they manage it by phone?"

"Good point. That eliminates enchanted weapons and a unicorn's horn, too."

"So much for offense. Defense is no better. The only recommendations are for various ointments around the windows and doors to prevent the incubus from passing over them, but that wouldn't work for a phone, either. Neither would putting my bed up on bricks."

"Bricks?"

"Some incubi are known to be short. But if Alejandro can make a cell phone work when it's turned off, he could probably handle a step ladder."

"Nothing else?"

"Women are advised to stay chaste."

Rocha made no comment, which was probably for the best.

I slammed the book shut. "I know you don't want to have to wait for my family to get back, but I don't think we have a choice."

"You can't contact them?"

"I don't think so." From previous years at the retreat, I knew they'd gone deep into the woods to form the circle and, as Ennis had warned me, had left all cell phones behind. Plus they'd probably set wards to keep themselves hidden. To get to them, I'd need to find a practitioner who was both powerful enough to track them down, and trustworthy enough for me to point in the right direction, and I didn't know one who wasn't already at the retreat.

"Okay, then we wait. And the phone comes with me."

"Agreed, but you've got to keep it away from anyone female."

"I've got a fireproof safe back at my house, and I'll lock the thing up until I hear from you."

"He'll probably keep trying to call."

"I'll stuff the safe with a pillow to muffle the noise if I have to—I'm not going to answer it."

"It's a plan." I walked him to the door, and was about to unlock it when somebody knocked on the glass from the outside. I peered through the blinds, and saw a teenaged girl in a Salem State hooded sweatshirt with a pierced nose and too much eyeliner. My guess was she was a wannabe practitioner, and since the store gets a nice share of its profits from wannabes, I opened the door and politely said, "Sorry, we're closed."

"It's her," she said.

"Excuse me?"

She went on. "Dark red hair, black T-shirt, and jeans. But no way she's five seven."

"She's got an earpiece," Rocha said. "She's on the phone with him!"

The girl held up her phone, snapped a picture of me, and ran down the sidewalk.

"How did she find us?" I demanded.

"Carmen's phone has GPS!" Rocha went out the door in pursuit, and the two of them were quickly out of sight.

"Shit!" I said, slamming the door shut. The bastard had tracked me down. While we'd been trying to find a way to get to him, he'd found a way to get to me.

I wasn't even surprised when the store phone rang a minute later. It wouldn't have been hard to seduce directory assistance into giving him the number.

The phone continued to ring. "Some things never change," I said to nobody in particular. "Here I am, afraid to answer the phone. Of course, this time I'm worried that I'll get fried instead of the phone, but—" I stopped.

Could it be that simple? Alejandro used a telephone to absorb life force or vitality or whatever you wanted to call that kind of energy. And whenever I talked on a phone, I destroyed it with some sort of energy. The more emotional I was, the more energy I produced, and I didn't think I'd ever been as scared or as pissed as I was that minute. Maybe it was that simple!

Resolutely I answered the phone. "What!?"

"Why did you abandon me, Maura," Alejandro asked with tones of velvet. "Weren't you enjoying yourself?"

"Can't you find a real girl to play with?" The phone popped and crackled loudly.

"But you are real. I've seen your photo. You're even more breathtaking than I imagined. Not a callow child, but a woman with experience and passion."

The way he said "passion" went right to my groin, but the idea of him having a photo of me from his minion's phone scared the sex appeal right out of it. "Jerking off to a photo—how lame is that?"

Crackling filled the line, and I heard a sound of surprise from Alejandro. I hoped it was because of pain. Pain would be good.

"What are you?" he snapped, no seduction in his voice at all.

"Somebody you shouldn't have pissed off!" I said, and for the first time, I actually wanted to send static through the phone line instead of trying to hold it back. It was as if a dam had burst, with something pouring from me instead of leaking out like water through a cracked glass.

Alejandro groaned.

"How's that for passion, asshole?"

There was a pause, then he croaked, "More."

"What?"

"Give me more! It's like nothing I ever . . ." His voice reverted to sexy huskiness. "You're the one I've been searching for. No woman has ever brought me such pleasure." It went on from there, hokey and cheesy, and I came so hard I slid to the floor to keep from falling. The burst of power I'd sent toward Alejandro hadn't weakened him—it had strengthened him and I was overwhelmed.

He kept talking, and everything he told me to do, I did. With each orgasm, I sent another wave of magic through the phone to him, and I could hear his moans of pleasure as he took more and more. Then he did it all over again. Power in and power out. Even though I could tell he was draining me, or maybe I was draining myself, I didn't want to stop. I couldn't.

Then suddenly there was a mouth on mine. At first I thought it was illusion, or that Alejandro had managed to insinuate himself through the phone. Then I realized it was Rocha. The kissing was real enough, vital enough, that I could pull myself away from Alejandro's voice, but I could tell it wouldn't last long. Kissing wasn't going to be enough.

My clothes were already in shreds, and I pulled at Rocha's with the hand that wasn't still clutching the phone to my ear. I got his pants unzipped and ground myself against him. He responded, but not enough, so I pulled him down onto me and into me. He took it from there. I was gratified to learn there was something about Rocha that wasn't medium. At Starbucks, he'd have been a venti.

Alejandro was still murmuring in my ear, but it was Rocha's body that brought me off that time. As I lay there panting, he wrenched the phone from my hand and threw it across the room.

I wriggled under him, but he wrapped himself around me so tightly I could barely breathe. Minutes passed, and I finally said, "I'm okay."

"Are you sure?"

"Yeah. But don't let go."

I could hear Alejandro calling for me, growing increasingly more demanding.

"What happened?" I asked Rocha.

"I ran after the girl who ratted us out, but she gave me the slip. Then four other girls came out from nowhere and started pushing at me, yelling and blocking me from getting back here. Distractions, I guess. I went the other way, then doubled back. The door was still unlocked, and I found you—"

"That was some good finding, too."

"Look, I wouldn't have . . . I mean, I—"

"Hey, I'm the one who unzipped your pants. I knew what I was doing."

"That's good. I didn't want to take advantage of you. I did try to take the phone away, but you wouldn't let go. So I unplugged it from the wall, and that didn't help. Then I yelled at you. I even splashed cold water on you."

"Is that why my hair's wet?"

"All that left was hitting you or . . . or what we did." He gave me a small grin. "My mother taught me I should never hit a woman."

"She might not have approved of our approach, either."

He grinned more widely.

Alejandro was getting more strident.

"What do we do now?" Rocha asked. "Can I let you go?"

"If you did, I would crawl over broken glass to get to that phone." I explained as best I could how Alejandro had reacted to my attempt to fry him through the phone. "I keep throwing energy at him, but he likes it."

"Throwing energy? Like magic? Does that mean you've got an Affinity after all?"

"I guess it does." I hadn't stopped long enough to realize it. "Hell of a way of finding out."

"How does it usually work?"

"It depends. Ennis made a rose bush bloom in December."

He nodded, and I decided it was the weirdest pillow talk I'd ever participated in, particularly since there was no pillow. But I needed distraction from Alejandro's voice.

Then there was blessed silence. "Did he hang up?" I asked.

"Maybe he gave up," Rocha said, but I noticed that he didn't get off me, which was just as well.

The voice started again, louder than before. "I need you, Maura. Let me pleasure you."

"Shit! He's turned on the speaker," I said.

"He can't get at you from a distance, can he?" Rocha asked.

"Yes, he can," I said, writhing under him. "He's pulling power from somewhere so he can keep draining me."

"How?"

I was too busy climaxing to answer, and I heard a low chuckle of satisfaction as my magic flowed to Alejandro.

Rocha pinched my arm hard—apparently his mother hadn't taught him not to do that. "Maura, stay with me! Where is he getting the power?"

"How would I know?" I snapped.

"If phones are your thing, use them! Damn it, are you a good witch or a bad witch?"

If I'd had a hand free, I'd have punched him, but as it was, all I could do was try to concentrate as Alejandro sent waves of eroticism into me. "It's different this time. Somebody else..."

"Another incubus?"

I shook my head before another orgasm ripped through me.

It took a much harder pinch to get my attention the next time. "More people. He's pulling power from more women!" Of course Alejandro could draw from more than one at a time. Hadn't Rocha said he'd been delayed by a quartet under the incubus's spell?

"Can you pull from them, too? Bypass his circuit?"

"Maybe..." I tried, but I was trying to do something for which I didn't even have words other than Rocha's electrical imagery—I would have to get the Kith to help me develop a new vocabulary if I lived long enough. "There!" I said in momentary triumph as I managed to go directly to the women. Only they were sending sex, too.

Another orgasm, another pinch. My arm was going to be black and blue. "That's no good. They're as turned on as I am."

"Can't you pull something else from them?" Rocha asked.

"All they're thinking about is sex!" Another five minutes, and it would be all I ever thought of, ever. I was building toward another climax, and the climaxes were becoming so intense they were nearly painful. I could tell that not only was Alejandro draining me, he was draining the other girls as well. Already one of them was nearly unconscious.

"Forget them," Rocha said. "Find somebody else."

"What? Who?"

Rocha managed to pull a black cell phone from his pants pocket without giving me a chance to squirm free.

"No more phones," I moaned.

"This one's mine," he said, pushing buttons. "And Alejandro hasn't got my number." When I came out of the next orgasm, the phone was next to my ear and a sublimely bored voice said, "This is Wanda in technical support. Who am I speaking to?"

"This is Maura. Don't hang up," I gasped, and used my newfound Affinity to pull that boredom right out of her. Then I pushed it toward Alejandro, and for the first time in what seemed like an eternity, the arousal abated.

"What's the nature of your problem, Maura?"

"Hold on! I dropped something." I pushed past Wanda, through the lines, and I could sense an office building full of people, all in various degrees of intense boredom. I pulled and pulled as much of it into me as I could, then shoved it at Alejandro. He screeched, the least sexy sound I'd ever heard, and I felt the other girls he was draining dropping out of the circuit.

But Alejandro wasn't giving up. After just a few seconds to recover, he started after me again, and I could feel my body starting to react.

"Hello, Maura," Wanda was saying. "Are you there?"

It was Rocha who said, "She's lost her warranty certificate. Can you explain how it works?"

Wanda sighed, and more boredom wafted from her. I sucked all I could from her, but I'd already taken all I could from the others in her building. So I went on through the networks and wires and whatever it was that carried voices through the air. I found the people who were waiting for an overdue bus or stuck in traffic, who were complaining about spreadsheets and proofreading at work or tedious homework assignments, who couldn't find anything worth watching on TV or any books to read. So much boredom, and I grabbed every bit of it and shot it at Alejandro as hard as I could, ignoring his entreaties and shrieks and then... Then there was nothing to hear but Wanda, who must have been reading the third page of text by then.

Rocha asked me, "Did it work?"

I waited, and then the most wonderful sound I'd ever heard came from Carmen's phone: a dial tone. "It worked!"

Rocha said, "Thank you, Wanda, that's all we need. Please tell your boss you're doing a terrific job." He hung up on her surprised thanks.

We stayed there a little while longer, just to make sure. Then slowly Rocha levered himself off me, pulled out Carmen's purple cell phone, and pressed redial. He grinned, then held the phone up to my ear.

A mechanical voice said, "The number you have called is no longer in service."

Only then did Rocha and I realize that I was practically naked and he still hadn't zipped his pants. It made for an awkward few minutes before we decided it was late and time for him to go.

A few days later, I was alone in the shop watching the clock. The Kith was due to shut down the circle at twilight, meaning that they'd be accessible by phone again. I was still waffling about who to call first. Was it going to be Aunt Hester, so I could tell her she'd been right about me all along, or Ennis, so I could tell her she'd been wrong about me all along? I hadn't heard from Rocha, and had decided I wasn't going to. It wasn't as though we'd had an actual date—screwing to save me from a rampaging incubus didn't really count.

Then the bell over the door tinkled, and Rocha stepped in carrying a dark blue gift bag with gold stars on it.

"Hey," he said.

"Hey."

"I brought you something. I thought about flowers, but I figured with your sister . . ."

"Yeah, flowers aren't my favorite thing."

He handed me the bag, then shuffled his feet as I pulled out what I could only assume was a top-of-the-line cell phone, all gleaming and shiny.

"It's beautiful. But you didn't have to—"

"Yeah, I did. For what you did for me and Carmen. I, um, programmed my phone numbers into it already. In case you want to call me."

I held the phone up to my ear as if I were talking on it. "Rocha? This is Maura. Are you free for dinner tonight?"

He smiled. "You bet. I'll pick you up at your shop." He leaned toward me to give me a much softer kiss than we'd shared before. Overall, I preferred it to the previous ones.

Then he said, "There's a case, too."

"Rocha, you're amazing." I reached back into the bag and found a sleek leather case, with a silver charm dangling from it. The charm was even engraved: Good Witch.

Robert Heinlein said, "Specialization is for insects," and **TONI L.P. KELNER** concurs, at least where her writing is concerned. Kelner is the author of the "Where are they now?" mysteries, featuring Boston-based freelance entertainment reporter Tilda Harper, and the Laura Fleming series, which won a *Romantic Times* Career Achievement Award. Her most recent novel is *Blast From the Past*. She also co-edits urban fantasy anthologies with Charlaine Harris. Their most recent is *Home Improvement: Undead Edition*, about supernatural beings taking time off. In between books, she's a prolific writer of short stories, including the Agatha Award winner, "Sleeping With the Plush." Kelner lives north of Boston with author/husband Stephen Kelner, two daughters, and two guinea pigs. She admits that she is addicted to her cell phone.

She provided this note about her story:

Most writers will tell you that story ideas are everywhere, but you know what's really ubiquitous? Cell phones. When was the last time you went out that you didn't see somebody with one? People talk while driving, grocery shopping, and watching their kids. They text during meetings and while getting their toenails painted. They check e-mail while waiting in line at McDonald's. At any given moment, people are making dinner plans, sending sexy photos, complaining about traffic, and laughing at dirty jokes. And as far as I can tell, thousands are telling each other how bored they are.

One cell phone company has a series of commercials about things going on at any given moment, everything from the number of text messages being sent, to lovers breaking up, from how many people were listening to music on their phones to how many were using theirs as flashlights.

All that data is just floating through the air. Except it's not just data—it's a whole lot of emotion.

Some of it must have been floating in my direction when Mark asked me to write a story for this collection. I'm a big fan of urban fantasy, both reading it and writing it, but there's so much good stuff out there that it's hard to come up with something original. I'd done vampires, and werewolves, and even vampires dating werewolves, but I'd never done a witch of any description. If only I could come up with a different source of power for a witch.

A witch looking for power . . . cell phones filling the air with powerful emotions . . . is it any surprise that I made the connection?

FINE PRINT

DIANA ROWLAND

One second I was sitting on the couch in my living room, mentally rehearsing what I wanted to say to my girlfriend. The next second the house shook as my front door exploded inward.

I let out a shocked yell and jumped up from my spot on the couch as shards of wood scattered far into the front hallway. I started to grab for my phone to call 911, but stopped in mid reach as a tall, drop-dead gorgeous woman dressed in red leather strode through the smoking hole that used to be the doorframe. Silky black hair flowed about her like a living creature and rage permeated every fiber of her being as she flung something at me, striking me hard in the chest.

"Ow! Shit! What the hell?" I staggered back a step, making an awkward grab to catch the object.

"Jason, you worthless fuck!" the woman snarled. "It's not in there. Where is it?"

I stared at her with a total lack of comprehension, then dropped my eyes to the thing that she'd thrown at me, bafflement increasing as I saw that it was a copy of *Black Magick Stories*—the magazine I edited. The October issue. I looked back up at the woman in shock as recognition abruptly clicked. "Rachel...?" It was my girlfriend, but she sure looked different. Sexier. Taller.

Meaner.

Oh shit. I'd had an odd suspicion that my girlfriend was more than she seemed, that perhaps she was hiding something from me, but I hadn't truly believed it could be anything that would allow her to change her appearance like this. I mean, why the hell would I? Some things were beyond the realm of rational thought.

I backed away from her, glad that the coffee table was between us. Not that it made a difference. She reached down and grabbed the table with one hand, flinging it against the wall as easily as tossing a pillow, then closed the distance between us before I could blink. In the next instant pain exploded through my face as she backhanded me hard enough to send me sprawling to the floor.

She had her boot planted in the middle of my chest before I could do more than let out a choked cry of shock. Under different circumstances I might have found it incredibly sexy. Right now I was scared shitless.

"You promised me my story would be in the Halloween issue!" Rachel raged, red flecks glowing in her crystal-blue eyes. "We had a contract!"

I let out an involuntary scream as she ground the point of her heel into my sternum. "I can explain!" I gabbled, terror beginning to overwhelm my confusion. "It's in the November issue instead!"

"Halloween is in October, you fucking moron!" She bared her teeth in a snarl. "Damn you to all the hells!" To my immense relief she removed her boot from my chest and crouched beside me. I took several ragged gasping breaths as I struggled to work moisture back into my mouth.

"But at least I'll have you to share the next few centuries with me," she said, a cruel smile curving her lips. "Though I don't think you'll enjoy the time."

I'd met Rachel at a science fiction convention earlier in the year, though I realize now that it had been far from a chance meeting. She'd no doubt orchestrated every aspect of our first encounter, even down to somehow giving the guy sitting next to me at the hotel bar a sudden case of the runs that had him dashing to the restroom.

She slid into the empty seat and gave me a smile that caught my attention. Hell, it wasn't just her smile that did it—she was damn pretty, with long brown hair, blue eyes, and a slender figure. She wasn't overly sexy—which was probably deliberate. If a model-gorgeous sex vixen had sat next to me, I'd have been too intimidated to even look at her, much less strike up a conversation.

I also wasn't exactly dressed for picking up hot sex vixens—my garb du jour was jeans and a "Fruity Oaty Bar" T-shirt.

"So," she said with a cheeky grin, "is it true that sleeping with the editor is a viable way to get published?"

I blinked at her in shock for several seconds. *Black Magick Stories* was a small—though well-respected—fiction magazine, and this was the first time I'd ever heard anyone suggest a possible exchange of sexual favors for publication. And here was someone I might actually want to exchange sexual favors with. Though, of course, that would be totally unethical...

She tipped back her head and let out a delightful peal of laughter. "I'm so sorry, I just couldn't resist. You looked so damn serious and in need of some shaking up." She stuck out her hand. "I'm Rachel. And don't worry, I won't ask you to publish any of my stories."

I took her hand and shook it obligingly. Her humor was infectious instead of insulting, and I found myself smiling at her.

"So does this mean that you won't sleep with me?" I cringed mentally as soon as the words were out of my mouth. I was never this forward, but to my relief she merely laughed again and winked.

"I'll answer that question at a later time. How 'bout I buy you a drink instead?"

I grinned and lifted my nearly empty beer. "Now that's the way to get published!"

By the second night of the convention she'd invited me to her hotel room. By the end of the convention I'd learned—to my delight—that, by bizarre coincidence, we lived in the same city. A week after we returned home she was firmly entrenched as my girlfriend, and I was in heaven.

I tried to make a dash for the door, but Rachel snagged me by my hair as easily as a mother dog snatching up a wayward puppy. "By all means, make this entertaining for me, Jason," she hissed as she dragged me over to the wall. "You've ruined a great deal of careful planning, and I'm going to need to find some way to regain my usual calm."

I clutched at her grip on my hair. "Rachel, wait...I can explain—" The rest of my sentence dissolved into a pained yelp as she hauled me upright. She lifted her other hand, and then suddenly she was holding a thick iron nail, six inches long and about a half inch in diameter.

My eyes widened as she raised the nail high. "Shit, Rachel, wait!"

Her lips pulled back from her teeth as her hand arced down toward me. I yelled something unintelligible and squeezed my eyes shut, every muscle in my body tensing in expectation of the feel of the metal driving into my flesh. A loud thunk rattled my teeth, but to my surprise there was no accompanying burst of agony anywhere in my body. I tentatively opened my eyes, legs almost shaking with relief to see that she'd driven the nail deep into the wall of my living room, over my head.

With her bare hands, I realized.

Oh shit....

It took her less than a minute to strip me of my clothing and tie me by my wrists to the nail. I made another pathetic attempt to escape, but she was faster and stronger than I'd ever imagined. She was also barely recognizable as the woman I'd been dating. The basic features were the same, but this Rachel was several inches taller, much bustier, with a narrow waist, longer hair, plumper lips...exactly the kind of woman I'd never have been able to work up the nerve to talk to.

She stepped back and regarded me as I hung from the spike in the wall. "Well, this will do for a start," she said with a shrug, full lips curving into a smile that made me want to run and hide under the bed. "And now for the real fun."

My fingers clenched in the sheets and I gave an involuntary shudder as Rachel slowly stroked up the inside of my thigh. "You...are a tease," I gasped, lifting my head enough to give her a shaky grin.

She responded with a laugh—not sultry and sexy, but one tinged with delight, as if she was amazed she could have this sort of effect on me.

"I take it you like what I'm doing?" she asked, giving me a mischievous smile.

"I'll tell you in a few minutes," I assured her.

She laughed again, just shy of a giggle, then lowered her head to let her tongue follow the path that her fingers had just traveled.

I groaned and let my head drop back, then sucked in my breath as she reached her destination. She seemed a little inexperienced, but she was eager and adventurous, and, truth be told, I was more comfortable and relaxed than if she'd been a seasoned pro in the sack.

But she was certainly good at what she doing right then and there. It seemed only minutes later that she brought me to the best damn orgasm I'd ever had in my life. I struggled to slow the slamming of my heart as she shifted up and snuggled into my side. She rested her head on my shoulder while I tried to catch my breath.

"You like that?" she murmured.

"Holy fuck," I said with a shaky laugh. "You could say that." I took a deep breath, fairly certain now that I wasn't about to die of a heart attack, then kissed her lightly. "I'm the luckiest guy in the world."

She shifted up to one elbow and gave me a grin. "Since I'm sleeping with you now, that means you'll publish all my stories, right?"

I gave a mock groan of despair. "I knew it! You're only dating me because you know that getting a story published in my fourth-tier magazine will bring you all the fame and fortune your heart desires."

"Curses! You've figured out my evil plot," she said, smacking me with a pillow. Then she leaned over and kissed me on the nose. "Don't sell yourself short, honey. *Black Magick Stories* is at least third tier."

"Bitch." I smiled and pulled her down on top of me. "Seriously, though, why haven't you let me see any of your stories?"

She lifted one shoulder in a shrug, her blue eyes sparkling with amusement. "Perhaps I was waiting until I had you completely under my sexual spell?"

"I'm there, trust me," I assured her. "Look, I can't promise that I'll put it in the magazine, but I'll at least give you an honest critique."

A strange fury flickered in her eyes, so quickly that I wasn't even sure I'd seen it. Then in the next second she leaned down and kissed me again, thoroughly enough that I completely forgot about the odd flash of anger. "Of course, baby," she murmured against my lips. "I understand perfectly. I'll do whatever I need to do to get a story in your magazine."

"I know what you are," I managed to croak out. "Y-you're a greater demon," I continued, my breath coming in labored pants as she trailed her sharp fingernails up the inside of my thigh. I was pretty sure she was drawing blood. My hands were already going numb from the ropes on my wrists, and my shoulders were on fire from the position I'd been tied in, but a sudden realization briefly distracted me from my physical predicament. "Oh my god. You need people to read your story so that you c-can come through and establish power on earth."

She paused the progress of her nails, to my relief. "And how did you figure that out?"

Shit. There went the sliver of hope that she'd deny it and I could keep pretending this wasn't happening. "Google," I gasped. "That poem...the one you insisted be untouched. I...I looked it up."

"Clever boy," she said, rewarding me with a tight smile. "Yes, I wish to establish a presence on earth and wield my full power while here. All I need is that one passage to be read...aloud... by a number of oblivious humans."

I gave a jerky nod. "Right, a-and you figured the readers of my magazine would do that?" I hated the way my voice shook, but at least she wasn't hurting me at the moment.

She shrugged. "Enough would."

"Why couldn't you just...make people read it?"

"No direct coercion is allowed in any stage of the process," she replied. "Incentives and encouragement are permitted." She gripped my hair at the back of my head and kissed me hard and deep, grinding herself against me. My whimper shifted to a groan as my body responded. This was pathetic. Here I was, about to die in some sort of hideous fashion, and I was getting turned on.

She released me and then crouched before me. A second later, I jerked at the feel of her tongue on my thigh, slowly working upward. I had a sick feeling she was licking up the blood that her nails had drawn, but my dick didn't seem to care, and by the time she made it up there I was at full attention. I expected her to do something vicious, but to my shock I felt her mouth slide over me.

"Oh fuck," I whimpered, squeezing my eyes shut as she continued to work me with her mouth and tongue. I was shaking, as much from what she was doing as from the terror of what she could do to me in this position. But she merely continued to stroke and suck until I was gasping and shaking, right on the brink of coming.

And then she stopped, leaving me practically keening in need. She laughed and pulled away, then stood while my dick throbbed and I whimpered like a helpless idiot. "And you, my darling Jason," she said with a throaty laugh, "were very easy to encourage."

☆   ☆   ☆

I looked up at Rachel over the last page of her manuscript. "Honey, this is"—I shook my head in amazement—"this is an incredible story."

A broad smile stretched across her face. "You think it's good? So you'll publish it?"

"It's a fantastic story!" I said fervently. "But, as much as it pains me to say it, you should try and sell this to one of the bigger magazines."

She shook her head slowly, eyes staying on me. "No, I want it in yours."

"Then I'm one hell of a lucky guy," I said. "Where'd you learn to write like that?"

"Oh, I didn't write it," she said with a casual shrug. "I used threats of torture and coerced an award-winning author into writing it for me."

I laughed at the joke. "Hey, whatever works, right?"

She grinned. "Whatever works. So you'll publish it?"

I gave an emphatic nod. "Hell yeah. It just needs a couple of tweaks. I'm not so sure about that poem in the middle and the bit where you tell the reader to say it aloud—"

A heartbeat later she was pulling the manuscript out of my hands and straddling me. "No changes," she said, nuzzling my neck and lightly nipping my earlobe.

I exhaled and dropped my head back. "Mmm...I suppose I could be encouraged to leave it as it is."

She gave a throaty laugh and slid a hand beneath my shirt. "And you'll put it in the Halloween issue?"

A shudder raced across my body and I could feel my nipple harden against her touch. Other parts of me were beginning to harden as well. "Um, sure, yeah. Halloween."

She unzipped my pants and began to slowly fondle me. "Can we go ahead and do the contract now?"

"Right now?" My voice might have squeaked a little.

She slid a hand into my hair, then pulled my head back and kissed me hard. "Right now, baby," she purred. "I just have a couple of details that need to be included. Let's get the technicalities out of the way, and then I can show you how grateful I am."

"But I don't understand why you're so angry!" I finally managed to say. "I fulfilled the contract. The story will be published, just like you wanted."

She took hold of my earlobe and dug her thumbnail into it, wringing a scream of pain from me. "The contract stated that it would be in the October issue," she hissed, fury filling her eyes again. "The November issue is too late, you stupid fuck."

I tried to shake my head, but the grip on my earlobe prevented it. "No, no, no. Please, I knew what I was doing. I swear! I...I wanted to help you. I told you, I'd figured out what you were." And the truly stupid part of this was that I was telling the truth. I'd looked up the passage and found out that it was part of a ritual for calling forth a greater demon. But I hadn't really believed it, of course. I'd just assumed that it was a big game to Rachel, and that it would be a fun thing to do for Halloween.

She released a fraction of the pressure on my earlobe. "What do you mean?" she demanded, eyes narrowing.

I took a shuddering breath. Maybe I would still survive this? If so I'd be the luckiest guy in the world. "Th-the publication schedule. The Halloween issue came out in September. That issue"—I jerked my chin toward the magazine that lay crumpled on the floor—"has been on the stand for weeks. It's about to be taken off, because the November issue comes out next week. Most magazines are like that. Haven't you ever noticed?"

"Gee, sorry," she sneered. "I've had a bit of trouble getting magazines delivered to my address in hell." She stepped back and put her hands on her hips, narrowing her eyes at me. "So...my story is in the November issue? And it will be out before Halloween?"

I gave a frantic nod. "Yes! Yes! I swear! It's been printed and everything. And...it's better for you this way," I babbled. "I knew that putting it in the Halloween issue wouldn't work for you. It would be too soon!"

A smile began to spread across her face—one that reminded me of my Rachel, not this demonic version of her. "Oh, sweetie, were you really thinking of me?"

Relief flooded through me. "I was! Please believe me." It was true enough. I was thinking of her—the human version of her. "Rachel...I love you." A pang went through me. I did love her. Okay, not so much the being tied to a wall and being tortured part, but she was still beautiful and sexy...

Hell, I could handle being boyfriend to a demon Rachel, too, right?

"I just wanted you to be happy," I sighed. "I was going to ask you to move in with me."

She bit her lip, then moved to me and gave me a long lingering kiss. "Oh, Jason, I . . . I don't know what to say. You've made my dreams come true." For an instant I thought she was going to wipe away a tear. "In just a few days, I'll have a link to earth. I'll take my place among the other demons who've preceded me. Genghis Kahn, Pol Pot, Bill Gates—"

What had I done? I gulped as sick fear coiled in my belly. "Are . . . are you planning to unleash a new operating system onto the world?"

She shook her head. "Oh, no, nothing like that." Her smile turned feral. "E-reader, baby. Print will soon be a distant memory, and I'll have total control over the world's reading material!"

I breathed a sigh of relief. "Oh, okay. And, so, we're cool, right?" I asked, twisting my wrists in the ropes.

She tilted her head. "Well, if it wasn't for you, this never would have worked out for me."

"Yeah, exactly!" I said, a measure of hope beginning to steal in. "I mean, I can understand that you can't move in with me now . . . but, um, you're not still mad at me, right? You can let me go?"

She gave a long sigh. "Unfortunately, your soul is still forfeit to me."

I stared at her in confusion as I tried to swallow back the rising horror. "Wh-what? But how can that be? I helped you!"

She kissed me again. "Putting it in the November issue really was thoughtful of you, baby," she said, "and I won't forget that. But you really gotta pay attention to the fine print. The contract specifically stated it would be published in the October issue." Her expression grew serious. "Love is love, but a contract is a contract. If I let you slide, it'll kill my reputation."

I was silent for several seconds, then took a deep breath. "In other words, in a way, you're asking me to move in with you . . . ?" I gave her a tentative grin.

She let out a peal of laughter. "Oh, sweetie, that's perfect!" She parted the ropes holding me with a fingernail, then cradled my face in her hands. "But won't it bother you that I own your soul?"

"Trust me," I said as I kissed her, "it'll be no different from any other relationship I've been in."

DIANA ROWLAND has lived her entire life below the Mason-Dixon line, uses "y'all" for second-person plural, and otherwise has no Southern accent (in her opinion). Despite having a degree in Math from Georgia Tech, she has worked as a bartender, a blackjack dealer, a pit boss, a street cop, a detective, a computer forensics specialist, a crime scene investigator, and a morgue assistant. She won the marksmanship award in her Police Academy class, has a black belt in Hapkido, has handled numerous dead bodies in various states of decomposition, and can't rollerblade to save her life.

She presently lives in South Louisiana with her husband and her daughter, where she is deeply grateful for the existence of air conditioning.

At my request, she supplied this afterword to her story.

For some reason I feel I should state up front that I did not sleep with Mark Van Name in order to sell this story to him.

I mean, not that he isn't a handsome and charming and terrific guy, but, well....

Ahem. Anyway! The seed of this story came from a random conversation among publishing professionals, during which some were wondering if there really were some writers so desperate to get published that they would sleep with an editor. A common enough trope—the "casting couch" type of thing—right? But it got me thinking . . . What would be the consequences for the editor? And what if getting published wasn't really the writer's ultimate goal?

UNAWARES

SARAH A. HOYT

I remembered my name and the color red. My name was Serena Reis. Red had been dripping, dripping from—

Memory failed. I struggled. Under me the floor was gritty, hard. There was a smell of must and disuse, a smell of sweat and a smell of—

Blood. As the thought formed, I smelled it again, strong and tangy-sweet. I sat up before I realized I wished to, my hands pushing against cold concrete to impel my body upward, my head whirling suddenly. My head hurt and it felt like it swayed. I could only think slowly and as though through cotton wool.

"Easy," a voice said. The sort of voice that makes one think of really dark chocolate, or of a hand running over black velvet. "Easy now. Slowly."

I felt hands on my arms—warm, strong. Masculine hands, but very soft.

There is someone here. There is—I remembered someone. A group of tall, dark figures, gathered around a naked, bleeding corpse. My stomach shot towards my mouth and I bit my lips together. I opened my eyes, but everything was dark. I only knew my eyes were open because the darkness was more textured than the space behind my eyelids. I squirmed against the hands holding my arms, but all I got for my pains was, "Easy. You'll be unsteady," as the hands helped—forced?—me to stand.

"Who . . . ?" I started to say, but my voice came out raspy, hoarse. I knew the corpse they'd gathered around. I'd known it in life. I'd dated it for the last six months. "Phil."

"Shh," the man said out of the darkness, holding my arms firm and piloting me up what felt like a set of winding steps. "Shh. Not now."

Just as he said that, he must have pushed a door with his back, because it opened and I was blinded by the scant light of a winter evening. Though there was no more lighting than the street lights—even the moon was obscured by heavy snow clouds—it felt like dazzling sunlight after the darkness of the . . . cellar? Yes, cellar, I thought as we came all the way out to stand on a broad sidewalk, near the door we'd just left. The door was painted red, and it was the only bit of the building that looked to have had any sort of upkeep in the last hundred years or so. The rest of it—massive, red brick, with a broad, boarded-up front door and a boarded-up row of windows at second-floor height—looked like it had been abandoned decades ago.

The man let go of my arms, and I turned around to look at him. I don't know what I expected. Probably one of the dark hooded forms I'd seen around the corpse. My heart pounded hard, and I thought I should run. But every movement brought a stabbing pain through my head and made me feel like I would throw up.

The man . . . wasn't hooded, though he did wear a black leather jacket, which contrasted nicely with a lot of tied-back blond hair and the sort of features that romance cover artists would die for.

He smiled, a wry twist of his lips. "You're perfectly safe with me."

Said the wolf to the lamb, I thought, but was too nauseous to say. Besides, I wasn't exactly equipped to fight for my life. For some reason it's not something that often falls to students of classical literature to do. Frankly, I wasn't normally even out alone this late. He looked behind me at the door and the smell vanished. "We should get away from here, though. Fast. Can you walk fast?"

I nodded, though I wasn't sure at all I was telling the truth. But I was half afraid he would offer to carry me, if I said no.

As it was, he put his arm around my waist and half supported me, half pulled me, walking fast down Colfax Avenue, the longest, straightest street in the west, until it veered off to pierce the heart of Denver.

As might be inevitable in a road that long and at the center of a city that was a collection of neighborhoods, it changed every two or three blocks. One block—the one where the cellar had been—would be all warehouses. Two blocks later there would be bodegas and hairdressers with Spanish names. The next set would be lofts and gentrified coffee bars. I realized we'd left all those behind and entered what I thought of as "normal Colfax"—the part of town I thought of as real Denver, near the bend at Colorado College. Oh, somewhat gentrified, but not so much that it had run out the old diner at the corner of Colfax and Race, or the head shop across the street.

My companion had slowed down the last block, which was good because I really felt like I might pass out at any minute. Now he piloted me through the door of the diner, past a little vestibule. He nodded to the woman behind the cashier's stand, and pulled me all the way to the back, to the corner booth, despite the sign over it saying it was reserved for parties of six or more.

No one stopped us, probably because the diner was half-empty. The clock on the wall said it was three o'clock and I frowned at it. The last I remembered was ten P.M.

I sat against the brown vinyl cushions, shivering a little, realizing I was wearing only a white T-shirt and jeans. Unless I'd lost months, as well as hours, it was January. Hell, I knew for a fact the snow had been about to fall, out there. What had possessed me to come out wearing summer clothes?

The blond man, still standing, pulled off his leather jacket and wrapped it around my shoulders, before sitting down across from me. With his jacket off, he looked, if possible, more intimidating. He also was wearing a T-shirt, but his bare arms had a wing tattooed on each of them. Beneath each wing, a single word: "Heaven" and "Bound."

"Hello, Uri," a waitress said, wiping the already clean table in the way waitresses do when ingratiating themselves with a big tipper. "What will it be tonight?"

"Coffee," he said. "Black." He might have been ordering naked odalisques on a bed of rose petals, the way he spoke. "And a slice of cheesecake."

The woman looked at me. She was faded and forty—at least—with hair dyed an unlikely shade of red, and eyes underlined by far too dark a pencil. But she was looking at me as if I was the fright. Perhaps I was. The way my head hurt, I must be awfully pale.

"She'll have tea," Uri said, as if he'd known me all my life, and knew my drinking preferences. I opened my mouth to protest, then realized anything else was likely to make me throw up, and only added, "And sugar, please." I'd read somewhere that hot, sweet tea was good for shock. And I thought I was in shock. Either that or very ill. And I hoped to all that was holy that I had imagined what I thought I'd seen in the cellar.

"How do you feel?" Uri asked, as the woman walked away.

"Dizzy," I said. "Nauseous. Who—"

He slid a card to me, across the table. It was one of those cheap business cards you can buy in a big sheet and run through your laser printer when you need half a dozen cards and don't mind the slightly serrated edge. It said "Heaven Bound" across the top, then "Uri Heaven," in slightly smaller type. The bottom line, small enough to hide embarrassment at what it said, proclaimed "Psychic investigations." At the very bottom of all, and in a smaller font still, was a phone number.

I picked up the card and ran my hand over the rough edge. "You're Uri Heaven?"

"Uriel," he said, and smiled dazzlingly. "Father liked names from the Bible."

So what's a boy with a nice biblical name like that, doing in a nightmare like this?

The waitress slid a cup and a plate of cheesecake in front of him, an empty cup, a bowl of various sweetener packages and a little teapot in front of me, and walked off to talk to one of the cooks at the counter. Uri took a sip of his coffee, put it down. He looked up at me, while I tried to avoid looking directly at him by ripping two packages of sugar open and dropping their contents into the cup.

But when he said, "What do you remember?" I couldn't help looking up. His eyes were not actually black, as I'd first thought, but dark, dark blue. Where the lights on the distant ceiling shone upon them, you could sort of see a depth, like looking into a lake on an overcast day. They looked worried. Very worried.

"I saw a corpse," I said. "And...and people around..."

He frowned. "I see. Did you know the corpse?"

"Phil," I said. "I...we share an apartment, you see? I...I came... he left a note," I said, finding my footing as I spoke. "Asking me to come to that address. At ten." I looked at the clock again, and it was now three-fifteen, which meant it probably wasn't a dream.

He inhaled deeply, then asked me the oddest question, "All right. Now tell me: were you wearing a jacket?"

An hour later, he accompanied me up the narrow staircase to my—and Phil's—second floor apartment, frowning worriedly at me. "Are you sure you want to stay here?" he asked. "Not...not in a hotel room?"

The fact that I was a student and lived on carefully husbanded money that left no surplus for a hotel room was not something I wanted to discuss with a complete stranger. In fact, the place I would spend the night was none of this stranger's business. Even if he had been a reasonable height—not towering over me by a good foot—and even if he hadn't looked muscular enough to feature in magazine ads for miracle supplements. Even if he had no tattoos. Even if he didn't wear a leather jacket. Or think he was a psychic investigator. Whatever that was.

I was starting to feel better, after the sugared tea, so it must have been mostly shock making me feel ill. And I was starting to come to my senses. I wouldn't have let him accompany me home, if I could have helped it. But there had been no way to shake him, short of physical violence, and I wasn't ready to do that. I'd managed to get away from him long enough to call the police from the old-fashioned phone in the hallway leading to the ladies' room back at the diner. I'd given the police the address of the building and told them I thought there had been a death there, and also Phil's name as the victim. If they checked—they were bound to check, right?—and found him, likely they'd come to my place and intercept us before he could do something funny like kidnap me.

But the hallway outside my apartment was empty, and the door looked locked and untouched. I took off Uri's jacket, handed it to Uri, told him, "Thank you so much, but I think I'll be all right now." I opened the door, rushed in, shut it and bolted it, in the practiced movements of someone who had gotten rid of many an insistent date.

I leaned against the door, breathing hard, thinking of what he'd said. That Phil had been a blood sacrifice by a cult of vampire-raisers. They were trying, my charming—and more than likely nuttier than a fruit cake—companion had said, to raise all the people who'd died of consumption in the city a hundred years ago and more. Consumption, or as we now called it, TB, made those who died of it likely to become vampires. And there had been a lot of deaths of tuberculosis all over the Rocky Mountains before penicillin. The place was known to be beneficial to sufferers of lung ailments. But still quite a few of them died.

But why would anyone want to raise vampires? I'd asked.

He'd shrugged and told me, as if this were the sort of thing everyone knew—perhaps through reading some Psychic Investigators' Journal that I didn't know about—that vampires were very strong, somewhat telepathic and endowed with a sex appeal out of proportion with what they looked like or who they might have been while alive. That these people intended to use them as something between executioners and a shock army.

I checked the locks on the door and looked around. Everything looked exactly as I had left it and as it normally did on a Friday night. There was the sofa that Phil and I had bought fifth-hand at the Goodwill store, seventies chic, in a curved design covered in fake brown leather that had seen better days. It had Phil's economics textbook open on it, with his highlighter resting on top.

Last I'd seen it, there had been a note on the sofa, too, asking me to meet him at that address on Colfax. Funny, I didn't remember taking the note with me, but it wasn't there. I looked around on the sofa, and checked my pockets, but it was gone. Mind you, Phil wasn't home, but then he often wasn't on a Friday night. If we weren't out, he often went off with the guys to see some movie I didn't want to see, or to a game or something. Friday was the night we often did separate stuff, since we were together the rest of the week.

And the police hadn't called. I looked at the answering machine and there was no light blinking. Pressed the button and it said no new messages. It wasn't just that I'd given them Phil's name— which was listed here. But my jacket had been there as well, with my student ID in the pocket. They would have called, either to avoid going there, or after going there. And it had taken half an hour to walk home. It had to be forty-five minutes since I'd called. They'd have called by now.

Had I dreamed it all?

Had I slipped on those stairs, passed out, had concussion and imagined the rest—remembered a scene from some horror movie with Phil's face on the corpse? By the time I had reached the bathroom and looked at myself in the mirror, I was fairly sure that's what had happened. Who Uri was and why he'd told me that entire tale was something I couldn't imagine, but anyone who made a living as a psychic investigator was probably ready to tell more than a few fantastical tales. Perhaps he'd thought I'd pay him to do a psychic investigation or look for Phil or something. Or perhaps he believed what he said.

I glared at the mirror above the chipped harvest-green sink. I looked extremely pale, but at least my pupils—as I glared at my reflection—seemed to be the same size, which meant there was no skull fracture. The back of my head, when I felt it gingerly with my fingertips, blazed into a burst of pain.

I'd asked Uri if I'd fainted from the sight of Phil's body or some sort of magic, but he'd shaken his head and told me, "No. They hit you on the head. You were supposed to be the . . . wake-up snack."

I shuddered. Charming imagination, that. I swallowed two aspirin, threw cold water on my face and wondered why the heck Phil had left me a note asking to meet him it the basement of a warehouse. Probably someone had something to sell and he wanted me to look at it. Likely a desk, as he'd been looking for one. I brushed my teeth.

He'd probably gotten done before I got there. And they'd left the door unlocked, and I'd slipped and fallen down the steps in the dark. Yeah, that made sense.

I realized Uri—if that was his real name—had never turned the lights on or a flashlight or something, and let me see that basement. Probably full of old furniture someone was disposing of. And if Uri thought I believed for a moment that when he'd put his hand over my tea, he'd been blessing it, or that this had any effect in making my concussion better, he had another thing coming. Heck, if the lid of the teapot hadn't been firmly shut, I'd have thought that he'd put something in it. Roofies or wallies, or windowees, or whatever the latest rape drug was.

But no, he was just one of those new-agey deluded souls who cleansed auras and talked about one's past lives. And he knew where I lived. Which was just wonderful. Of course, normally I wasn't here alone at night. And when Phil came dragging home tonight, he was going to get the talking-to of his lifetime, for having left before I arrived. And then he was going to promise me to forfeit his next two Fridays with the guys. He could bring them here for chips and TV or whatever, but I wanted company in case the delusional maniac came trolling around again to save me from vampires.

By the time I'd put on a nightshirt—actually an old, oversized T-shirt—I'd talked myself down from that, too. After all, Uri hadn't harmed me, and he could have, when I was so out of it. He might be a nut, but he was an inoffensive one. I'd be fine. And Phil would probably laugh at it.

I wanted to go to sleep, but then I'd just wake up with Phil coming in. Normally I'd get out my laptop and play free cell, but I was too tired for that, and I didn't think I could concentrate that well. Not with my head hurting so badly. So, I moved Phil's textbook and sprawled on the sofa watching late-night TV. I was trying to figure out what the thing advertised as a mop that could also double as a shovel could possibly be, when I must have fallen asleep, because I woke up with someone pounding on the door.

"Yeah?"

"It's me, babe." Calling me babe was one Phil's worse habits. But, hey, it could be gambling. Or instigating revolutions in small third-world countries. "I lost my key."

I didn't realize I'd been worried until I failed to be angry at Phil's losing the key. He did it about twice a month. Sometimes he lost my key too. And each time, it cost us over a hundred dollars for the landlord to have the lock reconfigured. If he stopped doing that, we could afford cable and I might have something to watch other than late-night commercials.

But at least Phil was alive, and the bizarre dream hadn't been true. I turned the TV off and went to open the door. Phil was leaning against the wall outside, looking at me with a slightly unfocused gaze. He was drunk. I was sure of it. Only drunkenness would account for his leaning on the wall like that. Besides, he gave me a slow, sloppy smile and said, "Man, you're a sight for sore eyes."

"Oh, good," I said. "What was it? The margarita special at what's-its-name in Lodo, again?"

He frowned, as though not sure what I meant. I took a deep breath and stepped back from the door. "Fine. Come in. I suppose there's no point arguing."

He... flowed in. It was odd. One minute he was leaning against the wall, looking too wasted to stand up properly, and the next minute, he'd come through the door in a single motion, as if he were made of liquid. He shut the door behind himself with a careless slap and smiled at me. His eyes were still unfocused though. "Never mind," I said. "Let's go to bed."

And like that he was on me, pinning me against the wall—his hands on my shoulders, kissing me as if he'd spent the last ten years trekking the Sahara and never meeting a woman or even a female camel.

Look, I'm not going to say that Phil was normally a slouch in that department, but he wasn't exactly Casanova, either. I wasn't his first girlfriend, but I was the second. He hadn't spent years practicing his kissing with experienced women of the world. But that is what it felt like now. His tongue flowed into my mouth— cold and skillful, twining my own tongue in a seductive way, and he sucked, just a little, and he leaned close and pushed me up against the wall with his body, so that I could feel every inch of his muscles . . .

The problem is, as he tried to shift my position—with his hands now on either side of my waist—he shoved my head against the wall. Right over the bump. I howled, and pulled back from the kiss, the moment broken.

And I realized something was very wrong. For one, Phil didn't smell of alcohol. For another, Phil didn't usually smell this good. It wasn't a smell I could define—something exotic, like . . . like a tropical plant. But he smelled irresistible and made me want to melt into his arms.

Of course, maybe it was the windowees that Uri had given me. Only he hadn't, and I knew he hadn't, too, and I remembered Uri saying that vampires were sexually irresistible, even if they hadn't been before. It was nonsense, it had to be nonsense. . . .

But I allowed Phil to start kissing me again and, while he did, I unzipped his leather jacket, as if I were just sort of playing and not sure what I was doing.

I unzipped it enough for it to part and for the collar he'd raised to fall. Looking down, as he kissed me, I should not have been able to see much of anything. But the slash across his throat was pretty damn hard to miss.

A slash across his throat and the drip, drip, drip of blood being collected into a bowl.

Pushed against the wall, pinned in on either side by the arms of a dangerous—zombie? vampire?—boyfriend, there was only one direction I could go. It was a direction, too, that most men don't think of stopping a woman going.

Down. My face scraping against his jacket, my body sliding down as if I meant to kneel. Only instead, I lurched sideways, and rolled away from him. Good thing I'd actually been good at gymnastics, though it had been a long time since I'd done anything of the sort. Very good thing, because Phil didn't even hesitate. He flowed towards me, moving as fast and soundlessly as he had at the door, reaching for me. And now he was making a roarlike sound, which should have been scary—and was—but also reminded me of a house cat throwing a fit. And his teeth glimmered in the light, displaying two long and quite pointy fangs. Vampire, then. Good to know. He must have been damn careful not to let me feel those while we were kissing.

I slid around furniture, evading him. We must have looked like a Victorian maiden and her unruly suitor. "So you're a vampire?" I said conversationally, hoping to distract him. But all he did was roar at me again.

We were dancing on either side of the sofa, this way and that. His arms were extended, like a goalie's trying to prevent me getting past him either way. Were those claws at the end of his fingers? I really didn't want to know. Bad enough the wide-open mouth, the fangs glimmering, the roaring.

I jumped—straight back, over the coffee table—then lifted the coffee table, holding it as a shield between him and myself. It was exactly like a lion-taming act, only much more dangerous, because he kept trying to reach around the table, and the table was heavy. I wasn't going to be able to stay like this very long. If I could reach the door...

But I realized that would only mean that I would careen down the stairs and Phil would catch me and suck me dry. The new, improved Phil moved much better than I ever had.

I could run into the kitchen and find something to skewer him with. Unfortunately neither of us was exactly a gourmet cook, and there was only one knife in there. I didn't think that vampires could be killed with a paring knife, could they? Heck, I didn't even have chopsticks in there. Perhaps the broom handle?

He must have read my mind, or anticipated my thoughts, because he moved that way, blocking my path to both the outside and the kitchen.

So, I ran the only way I could—into the bathroom. And grabbed the first thing I saw that looked like a stake—the toilet plunger. Wrong side out.

I heard Phil's feet pound towards the door and the snarl-hiss louder than ever, as he grabbed the door I was trying to close and pulled it not just out of my grasp but off the hinges, throwing it into the living room with such force I heard it crack and splinter.

And then he advanced on me, with a big smile—or at least with his fangs really showing. I knew the plunger would never work, but what the heck. I grabbed the rubber end and struck, hard, in the direction of his chest.

Vampire chests must be different, because it went in, the whole way. He looked down for a second, somewhere between surprised and puzzled.

And then he fell into a pile of dust on the floor, and I leaned back against the sink. Just long enough to realize that I could hear screams coming from downstairs, and the same sort of hiss-growl that Phil had made. I looked down at the pile of dust and Phil's empty jeans, T-shirt and—incongruous—wristwatch.

There were more of them. Phil had probably bitten people and made them vampires. Or they'd been awakened by the sacrifice. Which meant...

It didn't matter what it meant. As I recovered from my fright, I realized I couldn't let vampires roam the streets of Denver. For one, I thought, I liked this town. For another, whoever had created vampires and made Phil into a vampire had, in a way, killed Phil. He might not have been the best boyfriend ever, but he hadn't been too bad. And he certainly hadn't deserved to die. Besides, my mind added, somewhat more incoherently, a plague of vampires would be really bad for tourism.

My body hurting as if I were about a hundred years old, I forced myself to walk out of the bathroom to where Phil had, so helpfully, broken the door. It had splintered in so many pieces that only ten or so layers of paint held the century-old wood together. Pulling a decent stake out of the mess was not hard at all. Running down the stairs to the front hall was the work of a minute.

Uri stood in the hall, defending the building from—I blinked. They were definitely vampires. But the front two were—I'd swear—two of Denver's finest, male and female, in their uniforms. They looked alive and, like Phil, would pass for human if it weren't for the glittering fangs. Behind them there clustered a far-longer-deceased multitude. Those who retained any shreds of clothing seemed to be dressed in the remains of turn-of-the-century clothing. One of the men at the back even had a very shredded top hat set atop what must have once been glistening curls but were now just grave-dirt-caked curls. All of them were grave-dirt-caked, which made race, age and creed indistinguishable. The only thing about them that glimmered was their very sharp fangs.

And Uri was keeping them back with . . . a flaming sword. There was no other way to describe it. It was a sword, and long, and made of flame. Whenever it touched a vampire, the vampire crumbled to dust.

Except for the two police-officer vampires, who must have retained some of their training because, though they were clearly in the lead and inciting the others on, they managed to stay just out of reach of the flames.

I dove under his arm, and the sword, and managed to plunge my stake into the male officer's chest. He crumbled into dust, but the female officer had gotten the point and managed to get between me and Uri, grab me by the shoulders and pull me towards her.

I swung my arm around with the desperation of the lost, and plunged it into her back, right about where I thought her heart should be. She screamed and crumbled.

The army of the long undead, losing their leaders, hesitated. Uri advanced, swinging his flaming sword. Rank on rank, they fell before they could react.

Soon, we were in the hall of my apartment building, all alone.

"A few at the back ran away," I said. "I heard them."

"I know," he said and sighed. "Can't be helped."

The other thing I supposed couldn't be helped was how he looked. He still wore his leather jacket and tight, tight jeans. His features still looked like an illustrator's wet dream. But his hair had come loose of the ponytail and seemed to have acquired a life of its own. It writhed and shone, silvery gold, lighting the entire shabby hall and its collection of turn-of-the-century, in-wall mailboxes in a way it could never have been meant to be lit. At his back, seemingly growing right through the leather jacket, was a magnificent pair of wings—white and feathery and glowing.

He did something with the sword, and the flame went out, though I supposed something remained, because he slipped something into his pocket. But the wings and the hair remained, and as he raised his hand to touch his forehead, light seemed to leak between his fingers.

"Who are you?" I asked, and realized a little late I should have said what.

He didn't argue semantics, though. Instead, he gave me a level look. "Uriel," he said. "Archangel of the presence. I—" For a moment his gaze looked as unfocused as Phil's had been. Then he glared at the light glowing around his fingers, swallowed hard and looked at me. "You don't have any liquor?" he asked. "Or cigarettes?"

"What?"

"I... need it," he said. "To keep from ascending. You see... the form on Earth is unstable, and when I'm tired or... or exert myself too much, I revert to my most true form."

"Liquor?" I said. "Cigarettes?"

"Any carnal pleasure would do," he said, managing to sound very tired. "We... don't have those, normally. It... it reinforces the body."

I looked at his confused face, his glimmering body, now seemingly shining with an interior light that came even through the leather jacket, the very tight jeans. His wings fluttered and they weren't so much real feathers as light woven into feathers. I looked up to meet his very sad expression. "Don't you want to ascend?" I asked. "Isn't it to... go to heaven?"

He shook his head. "Not while there's danger threatening people in Denver. I came here because the shielding this high in the mountain was unstable and there was a chance of... breakthroughs of... magic and supernatural and... evil things. Like this. The place itself gives people ideas, and it's easier to fight them as they start. If I go to heaven, I'll leave the area to be taken over by evil."

"We don't... Phil didn't smoke and I don't either. And he only drank when he was out."

"Oh, but then..." The light was stronger around him.

Carnal pleasures. There was only one thing I could think to do—and I couldn't quite bring myself to ask. He could stop me any time. It was odd, on short notice, but he'd saved my life. Twice.

I took him by the hand and led him up the stairs. His hand was large and strong and very soft—skin never marred by the

touch of everyday life on Earth. I opened the door to my apartment, led him into it, closed the door behind us.

He shone softly, making the torn-up living room look like
something out of a dream. Even the bedroom—when I led him
there—with the unmade bed and the ratty bed cushions, looked
like something strange and wondrous, with him in it.

I unzipped his jacket and took it off, then his T-shirt. They
came off with no hint of catching at the wings—as though the
wings weren't quite material. Underneath, his skin was very soft,
a sort of pale gold, with a dusting of darker gold hair. I reached
up to pull his head down, my fingers twined in the writhing
hair, and kissed him hard. His mouth was soft, very warm, and
after a second he returned my kiss with an ardor that Phil could
never have matched, even as a vampire. He felt warm, and contact
with me warmed me, in a not-quite-physical fashion. It was like
kissing the rising sun, like holding fast onto a warming flame
that didn't burn.

When I managed to pull back and recover my breath, he
looked at me with something close to hunger. "I didn't know," I
said, babbling the first thing that crossed my mind, "that angels
could do anything like this. I thought angels were all holy and
wore...nightgownlike things."

He narrowed his eyes, but seemingly only to focus better on
me. "We're not...what we're painted. We're very ancient. Before
Christianity. Before Judaism. Men called us into existence when
they first started thinking of eternity. Conjured us as messengers
to the divine." He sighed. "We're not...good. Or perhaps it's easier
to say we're so good, most humans would perceive us as terrible."

I thought of him in that cellar, escorting me, the subtle hint
of menace even through the protection—which had led me to
imagine all sorts of terrible things about him. I thought of him
cutting at the vampires with his sword. Phil had talked until he
got into what I guess was blood lust. Vampires were sentient. An
angel who was goody-goody would not cut them down without
a thought. But Uri had.

My hands had found the button to his jeans. I was touching something eternal, something that I could never even fully
understand. But then...doesn't one always feel like that when
lovemaking is what it's meant to be?

We kissed and kissed again. He removed my clothes slowly,

reverently, as though I were a holy relic. His hands, soft-strong, ran along my body, wakening feelings I'd never even known could exist.

I don't remember his wings disappearing. Perhaps it happened while we were making love. I woke up to the grayish light of morning, to see him standing by the window, looking out. I knew the view well—the clustered rooftops of the older part of the city. At this time of year, doubtless with a fine dusting of snow making the whole look like holiday decor.

He looked tired and also inexplicably sad. The wings were gone, leaving only the tattoos of wings across his muscular arms. Heaven Bound. I guess it was the equivalent of Pikes Peak or Bust on the back of wagons climbing the mountain at the turn of the century. Perhaps he needed to remind himself he was headed back there, eventually, no matter how hard he fought it.

Uri looked at me and smiled a little, a crooked smile. "Thank you," he said. "I miss...I miss my rightful sphere but I can't go...yet."

I sat up in bed, and gathered the sheet around me, as though there was an inch of me he hadn't seen. "No," I said. "I'm sorry I called the police. I guess the officers went to check the place, just as Phil was waking up?"

He nodded. "The sacrifice himself often becomes a vampire," he said. "I wasn't sure, and he would be shielded by the forces of the ritual, so I couldn't get near him and make sure. And, of course, the others followed the scent on your jacket. I'm sorry I... had to deal with something else, and when I got back, I didn't realize your...the sacrifice had already made it up the stairs."

"I wonder..." I wondered if he'd stay with me, to protect me from those vampires that had escaped? But I imagined there were other dangers he was watching, other perils to defend Denver from. He'd alluded to many perils, not just this one. And if the vampires came for me, I could battle them. I thought I'd proven that.

He smiled again, sadly. "You'll do fine. You have my card, if you need me. But I don't think you will."

After a while he dressed and left, locking my door behind him. And I stayed on the bed, leaning back. Presently I'd have to go and sweep Phil up off the bathroom floor. I suspected soon enough shock and grief would set in.

But for the moment I'd lie there, cherishing the memory of two wings woven out of light and the soft wonder of touching eternity.

SARAH A. HOYT has published seventeen novels under various names. The most recent publications are *No Will But His*, a story of Kathryn Howard, *A French Polished Murder* (as Elise Hyatt), and her first space opera and possibly her favorite of her own books, *Darkship Thieves*. She's also the author of an urban fantasy series—*Draw One In The Dark*, *Gentleman Takes a Chance*—for Baen Books.

Her short fiction has been published by such magazines as *Dreams of Decadence*, *Amazing*, *Analog*, and *Asimov's*.

At my request, she supplied the following afterword:

In many ways, "Unawares" started on a hot muggy summer, when I was a young mother living in Columbia, South Carolina, with a one-year-old, without air conditioning, and with only one car shared between myself and my husband. We didn't know anyone and, having moved away from Charlotte, North Carolina, I'd lost the client list my incipient multilingual translation business had built over the last five years.

The plan, such as it was, was to devote myself to writing, but between the baby, my husband working sixteen-hour days, and the fact that we were nearly broke, most of the time I just sat around looking at the lake at the back of the yard and brooding over the various stories—none of them happy—associated with the property.

This is when my friend Charles (Quinn), who worked—still does—in a bookstore (though one in Colorado now) thought I needed a pick-me-up. In the past, the man had given me books about the Civil War, about Roman architecture, about strange experiments in biology undertaken by nineteenth-century madmen, or really about any crazy thing he could lay his hands on. Some years after this, by giving me a biography of Elvis Presley, he became responsible for the short story "Elvis Died For Your Sins." The novel started by his giving me The Day The Red Baron Died *is still in progress. I think he has a bet with himself on whether he can find a book so bizarre I won't read it or it won't inspire me to write something.*

In the summer of ninety-two, the book he chose was A Dictionary Of Angels. *And I think up till now Charles thinks he* has hit on the book too weird to be made into a story. That summer long, I sat on the back porch and found out things I never knew about angels—such as that they're much older than Christianity. Heck, they're older than Judaism. Odder too. The word "angel" comes from "messenger" in Greek, and as we know, messengers can come from anywhere, and bring any kind of news. They have to be tough, too, for the perils of the journey.

Even in modern days . . . well, you'll be surprised to find that most angels also have a demonic identity. (Think what a film noir that would make.) And though they show themselves as humans—often, at least—they can be very weird creatures with multiple eyes and more than one pair of wings. Then there's the whole fiery sword thing. In fact, when it comes down to it, angels are both more dangerous and more ambiguous than all the favorites of urban fantasy. Vampires and werewolves are very simple creatures by comparison and have nothing on these bad boys.

So this is where "Unawares" originated, in that back porch, looking at a lake that was said to be haunted and at which one of our neighbors shot regularly because she believed the fairies that lived under the lake had stolen her boyfriend.

I have started a novel, featuring Uriel as well, that will see the light of day in the fullness of time. I guess all these years I've been entertaining angels unawares.

OF SEX AND ZOMBIES

TICIA DRAKE ISOM

Weddings are supposed to be sedate, orderly affairs, full of flowers and sappy love songs. Standing shoulder to shoulder with my beloved, in all of our wedding finery, while facing zombies is not an auspicious beginning to a new life.

"Are we married or not?" Michael asked.

Our wedding officiate, human like Michael, lay dead between us. I shrugged. "No rings, no vows. I say not married."

"That blows!" Michael kicked a pimply-faced teenage zombie off the dais.

Every supernatural seems to hate the idea of fairies marrying humans, so I had expected some form of attack—just not from the undead.

Michael and I both reached for the nearest weapon, an ornate candelabrum with fat candles glowing at the top that stood as tall as I did.

"Ladies first." With a flourish, he relinquished his hold on it and jumped off the dais to find another weapon. He winked at me, and I watched as his tall, rangy figure disappeared into the fleeing crowd.

I kicked myself for not having a knife or revolver on me. I never go anywhere without some way to defend myself, but the thigh holster ruined the clinging line of my wedding dress, whose plunging neckline left no hiding place.

I grabbed the candelabrum and dropped it, cursing, as red welts appeared on my palm. Stupid wedding planner. Iron is poison to fairies.

I ripped a chunk of Swarovski-crystal-encrusted train from my dress and wrapped my hand in the protective cover before reaching for the iron candelabrum again.

I stand five foot six and I'm strong and healthy, but I'm no warrior or magician. My skill is glamour. Glamour is not going to stop a horde of zombies the way a machete or a semiautomatic will.

I hiked up my skirt with my left hand and clutched the candelabrum in my right.

Michael appeared at my side, his dark hair mussed, his tuxedo jacket missing. He clutched a metal folding chair in both hands.

I snickered.

"Yeah, yeah," he said. "Next time we get married, I'm bringing an Uzi!"

What can I say? Great minds think alike. I stepped into him and, thanks to my red-soled Louboutin shoes, which made me almost as tall as Michael, leaned over to kiss him.

His gaze darted to the right. "On your left!"

I spun and, throwing all my weight behind the swing, smashed the rushing zombie across the side of her head with my vanilla-scented bludgeon.

"Double-tap," Michael said.

I reduced the zombie to a bloody pulp.

Near the edge of the clearing, Alex, Michael's best man and Special Investigations partner, was herding the human guests out of harm's way. His werewolf form was scaring some of them more than the zombies. Alex is a big human. In werewolf form, he's huge.

The Fey Guard entered, Grig in the lead.

"Your boyfriend's here," Michael said.

"Would you be quiet? He's going to hear you."

"Just tell him you know he loves you. Maybe he'll back off. Of course, you're getting married and that hasn't stopped him rushing to your rescue...."

"More fighting, less talking." I rolled my eyes and nailed a zombie in a three-piece suit across the back of the head.

Michael crammed his chair into the gut of a charging middle-aged woman wearing a hospital gown and a toe tag.

"That's bad fighting manners, Sylvie," Michael said. "Never hit an opponent when their back is turned." He smashed his zombie across the back of its head once it fell to the ground. "It's rude."

"Bite me!" I hit my zombie again, watching as it, too, crashed to the ground.

I glanced at Michael's felled, toe-tagged zombie. No underwear. Great. "Could you at least close the back of your zombie's gown? She obviously didn't read the invitation. This wedding is semiformal."

"I'm not touching that!" Michael ripped another strip off my wedding train and covered the offensive sight.

"Hey!" I said.

"Have you looked at yourself, Sylvie? You've got more blood on you than Carrie did at her prom. That dress is toast."

I looked down and sighed. I loved this gown. "Point taken."

Grig rushed over and, with more ceremony than the situation warranted, dealt my already dead zombie a killing blow with his sword.

Grig was gorgeous; the trouble was, he knew it. With his long blond hair braided and tied back, his almost feminine features, and sharp green eyes, he represented the perfect fairy ideal to humans. He even managed to look great in the hideous Fey Guard puce green uniform.

He glanced at our dead minister as he took my ringless left hand in his. "The ceremony wasn't completed?"

I shook my head no.

He laid his hand on my shoulder. "Don't do anything stupid, and call me if you need me."

"Does he always have to touch you?" Michael said.

"Say what you want about his unwavering attention; he sure knows how to fight and make a girl feel special."

"I told you about that zombie!" Michael protested. "If that doesn't scream love, I don't know what does."

Fairies and zombies are not natural enemies. They don't prey on us, and we don't worry about them, because nothing dead or undead can enter Faery. Plus, the day a zombie can catch a fairy is the day we discover that chocolate is dietetic.

I glanced over at Michael and my heart melted. "If you didn't want to get married, you could have just said so," I said, grinning. "No need to call in the cavalry."

He laughed. "You're the one who was dragging her feet."

I stuck out my tongue at him.

"Incoming!" Michael yelled. "Duck!"

I ducked.

Michael struck this zombie so hard with the edge of the folding chair that its head sailed into the empty seats.

"Who loves you, baby?" Michael said.

Unfortunately, being headless didn't slow the zombie much. Michael knocked it off its feet with a roundhouse kick, and Grig swooped in and impaled it with his sword.

"A woman over there," Grig said, pointing to the crowd behind him, "said she saw a small child running toward the forest. She said he was all dressed up and holding a small pillow. Shall I go after him?"

Michael and I looked at each other in horror.

"No, I'll go," Michael said. "It sounds like our ring bearer." He glanced at me. "Will you deal with the cleaning crew and the police?"

"You shouldn't go by yourself," I said. "I'm going with you."

He ignored me and sprinted into the forest.

I stared after him, wondering if I should follow.

"Okay," Grig said, as if reading my thoughts. "If it makes you feel better, I'll go take care of him."

"Good idea," I said. "Make sure he comes back in one piece."

Grig started after Michael but stopped to deal with three zombies who were shambling toward us. "Go on," he said. "I'll take care of this bunch, then find Michael. You need to handle the police."

I nodded, squared my shoulders, hitched my ripped wedding dress securely over my arm, and stomped my way through the wreckage to the parking lot where everyone was congregating.

I ignored the paparazzi that clamored for my attention behind the police barriers. I glanced down at my destroyed gown and knew that the pictures on the front page tomorrow would not be my most flattering. Oh well. I shrugged off my momentary fit of vanity. Short of glamouring the whole world, there was nothing I could do about it.

I searched the familiar faces around me. I almost crowed with glee when I saw Alex, naked except for a tablecloth slung around his hips, standing in the crowd ahead of me. I elbowed my way through the people, ignoring their questions, until I reached Alex.

"Nice look," I said.

"I transformed too fast, trashed the tux." He raised an eyebrow at my dress. "You're looking a little worse for wear yourself." He glanced behind me. "Where's Michael?"

"He and Grig went into the forest to look for our ring bearer," I said.

"You mean him?" Alex pointed to a little boy standing with a police officer I didn't recognize.

"Yes," I said. "You know," I gave Alex the full benefit of my smile, "I have to run and tell Grig and Michael that the boy is safe. You'll be a dear and handle the police, won't you?"

Alex glared at me. "Don't try that glamour crap on me. It may work on Michael and other humans, but it doesn't affect werewolves; it just pisses me off."

I blinked and ducked my head so that Alex wouldn't see how much his remark hurt me.

Michael, Alex, and I met two years ago while they were tracking the Collector, a psychotic human whose hobby was capturing tree fairies and pinning them, while they were still alive, on display boards in his house. As the Fairy/Human Liaison, I was Alex's and Michael's contact and partner for the investigation. Michael and I connected instantly, and we fell in love. I continued to represent Faery through the trial just so Michael and I could spend as much time as possible together.

The case cemented our relationship, but it also brought to light the intense hatred of all things human by an alarming percentage of the fairy population. Ever since, I've been doing everything I can to prove that not all humans are as bad as the Collector, but it's an uphill battle.

In fact, the entire supernatural community seems to have a problem with Michael and my relationship. The only group supporting us is the humans, mostly because they're still excited that all of the supernatural creatures in children's books are real. It's been ten years since we came out of the closet, but to the humans, we're still as shiny as a new penny.

They call us "the Hidden."

The supernatural world's reply to that is, "Nothing exists that a human can't see." Big joke. Only some supers aren't laughing.

"You still don't trust me, do you?" I whispered. "What happened was a mistake. As soon as I realized that I'd glamoured Michael, I brought him back."

"He lost a part of his life because of you," Alex said.

"Two days," I said. "And I've said I'm sorry until I'm blue in the face. He's forgiven me. Why can't you?"

"I don't want to talk about it," he said, turning away from me. "Go," he added. "I'll deal with the police."

I knew this was the best I was likely to get for the time being. I headed out to find Michael and Grig.

A few yards into the forest, the gloomy darkness made me stop and blink. My eyes took a moment to adjust. When they did, I froze, not believing what I was seeing.

I screamed and charged. Six yards ahead of me, a zombie with an impossible frizz of red hair and a white lab coat was dragging Michael's unconscious body across the ground.

"Oof!" I tackled her, and she fell with a thud. I followed, teeth bared and nails clawed, ready to gouge her eyes out.

"Wait!" she gasped. "I'm just trying to help." She sniffled and wiped a hand across her face, adding a dirt smudge to the tear tracks running down her cheeks.

I stopped. Zombies can't speak.

In fact, as the red haze cleared from my eyes, I realized that zombies don't drag their meals either. A downed human is an instant all-you-can-eat buffet. "What are you doing?" I asked.

"Michael's been bitten. I'm hiding him from the cleaning crew."

"Bitten?" I said.

"By a zombie." She pointed to his newly bandaged shoulder.

My stomach dropped, and my vision blurred. A bite from a zombie is a death sentence. There is no cure. Once a zombie bites you, you're just another form of walking dead.

"No," I said. "We're getting married today."

She spoke, but I heard nothing. I couldn't move; I couldn't think; I couldn't even blink. This was my wedding day. It was supposed to be the happiest day of my life. The only violence that was supposed to happen involved an enormous cake and a sharp knife.

She slapped me across the face, hard, snapping me out of my paralysis.

"Help me with him," she demanded.

"Where's Grig?" I looked around. "He was going after Michael. We need help to move Michael without anyone seeing us."

"There's no one here but us," she said.

"Then I need to get help. Alex is strong and a friend."

"He's with the police, isn't he?"

"Yes."

"Then he won't do it. If he finds out Michael's been bitten, he'll follow police procedure: he'll kill him."

I gasped. "But he's Michael's partner."

"You know I'm right," she said. "There are rules and regulations about zombie attacks. Michael doesn't stand a chance unless we get him to someone who can save him."

"Save him? No one can save him."

"Maybe, but I know someone who just might be able to do it."

"You're a doctor," I said, noticing the black bag for the first time.

"Yes," she said. "Lucy Greene." She stuck out her hand, and we shook. "Of course, I already know who you two are."

"You realize the insurance doesn't kick in until we're married, right?" Michael's smile was lopsided and less cheeky than normal, but I felt a surge of happiness when I heard his voice.

"I paid extra for the 'in case of catastrophic wedding failure' coverage," I joked back, trying to hide the tears that threatened to fall.

"We should get someone over here to finish the ceremony, Sylvie. Then I'll have Alex take me out," he said.

"No!" I said. "We have to explore all the options first."

"There's nothing to be done, Sylvie," Michael said.

"Lucy says she knows someone who might be able to save you," I said.

Michael stared at her. "How is that possible?"

"Dr. Victor Swan," Lucy said, as if the name alone was enough of an answer.

Michael froze.

"Who's she talking about, Michael?"

"A crazy I put out of business a few years before I met you. He was getting his kicks torturing zombies. They changed the Geneva Convention because of him. He never went to jail, because he wasn't technically breaking any laws, but he lost his license to practice."

"He was a doctor?" I asked.

"Yeah. And a wizard." Michael shuddered. "I still have nightmares about what I saw there."

"He was trying to find a cure," Lucy said.

"That's what all the psychos say when you take away their toys. He's just another Frankenstein looking to make his fame and fortune off his monster."

"Every pioneer is considered a crackpot by some," she said. "Once they succeed, they're heroes."

"How do you know Swan?" I interrupted.

"I've been studying zombies and his work for many years," she said. "I'm part of the zombie disposal squad. Well, I'm a coroner for the city, and I volunteer with the corpse patrol."

Michael backed away from her. "Did he send you to steal my body?"

"No! He doesn't even know I'm here," she said.

"Why are you here?" Michael asked.

"I heard the alert on the police scanner and rushed over to see if I could help."

"Why would you do that?" I said.

Lucy blushed scarlet. "I've been following your exploits in the tabloids. It's so romantic. It's like a real-life Romeo and Juliet story with all the opposition you guys have faced." She gasped and went pale. "Except we're going to make sure you have a happier ending," she whispered.

"Victor won't help me," Michael said. "I told you: I busted him."

"He'll forgive you," she said. "He was trying to reverse the infection and find a cure. The only way he could do that was by trial and error."

"The experiments he performed on those helpless creatures were horrific."

"You're one of those helpless creatures now, Michael," Lucy pointed out. "Victor may be your only hope. No one else knows half as much about zombies as he does. Do you want to fight for your life and throw yourself on his mercy, or do you want to curl up into a defeated little ball and die?"

"He's a monster."

"Do you want his help or not?"

I held my breath as Michael thought. I wanted so badly to shake him until his teeth rattled, but I knew from experience that if I tried to force him to do something he wasn't ready to do, he'd do the opposite.

I couldn't afford that now. This was too important.

He looked at me. "What do you think, Sylvie?"

"Go for it," I said. "I'm willing to try anything."

"Then we'd better get moving." Lucy picked up her bag. "At the most, we have ten hours left to cure you or kill you. You two continue through the forest to the highway. I'll get my car and meet you up the road in ten minutes." She patted me on the arm and then jogged toward the parking lot.

I leaned my head against Michael's good shoulder. "This better work," I said. "I'm going to kick your ass if you die." I paused. I knew he'd hate the suggestion, and I'd resisted making it earlier, but I also knew it would work. "Or, we could go to Faery."

He kissed my forehead but said nothing.

It was probably better than arguing. "How are you feeling?" I asked, dreading his response.

"Surprisingly normal." He ran his hand through his hair. "A little tired, but I blame all the excitement."

He leaned into me. "Give us a kiss."

I slapped his arm playfully. "We have more important things to worry about right now."

"No." He stopped in his tracks. "You are the most important thing in the world to me. I'm doing this for you. I don't know how long I can hold on. Whether the priest finished the ceremony or not, this is our wedding day. I want to kiss my bride."

He gathered me into his arms. His lips were gentle, the kiss slowly deepening as we found comfort in each other. His hand slid down my back to grab my ass, pulling me close. He was rock hard.

I moaned and pressed closer.

"How very touching." A dry voice interrupted our solitude.

I jumped away from Michael with a guilty start.

"Grig," I sighed. "Where have you been? You were supposed to be protecting Michael."

He tapped his sword hilt. "More zombies followed the three you saw. I couldn't let them live."

He raised his nose in the air and sniffed, his eyes locking onto Michael. "I see I missed one. I'm sorry, Michael. I'll make this as quick and painless as possible." He drew his sword.

"No!" I lunged between the two of them, forcing Grig to back up.

"Are you taking him to Faery?" Grig asked.

"No," Michael said.

I lowered my eyes.

Grig shrugged. "Your choice."

"I refuse to be a pawn in Faery." Michael lifted my chin with his finger. "We've had this discussion."

"That was before the zombie bit you," I said. I didn't want to argue, but I couldn't help myself. Dr. Swan might be able to help him. In Faery, Michael would definitely live.

"I'd rather be dead than a prisoner never allowed or able to leave Faery."

The breath whooshed from my lungs. My eyes stung as tears blurred my vision. "But it would save you..." I whispered.

Michael gathered me to his chest, wrapping his arms tightly around me before pulling back and placing his hands on both sides of my face. He held me like that until I raised my eyes to meet his. He wiped away the tears with his thumbs.

"I love you, Sylvie. I want to spend the rest of my life with you, but that would be no life. I'd rather be dead than a slave."

I nodded, gave him a wobbly smile, and snuggled back into his embrace.

"I can't lose you," I whispered as I nuzzled his neck.

"We're not giving up without a fight," Michael said.

"In that case, I assume you have a plan?" Grig said. He quirked an eyebrow at me.

"We do," I said from the comfort of Michael's arms.

"Then I'm coming with you."

"Like hell you are!" Michael objected.

Grig ignored Michael and looked at me. "When he turns zombie, he'll need to be put down before he hurts you or anyone else. Do you think you can kill him?"

"No," I answered, stricken. I held Michael, tight.

"Let me be there to protect you," Grig said.

"She doesn't need you to protect her! I would never hurt her!" Michael said.

"You can't know that," Grig said.

Grig gave Michael a measured look before he turned back to me. "I'm going with you."

"Fine," I said. I would never say it aloud, but I was relieved that Grig would be there if things went horribly wrong.

When we got to the car, Lucy looked long and hard at Grig. "Don't I know you from somewhere?"

"We've never met," Grig said. He took Lucy's hand in his and kissed its back.

Lucy looked exhausted, almost empty as she got into the car. I worried about her driving, but we needed to get moving.

Michael's cell phone rang.

"Hey, Alex," he said. "Yeah, we're fine.... No, she forgot to tell me.... I'm glad he's safe.... Thanks, I appreciate that. We're heading home to change." He glanced at me. "No, it's not like that. We'll talk about this later. I'll check with you after we've cleaned up." He hung up and ran his hands through his hair.

"He's suspicious. He knows something is going on, but he doesn't know what," Michael said.

"Great," I said. "He thinks I'm up to something, doesn't he? I thought by agreeing to be your best man he was endorsing me and the wedding."

"Sylvie, werewolves are suspicious of everyone. You know that. That's what makes them such good cops."

"But I've done everything in my power to make him trust me."

"You can't make someone trust you, Sylvie. You earn it."

"One mistake, and I'm branded for life!"

"Alex was frantic."

"In my defense, I didn't realize I'd glamoured you," I said.

"I know, Sylvie. So does he. He's just afraid you'll do it again. He's trying to protect me."

I sighed. "You're right. We have to find out who's behind this before Alex has me arrested for kidnapping you."

"We can always play that game later if you want." Michael waggled his eyebrows at me.

"Brat." I said, smiling.

During the drive to our apartment, Michael and I crouched, out of sight, in the backseat.

The phone was ringing as we entered. "It's Alex," Michael said. "I'll let the machine get it."

After quick showers, it was time to gear up. "This time, I'll be prepared for anything." I slipped on my running shoes and stuffed a five-inch blade into the back pocket of my jeans. A loose sweatshirt and a ball cap completed my glamorous transformation.

Alex ambushed us as we left the building.

"What's going on?" he asked Michael. He looked at Lucy, Grig, and finally, me. "There's something you're not telling me."

"Alex, I didn't want to get you involved." Michael scrubbed a hand across his face. As soon as Michael moved his arm, the hair on Alex's nape stood straight up. Alex growled low in his throat.

"Zombie." He almost spat the word.

"Not yet," Michael said. "But soon, too soon." He closed his eyes. "We're going to visit Swan. See if he can help me."

"This happened when you went into the forest with the fairies," Alex said.

"It wasn't like that!" I said.

"They had nothing to do with this," Michael said.

"Right," Alex said. "It's just convenient and totally unrelated."

"Yes," Michael said. "Why would they be so obvious about it?"

Alex threw his head back and howled. The misery in that sound ripped my heart in two. When he was done, he looked Michael straight in the eyes and said, "How can I help?"

A tension I didn't even realize I was holding disappeared.

"You could get in big trouble, Alex," Michael said. "Just turn around and leave us to it."

"You're my partner and friend," Alex said. "Of course I'll stand with you. What can I do?"

"Thank you," Michael said. "Knowing you're on our side is enough."

"I'll make sure the police stay off your backs," Alex said. "Just keep me in the loop."

Traffic was slow once we neared Victor's house. I groaned when I saw why. I pulled the baseball cap lower over my eyes and slumped in my seat. Five media vans sat in front of the building.

"Great," I said. "Not only do we have to figure out who's behind this and cure you, but now we have to dodge paparazzi." I wanted to scream.

"Sylvie, we can glamour the people here and sneak into Victor's house," Grig said.

"Let's wait and see what's going on first," Michael said.

We watched in horror as two burly police officers forcibly escorted Victor, in handcuffs, out his front door.

The flash of the media's cameras was blinding. I could hear the press calling out "Why did you do it?" and "Where are they now?" as they crowded around Victor before the cops shoved him into the police car.

Victor kept his head down and never opened his mouth.

"Somebody made that connection pretty quickly," Michael said.

"Now what do we do?" Lucy said. "Victor was going to fix everything."

Michael pulled out his cell phone. "Alex. They just picked up Victor Swan. Could you have him put in a private investigation room until I get there? I want to question him about those zombies before anyone else talks to him." He paused. "I appreciate it. What? Good idea. Let me know what you find." He hung up.

"Victor didn't send those zombies after you," Lucy said.

Michael wiped a hand across his sweaty brow. "Prove it," he said.

Lucy lowered her head and said nothing.

Michael pulled me aside when we got to the station house. "Tonight, Alex and his pack are following the zombie trail to its origination point."

"They can trace the zombies to the source?" I said.

"Alex thinks so," he said, wiping his brow. "How do I look? Will I pass as uninfected?"

"Your eyes are a little bloodshot, and you look like you've just run a few blocks, but I'd still do you." I smoothed his sweaty hair before kissing him lightly. "Just to be safe, I'll throw a glamour around you."

"Let's do this then."

We walked, hand in hand, Grig and Lucy behind us, to the staff sergeant's desk.

"I'm here for Victor Swan," Michael said.

"We got a call," the sergeant said. "He's upstairs in Interrogation Room 3. Scum like Swan shouldn't be allowed to walk the streets."

"I couldn't agree more," Michael said.

Victor sat facing us, on the far side of a large table, his chair tilted back on two legs, his feet propped on the table.

"Lucy," he nodded at the redhead. "Have they brought you in about the zombies, too? Does he," he glared at Michael, "think you did it?"

"No," Lucy squeaked, blushing. "I ... I'm here to help. Michael's been bitten."

Victor raised an eyebrow. "Really?" He started laughing. "Fate must have a sense of humor after all. You clearly need my help now. Why should I bother?"

"I told you he'd say no." Michael turned to leave.

I grabbed his arm and forced him to look at me. "This is our only hope."

"Fuck," Michael said, running his hand through his hair. He paced the room before turning back to Victor.

"I'm giving my consent," Michael said. "The others never had a choice."

Victor opened his mouth to speak, then closed it again. Our eyes met.

"This could be good for you too, Victor," Lucy said. "If you cure him, people will realize you were right."

"Please," I spoke the word I knew Michael would never utter.

Victor turned to Michael. "You still think I'm a monster?"

Michael nodded. "I'm only here because of Sylvie."

"Well, you're truthful. I'll give you that." He paused.

"We have the resources of Faery at our disposal," Grig said. "We can make you rich beyond your wildest dreams."

"Tempting," said Victor. "But what I want, Faery can't give me." He looked at Michael. "I want my life back."

"No," Michael said.

"Then why should I even consider this? Everyone already believes I engineered the attack at your wedding. If I kill you while doing illegal experimentation on you, they'll throw the book at me."

"Please." I mouthed again.

"I want my name cleared first."

"He could be dead by then," I said.

Victor shrugged. "I won't do anything until you find the real culprit."

"Isn't there anything you can do before then?" Grig asked. "Not to cure him," he added at Victor's negative headshake. "To help us clear your name?"

"You want me to help clear my own name?" Victor scoffed.

"Who better?" Lucy said.

"Good point," he said. "I suppose we could do an Origins Spell."

"What's an Origins Spell?" Lucy asked.

"It's a spell cast to call the maker back to its spawn," Victor said.

"We already have werewolves doing that," Michael said.

"All the werewolves do is track the scent. I can bring the maker here."

"How?" Lucy asked.

"We use a vial of blood from one of the zombies, something organic from the site where you were attacked, and magic to bind it together."

"Can't you use my blood?" Michael asked.

"I could. However, that would be breaking the law, because

you're still a living zombie. Until you clear my name, I'm not taking any more chances. Lucy can get the blood from the zombies at the morgue."

"It won't be admissible in a court of law," Lucy said. "The laws are very strict about the use and misuse of magic. Too many witches have been caught altering evidence or manufacturing clues to frame innocent people."

"We'll worry about that later," Michael said.

"Can you do the spell here?" I asked.

"I can. In fact, I insist on it. I'm not leaving this room until you prove I had nothing to do with this attack." He set his chair flat on the ground. "I'll give you a list of what I'll need from my lab."

Michael turned to us. "Lucy, you're in charge of blood. Grig, will you get dirt and grass from the clearing?"

"Of course," Grig said. "I live to serve." He ran out.

"Sylvie, you and I will get the supplies from the lab."

"Use my car," said Lucy. "My offices are just around the corner. I'll walk." She tossed me her keys as she left.

I rummaged through my purse, found a pen and an old receipt, and set them on the table in front of Victor. "Write down exactly what we need."

"There is a way to slow the process, buy you a little more time," Victor said as he handed me the list.

"How?" I asked.

"Humans have a natural defense against the virus. By revving Michael's system, like an engine, it can supercharge his immune system. Every time his body goes through a build and release of energy, it starts the cycle again."

"Okay. Let's do that then," I said.

Victor laughed. "You need to do that. I don't do boys."

I started laughing. "You're kidding. You want us to . . . now?"

"I'm serious, Sylvie," Victor said. "Sex is the answer."

"No," Michael said. "I refuse to endanger Sylvie. What if I infected her?"

"You can't infect her," Victor said. "You're not undead yet."

"You're serious?" I said, still giggling.

"It works especially well when someone else is watching," he said.

"That's not going to be you," I said as I pulled Michael from the room.

"This is the first time all day that I feel like there's something I can do to help you," I said to Michael.

"Help away," Michael said as he led me, stumbling and still giggling, to a broom closet. The fear of being discovered added excitement and an element of danger to our play. We nibbled and nipped our way across every exposed piece of flesh, tearing at clothing in our haste to be together. Michael pushed aside my bra and drew my nipple into his mouth, sucking hard. I shuddered. I reached my hand down the front of his jeans, squeezing his rock-hard cock and stroking him with one hand while I pushed down his pants with the other.

"Come on, baby." Michael was busy too. His fingers slid into me, his fingers and mouth creating a rhythm that impeded my breathing. My mouth went dry, and I felt my body flush and spasm around his fingers. "Yes," he moaned against my breast. The sound reverberated through my body, making me twitch.

I groaned a protest as he removed his hand and mouth from my body, then groaned again as he grabbed my hips and lifted me before lowering me onto his cock. I exploded. Once. Twice. He continued to pound his way into me, his hands digging into my hips as he held me against the wall. When he finally went over the edge, I was a limp bundle in his arms.

"Look what I did!" I said, pointing to his ripped shirt.

"You're an animal," he said, kissing me. "Don't worry, it just adds to my zombie mystique."

I laughed. "Come on, Zombie Boy. Now that we've reset your clock, we have a crime to solve."

When we got to Victor's, police cordons blocked the property, and ZOMBIE FREAK was spray-painted, in dripping red letters, across his front door.

"Jail is probably the safest place for Victor right now," Michael said.

"They're treating him the same way the super community is treating us," I observed.

Michael said nothing as he opened the front door and entered the house.

I expected to see evidence of Victor's peculiar hobbies, but there was nothing unusual, just books everywhere with old comfortable chairs and overstuffed couches piled high with paperwork. We went into the basement laboratory and gathered the things on Victor's list. I crammed everything but the fishing rod into a cloth grocery bag I found in the kitchen.

We were the first to arrive back at the stationhouse.

"What happened to you?" I asked Grig as he walked in a few minutes later. "You look like you've been in a battle with a lawn-mower and lost." His pants were tattered and torn at the hem. "Where's your uniform jacket?"

"I don't want to talk about it."

There were long, ugly scratches across his chest and welts covering both arms. Luckily, fairies are quick healers. He'd be as good as new in a few hours.

"I'd make a joke about Toro mowers and your jacket as a cape, but I can see you're not in the mood," I said with a smile.

"Olé," said Michael.

"Your werewolf cop friend attacked me, if you must know. I had to defend myself. I'll be sending you the bill for a new uniform," Grig said. He handed two baggies to Victor.

"You saw Alex there?" I asked.

"They thought I had something to do with the zombies," Grig said.

"Did you?" Michael asked.

"You two just had sex, didn't you?" Grig asked in disgust. "I can smell it, and you're both acting like giddy schoolchildren. What if you infect her?" He snarled at Michael.

"No chance," Victor said. "And it's my fault. I told them to."

Grig snorted and stood as far away from us as he could in the small room.

"I wonder what's taking Lucy so long," Michael looked at his watch. "She should have been back before all of us. We're run-ning out of time."

"I'll go check on her," Grig said.

"We'll go with you," Michael said. He grabbed my hand, and we followed Grig from the room. Victor never even looked up.

"Why are we going with Grig?" I whispered to Michael.

"I don't trust him," Michael whispered back.

"Oh, please," I said. "Now you're being paranoid." I patted his arm, but I was nervous. Paranoia was a symptom. How much time did we have left?

Everything was fine until we reached Lucy's building.

I bumped into Michael as he stumbled getting out of the car. A tremor passed through his body as I clutched his shoulder to keep from falling.

"Michael?"

He didn't answer. He couldn't. A spasm distorted his face as another, more violent, tremor shook him from the top of his head to the soles of his feet. His face turned an alarming shade of red, and sweat exploded from every pore in his body, drenching his clothes.

"Michael!" I cried. He closed his eyes and sagged against me, the hectic color fading from his cheeks as his muscles relaxed.

"Blowjob?" He whispered.

I let out a choked sob of relief. "Let's find Lucy first," I said.

I put my arm through his, throwing a glamour around us as we walked into the building. Grig led us down the stairs to the morgue. There was no way anyone would see Michael as normal now. He was almost zombie.

The door to Lucy's office stood ajar. Grig pushed it further with the tip of his sword. It opened with a squeak, but that was the only sound.

"Lucy?" He called through the doorway. "Are you in here?"

"Yes." She burst into noisy sobs.

I pushed past Grig. Lucy sat in a heap on the floor. Broken glass and scattered paperwork surrounded her. Her office looked like a tornado had touched down in it.

"What happened?" asked Grig as he helped Lucy to her feet.

"I don't know," she said sniffling. "I remember coming in here to get the samples, and then I woke up on the floor with a headache the size of Montana."

"This can't be good." I pointed to an overturned container with the red-lettered warning BIOHAZARD stamped on all sides. The lock was missing, and there was nothing in it.

"They bit off more than they could chew when they opened that. The zombie pieces from your wedding were in there."

"Why?" I asked.

"Zombies need to be incinerated to destroy them. Hacking a zombie to pieces will only slow it. That box must have exploded with creepy-crawlies when they opened it. In fact..."

Lucy dropped to her knees and started crawling around the floor, pushing paper and other debris out of her way.

She looked up at us. "If one of the pieces got away, we'd still be able to use it for the spell. Help me look."

We all spent a fruitless ten minutes sifting through the over-turned office searching for specimens.

"Sylvie," Grig pulled me aside. "How well do you know Alex?"

I moved closer. "What do you mean?" I whispered.

Grig shrugged. "He knew we were coming here. His cohorts attacked me. What if he's behind the zombie attack?"

"That's ridiculous," I said. "He's Michael's partner."

Michael's phone rang.

"What?" He spat into it. "Damn it, Alex. Of course, the crime scene and the forest reek of fairy magic. The entire Fey Guard was there!" He threw the phone across the room; it shattered against the far wall.

"Michael's starting to fall apart, Sylvie," Grig said.

"No," I whispered.

"Grig's right, Sylvie." Michael slumped against the wall and scrubbed his hands over his face. "I'm losing myself. The paranoia. The hair-trigger temper," he sighed. "The sex didn't help. I'm turning even faster than normal. Grig needs to kill me before I hurt someone."

"NO!" I said. "I'll take you to Faery."

"It's too late," Grig said. "I'm sorry, Sylvie, but Michael's too far gone. Nothing dead can enter Faery. And he's definitely dead."

"I don't feel so good," Lucy said, swaying on her feet.

Grig caught her before she fell. "You two go to Victor. I'll look after her." He guided Lucy to her office chair, forcing her head between her knees.

Michael stumbled on the steps out of the building and rolled down them, landing in a heap at the bottom.

"Michael!" I rushed down the stairs after him.

"I can do this by myself!" He shoved me as he staggered to his feet. "Leave me alone!"

"We may not have much time left, Michael," I sobbed. "Please don't push me away."

He reached over and pulled me close. "I'm sorry," he said, burying his face in my neck. His skin was fever hot.

Michael was shambling by the time we got to Victor.

Victor paced the small room, mumbling under his breath after we told him the bad news.

"Get Alex," Michael mumbled. "Gun."

"No," I said. "We've come this far. We can do this. Don't give up on me." Under the harsh fluorescent lights, Michael looked awful. The circles under his eyes were black, and his eyes showed more red than blue. I glamoured the two-way mirror to make sure he never saw the zombie in his reflection.

"Alright," Victor said. "I'll use Michael's blood. There's no mistaking him for the living dead now anyway." He grabbed the edge of the table. "Help me move this thing."

We pushed the table against the wall. Victor removed all of the objects from the bag I'd brought from his lab and lined them up along the top of the table. He laid out a piece of papyrus and placed a chip of elephant tusk across its center.

"What does that do?" I asked.

"Do you know anything about fetishes or magic?" he asked.

"Not human magic," I said.

"Ahhh...Well, in this case, I want to lure our practitioner here with their senses. The ivory is for thought." He picked up the hawk's feather. "This is for sight." He placed it alongside the ivory. "For taste, I add a drop of mead. Just a touch of pheromone for smell." He drew the stopper from a little bottle, sniffing it, before dripping it along the feather. "I'll finish it with the sound of a siren's call"—he waved a tiny crystal vial under my nose before placing it in his pocket—"once I've closed the circle."

Victor pricked the tip of Michael's finger with a fountain pen; the pen sucked up the blood before it could drip to the floor.

"It's a leech pen," Victor explained at my look of disgust.

Victor used Michael's blood to scribble runes on the paper. Then, in a series of intricate moves, he folded the papyrus around its contents.

"It looks like a koi," I said.

"Oh, I almost forgot," he retrieved a fishing lure that had snagged in the bag and tied it to the outside of the koi, leaving the wicked barb jutting from the front like a harpoon.

"Voila!" He laid the completed charm in the middle of the floor next to the fishing rod and a little mound of dirt and grass from the clearing.

"Give me as much room as you can," he said. I grabbed Michael and backed into the far corner.

Victor drew a circle around himself with chalk. Then he attached the lure to the fishing rod. He began chanting something in a language I didn't understand. There was a rhythmic cadence to his humming.

The energy in the small space shifted.

The hair on my arms and the back of my neck stood on end. Electricity filled the air.

Taking the little crystal bottle from his pocket, he removed the glass stopper and used it to paint a blue smile across the face of the koi.

I heard nothing, but Michael jerked.

"Hold him, Sylvie." Victor's lips never moved. His voice was in my head.

I held Michael as Victor cast his lure. The bait dangled a foot from the floor.

Victor looked into space as he sat in the protected circle. A shiver ran across my body. There was more to him than met the eye.

Suddenly, the lure disappeared and the fishing line went taut.

"Gotcha!" Victor reeled in the line.

Lucy walked in.

"Perfect timing, Lucy," Victor grunted, sweat beading his brow. "Any second now, the person who perpetrated this atrocity will come walking through that door and clear my name."

Lucy said nothing, tears in her eyes. Victor pulled on the line again. Lucy moved forward. Victor watched her as he released the tension again. She relaxed. He gave a giant yank on the line, and Lucy fell forward, stopping as she hit the invisible barrier of the protective circle.

Lucy burst into tears. "I'm so sorry. I tried to tell you so many times. This is so out of control."

"This doesn't make any sense," I said, shaking my head. "If you released the zombies, why help us?"

Lucy's words came in a rush. "I still can't believe it. I left the room for just a minute. When I got back, the morgue was empty." She wiped her streaming eyes on her sleeve.

"You left a room full of zombies alone?" Victor asked.

"They weren't zombies," Lucy sobbed. "I ran all the tests. They showed no infection."

"You must have missed something," Victor said.

"I don't know," Lucy said. "All I know is that when I heard there were zombies on the loose, I rushed out to help."

"Why didn't you tell us sooner?" I yelled. "We could have saved hours! Look at Michael!"

"I was going to confess when I gave you the blood, but some-body knocked me out and destroyed the evidence."

"How convenient." I said.

"It's not my fault!" she said.

I took her down with a flying tackle. "Bitch!"

Victor pulled me off her before I could do her serious harm.

I turned my anger and frustration on him. "She started this whole fiasco. They arrested you because of her!"

"I know," he said. "And she'll pay for it. But right now, we need to . . ."

In the corner of the room, Michael let out an ear-splitting scream, then gasped, clutching his chest as he collapsed, convulsing, to the floor. His back arched like a bow, every muscle in his body rigid.

"Sex," I said.

"Too late," Victor said. "He's entering the last stage. His time is up. We have to get him out of here now."

Lucy picked up Michael's feet. "Grab the other end, Sylvie."

I pushed her away. "Haven't you done enough damage?" I said.

"I can help," she said.

"She knows as much as I do about zombies," Victor said. "Let her help."

I rubbed my hands across my face and slowly nodded. "Okay. Let's do it." I bent to pick up Michael's head.

"I can't leave," Victor said. "I'm still under arrest."

Shit. I laid Michael's head down again. I tried calling Alex, but his phone went straight to voicemail.

Michael began twitching on the floor, his face glowing with fever, his skin so dry it looked like it would crack if I touched it.

Panic and fear bubbled in me. I tamped them down. "Focus," I told myself, tearing my gaze from Michael.

I looked at Lucy. She stared back at me blankly.

I turned to Victor. "Magic?"

He shrugged. "Invisibility is always an option, but I don't have what I need."

"Can you fix Michael here?"

He shook his head. "Too many variables. I need all of my tools at my disposal to deal with whatever comes up."

"What do you mean?" I asked.

He looked me in the eyes. "I haven't succeeded in reversing the process yet. My work was interrupted."

My stomach dropped.

"One problem at a time," I said.

My brain kept replaying the word "invisible." It was the key. If we couldn't actually make Victor invisible, could we fake it?

My gaze fell on Michael. I flinched. His skin was pallid grey where it wasn't fever bright, emphasizing the dark circles around his eyes. Glamour would not be enough to get him out of the building without anybody realizing he was a zombie.

Could I glamour Michael and Victor invisible? No, too hard, but...

"Lucy, you and Victor are going to carry Michael down the stairs to your car. I'll walk ahead. You stay five feet behind me, no further, and no closer. Also, no talking or drawing attention to yourselves in any way; think invisible thoughts."

"Why?" they asked in unison.

"I'm going to boost my sex appeal so much that no one in the stationhouse will notice anything but me as we walk through. Whatever you do, don't look at me or make eye contact with anyone in the building.

"Here," I took a crinkled Kleenex from my purse. "Don't worry, it's clean." I ripped it into four pieces and handed two to each of them. "Wad these up and put them into your ears."

"Why?" Lucy asked.

"I'm going to use an enchantment song to add to the distraction."

Once I was sure they were both as protected as I could make them, I motioned for them to pick up Michael.

We headed out.

I gathered all of the fairy power I could muster. I ran my hands seductively across my breasts, down my stomach, and along my hips, adding a little shimmy to settle the glamour over me like a sexy, tight black dress. I tossed my head and set my shoulders back. As I led our little procession from the room, I started humming one of the oldest songs known to Faery. We've been using it to lure humans for as long as they've walked the earth.

I matched my body's rhythm to the beat of the music. My pulse quickened in response. I walked a little faster and let my hips sway. My breath hitched as I approached the stairs. I ran my hand along the smooth wooden handrail as I began my descent. A flush spread over my body, and tension mounted as I continued the song. The moment I came into view of the room downstairs, all activity stopped. I was the center of their universe.

I hoped that Lucy and Victor were right behind me, but I

couldn't risk a peek. I continued down the stairs, stroking the banister as I went.

I repeated the first verse of the song three times before we were safely at the car. The second verse would have enslaved everyone who heard it. I wanted to distract them, not have them following me to the ends of the earth.

When we pulled up in front of Victor's house, I was relieved to see there were no media vans around.

The camera flash came out of nowhere, blinding me.

"Care to make a statement?" The man stepped into view as he spoke.

"We don't have time for this," I said, trying to hold up Michael and maneuver around the reporter who was now blocking the entrance to Victor's house.

"Isn't that Michael Thomas?" He said.

I looked around for help. Lucy stood frozen, and I didn't see Victor anywhere.

"And aren't you—" The reporter slumped to the ground. Victor stood behind him, a frying pan in his hand.

"You can't just go around knocking people out!" I said.

Victor shrugged. "We'll give him an exclusive later," he said as he pulled the reporter's limp body up the front stairs and into the house.

Lucy and I followed with our own limp burden.

"He'll be safe in here," Victor said as he shoved a chair under the knob of the coat closet door, wedging it shut.

"Come on," he said, disappearing down the steps to the basement.

Before we could follow him, Grig stepped from behind the basement door. He closed and locked it. "Not so fast," he said.

"What are you doing?" I asked.

Victor pounded on the door.

"This travesty stops now," Grig said, blocking our path with his body. "Humans are pets, nothing more. You certainly can't marry one. You're going to marry me."

"I don't love you."

"Once he's out of the picture, you'll feel differently," Grig said.

"No, I won't." I stuck my face in his. "Even if you were the last male anything left in the worlds, I wouldn't marry you."

"You say that now," he said.

"And I'll say it forever." I sighed in exasperation. "Open the door, Grig. We're done talking."

"As you wish." Grig drew his sword and stabbed Michael through the middle of his chest.

I screamed and threw myself at Grig, but I was too late. Michael lay on the floor, his blood soaking the carpet beneath him.

"It was you," said Lucy. She was staring at Grig. "You attacked me in my office. And I met you earlier, too. At the morgue, just before I discovered that all the bodies were gone."

I froze and stared at Grig in horror.

My skin crawled when he smiled.

"Yes, but it didn't work the way I planned. The zombies stopped the ceremony but failed to kill Michael...."

"As you planned," I echoed. The world shifted under my feet. I felt dizzy. My ears roared.

"You were in the forest, too," Lucy said. "You must have glamoured me, but I remember now. You put the zombie in Michael's path."

Grig smiled. "I saw an opportunity and acted upon it. Humans are so easy to manipulate." He grabbed my arm and pulled me toward the front door.

I dug in my heels and tried to break free. "What are you doing?"

"Taking you back to Faery with me."

"No! I can't leave Michael."

"He'll be dead soon—if he's not already."

"Because of you!"

"Yes." He yanked my arm again.

I pulled my knife from my back pocket and stabbed Grig with it.

"You think this puny thing is going to stop me?" He ripped it from my hand and threw it across the room.

I grabbed the hallway doorjamb with my free hand, then screamed as he pried my fingers away.

The front door exploded in a shower of wood.

Alex lunged through and barreled into Grig and me. Grig fell to the floor with his sword trapped beneath him. He defended himself from the massive werewolf jaws, first with an umbrella and then with a flowerpot, the only weapons within his reach, as Alex growled and snapped at every move. I heard bones crunch in Grig's arm.

I scooted out of the way as fast as I could.

Grig landed a blow on the side of Alex's head with a doorstop. The werewolf rocked back on his haunches.

Alex locked his teeth around Grig's shoulder and threw him across the room.

Grig bounced against a bookshelf and collapsed to the floor. The bookcase and its contents crashed on top of him.

Alex licked my face with his werewolf tongue, then nudged me toward the basement.

I crawled backwards toward where Michael lay dead or dying. He wasn't there. I followed the trail of blood through the now open door to the basement. As soon as I was on the stairs, I closed the door on the furious fighting that had resumed in the living room.

Michael was strapped, naked, to an examination table in the middle of the lab. IV tubes snaked out of his neck, his arms, his thighs. Runes decorated his forehead and wrists. Colorful stones marked his chakra points. A gaping wound in his side dripped blood into a bucket under the table. Lucy leaned over him, pushing on his chest.

"Don't touch him," she said. "He's in stasis. As long as I keep up the chest compressions, he won't die."

Victor looked up from his work. "I have a theory," he said. "Fairies are immune to zombie contamination; correct?"

"Why do you think that?" I hedged. This was a forbidden topic.

"Grig never showed any ill effects from his encounter with the zombie parts in Lucy's office."

"Yes," I said, "but what does that have to do with Michael?"

"I want to drain his contaminated blood and replace it with fairy blood," Victor said.

"Faery law forbids this kind of transfusion," I said.

"So does human law," Victor said.

I sat down and rolled up my sleeve.

Michael started convulsing as soon as my blood hit his bloodstream.

"It's not working!" I cried. I sat as the strength left my legs.

"Give it a minute," Victor said, pushing me back down. "The infection is fighting the fairy blood."

"Michael, I need you," I said, leaning as close as I could, knowing that I couldn't touch him. "Fight this. Don't give up. I love you."

"His heart is beating on its own!" Lucy said.

I breathed a sigh of relief.

"Yes!" Victor said. "I was right. Your blood is winning! It's working."

"Sylvie, we're going to need more blood than you can give," Lucy said.

"Alex," I said, knowing that his werewolf hearing would bring him to my side in an instant. "Bring Grig down here, please. He needs to make a donation."

Even though Grig was barely conscious from his battle with Alex, it took three of us to restrain him for the procedure.

"He looks like the Tin Woodsman, Sylvie. Do you think we used too much duct tape?" Lucy asked.

"Did you have any trouble putting the IVs in?" I asked.

"No," she said.

"Then we used just the right amount."

"You'll never be allowed back into Faery, Sylvie!" Grig screamed. "I did this for you. If it wasn't me, it would have been some other fairy. I love you!"

"Oh look," I said, "we missed a spot." I slapped a piece of duct tape over Grig's mouth.

I turned to Alex. "How did you find us?" I asked.

"I followed the scent."

I threw my arms around his neck. "Thank you," I said.

After two hours, I couldn't keep to myself any more. "Are you sure Michael's going to be okay?" I asked.

"Look at his wounds, Sylvie," Victor said. "He's healing like a fairy."

"Why isn't he waking up?"

"I don't know," Victor said.

"What will happen to Grig?" Lucy asked.

"He'll go before the Fairy Council," I said, grateful for the distraction. "He may not even get in trouble. There are so many that will see his actions as justified."

"The human authorities may have something to say about that," Lucy said. "What do you think they'll do with you?"

"I don't know," I said. "But even if I never go back to Faery, Michael is worth it."

Michael reached up and grabbed my wrist.

"Am I dead?" Michael asked.

"No," Victor said. "We had to put so much fairy blood into you that I'm not quite sure what you are. You're not dead or undead, you're not fairy, but you're also not completely human. How do you feel?"

"Strange," Michael said.

"Good strange or bad strange?" I asked.

"Good," he said. "In fact, I feel better than I felt before the attack."

"Anything else?" Victor asked.

"You mean am I craving brains?" Michael said. He scanned all our faces slowly. "Now that you mention it, a little, yes."

You could have heard a pin drop in the room.

"What?" he said. "Too soon for zombie humor?"

TICIA DRAKE ISOM lives in Northern California with her family where, although temperatures are in the balmy 90s, it is not unusual to see her wearing Uggs in the middle of summer. Ticia loves to engage everyone she meets in thought-provoking conversation. Many people are convinced that she never actually sleeps. She believes that there is magic not only in words and the use of them, but in just about any situation. This is her first published work. You can follow her exploits on twitter @ticia42.

She responded to my request for an afterword with the following:

I love where questions take me. This story started with a simple one: What if a fairy fell in love with a zombie? That question originally led me to a dead-end outline, because my plot device, not my characters, was driving the story. The original outline involved the kidnapping of Victor Frankenstein (yes, Swan's name is a nod to the great doctor) and forcing him to cure Michael. The climax was angry townspeople chasing and killing the cured zombie. Yes, in my rough draft, Frankenstein's monster was a zombie. But, it never jelled for me—until I changed the focus to the characters and their plight. The idea of love overcoming overwhelming odds is not a new one. Nor is the idea of love with an inappropriate partner. Start throwing in unrequited love and some subterfuge and misdirection, however, and you have what I hope is an entertaining and more unusual tale. I love these characters and am now working on additional stories with them, because that's where the new questions are taking me.

LOVE KNOT

DANA CAMERON

Justine sat at the table and stared at the small parcel wrapped in plain brown paper. The only light came from a single bulb in the cheap motel lamp, but it was enough. She hated the sight of the package.

She pushed it farther from her, wincing as she did so. She was pretty sure something had been torn in her arm. The long-sleeved shirt meant to hide scratches on her shoulder and arms only stuck and made them itch worse.

She shifted her weight, gingerly, regretting it as she did so. Her back...her legs...simply everything ached. But she had to decide what to do with the hateful thing on the table. Now on her eightieth hour without sleep, the eightieth hour since the parcel had come into her possession, she could barely keep her eyes open. But she didn't dare fall asleep, not without deciding what to do.

She couldn't just throw the thing away. She'd already tried destroying it, with dire results. She was fearful of bringing it to the Family: despite the oaths she'd sworn and the loyalties she owed them, she couldn't trust them with it. Especially not them. If power corrupted even the best of people, then this thing...

No. She couldn't go to the Family, but if they found she'd had the box and hadn't brought it to them...

She shuddered, and *that* hurt all over.

Well, that was just one more item in a long list she couldn't let happen.

She had to do something. Whatever it was, it would be a chance.

She had an idea, rejected it, then reconsidered.

She was going to call Claudia.

Shit.

As Justine punched the number with a shaking hand, she tried not to think of what she would be doing to Claudia.

But if you couldn't bring this kind of trouble to your friends, well, you were just out of luck.

Four hours later, Claudia Steuben checked the security monitor in her kitchen before she answered the door. Her friend Justine looked every bit as bad as she'd sounded on the phone: her auburn hair was a tangled mess, her eyes were bloodshot, and her athletic figure drooped with fatigue. Her skirt and jacket were rumpled. She had no luggage besides a briefcase and a small, sturdy, plastic cooler.

She shoved her way past Claudia and went straight into the kitchen. She pulled out the carefully stacked and color-coded plastic containers from the refrigerator and threw them on the floor. She shoved the cooler into their place, then slammed the door shut. She walked, unseeing, past Claudia, collapsed on the couch, and began to cry.

Claudia watched for a moment, frowned briefly at the disrupted order of her kitchen, then nuked hot water for tea. She cleaned up the kitchen floor and threw out whatever wouldn't last in the freezer or on the counter so she would not have to reopen the refrigerator. When the tea water was ready, she set it to steep. She poured the tea into two mugs, laced them both with honey and lemon, then poured a stiff shot of whiskey into each one.

By the time she returned to the living room, Justine had calmed down. Her face was streaked with tears, and she stared straight ahead, only seeming to recognize Claudia when she was handed the mug.

"It's hot. Also spiked."

"Thanks."

They drank. Claudia curled up in the leather chair and waited for Justine to start talking.

After a long shuddering breath, Justine looked up. "I'm sorry."

"For what?"

"Look, that...thing...in the refrigerator...?"

"What is it?"

"It's dangerous. Worse than that. There are men after it. I don't know who they are, but they mean no good."

Claudia could be patient. "Why not bring it to the Family? Why not destroy it?"

"I can't. Neither of them. I've tried destroying it, and...I can't."

"You can't."

Justine shook her head. "You'll...you'll see what I mean. I don't dare hide it. And frankly, I think you'll understand why I can't bring it to the Family."

Claudia watched Justine carefully. Clinically. "And?"

The question was obvious. Why didn't Justine take care of the situation? It should have been well within her capabilities. Their Family—the Fangborn—was made up of vampires, werewolves, and others, all dedicated to tracking and destroying evil. The humans they protected never knew about them, though myths of monsters and murders swirled up around them. Justine's strength, speed, and intuition should have been more than enough to deal with whatever the problem was.

Justine's hands shook as they held the empty cup. "Claudia, I promise you. It was all I could do to evade them, and make it up here."

"So why bring it to me?"

"I trust you." Justine's eyes flicked away. "You'll find a way to deal with it."

Claudia nodded. Her friend was lying. "Deal with what?"

"You'll see." Justine set her cup down. Her color was better now, but she still looked desperately tired. "Take the cooler out of the refrigerator. Open it up. I want to reassure myself that the damn thing isn't witching me. I want to make sure it's real, that I'm not going crazy."

Which I'm not ruling out, Claudia thought. Justine looked like seven kinds of Hell.

Willing to humor her a little longer, Claudia retrieved the cooler from the fridge. It had a few sparkly stickers on the outside. Unicorns and stars. Claudia looked up.

"The kids got them out of the cereal," Justine explained.

Claudia nodded, feeling slightly ridiculous. "They're safe?"

"With their dad. I told them I had an out-of-town appraisal. Didn't want to worry them." Parenting was tough on Fangborn, even after their children understood their special role in the world.

Claudia nodded again. She put the cooler on the kitchen table. She swung the handle back and removed the lid carefully, noticing as she did so that Justine was unconsciously turning her head away, pressing herself back into the cushions of the couch.

What the Hell is in here?

She set the lid aside, and peeked in.

A small box wrapped in brown paper, taped up and addressed, as if it was ready to be mailed. The address was faded and illegible, and the tape had been replaced several times, leaving dark ghosts of the adhesive on the furred brown paper.

Claudia relaxed. It looked like nothing at all.

She fanged up, briefly, just enough to allow her nails to grow and strengthen, her skin to turn pale violet. She slashed the tape on the package, removed the paper, opened the cardboard box beneath. That done, she returned to her human form.

Inside was another box, this one much older than the cardboard she'd just discarded. This was nineteenth-century, carefully dovetailed, travel-stained, perhaps the size of a stack of three hardcover books. She didn't recognize the exotic wood.

Claudia lifted the top of that box and suddenly was relieved. Everything was going to be perfectly fine. She was completely on top of the situation. There was nothing to worry about. In fact, she felt like she'd had three quick shots of tequila.

Inside was an object wrapped in layers of antique cloth, nestled in layers of utterly modern acid-free paper.

Justine was standing across the kitchen table now, breathing shallowly, her eyes wide. Claudia glanced up. Justine looked much better now. Everything would be okay. Claudia reached out, brushed the hair from her friend's cheek.

Justine's hair smelled of orange blossom and honey. Claudia leaned over to breathe it in. Her lips brushed her friend's hair, her teeth grazed her ear. She could see Justine's neck muscles tighten, and the curve of her breast just below the collar of her silk shirt.

Startled, Claudia pulled back. Then she caught a look at Justine's shoes.

Ooh, Jimmy Choo! Pretty, pretty...

Justine kicked away her chair and grabbed Claudia's arm,

Changing into a sleek wolf-woman in a Chanel suit. The expenditure of power involved in Justine's Change shook Claudia to her vampire core, and in response, she Changed, too. Her eyes widened, her nose receded, the outline of scales appeared on her violet skin, and her fangs grew long and bright.

It was both better and worse. Claudia's Fangborn senses were heightened, but her head cleared, and she knew she was being heavily influenced. It wasn't the whiskey in the tea. Her tongue flicked out from between her fangs. She tasted the air and it was exquisite. Beguiling.

She also now understood that whatever was in the box was affecting her, affecting her so deeply that she was producing a level and complex of pheromones that would slow down an army. Ordinarily, it would be just enough to calm whoever she was trying to cure—that's what gave fictional vampires the charisma and allure they seemed to have in the movies and comic books. Now...

Justine had taken off her jacket and had undone the top button of her blouse when Claudia managed to damp down the chemicals she was producing. Justine growled, confused but relieved, and that allowed Claudia to concentrate even more. Vampires can produce a range of effects on other living creatures, and to a certain extent, control their own body chemistries and those of the people around them.

With an effort, Claudia got hold of herself, slammed the lid back on the box, and shoved it back into the cooler, panting. Justine collapsed onto a kitchen chair.

After a moment, she caught her breath, and blushing, buttoned her shirt. "See what I mean? It's not just me, is it?"

Claudia shook her head. And if Justine had been exposed to it for even longer than the drive from New York to Salem...

"When did you find it? Where did it come from?"

"The museum." Justine worked as a curator at one of the premier art museums in New York City. "It was my turn to be on the desk, you know, to answer questions the public might have. Identify the artifacts they bring in. Break the bad news that it's just Grandma's knockoff souvenir and not a real Romanov egg." She took a deep breath.

"A guy came in, and he looked like shit. I immediately thought 'junkie looking to sell an antique,' but he was okay: I didn't pick up any smell of drugs on him, or any trace of evil. I told him I'd look at

it, but he said he had an appointment. He barely stayed long enough
to give me his name and contact information. Practically knocked
a guard over, trying to get out. Then I thought: 'toxic divorce.'

"I opened the box."

Claudia reached out toward the cooler again, but Justine held
up a hand. "Please. Don't. I can't...I can't take any more."

Shaking off an unexpected regret, Claudia sat back down, controlled the impulse. "What happened?"

"At first I assumed that I was just, you know. Feeling the lack.
Two kids *will* put a speed bump in your sex life. But it wasn't
going away, and I found myself leaving work early. Since when
do I play hooky? It got worse. I started eyeballing guys on the
subway. I was actually contemplating following one home when
my stop came up. Thank God. I managed to get up to the apartment and lock myself in. Until Ben came home. I'm still worried
about what he thinks."

Claudia tilted her head. "You didn't tell Ben?"

"What, that I got a weird artifact at work, and suddenly, I was
horny as a teenager?"

Claudia hated the word "horny."

Justine continued. "My husband just took it as a pleasant surprise. We didn't quite break the bed before the kids got home
from day camp. The next day...the next day, I thought it was
just a quirk of hormones. But when I got back to the museum,
a couple of things happened. For one thing, even though I'd
packed the thing up in secure storage, there was an awful lot
of...friskiness...going on."

"It's been a wet summer, and it just turned sunny," Claudia
mused. "Could it be a delayed spring fever? And didn't you tell
me there were several couples working together?"

"Yeah, but this...was definitely beyond PDA. It wasn't so much
casual Friday as swollen, engorged Friday. Even with that thing
over there locked up, folks were getting positively rampant in
the back offices.

"Then I tried to call the guy back, give him my report. Unusual,
but not valuable, certainly not something the museum would consider purchasing. His name, the number, the address—all fakes."

Claudia digested this. People might abandon wrecked cars or
dump garbage by the side of the road, but why go to a museum
to lose something you didn't want?

"Then, I got the weirdest call. Someone asking to speak to the guy who left the box, using that fake name. I told them they had the wrong number, but then the caller got angry, said I'd be sorry I'd not been more helpful."

Justine took a deep breath. "I brought the thing—and the paperwork I'd filed on it—home with me. Maybe the guy who left it there thought it would be safe, but I didn't dare leave it at the museum."

Claudia nodded. If anyone could handle this, the Fangborn could. Better to keep civilians out of it, as much as they could.

"I left early again, and let me tell you, by the time I got done with him, Ben was no longer complaining about missing 'Dirty Jobs.' I'm sure he's still walking funny. I was about to tell him about it—after I'd hidden the thing so no one could find it—when I saw the newspaper. A man had been found, under a subway car. The body was unrecognizable, identification was through dental work."

"How do you know it was your guy?" Claudia said. "If you didn't know his real name?"

"He had my card in his pocket. Cousin Dmitri—down at one of the fire stations?—had been on the call. He palmed it and called me. Told me the guy, whoever it was, had been *tortured*. He noticed marks that weren't made by the train, and said the stink of whoever did it was pretty awful. I called in sick, grabbed the box, and told Ben I got a call from the Family, and would be back in a couple of days."

Claudia nodded.

Justine took a last sip of cold tea. "Someone bad is after this. I can't risk just leaving it somewhere. I've tried breaking it, but...I can't. Somehow, I can't. And now I realize the extent of its power, I don't dare hand it over to the Family."

Claudia got it right away. "So you came to me? Please tell me, it's not because I'm a vampire."

"It's not. It's just..."

"Honestly, Justine, if we can't keep our own Family from believing the myths—"

"It's not that you're a...it's not the vamp thing—"

The vamp thing, Claudia thought. *Wasn't that just like a werewolf? Fuzzy simpletons. No subtlety, not one of them.*

"It's not that." Justine shrugged miserably. "I didn't know what else to do. You have your head on the squarest of anyone I ever met. And . . . you're . . . you've . . . you've got good self-control," she finished lamely.

Claudia knew what she meant, knew her own appearance (professional, but tailored to the point of severity) and reputation (serious and studious) were often misinterpreted. She found this even more galling than the human beliefs about vampires and their reputed hypersexuality. "Go to Hell."

"No, seriously, I'm not being bitchy, it's just . . . if anyone's got the brains to deal with this, and the willpower to . . . not succumb . . . you do."

Brains and willpower don't automatically make one virginal, Claudia thought. But people sure assumed it did.

"Besides, everyone knows you're . . . seeing . . . whatshisname?"

"Fergus O'Malley." Seeing was about all they'd been doing. Claudia, having met Fergus during a difficult time, had wanted to take this relationship slowly. "He's out of town, at the moment. Did you find anything that did work? Anything that kept you from . . . giving in?"

Justine's face lightened and she answered eagerly. "Anything distracting is good. Something rote, if you can keep your mind on it. I did our quarterly taxes. That worked. Until I stopped."

Claudia nodded.

Justine tried to keep the hopefulness off her face. "Well?"

"I'll help you with this," Claudia said finally. "But for now, you need some sleep. I've made up the spare room—"

"No!"

"It's no trouble—"

"Another time, I'd take it in a heartbeat. But now . . ." Justine shook herself. "I just need to be away from people. I don't trust myself near *that* anymore, and I need sleep. Can . . . can I leave it here tonight?"

"Yes, of course, you may. Where will you—?"

"Blue Harbor Inn. It's actually wonderful, but the owner . . . well, he just gives you the impression you're messing up his beautifully run, historically significant house. Cold fish, your basic taciturn Yankee. He's *exactly* what I need right now."

Claudia made a face. *Another stereotype.* "Hey, I'm a Yankee and I have manners and I can be downright loquacious when I need to be. I know Mr. Dow—he's just rude. He must be a thousandy-seven."

Justine was ready to cry. "Claudia, fine, I'm sorry. I just... really need some sleep now."

Claudia nodded. "I'll see you first thing in the morning."

Ordinarily they would have hugged goodbye, but tonight they didn't, by unspoken agreement.

Well, Claudia thought as she closed and locked the door, *I've got the reputation. I might as well put it to work. It'll be easier, now that I'm alone.*

In the kitchen, she opened the cooler, stripped back the layers, then ran her fingertips around the edges of the top of the old wooden box. It resisted before it came off in her hands. She peeled back the acid-free paper, then steadied herself. Just as she'd discovered with Justine, there was real power emanating from the thing. The fabric, rotting and faded silk, centuries old, fell away to reveal another, smaller wooden box.

Claudia sensed the age of the nested box, would have sworn she felt it quiver in her hands. As if it were alive. Humming, almost vibrating, though she couldn't hear a thing. Whatever was putting out the power was in here.

It couldn't be alive, could it?

She felt herself grow warm. She was only delaying the inevitable. But the suspense about what the object might be was almost as pleasurable as knowing. The brink of discovery is intensely exciting, and there is always, always a moment of hesitation before revelation.

Claudia ran the back of her hand across her forehead, and then the back of her neck. Sweat slid along her spine as she ran down the list of things it might be. The box was oblong, so she immediately considered the possible contents: a Shiva lingam or Greek or Roman good-luck phalluses, or pre-Columbian pottery decorated with figures engaged in sexual activity. Then she wondered if it mightn't be older than that, and thought of the variety of Stone Age fertility goddesses.

The lid of this box was heavily inlaid, though the ivory had shrunk and cracked and discolored. It was smooth under her fingertips, and she had to sit down, because her knees would no longer support her. Her breath came in shallow gasps.

Finally, curiosity overcame prudence. She caught her breath and tore the box open.

And stared.

It was a vase.

There were no obscene figures, no runic inscriptions. Nothing in the least suggestive, from any point of view. It was porcelain, a white body with a blue floral decoration.

It was a perfectly ordinary bud vase, maybe nine inches tall, and two across at the base. Hexagonal, sides gently curved upward, it couldn't even be properly called phallic.

It was, in a word, "mumsy." A dust collector, out of date, pretty and curious and innocuous.

There must be something on the base, perhaps inside the thing.

Claudia picked it up—

POW.

Her head snapped back. She was flooded with wave after wave of warmth that started between her legs and radiated out. A rushing in her ears and the kitchen vanished, replaced with a delicious oblivion. She tasted salt and sweet and felt herself sag. She moaned.

With the last scrap of will she possessed, she hurled the vase across the room.

It careened off the wall, banged onto the stove, and bounced onto the floor.

There was no tinkle of broken pottery. There was no need to get the dustpan and brush. There was nothing to clean up.

Claudia, gasping, staggered to her feet. Porcelain, in her experience, did not survive flinging. It did not, as far as she understood, bounce.

She picked it up, and ran across the room. She slammed it into the marble counter top.

Nothing. Not so much as a crack.

Before the thing could completely cloud her judgment again, she seized a heavy aluminum frying pan and bashed the vase with every ounce of supernatural strength she possessed.

The frying pan was badly dented. Williams Sonoma would have wept to see its perfection marred. It would never again toast hazelnuts or sauté shallots or sear pork.

The vase was completely intact.

We are so screwed.

Claudia picked up the vase, and holding it as if it were radioactive, ran across the room and slammed it into its nest of boxes and wrappings. She stuffed the whole thing back into the cooler, then shoved that into the refrigerator.

As she leaned against the refrigerator door, out of breath, she reconsidered and took the thing to the deep freeze in the basement. Best not to take any chances.

It was not the first thing to be hidden in the padlocked freezer. It probably would not be the last.

There is no such thing as magic, she told herself, on the way back up the stairs. *We don't believe in it, not most of us, anyway. Our past, which is longer than that of humankind, would have produced physical evidence.*

The scientist in her reasoned: there are plenty of earthly, human objects we don't understand. We still don't know, entirely, how the pyramids were constructed. We don't understand why some ancient metals defy spectrum analysis. The Fangborn—we can't explain ourselves yet, or our place in this world, but it doesn't make us magic. There are a thousand unexplained things in the world; science just hadn't caught up with them ... or the knowledge hadn't survived the ravages of time.

Suggestion, she thought, though the idea was absurd. If she had to guess, after talking with Justine, she would have assumed a kind of psychological thrall. Perhaps she was missing subliminal clues, something outside their Fangborn abilities of detection?

But how could the vase look so normal, appear to be made of human materials that were well familiar to her, and yet resist destruction? Claudia could very nearly bend steel in her bare hands, and this thing...

Harmonics was another idea. Perhaps sound communicated directly with the parts of the brain involved in sexual desire and response.

Whatever it is, she thought, *it is terrible. Something that strips the will, clouds the mind, drives reason away.*

A terrible thing. In the wrong hands ... disastrous.

Justine was right not to go to the Family with it. They'd both seen the effect it had on supersensitive Fangborn. The Family was at a politically sensitive juncture right now: this thing would be the end of us all, Fangborn and human.

She remembered what she felt like, tearing through the wrappings to get to the vase. What it felt like to handle it.

She'd never smoked, but now she would have killed for a cigarette.

Claudia took the report to bed after a long, cold shower, and crawled in, shivering but clearheaded, to read.

She flipped past the description of the object on the forms in the front, noting that it had been assessed as "Dutch workmanship imitating Asian decoration for the export market." Which wasn't much of a clue as to its pedigree or manufacture; that would describe a thousand objects from any maker, any place...

She dozed off with the lights on.

The dreams were horrifying and wonderful.

As if to punish her for resisting or trying to destroy it, the vase exercised an awful vengeance. Though Claudia didn't believe in booty calls, if he'd been anywhere within a hundred miles, she would have called Fergus. Hells, if she'd known there were any willing males nearby, it would have been all over for them.

Fangborn have to be very careful mating with humans and Claudia was not sure her self-control was all it should be. Would ever be again.

She woke up in a sweat, trying to forget her dreams. After an hour, it was no good. She gave in. She opened the drawer and found Señor Peter Rabbit. She clicked it on. No dice: no batteries.

Claudia Steuben was a responsible environmentalist, but she'd forgotten to plug in the battery recharger. And after looting the remote control, the doorbell (God help anyone who came to the door tonight), and the flashlights, she failed to find the right-sized batteries. Finally she thought of the hurricane kit in the basement.

If this isn't an emergency, she thought, ripping out a fresh, nonrechargeable battery pack, *I don't know what is.*

Claudia woke from an uneasy sleep, about two hours later than she ordinarily would have. It had been a rough night.

Thank God it was summer. She had an early staff meeting at the office. Since it was August, she had no patients. With any luck, this ordeal would be over by the next time she had regular office hours. She didn't want to think what might happen to her own therapist's reserve and discretion after prolonged exposure to the vase.

She would drive to the meeting, get out ASAP, then find Justine. The two of them would get rid of the vase. Curiosity about its origins was banished by fear of this being unleashed on the world.

At first, she felt much better being outside, away from the terrible drive of the object in the freezer. The short commute from Salem to Lynnfield along Route 128 would be packed with annoyances that were anything but provocative.

The first one met her at the foot of her driveway. Landscapers were among Claudia's pet peeves—why did they have to start mowing, chopping, and mulching first thing in the morning? The racket, their unkempt appearances, the way their trucks took up an unreasonable amount of space on the narrow, twisting and busy roads of Salem, were constant sources of irritation.

She pulled over to tell them exactly which noise ordinances they were violating. She'd been meaning to for some time, in any case. *That one, over there. He was obviously the foreman or the team boss or whatever. Had to be. Look at the size of the brute, the sleeves were ripped off a dark green work shirt to accommodate his biceps. Not an ounce of fat on him, and he was sweating already, rivers running down the inside of his collar, getting lost in the dark chest hair...*

She froze.

What the Hell am I doing?

Claudia caught herself, turned, and all but ran back to the BMW, which was still idling. She tore out of the driveway, leaving the confused ground crew staring after her.

The guy in the green shirt yelled, "Hey lady! Did you want a card, or something?"

No cards, Claudia thought, shaking. *Definitely no "something." You wouldn't survive it, my friend. Not in the state I'm in.*

Being in the car helped—clearly, the residual effects of contact with the vase were enhanced by human proximity. She recalled Justine's warning and began conjugating Latin verbs. *Ero, eram, erat...*

Which worked until she got to the construction crew slowing the highway traffic on Route 128. They inspired desperate fantasies of faceless men, singly or in pairs. Then there was the distinguished man being driven in the Town Car—she could imagine the fine wool of his excellent suit tearing beneath her nails as she rode him into Boston, the coarse feel of his grey hair under her tongue as she licked the side of his head. The young driver of the empty school bus, straddling her on the back seat, the smells of ancient vinyl and petroleum and sticky spilled soda around them...

Claudia abandoned conjugating verbs and tried to recall the succession of Hittite kings: *Labarna, Hattusili, Mursili, Hantili, Zidanta, Ammuna, Huzziya, Telepinu...*

As long as she kept her eyes straight ahead and her brain distracted, she managed. Things took a turn for the worse when she had to pause next to the cop directing traffic around the roadwork—the uniform, the sunglasses, the gun, the *handcuffs....* All she had to do was roll down her window, give him a blast of her vampiric glamour, and the poor man would have leapt into the backseat where she would lash him down with the safety belt and then...

The cop, far from being under a sexual compulsion, rapped on the window and screamed at her to get a move on, startling her out of the reverie. The spell broken, she hit the gas and sped into the now-moving traffic.

Justine was right. There was no way the Family could manage something like this, no matter how good their intentions. Imagine the vampires, besotted by the vase, unable to control themselves, and then unable to control those Normal humans around them. Things would spiral out of control, into a beautiful, sexual chaos....

Okay, but we're not going to think about that now, are we? Claudia thought. *Because that would be the start of it.*

Thinking about starting the end of the world worked. Claudia forced herself to turn the radio to a shock-jock show she absolutely hated, and between that and jaw-grinding determination, she made it safely to the hospital.

She didn't dare stop at Starbucks. There was no way she was adding caffeine and energetic young baristas to this mix.

The hospital helped. Her empathetic sense registered the pain and grief and fear there, which diverted her from...everything else. She kept her head down over her clipboard, grateful at last for her reputation as a grind.

"Hi, Claudia," the receptionist, Marlene, called. "Staff meeting in ten."

Not looking up, Claudia mumbled something, and locked herself in her office.

The meeting was excruciating. Fifty minutes of iron-willed self-control and superhuman—Hell, super-Fangborn—concentration was needed. Claudia stared at her notebook, scribbling the alphabet in Greek (ancient and modern, upper case and lower). When questions were addressed to her, she kept the answers as brief as possible.

Finally the meeting was over. She was almost in her office when Dr. Schmidt came over. "You okay, Claud?"

"Just a little...something I ate." She noticed he washed with Tom's of Maine almond soap; his clothes smelled of Arm & Hammer. Intoxicating.

He waved a cupcake. "Then you probably shouldn't eat sugar and chocolate on top of it. I was going to tell you, Marlene has some left over from her birthday party."

She began to salivate as he described the party. She heard not a word of it. She couldn't take her eyes off the cupcake as he ate it. So chocolately there wasn't room for another bit of cocoa to be wedged into it. Frosting, white—she could smell the butter, vanilla, and was that just a hint of mint?

She watched, transfixed, as he reduced the overhanging frosting with little, nibbling bites. His tongue flicked out and he smoothed the edge of the frosting like he was licking an ice cream cone. He caught a large crumb that came away; it vanished into his mouth. Then he peeled the paper cup away from the cake, one pleat at a time, with a barely audible *pock* as the paper straightened.

He ate it with splendid and complete attention, his teeth, strong, straight, clean. Another day, his deliberateness and precision might have been an unnoticeable tic of personality: today, to Claudia, it had an admirable and consuming appeal.

She felt weak and sagged against the door. She couldn't stop thinking about his mouth and his...attention to detail.

"Anyway," he concluded, "you look like you could use some sun. Say, can you and your boyfriend get away to the beach this weekend?"

The thought of Fergus, their as-yet-unconsummated relationship, and a beach made her look up. She'd gotten to know Fergus in Aruba. Dr. Schmidt's cupcake was replaced by the memory of Fergus in a bathing suit, climbing out of the ocean, water running down his chest and belly, following trails into the waistband of his trunks.

With a wrench, Claudia turned her mind to the elements of the periodic table. *Hydrogen, helium, lithium, beryllium, boron...*

"I really think I need to get home," she managed to gasp, after a long moment.

"Get straight to bed, then," he agreed, then wagged a finger at her. "You take good care of yourself, Doctor."

Thinking of the battery charger on the counter at home, Claudia turned and fled.

☆   ☆   ☆

I'm going to kill Justine, Claudia fumed, on her way to the inn with the box. *She knew perfectly well what that thing would do to a vampire.*

She made the least of bad choices, the rational part of her brain tiredly reminded her.

She can bite me. But before that thought could jump the rails, she arrived at the inn.

Claudia relaxed. Mr. Dow was at the front. Something about him calmed her.

"Morning."

"Morning. I've come to see Justine Nash—"

"Can't."

"I'm sorry?"

"She never came home last night."

"Do you have any idea where she might be?"

Mr. Dow pursed his lips as he sorted the mail. "I never pry into my guests' comings and goings."

He's not even curious, Claudia thought. "Is there some way I could check her room? She was supposed to lend me a book." She stepped closer and used a little vampiric push, just enough subliminal influence to overcome his reticence.

He put his mail down, his eyes a little glassy. "Sure. No harm in that." He handed her the key, listing a little as he did so.

She opened the door. The room had been trashed. Someone had been looking for the object.

Her phone rang; it was Justine. She answered, and heard heavy, masculine breathing on the other end. "Who is this?"

"We have your friend. We want what she took from us."

Claudia stalled, trying to think. "Who is this? What are you talking about?"

"Your number shows up three times on this phone last night. We know she told you. Bring the box to Boston, tonight at eleven if you want to see her again." The voice gave an address and then hung up.

Claudia cursed briefly and thought furiously. She cast about the room for a trace of Justine's abductors. There were three of them, at least.

"I left after I didn't find my friend," she dictated to Mr. Dow, giving him a story to replace his reality. "I never went into her room." Tired and scared, she pushed just a little.

"I would never let you do that," he agreed, his dewlaps shaking with his head.

"The men who came here? Did you see them? Describe them to me."

"I didn't see any men."

"Okay. You were alone all morning."

"It's how I prefer it." He nodded with satisfaction. "Alone all morning."

It was then Claudia noticed that the terrible strain that had been hagriding her was gone. She looked at Mr. Dow with curiosity. Nothing there, no thoughts about sweeping him behind the desk and having her way with him. The idea was more than unappealing. Still susceptible to her chemical manipulation, the vase itself seemed to have no effect on him. Or her, near him.

He was still under her thrall, and stood smiling absently, waiting to be dismissed.

No time for speculation. She needed to get to Boston.

She sent him on his way, and had a quick look in the parking lot. It was gravel, and there were no tire tracks. She got into her car, and headed south.

Claudia thought about the disruptive power of the vase. Fangborn seemed to be unusually affected by it, but Normals—if Justine's account of the ruckus it had caused at the museum was any indication—were affected by it, even at a distance. Even when they didn't know where it was, or that it was even there. Everyone but Dow.

So imagine it in the hand of someone with a political agenda, of any kind. If it was ever analyzed, its secret found and harnessed, it would make a weapon of unspeakable power.

Your enemies would never even think of pushing the button; they'd never have the time. They'd never pick up a weapon. They'd never see you coming.

For a split second, Claudia thought: *What's so bad about that? Wasn't all the music and art and literature inspired by and devoted to crazy-making love? What if this is the key to world peace? What if this is the way to let the Fangborn reveal themselves to the Normals? What if we all learn to love our enemies?*

Right, she shook off the thought. *Get a grip. Love them right through the mattress or until you all die of terminal bedsores? Not very likely.*

This thing had to be absolutely destroyed.

☆   ☆   ☆

She spent the day observing the warehouse on the pier, but saw no way to set up a trap for Justine's captors without being seen by the legitimate traffic on the wharf. She returned after dark, closer to the appointed hour, and hid her car, but as early as she was, they were earlier. There was only one truck in the parking lot now. The truck was unmarked and unremarkable, but after she broke in, she found it was registered to the largest pharmaceutical company in the Northeast. Of course they'd want the object: if they could crack its secret, they'd rule the world.

She saw they'd left the door to the business office of the warehouse open for her, the way to them clearly lit, but she continued around the building anyway. She fanged up, the job keeping her focused, and she slung the backpack with the vase over her shoulder. She searched until she found a weather-beaten section of wall. Her fingers, now elongated into sharp claws, found the cracks in the brick and mortar and she climbed silently. A window showed there were at least six of them.

She listened, her keen ears picking up snippets of conversation. Apparently, the man who'd brought the vase to Justine had stolen it from the gang, who'd stolen it from a private collector in Switzerland. The original owner, quite mysterious about the object's origins, had made the mistake of showing it to the head of the pharmaceutical company's office in Berne, who instantly ordered its theft.

The men below knew what they were after, and its value, even if they didn't know who was after them.

There was no sign of Justine.

Claudia took a piton from the pouch on her belt and drove it between two bricks. The mortar crumbled, but it sank in and wouldn't move. She shrugged the backpack off, and, with a silent click, slid a carabiner attached to its handle over the loop of the piton.

The thing was safe enough, for now. Let them figure out how it got halfway up a sheer wall.

She climbed down, Changed back to her skinself, and went in the way they expected her to.

In addition to the six men she saw, there was another, clearly the leader. A tall blond, he was armed. She presumed the others were, too.

First things first. "Where's Justine?"

The leader was in the center of the room. As she approached, two of the others moved closer to her, never getting between her and his gun. She decided to call the one on the left Bruiser and the one to his right, Stretch.

The others she named Red, Knuckles, Scab, and One-Eye. Unimaginative, but mnemonic.

The leader stepped forward. "Where's the box?"

"Not until I get my friend back."

"She's only safe until I call in. If I don't call my man in ten minutes, with the box, she's dead."

"You're lying." And he was; Claudia could tell. His heart rate was up, and she detected the faint odor of anxiety. She realized he, Bruiser, and Stretch were battered and bleeding. From claw marks. Justine had Changed, fought her way out, escaped.

Claudia wondered whether Justine was okay. She could have used her friend's help.

"I don't need her." He lifted the pistol and aimed it at Claudia.

"Shoot me, and you never get the location of the . . . object."

"I can shoot you a little." He aimed at her knee. "Just a little. It doesn't have to be much—"

He was so sure of himself. He was a talker.

She thought, *Good.*

By the time his finger tightened on the trigger, Claudia had Changed halfway. The surprise of seeing her skin and hair turn violet, her fingers elongate into claws, and her face shift into something serpentine with two rows of sharp teeth, slowed the rest of them. She struck out at Bruiser, who was closest to her, landing a good uppercut on his chin. She pivoted and kicked Stretch, and when he bent over, she sunk her fangs into him.

She'd only meant to give him a jab of poison, a quick injection of venom that would keep him down and out of the fight.

It should have gone: Dart at the leader, two quick punches. Disable him, lose the gun. Guns leave trails that can be followed by the normal police. Punches and kicks and quick-healing vampire bites don't.

Spit poison at Red when he closed in, then twist, slamming him, blinded, into Knuckles, who would come from behind. Then two steps to kick Scab in the breadbasket, blocking One-Eye's punch before kneeing him in the head.

Interrogate the leader, using her chemical arsenal to get him to spill his guts.

That's how it should have gone. Claudia was good at this. And if she happened to exercise a little more self-control in her personal life to prevent the unjust employment of her powers, if she seemed to her Family and friends to be uptight, rigid, prudish, a little conservative, well, this was the part of the job where she loosened up.

But fatigue and worry caused her to misjudge.

What happened, alas, was this: As she bit into Stretch, her lips brushed his neck. The electric shock of his skin, the tiny hairs on the back of his neck standing straight up, the blood rushing over her tongue, made her gasp. She bit harder still, her tongue flicking, and the man collapsed, moaning. He tried to turn around to embrace her, but the friction of his body against hers had such an effect on Claudia that she released a flood of airborne chemicals, which knocked him to the ground, limp, spent.

That had the effect of rebounding on her, intensified by the power of the vase. Even a hundred feet away, it called to her, possessed her, drove her. She'd been exposed to it for so long, it no longer needed close proximity to work.

Oh, shit.

She tried to stop, but it was too late. She managed to block Red's punch, shoving him away. She kicked straight out in front, aiming for Knuckles's sternum, but her speed was off and while most of the kick connected, Knuckles stumbled forward, still holding onto her leg. She managed to stay standing, but he was now at her feet, one arm locked around her leg, his other hand sliding over her thigh, as he kissed her knee, utterly besotted.

The closer the others crowded, the worse it got. Their anger and aggression were channeled into sexual excitement. The more they got turned on, the more Claudia's empathy picked up on it. And then threw it back at them, amplified by the pernicious effect of the vase.

Red approached again, his pistol in his outstretched hand. He wept openly, adoringly, his other hand down the front of his pants.

Outraged at this breach of her control, Claudia slammed the pistol into his face. He went down with blood on his teeth, a smile on his lips, a stain on his jeans.

Scab said, "Oh, man. That bitch can fight."

One-Eye nodded, and reached over to caress Scab's face. They locked in a tight embrace, each struggling to take the clothes off the other while not breaking their kiss.

By this time, Claudia was blinded by her own desire/emotions/conflicts/lust. The more she tried to resist, the more tangled up things got. She knew she was supposed to stop the men, but now that they weren't actually attacking her, and were, in fact, pretty much willing to do whatever she wanted, she couldn't find it in herself to send them into unconsciousness.

Worse, all those desires, all those bodies, all that energy, all packed in together, were starting to feel very good to her.

She found herself giving in, and tried to resist. The heady combination of control and resistance only colored and heightened the experience for her.

What do you do when your strength is the very thing that is undoing you? Laying you bare, shedding your will—

For Christ's sake, Claudia! Focus!

Trying desperately not to watch One-Eye and Scab, Claudia felt herself pulled under by the waves of desire threatening to overwhelm her. She saw the leader was confused, but somehow, like Mr. Dow, unaffected. He screamed at his men, but getting no response, turned, heading for the door.

He'd get away, and Claudia couldn't let him escape with his knowledge of the object. With the tangle of men at her feet, she could barely move. She didn't really want to move...

What do you do when you can't go with strength? Go with weakness.

She focused on the power of the vase, and increased her attack tenfold. She absorbed the emotions of the men, and used that against them, too. Claudia gave in to her baser instincts, and let fly with every bit of glamour, chemical and pheromone, hint or suggestion in her vampire's arsenal. She might have invented a few new ones.

In the midst of it all, Claudia felt an extraordinary power coursing through her. She was a thousand places at once, an avenging angel in the depths of Hell, corrupting demons to the cause of good.

She pointed at the leader. In a powerful, echoing voice, not her own, she said: "That man could use a hug!"

Immediately, Red, Bruiser, and Knuckles tackled their leader, knocking him to the ground. Scab and One-Eye were crying, and Stretch had a blank look of joy. They cuddled their leader so effectively that he couldn't move. They snuggled him into submission.

The leader struggled under the onslaught of affection. "What the fuck—? What's wrong with you? She's a witch! Don't listen to her—"

Some little part of Claudia knew that she had to make this stop somehow. The more energy she absorbed, the more powerful she became, and the harder it was to wrest back her self-control. Either she would consume the whole world, as she drew others into her web, or eventually, she would die of sexual exhaustion and starvation.

She felt a buzzing against her hip. It broke her concentration on maintaining her spell, just the merest bit.

That's good, she thought. *My phone. It's a good distraction. I need a distraction. I need that. I need it . . . I need it to move down, and a little to the right. . . .*

The phone stopped vibrating and her disappointment was so great, it snapped her concentration. She fanged down, and suddenly, the flow of wonderful vibes was cut off. It didn't matter. Some of the men were unconscious, a few were weeping, and the rest just collapsed in a limp, damp, sated hamster pile on the floor.

Claudia staggered over to the wall, and shuddered. Her concentration was better now, and she found the leader, who was still squirming beneath his men. Somehow, like the innkeeper, he was unaffected by the presence of the object. He would be, however, affected by the chemicals she produced.

Better not to take any chances, she decided. Don't want to get that whole thing started again.

Before she could talk herself into getting close enough to glamour or bite him, she kicked him in the head. That shut him up and sent the three other men on him into orgasmic fits.

She went outside, and sagging against the wall, took out her phone. There was a message.

It was from Fergus. His lovely, growling brogue almost set Claudia off again.

"My flight was late, but I'm at Logan now. Call me, if it's not too late for me to see you." She pressed speed dial, and got him. "I'm at the waterfront. I need you." She gave the address and hung up.

She was still confident there was enough residual power in her voice to have Fergus come running.

By the time Fergus arrived, out of breath, Claudia had disarmed the men, and handcuffed them, using zip ties from her belt pouch. In a daisy chain along the wall, most of them were too stunned to say a word. All of them were still trying to figure out what had happened.

Claudia was on the phone. After a few more words, she hung up. Before Fergus could ask, Claudia began in a rush: "That was Justine. She's okay. They managed to get her into the back of their van by creating a roadblock, but after she came to, she Changed. They were on their way here when she came to, and busted out the back of the van. She made it off the highway to the Middlesex Fells, where she can heal undetected. We'll meet her back in Salem."

"Good," he said, puzzled. "But what do you need me for? You've got it under control, far as I can see."

Claudia took a deep breath. "I have to interrogate them, find out who else knows about this thing they were after. Then I have to wipe their memories. If you see me ... getting too deep, too involved, you need to stop me. Any way you can. If I can't wipe all of them, we'll have to kill them, and I'd rather we were able to hand them over to the police."

"Claudia, what—?"

"And then, once we can call the cops—I'll have them tell them that they were beat up by a rival antiquities gang—we'll split up. Meet me at the Charles Hotel in Harvard Square exactly one hour later."

"Um ... okay?"

She sighed. "I'll explain it all later. I swear, Fergus."

He looked at her, and nodded. "Man, you sure do know how to tease a guy."

"You have no idea."

Two hours later, Fergus O'Malley nodded to the doorman as he entered the Charles Hotel. He carried a battered overnight bag over one shoulder and a heavy shopping bag from Cardullo's. Not wanting to risk being even a little late, he'd bribed the cabby with an insane amount to get him to Harvard Square; then, being a gentleman, or at least knowing what was good for him, stopped at Cardullo's to buy a bottle of champagne. Then, thinking of his own proclivities, threw in a loaf of bread, smoked salmon, and crème fraiche. But since it was a celebration of sorts, he threw caution to the wind and asked for a tin of Sevruga, not bothering to inquire about the market price. But perhaps Claudia was more of a sweets girl—? He tried to remember whether she ordered dessert when they saw each other, and realizing time was wasting, grabbed a box of chocolates from Fauchon and some outrageously expensive apples.

The clerk observed the telltale groceries, the little bag from the pharmacy sticking out of his pocket, the burning desperation in Fergus's eyes and the impatient tapping of his foot, and decided that wishing the gentleman "good hunting" would be too cheeky.

"Have a good evening, sir." And he meant it. There was something about the guy...he usually went for blonds but had to resist the strongest urge to lean over the counter and run his fingers through the customer's dark hair. And a man with an Irish accent was almost too good to resist.

Fergus resisted looking at his watch again, while he waited for the elevator. He had no idea why he was so nervous: either Claudia would have sex with him tonight, or she wouldn't. He had been willing to follow her lead so far, and didn't think she was the kind to punish him for being a few minutes late, but he was not taking any chances.

The elevator door opened. A wretched thought hit him, and suddenly, Fergus's world came crashing down. Claudia wasn't inviting him to consummate their relationship, he realized. She'd asked him over to help wrap up the loose ends of the gig, deal with the aftermath, cover their tracks. He was acting like an adolescent idiot, and she—she of all people—would be able to tell.

Oh, God.

Then he braced himself. It would be hideously awkward, but maybe he should bring up the subject...they were both adults, they could...

He entered the elevator, and practiced what he'd say. *I don't want to rush you, and I'll wait as long as you want. You're worth waiting for. But I think we're both ready to try this—*

He practiced all the way down the hall; it sounded more and more lame, and he resigned himself to his lame-ness. The door to the hotel room opened. Claudia stood there in a white robe, her hair wet from the shower, the light of madness in her eyes, her fangs glinting.

He stammered, but started his speech. "I don't want to rush you—"

She grabbed the front of his shirt, pulled him toward her.

"You want to have sex?" Her voice was uncharacteristically husky. He nodded quickly. "Uh, yes, please."

"Good. I want sex. Let's have sex."

She pulled him all the way into the room, her lips fastening on his. His overnight case and the bag of groceries hit the floor. The apples rolled across the floor as, in between kisses, Claudia promised to repay him for the shirt she'd just ripped off him. The door slammed shut.

Three days later, they joined Justine back at her B&B. Justine entered the room to find Claudia and Fergus sitting on the bed, their fingers entwined. The box containing the vase, recently liberated from the safe at the Charles, was at their feet.

"Well." Justine gave Claudia a pointed look.

"Here's the plan," Claudia said, ignoring her. "Tell me if you have a better one, because this is pretty weak. We've tried everything from a junkyard car crusher, to acids, to explosives, and nothing's worked on the vase. All I can think to do now is take my brother Gerry's boat out as far as we can, load this thing down with weights, and lose it off the coast. With any luck, it won't be rediscovered until we have some way to combat it."

"But we need it! We need to take it to the Family," Fergus said.

The argument went round and round: if they couldn't destroy it, they couldn't trust anyone with it. Even involving Gerry was a risky move.

"It just can't be that hard to destroy," Fergus said, picking up the box.

He had it opened before either of the women knew what he was doing.

Claudia and Justine lunged toward him at the same time. "No!"

A voice came from behind the door. "Doesn't that look nice?"

Claudia, Justine, and Fergus turned. The innkeeper, Mr. Dow, was behind them. They exchanged uneasy glances; this was going to get messy. At least most of the guests were gone for the day—

"Just the thing for a little nosegay, right there in that corner."

Claudia was as astonished to hear him say so much, so positively, as she was to learn he knew the word "nosegay." She could only nod.

"I really like that," the innkeeper continued. "I'd be happy to buy it from you. Is it Chinese? Or an English copy?"

The vase seemed to have no effect on him, save one. For the first time since Claudia'd met him, a shy grin cracked his face.

She sputtered. She recalled the leader of the gang, who'd also shown no effect from the object. Maybe some people were just more resistant to it than others.

Justine said, "I don't know. I picked it up at a little shop in Boston."

"Well, it sure is pretty. They don't happen to have another, do they?"

"It was the last one," Claudia said. *I hope.*

"Oh, well." The innkeeper did not withdraw into his habitual taciturnity. He just whistled tunelessly, plucked a curtain back into place. "I guess I have to stop decorating some time. It's only that I'm about to retire, and my son will take over. He's a lot like me, and I thought if they had another, he'd like it. In any case, I'll be happy to bring you more towels, if you need them, Mrs. Nash."

"Oh, that would be lovely, Mr. Dow. You know," she glanced at Claudia, who nodded. "You know, now that I'm looking at it, I don't think it will go with my living room. The color's not quite right. I've had such a good time here that I'd like to give it to you."

Claudia stepped closer to him and pushed the flimsy story with a little blast of chemical conviction. Would that be enough to get him to take it? She even reached out to the vase for a little help, but there seemed to be a hollow place in the world, now. In Mr. Dow's presence, it was just a vase.

"Why, that's lovely of you!" he said. "Thank you!"

Fergus met Claudia's eyes. "I'd only ask that if you decide to sell it or give it away, you'd give us first refusal." Claudia nodded and kept encouraging the impulse.

"I'd never think of letting go," Dow said, and he meant it. "It's just too lovely."

None of them felt anything but relief.

A few months later, Claudia received an email from Justine, who reported that the vase was safe and sound. A temporary solution, hiding it in plain sight, they'd all agreed, but if it was neutralized by Dow and his family, it was the best they could do for the moment. Justine checked up on it periodically—just business, she'd told Claudia—but each time she'd brought her husband Ben and now they were expecting their third baby.

"Thought you'd get a kick out of this," Justine had written. There was a link to a "Hidden Treasures in Massachusetts" website. Blue Harbor Inn was voted "most romantic."

In addition to her award-winning archaeology mysteries, **DANA CAMERON**'s short stories have been nominated for the Edgar and Anthony awards and have won the Agatha and the Macavity. Dana introduced the Fangborn in "The Night Things Changed"; her second Fangborn story, "Swing Shift," is set in 1940s Boston. Dana lives in Massachusetts with her husband and benevolent feline overlords. She is hard at work on a Fangborn novel. Learn more about her at www.danacameron.com.

When I asked for an afterword, she supplied the following:

I knew I had to use my Fangborn world to write "Love Knot" because I wanted to address the notion of a vampire's hyper-sexuality and I wanted to do a story with Claudia, who first appeared in "The Night Things Changed." She's a good girl; she's smart, she's tough, and although I don't know entirely why she is so concerned about self-control (that may be another story!), I thought it would be fun to put her in the situation of having her considerable power enhanced. What would you do if you knew you had to be careful with your powers, but then came across something that increased them in a very . . . rewarding . . . fashion? The other thing that inspired the story was the idea of magic, or rather, the lack of it in this world. Claudia would tell you the Fangborn aren't magic, just as yet unexplained by science. What does a scientist do with something that seems to defy physics and logic? Sex may be one of the most basic urges in nature—explainable in biology, chemistry, and physics—but there's still some magic in it.

BEAUTY IS A WITCH

JOHN LAMBSHEAD

"Beauty is a witch, against whose charms
faith melteth into blood."
—William Shakespeare, *Much Ado About Nothing*

Rosalynne sighed. Here we go again, she thought. Fortunately, she had come prepared. She pulled a straw from her bag and raised it to her lips. She blew through the straw into Smith's face, enveloping him in a cloud of shimmering dust. Smith sneezed and looked puzzled.

"You have an important engagement elsewhere," Rosalynne said, locking eyes with him. "And you are late."

"Is, ah, that the time?" Smith asked looking at his watch. "I, er, have to go. You'll have to let me take you out to dinner another day. Let me know when you have the stuff."

Smith rose, clutching his briefcase like it contained his rich grandmother's only will. He almost ran out of the pub, tripping over another customer's legs in his rush.

"Bye," said Rosalynne, raising her glass to the bald, flabby, middle-aged, retreating figure.

The thought of a romantic dinner with Smith gave her goose pimples. She smoothed down her leather skirt over long and, even though she said so herself, slim and elegant legs. Rosalynne was far too curvy to be a fashion model but she had inherited blonde hair, high cheekbones and pale blue eyes from her Saxon forebears.

Magic came in many forms. Rosalynne could work the oldest spell of all on her clients when she dressed to impress, especially when those clients were men of a certain age. The only drawback was getting rid of them after they agreed to her terms.

The pub was like any other East End drinking hole that had yet to be gentrified. A large varnished bar dominated the room. Pint mugs hung from a wooden screen running along the top. A huge mirror behind the bar proclaimed the merits of Gordon's London Gin. Tables were scattered around and screened alcoves along the bar's walls allowed patrons to drink and converse with a degree of privacy.

East Londoners have a saying: "On the seventh day God rested by popping down the Whitechapel Road for a swift half at the Blind Beggar." The pub was built in the eighteenth century on the site of an even older coaching inn, which had itself accreted around a toll booth charging travelers on the old Roman road to Colchester.

Whitechapel was one of those places where the walls of the world stretched and thinned. Thoughts and more tangible things could slip through. Sensitives were attracted to Whitechapel and inspired to do great and terrible things, releasing powerful bursts of psychic energy that further distorted reality. The Blind Beggar was at the focus of this whirlpool so year by year, decade by decade, century by century, the pub slipped deeper into shadow.

Rosalynne finished her drink, feeling suddenly at a loss. The night was too young for her to return to her flat but she had nowhere else to go and no one she wanted to go with. She rose from her table and walked up to the bar.

"Hey, Henry, has that fat poufter been in tonight?" asked a customer perched on a barstool.

"Not yet, George," said the barman.

"Buy you a drink, love?" George asked.

"Thanks, Mr. Cornell, but I prefer to get my own," Rosalynne replied.

He laughed, "Your loss, love."

George Cornell was a powerful, heavy-set man, who would never have been considered handsome. He might have been sexy, in a thuggish sort of way, but for the ragged bullet hole in his forehead. He flickered slightly, outline blurring.

"Another, Rosalynne?" asked Henry.

She indicated assent and he poured a generous measure of gin into a glass.

"Not too much tonic, Henry," Rosalynne said. "My dentist claims the sugar content is bad for my teeth."

Henry nodded as if he had never heard the hoary old joke before. He moved methodically but surely, despite the sepia-stained bandage that completely covered his eyes.

"What's he doing in here?" she asked, indicating the other drinker with a swivel of her eyes. "I thought he had wound down."

Henry shrugged. "He appeared again just before you came in. There must be magic in the air tonight."

Henry gave Rosalynne a pointed look.

"Has that fat poufter been in tonight?" Cornell asked.

"Not yet, George," said Henry.

Rosalynne ignored the exchange. Eidolons tended to go around short loops. It was dangerous to interact too closely with one. You could get inserted into their pocket of reality.

Ronnie Kray, the fat poufter in question, had unsurprisingly taken great exception to being described as such and had expressed his displeasure with a Mauser 9 mm parabellum. This all happened in the Blind Beggar, one rainy night way back in the sixties.

"I wanted to have a word with you, Rosalynne. I've had to warn you before about using magic in the Beggar," Henry said.

Rosalynne cut across him, impatiently. "And I've had to warn you before that I do as I please, where I please, when I please, and anyone who has a problem with that can do the other thing. That goes double for some loser who has risen to the dizzy heights of bar staff in a naff East End boozer. Got that, blind man?"

Henry shrugged and said nothing but his jaw clenched until the skin was white.

Rosalynne smiled cruelly. It was not the first time she had slapped Henry down. It was a bit like shooting fish in a barrel but sometimes fish in a barrel were the only target around.

"I know what I'm doing," she said.

Henry stared blindly at her, then began to chuckle. Once started, he could not stop until he guffawed with uncontrollable mirth. Rosalynne was unnerved. She had never so much as seen him smile before.

"Oh, girly," said Henry, in a venomous tone. "What a high-spirited little chit of a thing you are. I had quite forgot what it was like to be young and so full of piss and vinegar. You know what you're doing?" Henry shook his head.

Rosalynne was angry now. How dare he patronize her?

"I may not be as old as you..." she said sarcastically, old being a synonym for senile in Rosalynne's dictionary.

"You are just another leaf in the autumn wind." Henry said, crushingly. "There's a point where a witch becomes ripe for burning. You're almost there."

It sounded like a threat: no—worse than a threat—a prediction.

"Hey, Henry! How about another drink?" asked Cornell loudly, banging his glass on the bar.

Henry moved to serve him.

A shiver ran down Rosalynne's spine. It was almost as if Henry knew something she didn't. Maybe it was just someone walking on her grave. She took her recharged glass into one of the partitioned alcoves along the wall.

The pub door banged and a blast of air from an older, colder London blew in. Rosalynne smelt sulphur and animal waste. A man strolled across the room and sat at a central table. He wore the clothes of a Victorian gentleman on an evening out. A red cravat at his neck was a splash of color against an all black outfit of top hat and double-breasted frock coat. He carried a carpetbag in his left hand and in his right, an ebony walking cane topped with a silver pommel.

The gentleman kept his top hat on. He tapped the cane on the floor thrice and signaled Henry with an upraised finger. Rosalynne waited for the explosion. To her astonishment, the barman meekly poured out a glass of port from a crystal decanter and carried it to his table.

Top Hat drank deeply. He caught Rosalynne watching him and tipped his hat to her. His eyes ran arrogantly down the curves of her body, lingering on her legs. Rosalynne was used to being the focus of unwelcome male attention and had developed an automatic response.

She glared at Top Hat, which was the signal for him to direct his lecherous intentions elsewhere. He slowly worked his way back up until he locked eyes with her. There was something cold and predatory in his gaze that made her think of snakes. She looked away first.

In the nineteenth century, the world's desperate poor crowded into Whitechapel's slum housing, forming a Dickensian "rookery," a concentrated pit of human misery and despair festering at the heart of the greatest and richest city in history. Gentlemen from West London would come to enjoy themselves drinking, gambling and whoring in Whitechapel's sixty-two brothels—gentlemen like the man in the top hat.

The bar abruptly went very quiet. That was not a good sign. She peeked through a gap in the alcove partition so she could see the length of the room without being visible. Two people, a man and a woman, stood in the pub doorway. The man was dressed in a perfectly fitting, classic pin-striped suit that murmured Savile Row. It was the sort of suit that implied Armani was nouveau riche. The clothes, the haircut, the bearing, not to mention his level of fitness made her think of an army officer. He should have been completely discordant in the Beggar but he radiated such self-assurance that it was everyone else who looked out of place.

In contrast, his companion fitted in just fine. She was tall, slim and genuinely beautiful, with a perfect complexion and bright green eyes. Rosalynne disliked her on sight. The woman's dark, straight hair framed a pale-skinned face that contrasted sharply against her black-leather biker outfit.

The man took a flat silver case from a breast pocket, nonchalantly pulled out a cigarette, and tapped the end on the case. His eyes swept the occupants of the bar. Rosalynne shrank back into her alcove, her apprehension turning to outright fear. He lit the cigarette in direct contravention of the United Kingdom's health and safety laws. No one protested.

The man and woman walked methodically down the alcoves, examining the occupants carefully before moving on. He was cool and businesslike, almost casual, but his companion moved like a lioness stalking zebra in the long grass.

A coil of fear slithered in Rosalynne's stomach like a chilled roundworm. She knew of these people by reputation. Every magical freelancer in London knew of Major Jameson and Karla, the Commission's London enforcers.

Rosalynne had no reason to think that they were after her. Nevertheless, her stomach gave another little lurch because she remembered being trapped. She remembered the police interrogation room. She remembered the smell of stale tea, sweat and mould. Most of all, she remembered the fear.

☆   ☆   ☆

"Who was in it with you? Who did the actual hacking?" asked the police interrogator.

"No one," she replied. "I worked alone."

The police interrogator leaned forward, chin thrust out aggressively.

"Come off it," he said. "You don't have the computer skills to hack into a sausage roll let alone a bank. You left a clear trail right back to your own account. You claim you worked alone, right, so how did you hack the computer?"

"You wouldn't believe me if I told you," said Rosalynne, perfectly truthful.

"I suppose you are protecting some boyfriend," said the policeman. "Silly little girl. Lover boy will be shagging a new bird when you are slopping out your cell and fighting off butch lesbos in the showers. A pretty little thing like you will be in demand amongst the lifers."

She did not answer. What was there to say?

The policeman got up and walked to the door but, before he left, he turned and had one last try. "They will throw the book at you if you don't cooperate."

She shrugged, displaying an insouciance that she did not feel. Inside, she was terrified.

"Well, suit yourself. Have a nice time banged up in one of Her Majesty's holiday camps."

Rosalynne was left alone for what seemed hours, but was probably only ten minutes. A middle-aged man in a suit entered and sat down in the policeman's vacated chair. He offered her a fag. She was about to refuse, then remembered that it might be her last for some time. He smiled at her like a kindly uncle proffering a birthday present and lit the cigarette. Rosalynne drew the hot smoke deep into her lungs and held it, letting the nicotine rush through her veins. She fully intended to give up, one day, but it never seemed to be the right time.

"You are in a bit of a pickle, aren't you, my dear? If you don't talk they will double your sentence, but you could end up sedated in a loony bin if you tell the truth."

She tried to hide her surprise.

"Magic and electronics have odd interactions," the man mused. "Something to do with consciousness and quantum mechanics, so they tell me. Don't understand a word of it myself but it's amazing how a spell can bugger up a computer system."

He beamed at her. She did not reply.

"You have a way out," he said, talking very precisely as if to a small child. "I work for an NDGO called the Commission."

She looked blankly at him. She had no idea what Commission he meant. NDGO sounded like the authorities. The establishment and Rosalynne were not entirely compatible. This was not her first brush with them.

"Non-Departmental Government Organization," he said, confirming her suspicions. "We have room for a bright girl with magical talent. Join us and I could arrange to have your sentence suspended."

Rosalynne stalled by sucking in another lungful. She had absolutely no intention of wasting her skills as a wage slave. No one ever got rich working for someone else. In her opinion, people who labored for the common good were either mugs or just too gutless to branch out on their own. She thought about taking up his offer and then pulling a disappearing act but decided it was too risky. She had no idea of the extent of the Commission's powers but they must have a long reach if they could fix a trial. Maybe it was best not to annoy them.

"Thanks but no thanks," Rosalynne heard herself say. "I don't think that I would make a good civil servant."

"Very well, serve your time," said the man. The smile left his face and his eyes became very hard, the avuncular persona dissipating like morning mist. "No more magical crimes when you get out or we will be the people who come for you, not the police. You won't like who we send and they won't put you back in a cell. Our agents solve problems permanently. Do you understand?"

"Yes," she had replied, compliantly.

"Good," he said as he left. "I am glad you have learnt your lesson."

Rosalynne smiled submissively after him but really she was disdainful and angry. Who the hell did he think he was? Did he really think he could intimidate her with silly death threats? This was England and she had rights. She was sure she had rights.

She had learnt her lesson. From now on, she would watch her trail and work for cash payment only.

☆ ☆ ☆

Rosalynne's mind raced, trying to devise a way out. Keep calm, she told herself. Don't give yourself away by acting suspiciously; they probably aren't looking for you anyway. Her stomach still lurched as the fear-worm took a bite out of the lining. Jameson and Karla were two alcoves away. Should she run or try to bluff it out?

A man stood up suddenly, throwing aside his table. He twisted, vanished and in his place something beastlike roared. It leapt, claws slashing at Jameson's throat. The enforcer twisted, right hand reaching beneath his jacket. The heavy, charging body knocked Jameson over. A dull-black, bulky pistol flew out of his grasp, skittering across the floor. The beast landed on its back legs, claws scrabbling on varnished wood. Gaining purchase, it sprang at Jameson, who rolled over towards his gun. The beast howled in triumph. Jameson would never make it.

A black streak intercepted the monster in midair, smashing it aside. Karla and the beast rolled over in a tangle of legs and arms. As they separated, Karla did something that was too fast for Rosalynne to see but the beast howled in pain and anger. It fell on its back and rolled over, growling and showing its fangs. Karla flipped gracefully onto her feet. She snarled back, her open mouth revealing impossibly long canines.

The beast charged her on all fours. She caught it by the throat with her right hand; her fingers, her claws sinking deep into fur and flesh. She pushed it upright until it was dancing on its back legs. It snapped at her face. Karla intercepted the beast's snout with her left hand, holding its jaws closed. Slowly, she forced the beast's head back, bending its thick neck to a more and more extreme angle.

Rosalynne saw stark terror in the beast's eyes. Its front claws ripped at Karla, tearing open the leather jacket. Blood ran down her breasts. Her face never changed expression but her eyes glittered metallic green.

There was a deep thump of displaced air that Rosalynne felt more than heard. The beast's back exploded in gore. Jameson stood in the classic pistol shooter's position, body turned sideways, arm outstretched, looking down the gun. He fired again. The gun made a *whump* noise and jolted his arm. Blue electrical flashes sparkled around the barrel.

The beast rocked in Karla's grip. She pushed it away contemptuously, like a woman disposing of a disappointing lover. It smashed a table as it fell, causing a shriek of splintering wood, but the monster still would not die. It tried to crawl away on its front paws, its paralyzed rear legs dragging uselessly behind.

Jameson walked deliberately round to the front of the beast and pointed the bulky pistol at it. The monster gave one last snarl of defiance. Jameson shot it in the head. The beast collapsed, finally stilled. Blood ran out of its eyes.

Rosalynne eyed Jameson's weapon. She smelt tube trains, an acrid tang of ozone quite unlike the friendly Guy Fawkes firework-night smell that she associated with firearms. The pistol hit like a sledgehammer, however it worked. Her eyes darted around the room, looking for a chance to escape. Maybe they had come for the monster? Maybe they were not interested in her at all?

"That was my kill. I could have taken him," Karla said to Jameson, her metallic green eyes narrowed. Her hands were still extended into claws and the long canines thickened her speech.

"Of course you could," Jameson said, diplomatically. "But I could not bear to see you hurt."

He sounded like a man mollifying a lover. Karla seemed to soften, the metallic shine in her eyes dulling back to a deep emerald green. Her teeth retracted, the claws became fingers and she looked like a woman again. The leather jacket was irretrievably ruined but she had already stopped bleeding.

Jameson turned the body over onto its back—the naked body of a short thickset man. "Who the hell is he?"

Karla shrugged. "Were," she said, in a voice like a breath of tropical breeze.

Even Rosalynne found it sexy and she had not the slightest interest in women. Then the important part of their conversation struck her. Jameson did not know who the monster was. He was after someone else. The shape-changer had barely slowed the Commission's torpedoes down. What chance would she have?

"I wonder why he attacked us?" asked Jameson. "Guilty conscience, I suppose."

Karla did not reply or acknowledge the remark. If anything, she looked bored. She was unnaturally still, more like an inert machine than something alive.

The Beggar's clientele came to life like a bunch of extras when the director calls action. The curious gathered around to examine the body while the circumspect gravitated towards the way out.

This was Rosalynne's chance to get away in the confusion. She slid out of her alcove, stooping to render her lightly built frame even less inconspicuous. She kept her head well down and concentrated on covering ground.

Someone stuck something between her legs. Rosalynne tripped and fell headlong, bursting through the crowd and falling facedown in the monster's blood. The top-hatted letch withdrew his stick. He giggled childishly like the third hick in a rural horror movie.

"Hello, Rosalynne, we were looking for you," said a male voice.

She looked up to see Jameson, gun in hand, between her and the door.

"Oh, bugger!" Rosalynne said, with deep feeling. "What have I done to attract the Commission's attention?"

She could hear the whine in her voice. She sounded like a small-time villain having his collar felt. Not me, Guv, she seemed to be saying, I ain't done nothing, I wasn't even there.

"What haven't you done, Rosalynne?" Jameson asked, rhetorically. "Your little forays into the City's computer systems are causing chaos. You remember the run on Newcastle Rock?"

Rosalynne considered. She did have some vague memory of people queuing for miles outside branches of a bank somewhere up in the northern provinces.

"The Chancellor of the Exchequer wants someone's head on a block," Jameson said, pointing the gun. "And guess who's in the frame."

Rosalynne reacted with blind panic and took off through the crowd's legs. She gambled on Jameson not risking collateral damage by taking a shot through the bystanders. Unfortunately, she ran in the wrong direction, away from the door. She headed for the bar with the vague idea of putting solid wood between her and the gun. She never made it, never even came close.

"Karla!" Jameson yelled, like a man unleashing an attack dog.

Adrenaline surge speeded up Rosalynne's mind. Everyone seemed to be moving in slow motion, everyone except Karla; she was still terrifyingly fast. Throwing aside a table, Karla was on Rosalynne like a terrier after a rat.

Rosalynne ripped the posy from her jacket lapel. In one fluid motion she turned and threw it at Karla.

The herbs ignited in a cold flash that sent a directional shock wave away from Rosalynne. Karla bore the brunt of the impact but the wave rippled through the room, knocking over people, tables and chairs.

Rosalynne threw herself over the bar. Something went past her ear with a crack. That was no warning shot. Jameson was trying to kill her. The mirror behind the bar shattered in a blizzard of glass shards. She landed heavily on her back behind the bar. A jagged piece stuck in the wooden floor. It was funny what the mind seized on when paralyzed with fear. "Ink Gord" was inscribed on the glass. Breaking a mirror was bad luck.

Henry looked down at her sightlessly and slowly shook his head.

Something stuck its head out of the broken mirror, something that looked like a gargoyle with stubby wings and a single horn on the end of its nose. Its skin cracked as it moved, releasing puffs of purple vapor that ignited into flickering green flames. It partly hopped and partly flew with a single downward wingbeat, down onto the top of the bar.

Rosalynne rolled over.

The gargoyle waved a stubby arm. "Hello, Henry," it said in a voice that sounded like moving tectonic plates.

There was another thump and the bar panel beside Rosalynne splintered. A missile like a crossbow bolt with inlaid iron strips burst through and stuck in the wall behind. So much for putting solid wood between her and Jameson: the bolt would have gutted her if she had not moved.

Rosalynne screamed. Stupid, stupid, she berated herself. It signaled to Jameson that she was still alive. The gargoyle noticed her, cocking its head on one side like a bird of prey. Its beak split in a broad grin, which was a disturbing anatomical feat in itself, and it wolf-whistled like a white-van driver.

"What a beauty," it said, admiringly.

Rosalynne scrabbled along desperately on her hands and knees behind the bar. Another missile burst through the spot she had just vacated. The gargoyle admired the rear view as she crawled past and whistled again.

"You'll do. Yes, you'll do very nicely." Its voice was becoming smoother, more baritone, as if it were adjusting to the world.

Rosalynne resisted the urge to stop and pull her skirt down. It wasn't fair! Everyone had it in for her. All she was trying to do was earn a pound or two. Why wouldn't they all just leave her alone? She had but a moment to escape before Jameson, or—worse still—Karla, came over the bar after her.

She jumped up and hurled herself headfirst through the broken mirror.

"Goodbye, Rosalynne," Henry said. It sounded like a valediction.

Rosalynne fell on her bottom into something squelchy. A choking fog seared her throat. She smelt steam engines and the air was thick with a rich mix of organic odors. Stale urine was the dominant constituent.

This was not London or, at least, not her London. It was too quiet. Where was the background drone of cars, jets and trains? Come to that, where was the pub?

The Beggar had disappeared: no pub, no bar, no mirror. There was nothing behind her but a narrow, twisting alley. Rickety houses leaned in from each side. Thick fog reinforced the murk. Brown and dirty-green vapor tendrils curled around the alley like eels.

Rosalyn thought quickly. She'd leapt through a gate to the otherworld. Would Jameson come after her? She thought not. Anything could have been on the other side of that mirror. From the look of the gargoyle, a pool of boiling sulphur was a distinct possibility. Jameson would not take the chance. Why should he? In his view, she was probably already dead. That thought caused her to shake with post-traumatic stress. No, they wouldn't follow her, she told herself, calming down.

Only the threat of immediate and messy execution could have prompted her to take the awful gamble of jumping blind through a gate. She remembered Karla, her speed, her strength, her fangs, and started shaking again.

Rosalynne waited until her tremors subsided, while considering her options. Returning to the Beggar was problematical but the otherworld was a dangerous place. Rosalynne chose the lesser of two terrors. She would take her chances with the Commission.

The gate back to the Beggar must still be there. She just had to open it to get back. She went through the various herbs and items that she had in her bag, selecting what she needed.

Rosalynne drew a stylized door on the wooden side of a building, using chalk quarried from London's North Downs. Then she tipped ground-up mugwort into her left hand. Mugwort identified the weak points in reality. The Bible said that St. John wore a girdle of the herb on his journey through the wilderness. She cut an incision into her left hand with her athame and let her blood mingle with the herb.

Blood magic could be dangerously unpredictable, but she had no other way of powering the spell. Odysseus had used blood magic to open a gate to the otherworld because it worked. Rosalynne slipped into self hypnosis.

Something jogged Rosalynne out of her trance. She replayed the last few moments in her head. A giggle, she had heard a giggle. She spun around to find she had been wrong. Someone had come after her.

A sword stick punched through her upper shoulder, grating against her collarbone. Blood flooded down her blouse. She tried to move but the pain was excruciating. The letch in the top hat let go of his sword stick. It stuck fast, pinning her against the wall.

Top Hat giggled again. "Not so hoity-toity now, pretty witch, are we?"

He took a large knife out of his carpetbag and moved slowly towards her, waving it backwards and forwards like a cobra.

"Oh, we're going to have such fun, my beauty," Top Hat said.

Cold evil flowed off him, like vapor from a bottle of liquid nitrogen. Rosalynne shuddered, tearing the flesh around the sword stick. A sharp pain bit into her shoulder and she was free.

She threw the blood-activated mugwort at him.

It hit him in a shower of sparks. Her concentration had been broken so the spell misfired. It didn't open a gate but the result was almost as useful. Top Hat froze in a shimmer of light, like an ant in amber.

Rosalynne took the opportunity to leg it before the spell collapsed. She ran for her life. She ran along winding alleys, trying to dodge around the larger or more obnoxious piles of waste, splashing through them when she couldn't. She was hopelessly lost when she stopped, gasping, out of breath. She nursed a stitch of pain in her side to match the one in her shoulder.

Rosalynne examined her wound, which turned out to be embarrassingly superficial. What was far more of a concern was that she had used up all her mugwort. She needed more to open a gate to home.

She took stock of her surroundings. Doorways and windows broke the lines of the brick and wooden walls. Dim lights flickered in some of the windows but most were dark. None looked particularly inviting. In one doorway, a bundle of rags stirred and held out a grimy hand as she passed. She ignored it. Rosalynne saw no advantage in funding beggars.

The alley fed into a square that was almost solid with lean-to shacks and stalls. She elected to walk around the perimeter where sufficient space had been left for the passage of hand carts. People jostled for space everywhere, the men dressed in dirty shapeless jackets and trousers, the women in long dresses. The more prosperous had threadbare overcoats that hung down to their ankles. Costermongers shouted their wares in a confusing babble of sound: apples, matches, gloves and pies.

Rosalynne had to constantly sidestep around people. She passed another alley. A bully had a woman pinned against the wall with her skirt hitched up. He thrust rhythmically between her legs. Neither made a sound. The bully posed no threat to Rosalynne so she ignored the couple and pressed on to the corner of the square.

Through the shifting bodies she saw a tall, blind man round the corner. He tapped with a cane to find his way through the crowd. A dirty bandage covered his eyes.

"Henry!" Rosalynne shouted over the babble of voices. "Henry, wait."

Hope flashed through her like a bright flame. Henry knew his way around London's otherworld. He could help her home. The blind man cocked his head to one side, as if he had heard her. Rosalynne broke into a jog trot.

"Watch where you're going, Judy," said a male voice. She cannoned off a bulky figure, tripped, and rolled under a stall.

A stick prodded her in the ribs. "Hoister, thief," said a female voice. Others took up the hue and cry.

Rosalynne did what she had done all her life; when she could not hide, she ran. She twisted and ducked, evading grasping hands. Howls of protest rose in her wake as she dodged around bodies and jumped over obstacles.

When she reached the corner, Henry had disappeared. A narrow street exited from the square. She dived down it. A ditch in the center of the street drained the waste from paved footpaths on each side. Rosalynne gratefully used the pavement. Her suede boots were ruined and she was pretty certain that she had voided their guarantee. Jimmy Choos were not intended for the otherworld.

Most of the shops along the street sold items that were of little use to her, things like fabrics or food. She had no intention of eating or drinking anything. Food in the otherworld had contaminants far more dangerous than cholera, not that she fancied cholera either, come to that. She rounded a bend just in time to catch a glimpse of Henry's back entering a shop.

A flickering gaslight illuminated the shop sign—Nell's Old Curiosity Shop. Rosalynne groaned. Bloody Dickens! Great works of art caused their own shadows in the otherworld, or maybe it was the other way round. Somewhere Long John Silver and Captain Flint probably still plundered the seven seas. Personally, Rosalynne loathed Dickens' cloyingly sentimental stories about born losers. She was of one mind with Oscar Wilde: "One would have to have a heart of stone to read the death of little Nell without dissolving into tears...of laughter."

A bell mounted on a coiled spring dinged as she opened the door. The wooden floor was at a lower level than the outside street. Cabinets and piles of junk were scattered at random. There was no sign of Henry, no sign of anyone. A stuffed owl hung on string from the ceiling. She gave it a gentle pat to make it swing. It twisted its neck round to look at her and hooted indignantly. A tray offered spiders' webs for sale in matchboxes.

She found a globe on a little wooden pedestal and gave it an experimental spin. Her finger stopped it at random, resting on the west coast of North America. An invisible pen wrote a name on the map by her finger—Portus Novae Albionis. She swiveled the globe around and found a large island in the North Atlantic. She touched it with her finger and the invisible pen wrote Atlantis.

"It will show lost Lemuria as well," said a voice. An arm reached over Rosalynne's shoulder and demonstrated. The arm belonged to a young man in a white, high-collared shirt.

"Kit, I presume?" asked Rosalynne, resignedly.

"Alfred," he replied. "Alfred Pumplecheck."

"Good grief," Rosalynne said. "How did Dickens get away with those names?"

"Can I help you, madam?" asked Pumplecheck, icily.

"As it happens, you can," Rosalynne replied. "A blind man came into your shop a few moments ago. I need to talk to him."

Pumplecheck tilted his head to one side. "Blind man?" he asked.

"Blind man," Rosalynne repeated slowly, pronouncing each syllable carefully, as if she were talking to the village idiot. "You know, white cane, bandage round the eyes, that sort of thing."

"You are my first patron for some time, madam," said Pumplecheck.

He sounded very sure but Rosalynne searched the small shop. She did not find Henry nor did she locate any way out other than the front door. She needed to think.

"Are you interested in any of the curios, madam?" Pumplecheck asked, breaking her concentration.

"Have you any mugwort?" Rosalynne asked, more in hope than expectation.

He burrowed under a pile of magazines, throwing copies in all directions. Rosalynne caught one. It was an issue of London Society featuring a new exploit of Sherlock Holmes as recorded by Doctor Watson, his faithful Boswell. Pumplecheck gave a cry of triumph and retrieved a small wooden box with an elephant carved on the lid. He thrust it under her nose and flipped up the top. It contained dried plant material. Rosalynne tasted a bit with the tip of her tongue. Result, she thought triumphantly, mugwort.

"I believe that is what you require," he said.

They haggled for some time but he finally took her daemon-bane amulet in exchange. Rosalynne regretted its loss but she was desperate. Pumplecheck could have held out for almost everything she had, up to and including her favors. She spat into her hand and rubbed a small portion of mugwort in to make a paste. This she smeared in a careful geometric pattern across a rose quartz crystal. She focused hard on the stone, building up energy.

Power flowed into the crystal, merging with its natural resonant frequency to create a complex signal. She waved the crystal around her like Spock's tricorder. The oscillation frequency peaked when she pointed in a certain direction. Relief surged through Rosalynne. She had found a gate. Now all she had to do was go and open it.

A man reeled out of a door. He bumped into Rosalynne, steadying himself with a hand on her shoulder.

"What a strawberry tart," the man said, enveloping her in a miasma of bad breath and rotgut gin.

He peered into her face, "You're a cut above the usual tail. How much for a blower?"

He lunged at her. She pivoted using his own weight and momentum to throw him facedown in the drain. He hit with a splash and failed to get up. Rosalynne strode away without looking back. The so-and-so could drown in his own vomit for all she cared.

The crystal guided her deeper into the Whitechapel rookery, a hive of fetid alleys and grimy buildings. She heard a rhythmic tapping ahead of her but could see nothing through the murk. It sounded different from a gentleman's stick but she gripped her athame tightly. The little knife was not much of a weapon against a sword stick but better than nothing. The tapping got closer. It had a weird double rap.

A figure loomed out of the murk. Rosalynne shrank back into a doorway. She concentrated on a spell to make herself inconspicuous, softly intoning the words under her breath. The man got closer. He swung himself forward with a crutch under each arm, right crutch first then second alongside, making the *tock-tock* sound. A knee-length coat flapped between the crutches but the man had no knees because he had no legs. He balanced adroitly as if the crutches were stilts.

When he reached Rosalynne, he turned to face her, pivoting on one crutch. So much for the efficacy of the hiding spell. She resolved to excise it from her Book of Shadows just as soon as she was home.

"Alms, fair lady, alms." He shook his head, causing a jangle of coins from a bag slung around his neck.

She was angry that she had been frightened by a bloody crippled beggar. Rosalynne being Rosalynne, she turned her fear into anger and focused it on the beggar.

"Sod off, you creep," she said.

"Lousy, glim-raddled dollymop." He hopped closer, his face twisting in rage.

A perfectly formed, miniature leg swung out of the man's long coat. A rusty chiv, tied to the beggar's foot, sliced up to disembowel her. It was a well-practiced move that must have often been decisive.

Rosalynne blocked the thrust with her athame. The blades clashed with a metallic clang. Her knife lodged fast in the chiv's lashings. She heaved upwards, throwing the beggar backwards off his crutches.

Rosalynne fled.

"Help me up, you pox-rotten bitch."

She risked a glance. The beggar struggled on his back, little legs waggling in the air like an upturned cockroach. She made the traditional two-fingered English salute before resuming her flight. Rosalynne rounded a corner to find the blind beggar leaning against a wall.

"Henry?" she asked.

"You look tired, beauty," the blind beggar replied.

It wasn't Henry's voice. The blind beggar had a rich baritone.

"You're the daemon," said Rosalynne, edging away.

"There's no fooling you, beauty," said the daemon, mockingly.

She automatically reached into her bag for her daemonbane amulet. The daemon smiled at her encouragingly. The amulet wasn't in her bag. It was in the daemon's hand.

"You were the shopkeeper, as well," she said.

"Albert Pumplecheck at your service, madam," it bowed, morphing into the shopkeeper. "I can't believe you swallowed that name."

It slapped its thigh, chortling.

"Were you looking for this?" it asked.

The daemon dangled her amulet in front of her face. She grabbed the charm but it was a trick. The amulet turned into a slimy toad in her hand.

"Yuk," she said, dropping it.

The toad hopped off with an outraged croak. The daemon laughed like Vincent Price in a low budget movie. It changed again, this time into the form of a tall, fit man with jet black hair and a sardonically handsome face.

"I like this shape," it said. "What do you think? Cat got your tongue, witch? Oh well, I think it suits me."

The catchphrase from the Fast Show's gay tailors popped into her head, "Suits you, sir," Focus, girl, she thought. This thing's dangerous and it's stalking you.

"You are so delightfully naive, beauty. I like that in a woman," it said. "It adds to your charms. We will have such fun together."

He rubbed his hands together, enthusiastically.

Rosalynne ground her teeth together. This bloody daemon was getting on her tits. It was a supercilious, sexist pig of monumental proportions, even when judged against the low standard set by the average London male. She got a grip on her emotions. It was deliberately goading her.

"What do you want?" she asked, in an attempt to get to the point.

"You are in a bit of a bind, witch," the daemon said. "How would you like me to take you home?"

Rosalynne dismissed the offer out of hand. Daemons didn't do favors for free. They made bargains and humans inevitably got the worst of the deal. It didn't seem to realize that it had already provided her with the means to escape the otherworld. Let it keep the amulet; she had the mugwort.

"No, thank you," she replied, politely. Only a fool was rude to a daemon.

"Ah well," it said, waving a hand languidly. "Please yourself. Just whistle if you change your mind. You know how to whistle, don't you?"

The daemon did its Vincent Price impression again.

"I suppose you were the top-hatted letch as well, just throwing a scare into me to get me running?" she asked.

"Actually, no!" said the daemon. "I assumed you would run without needing to be prodded."

A high-pitched giggle sounded behind her. Rosalynne did her startled rabbit impression and shot past the grinning daemon. She soon slowed down when a stitch stabbed at her stomach. She was hungry, she was thirsty and her feet ached. Why had she worn high heels? She bent over to catch her breath.

The top-hatted psycho strode out of the smog, like he was taking a constitutional in Regent's Park. Rosalynne groaned and trotted off. Ten meters further on, the alley was blocked by a great heap of rotten waste. She tried climbing over it but fell when she clasped a branch that proved to be a leg loosely attached to a dog's rotting corpse. Top Hat leered at her as she rolled on the ground. He opened the carpetbag and produced the shiny knife.

"Beautiful witch for the cutting," he chanted, in a singsong voice.

A metal ring jarred her wounded shoulder when she rolled over to get up. She took a firm grip on it and pulled, lifting a wooden trapdoor that had been hidden by muck. Rosalynne threw herself through headfirst, almost breaking her neck from the long drop onto a hard earth floor. The trapdoor crashed shut behind her.

The cellar was lit by flames from a fireplace against one wall. A family with two young children and a baby warmed themselves in front of it. The woman gazed listlessly at Rosalynne. Her man lay flat on his back, a dry cough wracking his emaciated body.

Two women in rags huddled together in a corner. They looked

seventy but were probably nearer seventeen. One's face was already pox-scarred. A man lay on his side beside an empty bottle.

The cellar looked like a scene for hell in the flickering red and orange firelight. The trapdoor above Rosalynne opened. She saw a top hat silhouetted against the light. She ran for a vertical wooden ladder in a corner. As she climbed, a heavy body thumped down into the cellar. It giggled: she climbed.

There was another trapdoor at the top of the ladder. She pushed it open with her shoulder and scrambled through. At the top, she dropped the trapdoor shut, slamming it on a sword stick that thrust through the gap.

Rosalynne fled down a narrow corridor. She flung open a door at random. The room was lined with parallel ropes. A dozen or more bodies were suspended on them. The ropes ran under their armpits, holding them vertically upright with their feet dragging on the floor. To her horror, some of the bodies stirred. The nearest opened his eyes.

"Piss off, dollymop. I'm trying to sleep."

She ran on, pounding up a staircase, round a corner, then up another flight. There was a door at the top. It opened outwards and she ran through—into empty space above a yard. Rosalynne felt like a protagonist in a Warner Brothers cartoon, except she dropped like a shot grouse. She hit a rope and bounced. She grabbed it desperately, hanging on for her life.

She was head-down over a huge copper vat. It was filled with strips of leather hanging in bubbling green liquid. The smell would have choked a ferret. Smoke and yellow-green steam billowed around her, leaving no doubt as to the purpose of the vat. Someone was tanning leather in boiling urine.

Rosalynne lay tangled in a rope bridge that spanned the gap to a house across the yard. There was a single rope to walk on and one for each hand. She hauled herself up and shuffled gingerly across. It was not easy. Her feet kept trying to rotate over her head. Rosalynne was a city girl. Rope bridges had never entered her curriculum.

Somehow she made it to the other side. The ropes were attached to hooks screwed into the wooden wall around a small wooden platform under a loading bay. The platform creaked alarmingly under her weight. Rosalynne was exhausted. Running was no longer an option. She had to finish this, one way or another.

Top Hat appeared in the far doorway. He pointed a finger at

her like a gun barrel, then stepped onto the rope. He made far better time across the rope bridge than she had. The bastard had probably been a boy scout. She watched with resignation, like a trapped rabbit in front of a stoat.

Rosalynne sprang to life when he was about a third of the way across. She sawed frantically on the footrope with her athame. The small knife was hardly ideal for the purpose but the rope was old and cut easily. It parted when Top Hat was only half-way across. He hung from the remaining ropes by his hands, his stick and bag dropping into the vat with a plop. A puff of fetid, ammonia-rich steam wafted up.

Top Hat kept on coming, swinging from hand to hand like a demented gibbon. Rosalynne resumed sawing on the next rope. When it parted, he almost fell, swinging wildly by one hand until he got a two-handed grip on the last rope. If anything, he increased speed, handing himself along the single line in a smooth motion.

Rosalynne cut frantically but the last rope was in better condition and resisted the knife. Top Hat swung onto the wooden platform, reaching out for her. The rotten wood gave under their combined weight, pitching them both into space.

Top Hat fell backwards into the boiling urine. An eruption of steam blotted out his death throes but Rosalynne heard the screams. She grabbed the remaining strand of the bridge, swinging clear of the building.

She managed to turn around and began inching her way back along the rope. To her horror, she had done her work too well, and strands unraveled where she had hacked at it. She crossed the cut and had almost reached the remains of the platform when the rope parted.

Rosalynne crashed down against the side of the building. The rope slipped through her hands, burning the skin. Somehow she braked her fall until she hung above the vat. She could not climb up. She could barely hold on. Her grip relaxed for a second and she dropped another centimeter, stripping more flesh. Blood made the rope slippery.

Rosalynne was a natural optimist but this was too much. To drown in scalding urine after all she had endured. It just wasn't fair. She began to cry at the injustice.

The daemon sat down in the loading bay, dangling its legs over the drop. It was in its tall, dark and handsome guise.

"Look at all this broken wood," it said to Rosalynne in a conversational voice. "This building is a disgrace. I could get splinters."

"Haul me up, please," Rosalynne pleaded.

"Do you want to bargain for my help?" asked the daemon, carefully.

"No!" Rosalynne replied.

Never, never deal with a daemon—that was the rule—there was always a price and the daemon always got the better of the bargain. Rosalynne looked down. The top hat surfaced on an upsurge of hot urine, rolled over, and sank down again. There was no sign of a body. She slipped another centimeter down the rope.

"Yes," Rosalynne blubbed. "Yes, yes, yes. You win. Hurry, I can't hold on any longer."

"Then let's get down to business," it said. "The contract!"

The daemon snapped its fingers and produced a rolled-up parchment. It pulled the red ribbon and the parchment unrolled, all two meters of it.

"Shall I go through the subclauses for you, to make sure you understand the small print?" said the daemon considerately, taking a pair of reading glasses out of a breast pocket.

"No, no, I agree," Rosalynne said. "For the Goddess' sake, hurry up."

She couldn't feel her hands. Her fingers were completely numb.

"Excellent, then sign at the bottom,"

"How?" asked Rosalynne. "You may have noticed that I have a problem."

"Just say—I sign," the daemon replied.

"I sign," Rosalynne said, desperately.

Her fingers finally gave way and she fell.

Rosalynne woke up screaming in her bed, in her flat, in London. She put her hands over her face—her hands, oh Goddess, her hands. She took a deep breath and looked at them. They were unmarked. Her shoulder didn't hurt; it wasn't even scarred. She should be filthy dirty, but she wasn't. She lay back on crisp cotton sheets that smelled faintly of washing powder.

It couldn't have been a dream, she thought. It was all so real. The nightmare chase through a Dickensian rookery, the psycho with the giggle, the daemon—oh, Goddess, she had made a bargain with a daemon! What had she agreed to? Her thoughts went round like clothes in a tumble drier.

Her Jimmy Choos stood beside the bed, unmarked. Why weren't they ruined? It couldn't have all been a nightmare, could it?

Like many crooks, Rosalynne had a high capacity for optimistic self-delusion. Deep down she knew that truth was what you believed it to be and the events of the night before were already fading. She jumped out of bed and pulled on a wrap. Light streamed in when she threw back the curtains. Her bedside clock showed that it was almost midday. She went into the bathroom and ran the hot tap. She squirted a generous portion of Foxy Lady body oil into the steaming water, savoring the rich scent of musk and jasmine.

Rosalynne flashed back, hanging over bubbling urine. She couldn't get her breath. She gripped the bath with both hands until her knuckles whitened. Slowly, she got her breathing under control. She had not had a panic attack for months. When each breath was slow and deep she straightened up. She should take more care of herself. This wasn't good.

Rosalynne examined herself in the mirror. Maybe she was putting on a little weight? Henry had put too much tonic water in her gin. That thought reminded her of the Blind Beggar and the daemon. She dismissed the heretical memory. Maybe it was all a nightmare, or some sort of magical attack from an enemy too gutless to take her on face to face? That made sense.

Rosalynne slipped the wrap off her shoulders to make a more intimate examination. Her reflection had a smudge on her left breast. She rubbed a hand over the blemish, but it didn't come off. She looked down, lifting her breast. It wasn't a smudge; it was a tattoo, a tattoo of a gargoyle with stubby wings and a single horn on its nose. She pulled the gown around her body.

"Oh, bugger!" Rosalynne said, softly. She had a daemon mark, what Aleister Crowley called the Mark of the Beast. At one time, you could get burnt just for having such a thing. The clergy believed it signified a pact with the devil or one of his minions. The clergy were not entirely deluded.

Rosalynne took a deep breath.

"Oh sodding bugger," she said, sincerity making up for lack of imagination.

She slid her wrap open and checked the gargoyle again. It turned its head to look up at her and winked. She felt a pull as if an invisible rope was tugging at her stomach. The contractions built up in waves, like giving birth. It ended in one almighty wrench that felt like she was being pulled inside out, like a rubber glove.

Rosalynne felt the resumption of the panic attack. She bent over on the bath to catch her breath. Someone goosed her. She jumped, squeaking indignantly, panic attack forgotten. The daemon, in his mister tall, dark and handsome form, leaned against the wall. He wore the same sardonic smile. She licked her lips.

"I'm your pathway to this world. That's what you wanted from me. You couldn't get in without having a native familiar. How long did I sign up for?" she asked.

"Only the standard short contract for a thousand days. A witch's life isn't worth more," it replied.

"Three years," she said, doing a rough calculation.

"One thousand Black Citadel days," said the daemon, smugly. "About fifty London years, I fancy."

"What!" Rosalynne said. "Fifty years as a door."

"Not just a door, beautiful witch, although that is a useful attribute," said the daemon. "I own you body and soul for the duration of the contract, the most beautiful, valuable jewel in my collection."

Rosalynne didn't like the way it lingered on the word "body" and pulled her wrap tighter.

"You set it all up to ensnare me. You planned everything," she said.

"Down to the last detail, beauty," the daemon said. "I ran you like a rat in a maze."

"But how could you know that I would use high-energy magic against Karla in the Beggar?" Rosalynne asked. "That opened the door for you. Without that, you couldn't have got into the pub in the first place. You couldn't have known that Jameson would search for me there, unless..."

She looked at the grinning daemon with dawning comprehension. "Unless Henry tipped them off and set the whole thing up."

"You get there in the end, beauty," the daemon said. "Henry owed me a favor and you had pissed him off once too often."

"But I could have been killed," Rosalynne said.

The daemon shrugged. "You wouldn't have been much use to me if you couldn't look after yourself. Henry reckoned you were a survivor, completely amoral and ruthless. I think he likes you.

He wants to borrow you but I don't share my possessions. Well, not unless I get a really good offer."

The daemon advanced on her. Rosalynne retreated step by step until she was against the wall. It stepped in really close and kissed her on the lips. She tried to punch but it held her wrists. It was incredibly strong. It pushed her arms over her head and pinned them against the wall with one hand, pushing her wrap open with the other.

She kicked between its legs but it was quick, as fast as Karla. It turned its thigh and she bruised her knee on hard-packed muscle. It stroked the underside of her breast and kissed her again.

"The most beautiful, valuable jewel in my collection," it repeated, almost fondly.

It caressed her breast. When its thumb rubbed over the daemon mark, waves of pleasure rippled up and down her body. Her knees turned to jelly. It let go of her arms and she draped them around its neck.

"Bastard," she said.

It was naked. How had that happened? She offered no resistance when strong hands parted her thighs. He slid into her and she surrendered to him, collapsing on his hard, masculine body.

"You bastard," she repeated, in case he hadn't got the message first time around. She kissed him savagely.

"What a beauty," he said, when she came up for air.

Rosalynne lay back in her bath listening to the hiss of popping bubbles. She ached all over, a satisfied, fulfilled sort of ache, like one got at the end of a successful gym session. The bastard had enjoyed her body, thoroughly.

She had difficulty sorting her emotions out. She had never surrendered completely to a man, never given anyone that power over her. It was wonderful and terrifying, all at the same time. She had given herself to a daemon, not a man. Was that better or worse? She couldn't decide. He owned her body and soul, for the next fifty years. Then there was the matter of Henry and what retribution she could deliver for his treachery. Bastards, all men were bastards.

The Commission wouldn't give up until they had a body. The name on her flat's lease was an alias but, sooner or later, they would find her. Rosalynne blinked back tears; her beautiful flat was her home, her refuge, and she didn't want to leave. She had worked so hard for it. It just was not fair. She always had to run.

Rosalynne looked down at the gargoyle mark on her breast. It winked at her suggestively, and she felt the tug of her magical connection with her daemon, her owner. Bastard!

She would have to flee. She had no chance against the Commission's enforcers. She played back her encounter with them in her mind. Jameson was dangerous but Karla was bloody terrifying.

She remembered the possessive way Karla had looked at Jameson and a new idea occurred to her, an odd and interesting idea. Her daemon was very pleased with his new possession. How would her daemon, her very powerful daemon, react to a threat against his beautiful witch?

Rosalynne had spent her whole life in the shadows hiding, running when she couldn't hide. Maybe she did not have to hide anymore? There was more than one sort of power. It remained to be seen who owned whom.

A slow grin spread across her face. The gargoyle on her breast winked at her and she winked back. She lowered herself deeper into the bath water, blowing bubbles while making plans.

After all, beauty is a witch.

JOHN LAMBSHEAD was born in Cornwall in the 50s in the seaside resort of Newquay. He was educated in London at Brunel University and worked as a British Museum research scientist until his recent semiretirement, publishing many scientific papers. He has always had a second life, story-boarding computer games and writing radio plays, popular military history, and, latterly, fantasy. His first novel, *Lucy's Blade*, was published by Baen in 2006. He is married with two grown-up daughters.

He supplied these notes about his story:

"Beauty is a Witch" is a story about London, East London, the industrial city east of London Town and north of the Thames, that dates back to Medieval times. This is the city unvisited by the tourist. It has been the home of poverty, criminality, and depravity on an unimaginable scale. East London names like Jack

the Ripper (1888) and the Kray Twins, leaders of Britain's most feared organized crime syndicate in the 1960s, still resonate in popular culture. It is the traditional entry point for immigrant waves to the UK. Huguenot, Irish, Jews, Lebanese, Turks have all lived there and left their mark. The current newcomers are Bangladeshi.

There is a real Blind Beggar pub in Whitechapel, but you will find it quite unlike my entirely fictional description. The original blind beggar was Henry de Montfort, son of Simon de Montfort who set up the first elected parliament in Europe. Legend has it that Henry was blinded at the battle of Evesham and wandered as a beggar until he reached Bethnal Green, where he begged on the old Roman road. He was befriended by a baroness with whom he had a child, Besse—who gave her name to Besse Road. Booth launched the Salvation Army outside the Blind Beggar, and Ronnie Kray really did shoot George Cornell to death in the bar. Cornell was associated with the rival South London Richardson crime syndicate—the torture gang.

East London is now home to gleaming towers of chrome and glass, the largest financial center in the world. They still gamble there, but now with trillions of dollars rather than a handful of gold sovereigns. The girls still ply the oldest trade, but the modern belle de jours charge three hundred pounds an hour and the cost of a luxury hotel room and taxi. It's a far cry from the penny knee-trembler in a dirty alley. Cocaine has replaced gin as life's little helper. Criminals still flourish but they use computers rather than razors.

Old East London is still there, if you know where to look: a plaque on a modern building, or a piece of wall that survived both the Blitz and Heseltine's bulldozers. If you look carefully out of the corner of your eye, as the sun drops over the Thames into Kent, you may catch the shadow of a top hat and cane or a trilby and pistol. If you are really fortunate you might see a blind beggar on the Roman road. If you do, give him a couple of pounds—for luck.

THE LONG DARK NIGHT
OF DIEGO CHAN

MARK L. VAN NAME

"Sam's gone over," the first line of the text message said.

"You said you'd help if it ever came to this," the second continued.

"It has."

"Barbara."

Diego Chan kept running but reversed direction and headed back to the Super 8 that was passing for home this week. His legs carried him easily, his heart beat a steady rhythm, and his muscles moved smoothly and with power. He brushed the sweat from his eyes and thumbed a response, "Okay." He sent it on its way through the three redirectors that would mask its origins before it reached her.

He pulled up the tracking display on his phone: five miles out, a hair over seven minutes a mile so far, over thirty-five minutes to make it back. Not good enough. He pushed harder but not so hard that anyone would notice. That wouldn't buy him much time, but if she was right, the clock had started ticking a while ago.

The morning sun was still coming into its own when he reached the motel thirty-one minutes later.

"I can't believe he chose this," Barbara said. "He was sick, real sick—pancreatic cancer—and he knew he was probably going to die, but he had decided to fight it. He'd been at it for two months."

Chan froze. Sam hadn't contacted him. Once, Sam would

193

have told him anything that mattered. That was a long time ago, though. A long time.

"Did you hear me?" she said.

"Yes." Chan moved the phone to his right hand and resumed toweling himself dry. "Did he file new paperwork?"

"No," she said. "What you have is all there is. That's part of why I'm sure. The rest is..." she paused, "you know, he's just too strong. Even sick." She paused again as her voice caught. "If he did decide he wanted to change, he'd talk to me first. I know he would."

"Yes," Chan said. "He would." He put the phone back in his left hand as he began to dress. "Why do you think this happened, that one of them took him?"

"He'd mentioned approaches from some guy, Matt something, somebody he said you both knew from a long time ago. Said the guy had heard about his cancer and wouldn't give up. Asked him to come to a club he owned."

Yeah, a long time, as far back as Chan had memories, all the way to the first foster home. When Matt had decided to make the move, Chan hadn't liked it, but Matt had done it straight, filed the paperwork, gone over, what, maybe six years ago now.

"When?" Chan said.

"I can't be sure," she said, "but they usually leave the restaurant about one, sometimes two, so after that." Her voice trailed off. "He's never come home later than three. Never."

From anyone else, Chan would have considered this an over-reaction, encouraged them to wait a day for the missing person to show up, but not Barbara. Sam was never late and kept every appointment.

Chan checked the time: 7:00 A.M. here in Raleigh, 4:00 in San Francisco. Sam leaves no earlier than one, no later than two, so roughly a two- to three-hour window from when he left work to now. Matt would play it smart, ask to talk to Sam, lure him over, maybe spend an hour doing all of that. One to two hours already ticked off. Twenty-two he could reasonably count on, twenty-three if he was lucky.

No. No point in counting on luck. Twenty-two hours.

"What's the name of Matt's club?" he said.

"Changes." she said. "It's, uh, a sex club. Serves everybody. He runs it, makes the *Chronicle* now and then, keeps it clean and on the level. They say."

Chan nodded. That was good: He had somewhere to start.

"I'll catch the first flight I can," he said.

"Will that be soon enough? We only have"—she choked back a sob—"before..."

"I think so," Chan said, "but that doesn't matter. It's all I can do, so we have to assume it will be." He paused. "Sam's gone either way. You understand that, right?"

"Yeah," she said, "I do, but this is what he would have wanted. He always said that."

"Yes," Chan said, "he did." He terminated the call.

He opened a browser on his laptop to search for flights.

"I'm coming," he said to the still, empty room.

The American Airlines terminal at Raleigh-Durham International Airport sported the same chrome and wood and glass design of every major airport with a redesign within the last five years. Chan liked it well enough when he bothered to look at it, but mostly he didn't notice it. He wasn't on a job, but he might as well have been, so he focused on the people and watched for signs of trouble. He had to assume that Matt would know Barbara would call him, but he had no reason to believe Matt would know where he was. Still, it always paid to be careful.

He needed to be rested when he arrived, so he blew almost two grand on a one-way first-class ticket on the 10:15 via Chicago, then forked over the day fee for the Admiral's Club. He crammed himself into a corner chair where he could watch the door. No way had they designed these things for people his size; at six four and 240, he rarely found comfortable seats.

Decision time.

He could try it on his own, but that would cost time, maybe a lot of it, to acquire what he'd need to invade a club that he had to assume would be full of them. If he asked for help, though, he'd owe his occasional employer.

Chan hated owing anything to anyone.

He was wasting time. He already knew the answer. He'd promised Sam, so he had to do everything in his power to keep that promise.

He booted his laptop, brought up a clock, sent the message with the number of the mobile he was about to destroy, and waited.

The phone rang two minutes later.

He pressed the connect button but said nothing.

Silence.

After thirty seconds, he said, "I need a package and some data."

"We have no current contract," a scrambled voice replied.

Chan waited. They both knew how this would go, so there was no point in playing.

After a few seconds, the voice laughed, a sound more like car fenders screeching on impact than human laughter. "It'll come out of the next job."

"Yes."

"How complete a package?"

Chan glanced at his nearly empty backpack. Between jobs, he never carried more than the pack could hold, and he rarely took that much. Aside from his documentation, the usual travel basics, a few wads of cash, and the slim, waterproof envelope of key papers—one of which was Sam's—he had nothing he'd need.

"Complete." He shrugged. The heavy leather jacket slid over him, so worn and smooth it moved liked water. "I have a jacket; that's it."

After a pause, the voice said, "Will this come back on us?"

"No. The paperwork is good."

"Where?"

"San Francisco."

"The data?"

"All filed paperwork for Sam Flynn, plus background on Matt Gresham."

The pause was longer this time. "Matt Gresham is involved in this?"

Chan sighed. "Is that a problem?"

The car fenders screeched again. "No, but if you end up canceling him, we might make a little profit on this."

"It's only him if he forces it to go that way. It's not my goal."

"Then we'll hope for the worst."

Chan said nothing. The easiest way to get in trouble with these people was to talk. The less he said, the less likely he was to screw up.

"Intercontinental Hotel. A room will be waiting in your name. It'll be there."

After a pause, the voice added, "You know you owe us, right."

It wasn't a question.

The call ended.

Chan went into the men's restroom, closed the door of the rearmost stall, and smashed the phone. He broke the SIM card in half, then flushed those two pieces. Habit. Probably unnecessary now, but not harmful, either.

9:35 A.M.

6:35 there.

Twenty-plus hours.

He headed for the gate.

On the first plane, Chan bought Internet access with a credit card in an identity so thin it would rip easier than a wet sheet of notepaper.

Barbara was right: nothing about the Changes club was secret. Its web site offered an event listing, membership plans and costs, the disclaimer forms you'd have to sign to enter, customer testimonials, photos of all the rooms—play spaces, it called them—and even a floor plan. Formerly a theater, it sprawled across three levels: balcony, main, and basement. Every floor had at least one room with dirt for burial and rebirth play.

Great. Lots to search.

Matt's picture graced half a dozen pages that explained how very safe you could be there as you indulged your wildest dreams. Sex club. Kink club. All in private or in public, as you chose. Watch, play, or do both. Regularly inspected and licensed by city and state health authorities. Full bar, alcohol and blood. On-site security and medical staff. Humans and vampires playing together. Open from ten to sunrise.

Its neighbors—strip shows, cheap hotels, two diners open late—gave endorsements that included thin pitches for their own goods and services.

Chan enlarged his search to include articles about the club. News services attacked it in slow times but lost their energy for the fight faster than three-pack-a-day smokers sprinting up Lombard Street. No one had ever found any evidence of anyone being turned there without the proper paperwork. Members and even a couple of former beat cops gave testimonials when it won an online vote for being the safest of the late-night San Francisco clubs. Not a single news story mentioned a fight or an arrest inside it.

All of that information proved only that Matt was smart, which Chan already knew.

He also knew but had no way to prove that Matt had taken Sam. Since before he'd turned, Matt had been evangelical on the benefits and how good it was. He'd want to save Sam—and to have Sam join him.

No, Chan had no doubt that Matt had Sam. The question was, which risk was greater for Matt: leaving the club in the wee hours to go somewhere at the key time, or bringing Sam there.

Matt hated variables he couldn't control, so he'd prefer Sam be there, but then he'd be taking on other risks: finding a safe burial spot, minimizing the number of people who knew, and making sure no one checking the club found out. Meeting Sam elsewhere might be a simpler answer.

No way to know by staring at the screen.

Chan would have to ask Matt.

When they announced the descent into Chicago, Chan turned off the laptop. He knew all he could about the club without going there.

Chan dozed the second leg and left it feeling as rested as he reasonably could given that even the first-class seats weren't a good fit for him. He'd normally invest the first few days in a new place making sure no one was tracking him, but he didn't have the time. The plane landed slightly late, so he didn't make it to the cab line until 4:45, which put him smack in the middle of the worst of the rush-hour traffic.

He walked into the gleaming glass tower of the Intercontinental a few minutes before six.

Eight hours to go, give or take.

He fought the urge to rush everyone he encountered. It wouldn't help, and it could attract attention to him or even slow him.

At the check-in desk, he gave his name and asked if they'd bring the package from his room so he could keep waiting for his friends in the lobby.

Their smiles never wavered. An earthquake wouldn't change their expressions; it was that kind of hotel.

He tipped the bellman a twenty and grabbed the heavy, locked duffel bag from the guy's two hands with one of his. He headed for the bar and kept on going past it, through the restaurant and out the side door. The short time meant he had to ask for the package, but he didn't have to trust his occasional employer to give him a room. He could expect them to be watching him, because if they thought they might be able to make money off him, they'd try to steer events their way. With no definite engagement on the line, however, the surveillance team wouldn't be large.

Chan quick-walked to the corner, turned, and cut through the parking garage. On the other side, he caught the light, crossed the street, entered the multistory mall, and crammed himself into an elevator with a mother with two little boys, one on each arm.

They stared at him.

He ignored them.

When the doors opened on the top floor, the mother rushed them out of the elevator.

He rode it back down one level, stepped out, and followed signs to a luggage store. They'd have a tracker in the bag to help the follow team. It's what he would have done. With a small team, they'd use it to know when he left the mall. They might also have observers on the exits, but they wouldn't risk following him in a five-story structure: too much turf to cover. He bought a huge, red, rolling suitcase composed of some polycarbonate material so light it weighed less than his reinforced jacket. It cost all the cash in his wallet, but he had ten grand more in the backpack.

At a big-and-tall store a floor further down, he picked up a tweed sport coat that billowed around his waist but fit his shoulders and was tight but tolerable on his arms.

He snagged a Giants cap and XXXL T-shirt from a templelike shop dedicated to the team.

An electronics store sold him a prepaid mobile phone.

He bought clear spectacles at an eyewear kiosk.

In a public restroom he went to the handicap stall. The duffel's locks were keyed to his last payment account, as usual. He transferred the contents of the bag one at a time into the suitcase, checking each one carefully for tracking chips. The short sword's handle might hide one, but his experience was that inserting a chip there was more trouble than it was worth, so he didn't worry about it. Ditto for the dozen purpleheart wood stakes. He tossed out the bands on the five stacks of twenty hundreds. The bills would be traceable, of course, but not as quickly as Chan would finish here.

He added his backpack, shirt, and leather jacket to the big suitcase. He closed the suitcase and folded the duffel. He tore the tags off his new clothing and donned the T-shirt and sport coat. He tied his hair in a ponytail and tucked it under the cap. He put on the glasses.

He checked himself in the restroom mirror. He was too big to blend in easily, but with a bit of a slouch to cut some height, he could pass for an overweight local fan, at least from a distance.

He stuffed the duffel in the first trashcan he passed.

He bought a giant red slushie in a transparent cup and sipped it very slowly as he rode the escalators to the bottom floor and ambled out of the mall. No one on the run drinks a slushie.

If they were looking for him, they'd now have trouble finding him. They'd know he'd end up at Changes, but at least he could establish a private base of operations.

If Matt was expecting him, and Chan had to assume he was, anyone Matt sent would be unlikely to recognize him. It was still daylight, though just barely, so Matt himself certainly wouldn't be out.

Both his employers and Matt would expect him to keep a low profile, so he did the opposite: walked to Union Square and checked into the Westin St. Francis with another paper-thin ID. With a few sad comments about a rough divorce and a big cash deposit, he persuaded the guy at the desk to record but not charge the long-dead credit card he showed them.

He'd need more throwaway identities after this was over.

He chose a suite near the stairs and was finally settled in it at 8:15. An hour and a half before he had to leave so he'd arrive at Changes just as it opened, then four hours to find Sam.

Not much time, but all he was going to have.

Maybe it did happen later, maybe closer to three or even four, and he'd have that extra hour or two.

He shook his head. He wanted the extra time so badly that he kept circling back to it, but wanting it didn't make it real. Stick with the worst case. Let the good news surprise you.

He ordered the room service club sandwich, stretched until it came, and then wolfed down it and two bottles of water. As he ate, he studied the Changes site one last time and made sure he had memorized the routes to it and all the available interior detail. The data was far from perfect, but it was all he had.

He stood under a long hot shower and pushed everything out of his mind except what he had to do.

At 9:15, he loaded his jacket with everything he could from the package. The slots and clasps in the sleeves held the stakes and baton firmly.

At 9:40, he walked out of the front of the hotel.

Night owned the city now. The streets fought back with neon and crowds and cars and trolleys, but before it surrendered to the morning sun the night would claim victory, first in the suburbs, then in the rougher areas, and eventually even here, in the heart of the urban resistance.

Chan turned left and left again at the corner. About a mile to walk, twenty minutes to do it, plenty of time to check out the area around Changes before he entered it.

One more street to cross, then a turn at the next one, and the club would come into view down the road on his left. Chan's constant stride had carried him a step into that street when he noticed an alley ahead on his left.

If he were Matt and thought he was coming, he'd consider an ambush. No point in letting potential trouble into the club if you could help it.

He backed out of the street and slid to his left until he was in the shadow of an awning over a dark doorway.

He slowed his breathing, closed his eyes, and listened. Cars rolling past. A light breeze channeling through the streets. Settling sounds he couldn't identify.

Nothing from across the street.

That didn't mean anything, though; he was too far away to hear them if they were trying to keep quiet.

He'd have to move closer.

A car rolled down the street in front of him, the woman driving it talking on her mobile and gesturing with her other hand, the car apparently steering itself.

He crossed as it passed, using its sonic wake to cover any sounds he might make.

He slowed as he touched the sidewalk and moved slowly ahead. He was wasting precious time if no one was there, but he'd lose far more if he walked into an ambush unprepared.

He edged carefully along the wall and stopped a few inches from the opening to the alley.

He listened again.

Nothing for a few seconds. A murmur. Swallowing. A mumbled, "Thanks."

It could be some guys enjoying the night, but then they'd be unlikely to be so quiet. They might not have anything to do with him, might be muggers waiting for traffic. He could engage them, or he could try to cross down a block. He didn't mind fighting, even expected to have to fight before the night was over, but he didn't care about thieves plying their trade.

He backed slowly along the wall until he reached the corner, then walked down a block. He kept his pace slow. If the people in the alley were waiting for him, how would they have known he was coming this way? Had he failed to spot a tail?

Unlikely, but possible.

Matt would have figured he would come and known it had to be tonight. He might have put teams on all four approach vectors. If the ambushes worked, Matt won. If they failed, as long as the attackers weren't important to him, Matt won that way, too, because Chan lost time.

The other alley entrance would tell the story.

At the end of the block, Chan again edged to the alley opening, stopped, and listened.

This group was far less professional than the first one. Whispered conversation. Intake on a cigarette. A chuckle.

Decision time.

He could slip by them, or he could confront them. If he dealt with them, they'd alert Matt, but there was no down side in that; Matt knew he was coming. Of course, they might hurt him, but he doubted it. He knew the worst he could be facing; they did not. Plus, odds were good that if he didn't take them out now, he'd see them later. When he reached the club, Matt could call them as reinforcements.

Of course, if he was entirely wrong, if this alley was a neighborhood hangout area, then attacking them would be hurting innocents. If it was a target-rich zone for muggers, he'd be wasting time.

He'd give them a fair chance: Show himself, and let them move first.

He moved back around the corner of the building to prepare. He tied back his hair and rolled his neck and shoulders. He unclipped the holder on the baton in his right jacket sleeve, slid it into his hand, and slowly pulled it open. The lock engaged with a small metallic pop.

He crouched and waited. No way to know if anyone had heard the sound.

No one came.

He let down a purpleheart stake from his left sleeve. If they were human, it made a fine club.

He stood and zipped up his jacket for maximum protection. Its thin Kevlar lining would be little help against high-velocity bullets or direct thrusts with good blades, but every bit of protection was good.

He walked quietly to the edge of the alley, inhaled and focused himself, and stepped into a pool of shadows at its end. His boots hit the street loudly.

Three men swiveled as one to face him. All were tall, over six feet. The two on the sides were also big, guys who hit a gym regularly, while the middle one was weedy thin.

The one on the right was passing a butt to the one on the left but dropped it instantly when Chan appeared.

"Looking for me?" Chan said.

Recognition flared in the eyes of the one on the left.

"Run away," Chan said, "and I won't hurt you."

The guy on the left reached into his pocket. The man in the center backed up a step. The one on the right was better prepared and flicked open a knife, the sound distinctive in the sudden quiet.

That was enough evidence for Chan.

He rushed them, spreading his arms slightly and pulling them back as he covered the three yards to the men.

He swung the stake hard at the knees of the man on the left and felt the shock up to his shoulder as the wood connected with bone. The man was falling, his scream just beginning, as a half second later, Chan slammed the front of both knees of the guy on the right with the baton. The man dropped his knife as he fell.

Chan had expected to barrel into the one in the middle, but the guy leapt backward several feet as Chan straightened and stopped.

Too fast. The guy was too fast for human.

Chan backed up a step as the man smiled and bared his fangs. Cocky. Good.

The three men at the other end of the alley ran toward them, but the vamp held up his right hand, and they stopped.

Chan backed up another step, then another. The vamp watched him like a cat stalking a mouse retreating into a corner from which there was no escape.

Chan took one more step, then turned to his right and bolted around the corner. He glanced as he moved; the vamp was smiling.

The moment he was out of sight, Chan did a one-eighty and crouched.

The vamp rounded the corner a fraction of a second later, running faster than any Olympic sprinter.

Chan moved faster still as he jammed the stake up through the rib cage and into the heart of the vampire. Though the vampire was indeed very thin, he was moving fast enough that his momentum helped the stake pierce his heart and carried him and Chan to the ground.

Chan rolled away from the vampire as he dissolved into a small pile of fetid black dust. The humans whose knees he'd shattered were moaning and calling for help.

A deep male voice from down the alley called over their pleas, "Jimmy, stop playing with him."

Chan stood, doubled over as if hurt, and walked back to the entrance to the alley. "Jimmy's gone," he said. "Run away."

The three men stared at him. The one on the left bared his fangs and howled. "Jimmy was my friend," he said, "before and after the change."

Chan stayed bent; every little edge helped, even when he doubted he needed it. "Then he should have left me alone. You could still leave."

The vampire shook his head. "It was supposed to be quick. Now, it won't be."

Chan said nothing. He'd learned all that would matter in the next minute or two. Either Matt hadn't told them everything he knew about Chan, or Jimmy had been very stupid indeed.

The vampire nodded.

The other two ran toward him.

Good news: They moved at human speeds, so there was only the one remaining vampire.

Bad news: He was smarter than dead Jimmy. He hung back to see how Chan handled himself.

The two men on the ground were struggling to stand. Chan had hit only one knee of the man on the left, so unfortunately he might be able to make it to his feet. The other one couldn't find a way to do more than sit, so Chan had probably busted both of his knees.

Chan wanted to take out the other knee of the one who might get up, in case he decided to try to go for a weapon or help, but there was no time. He remained bent and considered backing around the corner, but he liked the clear view of all approaches that his current position gave him. Plus, they were unlikely to come as quickly into the same trap he'd used before.

He held his ground but extended his arms and weapons along his legs.

The two men spread so that they'd approach from his ten and two. Each pulled a knife as he ran, neither one big, blades maybe four inches long, but enough to do a lot of damage if they made contact.

Chan shifted two steps closer to the wall and put his back to it to cut their approach angles and to use the guys on the ground to slow them. He stepped forward, moved his right leg backward so it was against the wall, and tensed it.

Three yards out, the one on the right changed direction to avoid the fallen men.

Good. The two of them were now within a yard of each other.

Chan straightened partway as if preparing to fight the two men.

They stopped ten feet out and spread, one going into the street and one coming straight at him.

He glanced up the alley. The vampire hadn't moved and was watching them closely.

The one on the street stepped closer to him.

Chan pushed hard off the wall and launched himself at the guy in the street. As he moved, he swung the baton in a wide arc toward the man's shoulder. The guy managed to stab at Chan with his knife, but before he could finish the thrust, the baton smashed his shoulder and Chan was beside him. Chan wrapped his arm around the guy's throat and spun behind him.

The other guy yelled, a wordless cry of anger and frustration, raised his knife, and rushed forward. Chan pushed his captive into the attacker and followed the body shield forward. When the attacker stepped to his right to avoid his friend, Chan smashed him in the stomach with the edge of the purpleheart stake.

The guy doubled over.

Chan kicked the man in front of him, then turned and slammed his baton into the back of the man's knee.

The guy fell with a scream, screamed again as his injured knee hit the ground, and rolled onto his back.

Chan checked the vampire again. He still hadn't moved.

The man whose shoulder Chan had injured dropped his knife and held up his good arm. "No more," he said. "Please."

"Too late," Chan said. He stepped forward and swung the baton hard enough at the guy's knees that his feet went out from under him and he fell face-first onto the alley.

Chan moved into the center of the alley. He glanced at the four men on the ground. Each had at least one bad knee. The one he'd just hit was unconscious. They wouldn't bother him or anyone else for quite some time. He faced the vampire at the other end of the alley and never looked away from the guy's face as he worked. He shoved the baton closed, pushed it quickly into its slot in his sleeve, and snapped shut its clasp. He unsnapped the hold on the short sword on his right sleeve and caught its handle as the sword fell out of his sleeve.

The vampire strolled toward him. If he'd seen Chan change weapons, he gave no sign of having noticed the move. He smiled and spoke. "If my boss's insurance premiums go up because of what you did to those idiots, he's going to be pissed. He's no fun when he's angry."

"Last chance," Chan said. "Walk away."

The vampire laughed. "You're good—for a human—but you're not one of us. You're the one who should be running."

"Too bad you can't ask Jimmy how good I am," Chan said. He crouched as if bracing for an attack and focused hard on the center of the vampire's body; the guy would stop playing sometime very soon.

The vampire snarled, showed his fangs again, and darted forward.

Playtime was definitely over.

The vampire accelerated inhumanly rapidly and was two yards away from Chan within seconds.

When the vampire was a yard out, his outstretched fingers almost touching Chan, Chan leapt, also inhumanly fast, right over the guy's head. As he rose, Chan pivoted so he was facing the guy's back.

The vampire sputtered a quizzical "Wha—?" as he turned to come again at Chan.

Too late.

Chan swung the short sword as hard as he could at the vampire's neck. He aimed for the center of the throat but blew the angle and buried the sword deep into the intersection of the neck and the left shoulder. Chan let go of the sword as the vampire screamed and kept coming.

The vampire's shoulder slammed into Chan and knocked him back several yards and onto his back.

Chan rolled backwards and into a crouch.

The vampire screamed again and with his right arm pulled the sword out of his shoulder.

Chan charged and buried the stake into the vampire's chest. He missed the heart, but his momentum carried him into the vampire with enough force that the guy went down and Chan stumbled past him a step.

The cut was healing but the vampire's left arm was still useless, so he dropped the sword and reached for the stake in his chest.

Chan pivoted, grabbed the sword, and swung it hard enough to cut off the vampire's right hand.

The vampire screamed again. "What are you?" he said. His hand began to grow back.

Chan unclasped the hold on another stake in his left sleeve. He stood on the vampire's neck as he positioned the stake over the heart.

"I don't exactly know," Chan said, telling the vampire a truth he wouldn't live long enough to appreciate. He shoved the stake into the vampire's heart. As the vampire turned to dust, he added, "Not one of you."

Chan paused to bring his breathing under control and surveyed the alley. The four men were still down, two of them unconscious, the other two watching him. He gathered both stakes and the sword while he considered what to do with them. None of them looked to be in any shape to fight with him. If he left them, however, they might call for help from Matt. He couldn't have that.

He also had to assume that two more teams awaited him on a similar alley on the other side of the street from Changes. He could make his way around a few blocks and take out those teams, but that would consume even more of his increasingly short time. They wouldn't fight him in front of the club, but they might join Matt's men inside. He also had to admit the possibility that one of the other teams was enough better than these two that they could actually hurt him.

"Please," the man nearest to him said. The man held up his hands in surrender. "We're done."

Chan decided he needed to start searching the club more than he needed to further reduce the opposition.

He rifled the pockets of all four men and removed all the knives and mobile phones. The knives were all cheap crap, not a professional blade in the bunch, nothing worth taking. None of the men was smart or professional enough to carry a gun or even a baton. He threw the knives down the alley and smashed all of the phones except one.

Matt couldn't have believed these guys could stop him, so his goal must have been to use them to waste his time. They'd managed to do that, but not a lot of it.

Chan took the phone to the nearest conscious man and knelt beside him.

The guy pushed backward in fear.

"Call 9-1-1," Chan said. "Tell them where you are, that four of you are down. Say a big vampire attacked you but ran off when some strangers saw him bending over you. Stick to that story when they show up, or I'll find you again."

The guy nodded and reached for the phone.

Chan held onto it. "What did Matt tell you about me?"

The man pulled back his hand. "What Matt? We were just working this alley."

Chan laid the flat side of the sword across the man's neck. "One last time, and then I kill you and ask the next guy. What did Matt tell you about me?"

"Almost nothing! I swear!" The words came out as fast as the man could speak. "A big guy, six four, two-fifty, who might walk by the alley. Said you'd stop, we wouldn't have to make you. We're supposed to make sure you don't go anywhere else."

Chan nodded. "Anything more?"

The man shook his head. "No! That's all of it."

Chan handed him the phone. "Make the call."

When the man finished, Chan stood, smashed the phone under the heel of his right boot, and left.

He waited at the end of the alley nearest Changes until the sirens drew closer. He peeked around the corner at the front of the club. At least two dozen people stood in line, waiting their turn to do the necessary paperwork and enter. He turned right out of the alley and walked to the back of the line.

The people weren't what he'd expected. His only previous contacts with sex clubs had come through TV shows and movies, where all the attendees wore skimpy outfits and were beautiful actors and actresses. These men and couples—no single women—ranged in age from twenties to sixties and in size from bony to obese. Most fell on the older, heavier end of the spectrum.

An SFPD patrol car raced up the street and turned right into the alley.

Like everyone else, he leaned to his right, gawked at it, and then returned to waiting.

The night was brisk, so most of the people wore sweaters or coats. A few of the women wore high heels, and a few others carried them, but most were in comfortable shoes. Sneakers and casual leather shoes were the norm for the men. Ethnicity ran the gamut in classic San Francisco rainbow fashion. His own Hispanic/Asian/Caucasian coloring did not draw any particular attention. Nor did his long hair, which at six inches below his shoulder was still shorter than the hair of several other men in the line.

More people joined the queue behind him. Matt had to be happy with business.

Chan spotted two cameras monitoring the double-door entrance and another focused on the cashier windows.

Many of the people were obviously members; at the front of the line, they showed ID, got wristbands, and strolled straight inside. Three club staffers, each wearing black shirts with a neon green "Changes" in large Gothic type on both their fronts and backs, shunted newbies aside, handed them clipboards, and talked with them. When the newbies finished, they headed to one of the two available cashiers and paid their fees.

Flash back ten or twenty years, and the crowd would have been buying tickets for a show at the former movie theater. Go further back, and the performances had probably been live.

If anyone in line was a vampire, Chan couldn't tell from any external evidence, but that meant nothing.

When Chan was four people from the front, Matt appeared in the doorway, walked straight to him, and stuck out his hand.

"Diego Chan," he said, his smile broad and his fangs barely extended, "how nice to see you. What's it been: maybe five, six years?"

Matt looked exactly the same age as when Chan had last seen him, which of course he would, because he'd gone over right after that. Chan had tried to talk him out of it, but Matt had long before that time decided that the shot at immortality was more than worth the trade-offs.

Chan stared at Matt's hand until he dropped it.

"Does it have to be like that, Diego?" Matt said. His smile disappeared. "We go back, you and I. We were friends."

Chan stared into Matt's eyes. "Yeah, we were. No, it doesn't have to be that way. You know what I want, so let me have it, and we'll be done."

Matt smiled again. "I'd like to be able to say I don't know, but I do. There's just one problem: I have no idea where Sam is. He's been visiting frequently for a while now, usually right after he closed the restaurant, but when he didn't show last night, I knew Barbara would jump to the wrong conclusion and call you."

"So you set up those teams to waste my time?"

Matt's smile never wavered, but his pupils contracted. "I have no idea what you're talking about, Diego. All I know is what I said: Sam didn't appear last night, so I figured Barbara would blame me and contact you. As apparently she did."

"You always wanted us both to join you," Chan said. "Why'd you decide to force the issue now?"

Matt shook his head slowly. "Such prejudice. It's sad. Really, it is. One more time: I don't know why Sam didn't visit last night, or where he is now."

"So you won't mind if I come in and look around?"

"Not at all." Matt pulled several sheets of folded paper from the inside pocket of his deep navy jacket. "We are, of course, subject to a great many San Francisco regulations, so you'll have to sign the standard paperwork and pay the usual fifty-buck, single-male-visitor fee." Matt made a show of looking around. "Unless, of course, you've brought a female guest or"—Matt stared back at Chan's face—"you'd like to join as a permanent member."

Chan shook his head and took the papers.

One explained the rules. No is no. Use condoms. Don't masturbate onto anyone else. Blood games with vampires is acceptable but no turning on the premises, even if the human brought the proper paperwork. On and on the page-long list went, and though some of it baffled him, none of it applied to him.

Another detailed the fees. More irrelevant information.

A form that absolved Changes of all liability no matter what happened.

Another that required your real name and address, with a photocopy of your ID.

A privacy statement.

Chan signed all the forms, supplied his ID, and paid the fee.

The cashier clipped a bright red band on his left wrist. "You're all set," she said. "Have a great time!"

Matt chatted up the people in the line and occasionally handed out coupons for free drinks. He smiled and laughed and touched arms and clapped shoulders and was generally so social that Chan couldn't resist admiring the ease with which he worked with people. Chan would rather fight them all at once than do what Matt was doing.

When Chan opened the door to enter the club, Matt appeared in front of him and blocked his path.

"This isn't your kind of scene," Matt said. "I haven't seen you in years, but I'm sure of that. I can still give your money back."

"Sam's not here, right?" Chan said.

"Correct." Matt sighed. "As I told you."

"So why do you care if I go in?"

"I don't want you messing up my club, Diego." Matt lowered his voice. "This place is a money machine, and it's squeaky clean."

"If Sam's not here," Chan said, "then all I'll do is search the place."

"Fine," Matt said. For the first time, he looked concerned. "You and I used to be friends, and Sam and I still are. I know you're wasting your time. I'd rather you look for him somewhere you might find him."

"If you're so worried," Chan said, "you should be out searching, and you definitely shouldn't be wasting my time now." Chan shook his head at his own stupidity. With every action he took, Matt managed to delay him. Chan needed to stop playing along and get on with the job. "I've paid my fee and filled out the paperwork. Are you going to get out of my way, or are we going to get into it out here?"

Matt put his hand on Chan's arm. "You're more like us than them," he said. "What you're capable of. Hell, what you do." He paused until Chan met his gaze. "You always have been."

Chan shook his head. "No," he said, "not in any way that really matters. Never have been, never will be. Now, move."

For a second, Matt's eyes glittered and he parted his lips slightly. Then he sighed and stepped aside. "Knock yourself out."

Chan stepped inside.

Sound assaulted him, music that mixed a throbbing beat with moans and cries and occasionally something that might have been a word.

Everyone in the entry room paused, checked out Chan quickly, and then returned to their conversations. Chan moved to his right so he was out of the entry path, and stopped.

Matt followed.

The crowd again paused, stared, and resumed. A fresh meat ritual.

Chan stared at him.

Matt held up his hands and laughed. "Fine, fine. Whatever you want. I thought you might appreciate having someone show you around, but if you want to be on your own, go for it. Do what you need to do. If you want me, any of the staff should be able to find me. You can spot them by their shirts."

He left.

A clock over a bar to Chan's left read 11:55. He had some time, almost certainly around two hours, but that wasn't a lot. People stood around talking and drinking. Many were naked, others wore only underwear, and a few were still in street clothes. One bartender worked the human crowd from a fairly extensive wall stock. The other served the vampires; his drinks were all below the counter. Except for the nudity, the crowd looked and behaved no differently from the after-work gatherers at most bars in any big city.

Nothing to learn here.

Ahead of Chan were five ways out of the room: two that led up, two that went ahead into the main floor, and one with stairs to the basement. Red velvet curtains hung over each of them.

The basement was the most likely place, because it would have been the simplest, but Matt would know he'd think that. No, he'd start at the top and work to the bottom.

Fewer people blocked the entrance to the stairs on the right, so he headed up them. So narrow that his shoulders touched the walls on both sides, the stairwell was an ideal place for an ambush, so Chan was glad when he reached the top. He moved forward a few yards, flattened himself as much as he could against the side wall, and surveyed the area.

The floor plan he'd studied had depicted the place accurately.

The front two-thirds of this former balcony was entirely empty and afforded a clear view into everything on the main level. The center down there was a large open space where theater seats had once stood in rows. Now, each side boasted two rooms past the bar and many small clusters of furniture in the rest of the space. Each of those four rooms afforded onlookers a great view with windows that filled most of each of their audience-facing walls. In the one nearest the bar on each side, naked couples were kissing and petting and waving to those watching them. They were showing off at least as much as they were having sex. The other two rooms were set up for burial games, with four-foot-high enclosed dirt beds that in another setting would have been flowerbeds. One of those rooms stood empty. In the other, a short female vampire with a giant mane of wild black hair sucked delicately from the shoulder of a hairless man Chan's size who was kneeling in a hole in the dirt bed and staring up as if seeing heaven. A drop of blood ran down the man's chest to almost his nipple before the vampire noticed it and caught it on her fingertip.

Chan would have to check out both of those rooms after he finished up here.

All the groups of chairs and small tables that sat in haphazard fashion here and there in the large open area faced an old wooden stage at the end of the room. The only furniture not oriented forward was a sofa that faced the entrance from the bar. On it, a naked, pudgy man in his sixties sprawled nude for all to view. He stroked his cock and smiled at each woman who entered. For the short time Chan watched, no one encouraged the man, but no one seemed at all put off by him, either.

Four staffers in the club's black shirts leaned against walls and occasionally changed positions, their eyes always scanning the crowd.

Men and women in various stages of undress occupied about half the chairs on that level. On the stage, two women danced naked with one another, coming together to grind and to kiss, then backing away, facing the crowd, and gyrating. Half-hearted cheers rewarded their efforts now and again, but the dancers were lost in the motion and each other and never noticed.

A two-yard-wide balcony ahead of Chan led along the right-hand wall and down some steps to the stage. A similar balcony ran along the opposite wall.

To Chan's left and ahead of him stood a cluster of dark spaces lit here and there by dim yellow and red bulbs. He followed a hallway beside the stairway past a pair of restrooms and one guy in a Changes shirt to the frontmost room, a round space with a leather sofa wrapping the closed part of its perimeter. Two men sat on either side of a woman, each holding one exposed breast. One kissed her deeply and then turned her head so the other could follow suit. The center of the room was a pit filled with dirt and a mock headstone that read, "Coming soon."

The threesome glanced up at Chan. The woman raised her right hand and beckoned him to her.

Chan ignored her and stuck his hand into the pit. He hit bottom before the dirt hit his shoulder. Unlikely, but it pays to check, so he released the baton and dragged it through enough of the dirt that there was no way it was hiding a body. Satisfied, he replaced the baton and moved to the next room.

A heavyset woman kneeling in front of a seated older man gave him head while half a dozen men watched. All but two were stroking their cocks. The "Don't masturbate onto anyone else" rule now made a lot of sense. The room held no dirt, so Chan moved on.

The five other small upstairs areas also housed groups ranging from four to ten people, typically with two or three engaged in some kind of sex and the rest, usually the ubiquitous masturbating men, watching intently. None of the spaces held dirt.

Before he headed to the main floor, Chan even checked the two unisex restrooms, but each was only a tiny utilitarian space with a toilet, a sink, a paper towel dispenser, a wicker trash can, and a large box of condoms.

Chan headed down the left-wall balcony and onto the stage. It was reasonably deep, about twenty feet, and ended in an exposed brick wall. There was no backstage area. He checked above him, to where lights once would have hung, but all that remained was a lot of empty black-metal rigging.

Four women now shared the stage. He ignored them as he walked slowly along the back wall, thumping gently on the brick with the heavily calloused knuckles of his left hand. No hidden doorway.

Chan made his way to the room ahead of him that housed the raised dirt pit, the one where the vampire woman had been drinking from the large hairless man. As he rounded the corner of the room, he saw through the large window that the two of them were still there, though she was now sitting in a chair with the man curled at her feet. The onlookers had dispersed, the show over. Chan opened the door and entered the room.

The vampire smiled at him. "I'm full right now. Sorry."

Chan said nothing but kept an eye on her as he checked the dirt as he had the pit upstairs.

Her expression changed from sated to nervous as he poked around in the dirt.

That raised his hopes, but he found nothing.

As he wiped his sleeve clean, she crooked a finger at him. "We could always play later," she said.

He stepped toward the door.

"Come here," she said, "and I'll tell you just how much fun we could have."

Chan shook his head and took another step.

She looked down and whispered, so softly he barely heard her, "Sam."

He stopped, turned, and reached for her throat. "What—"

She grabbed his outstretched arm and yanked him toward her. "Like to play rough, do you?" As his head neared hers and his other arm grabbed her throat, she whispered, "They're watching. Act as if you're pulling back." She laughed and in a normal tone said, "Not as strong as you look." She licked his cheek and then his ear. She paused there and continued in a rushed whisper interrupted every few words by another lick, "Matt turned Sam and put him in the little park near the Hyatt across from the Ferry Building. There are three guards. Finish searching here so Matt doesn't know I spoke to you. Then go get Sam. I liked him. He didn't deserve this."

Chan turned his head so he could look her in the eyes. Her fear was clear.

"Too good to play with me?" she said. "Even after all that?" She pushed him away. "Fine. Go." Under her breath, she added, "Threaten me."

Chan nodded. He pushed on the wall to clear space between him and then grabbed her throat. "Don't ever touch me again," he said.

She smiled. "Whatever."

Chan walked out of the room and toward its counterpart on the other side of the big space. That one was empty, but he'd planned to check its dirt pit, so he maintained his route. He could leave now for that park and give himself more time there to handle the guards. If she was lying, however, he could end up spending so much time getting there and dealing with the guards that he'd miss Sam back here. On the other hand, if Sam was here, it would make no sense for her to encourage him to continue his search. She hadn't appeared to be lying, but vampires were notoriously good at deceit.

Quickly finishing the search here was as good a choice as he could make. If she was telling the truth, he'd waste a minimum amount of time, and he might give her a chance to get away from Matt and to safety. If she was lying and Sam was here, he had a chance to find him.

Chan headed back to the front of the main floor and from there to the stairs that ran along the right wall and down to the basement.

Where the main floor was high ceilings and spaces open for easy viewing, this level was a warren of small, dark rooms with limited access. He walked the perimeter first to get a sense of the area. Draped rooms barely large enough for two occupants lined the right, rear, and left walls. Most were open. He briefly pushed aside the drapes of those with occupants, most of whom were engaged in various kinds of sex and didn't let his interruption stop them. All of these rooms, like the hallways, had concrete floors.

A single wide room ran across the front portion of the basement. In its center stood a three-foot-tall faux stone altar made of wood and paint. It looked like it had started life as a giant wooden box, the sort of thing that might have held a piece of heavy machinery before someone turned it on its side, painted it so it resembled an ancient stone altar, and slapped a four-by-eight piece of three-quarter-inch plywood on top of it. A short, fat man was tied spread-eagle to four eyelets in the altar top, whose edges hung half a foot on each side over the base. Two women stood on either side of him and swatted him gently with small whips. Another dozen people ringed the altar and egged them on, urging them to hit him harder, to see what he could take. Matt stood in the far corner of the room watching the scene; three large male staffers filled the other corners.

Chan raised an eyebrow at Matt.

Matt shrugged.

Chan eased around the crowd and over to Matt. "What makes this worth your time?"

A large smacking sound caught Chan's attention. One of the women had switched to a heavier whip and was using it on the man's thighs. He grunted with obvious pain each time she hit him.

Matt leaned closer to Chan. "If anyone's going to get carried away and do something stupid, they're usually going to do it here. Those women are regulars; the guy's a newbie. He thinks he can take a lot, but he can't take what they can give him. The one with the big whip has a tendency to become . . . enthusiastic. We're down a few staffers tonight, so I'm helping make sure everyone exits gracefully when he says he's had enough."

Chan shook his head. "What a way to make money."

"It's a way to make a lot of money," Matt said.

"Enjoy your games. If Sam's here, I'll find him."

"I already told you," Matt said. "He's not."

Chan headed out of there to the rows of play spaces, four on a side, that formed the center of the basement. The corner rooms all offered dirt play areas. The rest held beds and slings and metal crosses and other stuff Chan didn't recognize, all of it on concrete floors. None of the corners was occupied, so Chan was able to search them quickly. He picked up his pace, time slipping away from him. The two staffers patrolling these spaces shook their heads as he poked the dirt holes but left him alone.

He found nothing.

The woman vampire had been right, and now he'd wasted more precious time. It was nearly one, so he had only an hour left, maybe two, but maybe even less.

He took the stairs two at a time to the main level and pushed his way through the crowded bar and out the main doors.

No cabs were in sight.

He pulled out his phone to look up the number of a cab company and order one, but before he could complete the search, a white and green taxi pulled to the curb in front of the club. Two men and a woman climbed out of the back seat.

As they were paying the cabbie, Chan cut in front of the two men who were about to get into the vehicle.

"I need this cab," he said.

"So do we," the nearer one said. He pointed at half a dozen other people who were waiting behind him. "And so do all those people."

Chan stepped between him and the car. "Not as much as I do." He pulled his money clip from his right front pants pocket and peeled off a bunch of twenties. "For your ride and theirs." He swung into the cab and flashed a hundred at the driver. "Ignore them. Take me to the garden behind the Hyatt across from the Ferry Building. Get me there as fast as you can, and this is yours."

The woman nodded and gunned the car forward. "What's so important there?"

Chan stared at the rearview mirror until she caught his eye.

"No problem," she said. "Do you mind if I play music?"

"Yes," he said.

She shrugged. "Your money, your ride."

He nodded, partly in agreement with her, partly by reflex, most of his attention directed inward. He would search for signs of recent digging. There should be guards, probably near the grave. Matt would have to make an appearance for Sam to finish, but until he did he would have men in place. He'd hate losing that control over the process, but it was the only way he could run the club as usual—and misdirect Chan with his presence there.

It had almost worked. If the vampire hadn't tipped him, Chan would still be there, growing ever more frantic because he'd searched everywhere there was any dirt at all, everywhere there even might be dirt.

Chan took a deep breath, closed his eyes, and rolled his neck on his shoulders.

The cab sped down the wide street toward the bay.

He'd be there soon enough. There was time. He might be cutting it close, but the tip had saved him. If the two teams in the alley were any indication at all of the quality of Matt's people, handling the guards would neither be much trouble nor take much time.

Matt's people.

Something about them bothered him.

He'd seen only two upstairs, another four on the main floor, two more walking the basement halls.

And three more, plus Matt, in that one room.

Four of them, a dozen onlookers watching two women whip a man tied to a raised wooden altar.

Raised.

Raised three feet off the ground.

With a four-by-eight plywood top.

A three-foot-deep, three-foot-wide, seven-foot-long container, plenty big enough to hold a shallow grave's worth of dirt.

And a body.

Damn.

"Take me back to Changes," Chan said, "as fast as you can."

"We're almost at the Hyatt."

He peeled off another hundred and handed it to her. "For this part of the trip. Another when we get back."

"Mister, are you okay?" she said. "I mean, I appreciate it, but if you're sick—"

He leaned forward and cut her off. "Drive! I'm fine, but I have to get back there. Now!"

"Okay," she said. "It's your money."

Chan clenched his fists and pounded them hard onto his thighs. Stupid. He'd bought the vampire's story. He'd bought Matt's safety explanation. Matt had played him perfectly.

He had to hope his original estimates were right and he still had time.

To focus himself, he visualized each step. Get there. Pay the cab. In the front door. To the stairs on the right. Down them. Back to the room. Deal with whatever he found there.

He couldn't see past that, because he didn't know what he'd find.

He didn't even know if he could take four of them in that small a space. Matt would close the area, and Chan would be alone in it with all four of them.

He'd have to figure it out.

The driver pushed the car faster through the streets.

He'd be there soon.

He hoped it would be soon enough.

He dropped the second hundred on the seat next to the cabbie and was out of the car before she could pick it up. He wanted to sprint for the door but made himself walk instead. Matt could have alerted his staff, so they'd be looking for any excuse to throw him out—any excuse that the other people in the club would buy. Matt wouldn't risk a scene in front of all those customers.

At the front door, Chan showed his wristband to the man by the door and said, "Forgot to say goodbye."

The guy made a show of inspecting the band but finally waved in Chan when the people behind him in line started to complain.

Chan headed for a group of three men and three women crowded in a corner, drinking and laughing. As he approached them, he pulled out his money clip. "Sorry to interrupt," he said, "but I could really use your help."

Their conversation stopped. They all stared at him as if he had pissed on their shoes.

He held up his money clip so they could easily see the thick wad of hundreds. "I've giving a friend of mine a special show in the basement," he said. "He loves an audience, and I want to make this great for him. Would you be willing to come watch?"

"Just watch?" the woman nearest him on his right said. In her incredibly tall, see-through heels she stood almost eye to eye with him. "We don't play outside our group."

Chan nodded. "Just watch." He cleared his throat. "Look, this is really important to me, so I'm willing to give a hundred each to the first dozen people who come with me. No obligation. I'm not soliciting anything. I just want an audience." He peeled off six of the bills. "That's it."

"Are you some kind of cop?" the woman said. "We don't need that shit here. We're not doing anything wrong. You're not going to entrap us."

Chan couldn't afford to invest more time. He stuffed the money in his pants and held up his hands. "No, I'm not," he said. "Forget the money if it bothers you. I want an audience. That's it."

The woman made eye contact with each of the others in turn and then shrugged. "Sure, we're game. If it turns out to be fun, you can buy us drinks later. If you're bullshitting us, though, we'll tell everyone we know about you, and you'll find this place a whole lot colder the next time you visit."

"Thanks," he said. He wasn't willing to spend more time finding others. Six would have to do. "Follow me."

He led them down the stairs into the basement and straight to the large room. Floor-to-ceiling faded black drapes had been pulled from each side to cover it completely. A CLOSED FOR CLEANING sign hung from the ties that held the two drapes together in the center. One of the men in a Changes shirt stood, arms crossed and legs spread, beside the sign. His eyes flickered in recognition when he saw Chan, but he otherwise did not react.

"I thought you said—" the tall woman said to Chan.

He cut her off. "It's invitation-only." He picked up speed, feinted toward the man, and then walked into the room in the gap between the left side of the drapes and the wall. "Come on in."

"You can't—" the staffer by the center of the drapes began.

Chan didn't hear the rest because he was inside, holding the curtain aside, yelling "Follow me," to the people with him, turning his head, and seeing in an instant—

—the painted plywood lid of the altar leaning against the far wall of the room—

—Matt standing beside the coffin and looking down into it, a gentle smile on his face—

—a hand pushing out of the dirt—

—two men in Changes shirts turning toward him—

Many things happened at once: Chan ran to Matt. Matt noticed him. The first of the onlookers burst in. The staffer from outside parted the curtains. The other two stepped toward Chan.

Chan grabbed Matt's shoulder and pulled the Do Not Turn order from his inside jacket pocket at the same time.

Matt opened his mouth to speak and raised his hand to hit Chan.

Chan leaned close enough to Matt's ear that he could whisper into it. "Don't," he said. "It's over. I have his instructions. They're legal. Let me do what I have to do, and nothing happens to your business."

"I could kill you," Matt whispered back.

Chan crooked his head at the people watching them from the corner. "In front of them?"

Matt lowered his hand and shook his head. "You don't know what you're taking away from him," he said.

"Yes," Chan said. His words caught for a second in his throat. "Yes, I do."

Three more people poked their heads around the opposite corner of the drapes. "Hey, what's going on?"

Matt glared at him for a second. "I hope you remember this for a very long time."

"I will," Chan said. "You know I will."

Matt nodded. "Sorry for all the drama here, folks," he said. "It's just part of the show."

A second hand pushed its way out of the dirt.

Chan released his grip and turned to face the crowd. "As it turns out," he said, "we're not quite ready here. Sorry."

"Whatever," the tall woman said. "You promised us drinks."

"They're on the house," Matt said. "Gentlemen," he motioned toward the two staffers who had crept closer to Chan, "please take these fine folks upstairs and make sure we comp them for the rest of the night."

"Are you coming with us?" the tall woman said, staring at Chan.

"No," he said, "but my friend here will join you." He clapped Matt on the back. "I need to finish up here."

Matt stared at Chan for a moment before he said to the man by the drapes, "Give him all the time he needs in here, and make sure no one disturbs him." He motioned to the other two staffers and walked toward the onlookers. "Shall we all go get those drinks?"

He held aside the corner drapes as all the people filed out. As he turned to follow the last one, he paused and looked back at Chan. "I was trying to help him."

"Not your choice," Chan said.

Matt shook his head. "You'll understand one day, and then you'll realize what you've done to him." He paused. "Don't come back here, Diego. Not ever."

Chan nodded. "I hope I won't need to."

Matt left.

The arms now extended from the dirt past the elbows. Chan stared at them for a moment and took a slow, deep breath.

No point in delaying this.

He undid the clasp holding one of the stakes in his sleeve, pulled it out, and put the piece of purpleheart through his belt. He grabbed the two elbows and pulled upward until Sam was sitting in front of him, his entire torso visible above the dirt. Sam was fully clothed. A red dish towel covered his friend's face.

Chan removed it.

Sam opened his eyes and immediately squeezed them shut. After a few seconds, he eased them open again, letting in the dim light slowly. He swiveled his head back and forth, his eyes wild, his jaw working but no words coming out.

Chan noticed a small cup of water on the left end of the edge of the altar and put it in Sam's hands.

Sam chugged the water.

Three seconds later, he grabbed his stomach, bent forward, and threw up the water onto the dirt in front of him. "Oh, God," Sam said. "That's not right. Why did that hurt so much?"

Chan shook his head and waited.

Sam scanned the room again, this time more slowly, and then focused on Chan. "So this it?" he said. "Matt turned me, and it worked? You see it, but until it happens to you..." His body trembled at the memory.

"Yeah."

"Where is he?"

"Gone," Chan said. "It's just us."

"I feel sick," Sam said. "Weak. Really weak. I thought they were strong."

"They are. You would be. You need to drink first, though."

Sam nodded. His eyes went to Chan's neck, as if he could see the pulsing of the blood right through the jacket's collar and Chan's long hair. When his eyes again met Chan's, his fangs had extended. "Would you let me?"

"No," Chan said. He held up the Do Not Turn statement that Matt had filed with the San Francisco authority four years earlier. "I'm here to respect your wishes."

Sam glanced at Chan's waist and saw the stake. "You mean, you're here to kill me."

Chan wouldn't let himself look away. "Yes. Matt turned you against your wishes, and I'm here to fix that. You always said you never wanted to live as one of them."

"I'm not so sure of that now."

"You went over and over this with me. You signed the statement. You made me take a copy. You made me promise I'd come if anyone ever turned you against your will." Chan put away the paper. "I'm here."

"I was dying," Sam said. "Now I'm not. That changes a lot."

"You knew you were dying for two months," Chan said. "You could have retracted the statement. You could have given Matt legal permission to change you. You didn't."

Sam shook his head. "I don't care about all of that. That's over. Now, I don't want to die." He grabbed Chan's left arm, his grip stronger than Chan had expected. "Now, I need to eat. You're my friend. Help me. I won't take much."

"Do you remember why you signed this statement?" Chan said. "Why you didn't want to live this way? Why you asked me to help? Why you told Barbara to contact me?"

"I don't care!" Sam said. "I don't care about you or about her or about any of that crap! I just need to eat! Help me, or get Matt. He's a real friend, not some drift-in, drift-out ghost from my past. He'll let me feed."

Chan nodded. He pushed off Sam's hand and stood. He extended his left arm. "Lean back," he said.

Sam extended his fangs fully. "I was wrong," he said. "I'm sorry. You are a true friend." Sam grabbed Chan's arm with his right hand to pull it closer.

"Yes," Chan said. "Yes, I am." He pulled on his jacket sleeve to expose the veins in his wrist.

Sam opened his mouth, Chan's left wrist only a few inches away.

With his right hand, moving as fast as he could, faster than even Sam knew he could, faster than Sam would have been able to move even if he had already fed and completed the change, Chan pulled the purpleheart stake from his belt and slammed it into Sam's chest.

The impact pushed Sam back onto the dirt. He screamed as he released Chan.

Chan used the heel of his left hand to slam the stake further into Sam.

He felt Sam's death shudder through the wood.

Sam turned to dust.

Chan stood in the dark room. The drapes rustled as the staffer on the other side of the curtain glanced in and then looked away. The music playing outside thrummed a steady beat he finally noticed again. He put the stake back up his sleeve. He bowed his head and closed his eyes, not sure what to say, what could matter now.

Sam was right on one point. He had been the friend who'd drifted in and out, visiting every few years, and then only when work brought him nearby. Through it all, though, Chan had always considered Sam his closest friend, one of the two people who'd known him as long as he'd known himself, since the day they'd met in the orphanage and Chan's memories had begun. Matt had been there, too, but Sam and Chan had agreed that when Matt had made the change, he'd given up their friendship in the process.

Chan walked out of the room, up the stairs, through the bar, and onto the street. He passed Matt, but they didn't make eye contact.

The club's lights flooded the street with enough illumination that Chan could see every face clearly in the orange-and-yellow-tinted glare, but he ignored them all. He stopped long enough to text a message to Barbara:

"Sam's gone."

He wanted to throw away the phone then, rip off his jacket, discard everything on him, and run, run just to be anywhere else. Instead, he forced himself to stay still. He thought of the man his friend had been, and then he added two more lines:

"He told me to thank you for sending me.

"His last words were that I should tell you he loved you."

Chan tucked his phone into his jacket and walked away from the club, away from his past, and into what remained of the night.

MARK L. VAN NAME has published four novels (*One Jump Ahead*, *Slanted Jack*, *Overthrowing Heaven*, and *Children No More*) as well as an omnibus collection of his first two books (*Jump Gate Twist*); edited or co-edited two previous anthologies (*Intersections: The Sycamore Hill Anthology* and *Transhuman*), and written many short stories. He is the CEO of a fact-based marketing and technology assessment firm, Principled Technologies, Inc., and has worked with computer technology for his entire professional career. He has published over a thousand articles in the computer trade press, as well as a broad assortment of essays and reviews. He has also created and performed three spoken-word shows: *Science Magic Sex*; *Wake Up Horny, Wake Up Angry*; and *Mr. Poor Choices*. For more information, visit his web site, www.marklvanname.com, or follow his blog, markvanname.blogspot.com.

His afterword:

Diego Chan and his world have been knocking around in my head for quite some time now. This story is their debut.

Like so many other urban fantasy settings, his world is one in which vampires and other creatures exist, but in it, as in ours, government regulations and political groups and all the other complicating factors of everyday life play important roles.

Diego is also a character who fascinates me, a man who makes his living in an unusual way and who lives a very different life from most of us.

The heart of this story, though, is none of that. In this tale, Diego has to deal in a very brutal way with the loss of a very close friend, a friend who ended up on a path Diego could not support. Many, probably most of us have had that experience, watching someone who mattered greatly to us turn down a road we would not follow. Saying a final goodbye, really writing off such a person, is incredibly hard—even when the act is not the extreme one that Diego has to take.

As time permits, I plan to write a series of books in which Diego discovers just what he is and, ultimately, why he is what he is.

BORN UNDER A BAD SIGN

CAITLIN KITTREDGE

Outside Lawrence, Kansas
1947

I am reborn in fire.

I am a fallen star, burning up, steam rising from my skin.

Naked under a night sky that unfurls endlessly, untainted by mountains or cities, I stay very still. Even then, I don't know what's really happened.

It takes me some time. After I sit up, draw my knees to my breasts, feel the frozen dirt under my flanks. See the twenty-foot circle my arrival has burned into the winter-dead cornfield. Watch stray snowflakes melt before they even get within a foot of my skin.

My bare skin. My flawless, new bare skin.

I manage to get up after a while. I'm sick and empty. My nerves burn and my bones ash and my skin gives off radiant heat that leaves a trail of black footprints branded into the mean, ice-crusted snow.

I look up. Up at the stars, Orion and Scorpio and Ursa Major spinning over the flat, featureless land all around. The stars are older than me. But not by much.

There's a road. A state route, paved and slick with black ice. I stay on the edge. I don't know the fragility of this new form, cooling like an ingot just from the furnace. I've lost everything. I am completely new. I could, for all I know, be completely human.

Fuck, I hope not.

I walk. There is no sound, nothing but the wind and the clouds and the crackling cold.

I'm cold.

I've never been cold before.

After a time, a truck comes. A rattlebone Ford, pitted with rust, driven by a man in a feed cap. He stares at me. I stare at him.

"Where do you think you're going?" he asks, finally.

I look down the road. It's a ribbon of ink across the dirty page of this place. I suppose it's as good a road as any. "Wherever you are," I said. His open mouth joins his stare.

"I'm headed for Topeka," he manages.

I walk around the truck. The engine shudders and rattles. The fan belt shrieks. I get in the passenger side. "Topeka sounds all right with me," I say.

He grinds the gears hard enough to bring out a little smoke. There's a variety program on the radio. A man is singing about a woman who did him wrong. I sympathize, even though I'm the woman.

The road rolls on. My savior watches the road. I watch him.

I see the sin on his soul, the burden and the stain. I see the young girls in diners and truck stops. I see their twisted faces and his nubby hands on their necks. I see the red knot at his center, the murderous impulse.

Maybe I'm not human yet. Not entirely.

I wrap the man's jacket around myself as we drive. He asks me questions. I don't answer.

I see his last girl, rolled in a tarp in the bed of this rusty truck, and left behind in a cornfield just like mine. I feel the hunting knife in the pocket of this jacket.

I watch him drive then, switching gears until I'm sure I've got it.

A sign whips by. A hundred fifty-two miles to Topeka.

I touch the edge of the knife.

I might be all right here on earth after all.

Eden, Kansas
Five years later

1.

Across the room, I watched my reflection in the mirror. I'd started the night with my hair rolled up and the nicer of my two decent dresses washed and pressed. My dress was on the floor by the wardrobe. My hair fell into my face, cutting dark lines across my vision.

The bare mattress rubbed against my bare stomach. The guy behind me—Ron or Sean, I couldn't remember—dug his fingers into my hip bones and pushed me against the edge of the mattress with each thrust.

It hurt, but not bad. I'd been hurt a lot worse. I'd started this life hurting, burning alive. And Ron or Sean didn't even want anything too special—a little shoving, ripping my underthings, fingers clawing runs in my stockings and popping the elastic on my garters while he'd held me down on the bed. He didn't have any particular sin on him, besides being drunk and horny. He was a country boy, passing through Eden on his way to somewhere better. Most of Maybelle's customers were just like him. Passing through.

He grunted. "Come on, baby." His rhythm increased. I tried to keep from rolling my eyes in the mirror. Ron or Sean wasn't going to win any prizes for longevity. I made some obliging noises, and tossed my head a little bit so my ruined curls waterfalled down my back.

Ron or Sean slumped against me, hot sour-mash breath on my neck, his chest pressed against my back. After a few heartbeats he straightened and pulled up his pants, buckling his cheap belt and fishing around on the floor for his cheap shirt. Doris had turned up her nose at Ron/Sean when he'd come in. He looked poor. He was poor. But he was also grateful, and the grateful ones paid you, every time.

"Damn, honey," he said. I rolled over and sat on the edge of my bed. My garter belt was the only thing still on me, but I put it back in place. Straightened my seams, and fished my hairpins out of the sheets.

"You ever come through Eden again, you come on back," I said. "You're a real nice guy."

Ron or Sean grinned at me. His teeth were crooked and brown. Arkansas farm boy's teeth. Ah, there it was. He didn't get dates with nice girls. Girls who cared if you looked like Cary Grant versus Robert Mitchum. "You just bet I will, babe," he said, and put a ten down on the dresser before he grabbed his hat and left.

I picked up the money and shoved it into the old sock that served as my safe deposit box, taking out four half dollars to give Maybelle her cut.

The arthritic grandfather clock down in the parlor was chiming two A.M. I got a robe and pulled my hair back any which way.

I was off the clock. I went downstairs to find a drink.

2.

Let me tell you a little secret about angels. Not all of us are good. Not even half of us. The word "angel" isn't even proper. It's Greek, a derivative of *angaros*, "messenger." "Harbinger" is a better word.

And we fall. We fall all the time. Seraphs are delicate creatures, and when sin enters them they can't sustain like a human. We fall. I did.

See, there isn't God in the angry-daddy-in-the-sky way humans understand. There is a Hell, of course. And a City. Where I lived, with the other seraphs. All that separates a seraph from a demon is a little bit of wickedness in their heart. A little bit of red, human blood beating in their veins.

There are spheres, but not in the elegant, impassable way you're imagining. The City and Hell and Earth are more like passengers crammed together on a railway car, overlapping, purses spilling into each other's laps, spare change rolling up the aisles.

So yeah, there are angels. Angels and demons and everything in between that has a bit of one bloodline or the other. And believe you me, some of the nastiest motherfuckers in this sphere come from angel blood.

Don't let it worry you. Chances are, you'll never meet or see one of us. Chances are.

There are a lot more than seven sins. Used to be, it took a lot for an angel to fall. It took an act of extreme cruelty, an act worthy of a human. Lucifer was real. I've looked into his eyes and touched his hand, to give me strength before battle. He was beautiful, because we were all beautiful. All shades and colors of it. Beauty is predatory camouflage. Because we're all predators, make no mistake. Lucifer was beautiful, a warrior and a thinker.

He still started a war. He still lost. And he still fell. Other than that, though, consider most of the holy books long, boring bedtime stories. Nothing is as clear-cut as all that Old Testament junk.

As the spheres weaken and the lines bleed, more and more of us fall. Some go straight through and end up in Hell, become demons or Nothingness, part of the howling void in between everything. More of us end up here on Earth, in shadow-bodies of ourselves, with shadow-wings and shadow-vision that lets us see sin, stripped of the majesty of the City.

We hurt and bleed and get hungry, need money like everyone else.

I could go on and on, about fallen angels and demons and my personal theory about the Great War, about how it tore something fundamental open between the spheres, the suffering of six million souls, the blood of two million more, Oppenheimer and his bomb. I could talk about my time in the City, and why I fell.

It's not important. Just remember: There are angels and demons and we walk among you.

We see you, even if you don't see us.

And God? Doesn't give a shit.

3.

I slept late, because that's what you do in a whorehouse—go to bed when you see the sun and wake up when it's mostly gone. At least in winter, in Kansas. By three P.M. the light was already long and slow, draining out of the world.

Of course, Maybelle's was a nice whorehouse. Better than the first rathole I'd worked at, in Topeka, where a man named Allendale ran the place, beat the whores, shot them up with dope, and generally made life a living hell. May didn't stand for any doping, and she didn't let johns beat us, unless they paid a whole hell of a lot.

Doc Pritchard was there when I came down. I hadn't bothered to put clothes on, beyond my cream silk robe. My makeup was all over my face, a map of last night. I got coffee and went to stand in line. Doc Pritchard came every few months and gave us penicillin, a glance down our throats, and the usual stuff. He took his pay in trade, off the books. He was a real doctor, better than the vet Allendale had called when a john beat a girl named Nadine half to death. Pritchard had a practice somewhere over toward Eden proper, and a respectable wife who had no idea that when he said he was treating poor farmers, he really meant whores.

He came other times, too, to set broken bones and to take care of the problems that came with working in a place like May's. Those calls cost extra. Doc Pritchard liked us to tell him he'd been bad.

"Don't you look a sight." Betty pulled a cigarette from behind her ear and gave it to me.

"Right back at you," I said. Betty was bottle red, from somewhere south of Kansas, and built like a house. She had the biggest tits of any human I'd ever laid eyes on. If a john paid for two, Betty and I usually took it. It was good money, and if he tried anything funny there would be one spare girl to scream. Theoretically.

"Snowing again," she said, and exhaled. Her hair was pinned up, waiting to fall down in soft curls that begged your fingers to run through them.

"Thrilling," I murmured. The snow was fat wet flakes, the kind that entombs houses and highways, cuts you off from every other living thing. If it kept up, there wouldn't be any business tonight. I might actually get some sleep, though I'd be down cash for the week.

"Elizabeth," Doc Pritchard called. "I'm ready for you. And put that out."

Betty smirked at me and sashayed into the parlor where Pritchard ran his exams, trailing smoke.

I felt the friction burns on my stomach from the night before. I couldn't get pregnant, but I could get hurt.

Most nights I tried not to think about it.

The kitchen was the end of the long main hall in May's shuddering seventy-year-old farmhouse, and I could hear a radio. Frankie, the big man she employed to keep johns in line and do some cooking and repairing, was moving around humming to himself. Cold draft wound around my ankles. May's house was tight as a two-dollar street hooker after Fleet Week.

But it was a place, and I'd done all right here. My looks weren't anything like Betty's. I was on the small side, dark-haired and pale-skinned. Something like I'd been back in the City. The shadow-body. I looked vulnerable. Some men like that. Some kinds of men, who aren't the kind a good girl would want to get mixed up with. Men where you can see the sin on them bright as a Klieg light, and twice as hot.

I smoked, and waited my turn, and listened to the radio. Somebody had killed a family over in Lawrence. Somebody else had won a baseball game against Kansas City.

And now, back to the music.

4.

I always liked walking in the snow. It was like walking in the sky, white and alone, except for your footprints.

Two thirds of a mile down the road, at a crossroads with the state highway, there was a filling station, and I went to get me a candy bar and Betty a magazine and both of us more cigarettes. Frankie would've gone, taken May's old Packard, but I liked the walk. Wrapped up in a coat and some boots that were too big, the flakes drifted onto me, and the blacktop. By dark, the snow would be deep. By midnight, it would cover the whole world, as far as the eye could see.

The filling station had a neon sign on a pole, a jackrabbit that ran in place all hours of the day and night. You could just see the sign from the attic of May's house. The station couldn't see us at all. Whores out of sight, whores out of mind. Or something like that.

The clerk never looked me in the eye when I bought things. The fact I paid was the only reason he let me in the place. He was what people called "God-fearing." He beat his wife and his daughter too, the sad hollow-eyed women who lived behind the station in the ramshackle little cottage with peeling paint the same color as the sky. He'd lost a son on Omaha Beach. I didn't feel particularly sorry for him.

He grunted when I put the chocolate and the *Parade* and the two packs of Lucky Strikes on the scarred counter.

"Supposed to be a foot and a half by morning," I said. I don't know why I bothered.

"You should give that up," he said, pushing the pack of smokes at me. "Nice girls don't smoke."

"Guess it's a good thing I'm not carrying that particular affliction," I said. "Niceness."

I don't know why I even opened my mouth. When I fell, the fight fell right out of me. I treated myself like a human. Fragile and fallible and human. I didn't pick fights. Fights meant pain, and I'd bled enough in my time.

"Whore," the attendant said. Like it was supposed to cut into my flesh.

"Good eye," I said. The bell rang happily when it released me back into the snow.

At the edge of the gravel lot, a car waited. I say waited because it crouched, engine running, cloud of vapor streaming from the tailpipe, gleaming chrome teeth and hardened black body ready to spring forward. Against the car waited a man, a tall thin shadow on the twilight snow.

"You sure are a long way from home," he said. His suit was black and his teeth were white, like the cigarette clamped between them.

I stopped before him, and cocked my hip. "Likewise."

The man in black unfolded himself from his car. The Buick purred on, even though no gasoline ran through its veins. Not that car. Never.

"You ditched the wings," the man in black said.

"You used to be taller," I shot back.

The man in black patted the Buick's flank. "Things change."

"I suppose they do," I said. "What are you doing in Kansas?"

The man in black dropped his cigarette into the snow, and walked out into the crossroads. The snow was everywhere now, and his dark eyes, all darkness, no white, were like coals. "Same thing I always am," he said. "You should go. Just keep walking."

I looked back toward May's. The paper bag tucked up under my arm got heavy. "Why do you care?"

"Because I'm not them, upstairs or down," the man in black said. "I don't have a dog in their fight. But there's bad blood coming down the road. Real bad blood." He turned on his heel. "Can you taste it?"

I turned my face into the wind, same as him. "That's not me any more."

"No." The man in black lit a fresh cigarette. "Suppose not." He came back, passed me, and stopped. His thumb ran down my jawbone. "Last chance, kid. Walk away."

I met those eyes, the black eyes that were older than any of the stars in the sky. "I've gone far enough."

The snow was already around my ankles, but I lifted up my feet and walked. Death stayed at the crossroads, watching me go.

5.

Betty smoked like she fucked—hard and straight ahead. "Shit. We aren't gonna get a single paying gentleman caller tonight."

"Do you have to talk like a sailor?" Doris sighed. She sighed like a schoolteacher. Probably had been one. She hated the rest of us enough to have had a better life a while back, and to still resent it being gone.

"I don't know. You have to be a dumb twat all the time?" Betty asked her.

I had the window seat. The girl in the window seat watched for cars and customers. I'd prettied up, put on a merry widow a traveling garment salesman had given me on his way through from Detroit to Fort Worth. He'd wanted me to lie still and pretend I was a virgin. Cry a little when he was done. I bit the inside of my own cheek to coax some tears.

Done my hair, painted up my lips red like flowers that wouldn't come until spring, made sure my seams were razor-straight, but I'd never been gladder for a dead night.

I didn't owe May any loyalty. She was a madam and she took her cut. She had a straight razor to make sure the girls didn't hold out.

I didn't owe Betty, even though she'd always treated me like her own. I should have walked.

Why the hell didn't I walk like the man in black said?

I still don't know the answer to that one. Another tip: angels don't have all the answers. Not even close.

6.

None of us saw the car pull up. The yard was empty and then it was there, in the dark, a darker spot of fenders and chrome and reflective glass against the twilight blue snow. An old Cadillac—rounded top, gleaming clean, long black hood shaped like a coffin.

Hands beat on the door, and Frankie stirred himself from the armchair by the fireplace. "All right, all right," he said. "Hold your horses."

All around the parlor, we fluttered and settled, smoothing down skirts, adjusting bosoms, straightening hair and seams. Customers were customers, and to come out in this weather they must be extra special grade-A horny. Some of us were making money tonight. Doris smirked at me while she pulled her robe further up her thighs. Betty stubbed out her cigarette, so the men coming in would have to light one for her.

Frankie's voice rose in the front hall, just a word or two. No, wait.

A wet snap echoed off May's high cobwebbed ceilings, like someone had stepped on a green sapling branch. A heavier, messier sound followed, the sound of two hundred and thirty pounds of ex-prizefighter limply hitting the front hall floor. The door slammed. May got out of her chair at the same time. Footsteps thudded toward the drawing room. I said, "May, don't," because I may just be a shadow-body now, but I still knew killing when I heard it. All four things happened at once.

Then, three men were in the drawing room, making the space too tight and hot and close. The one in front, the tallest but also the thinnest, held a big silver automatic down at his side. He told May, "Don't scream."

"Oh, my God," Betty said, matter of factly. The man's gun flew up like a dart. It was nickel-plated, a Colt army officer model.

"Shut your mouth, whore," he said. He put his eyes back on May. "This everyone in the house?"

"Yeah," said May without missing a beat. "You already met Frankie."

Doris let out a sob, hands over her mouth. The Colt came up again. "I said shut up!"

"There's no need for all this." May was talking low and fast, soothing as the carney fortune-teller she'd been in her young, pretty days. Bought the house with the profits. Opened a business for herself. "We're all friends here. Why don't you fellas sit down, have a few drinks? Everything on the house. You boys look like you need some R and R..."

The man turned the gun grip first and hit May across the mouth. She fell, on her side, hand on her jaw. Her teeth were dark and bloody as her lip peeled back. Fat tears grouped in her eyes but she didn't make a sound. The bruise was fat and square and it would linger for weeks. If they shot her, she'd be buried with it.

Everything went nuts then. Girls screamed, hands flying up like a cluster of doves to clasp mouths and eyes. The only one who didn't lose her wig was Betty, and she just sat like a stone, lips parted and eyes all pupil.

"Now let's try this again," the man said. "My name is Gil. This here is Buzz and Eddie. We're going to be waiting out the blizzard with you lovely ladies, and the lovelier you are, the less I'll have to do things like this."

His foot, black-booted, still wet with melted snow, went into May's gut. She let out a billowy wheeze, and curled into a ball. Still not a sound. May was tough as they came.

"You with me, ladies?" Gil asked the room at large. His eyes settled on Betty, the only one who hadn't fled to the far sofa, under the portrait of May's great-great-grandmother. "How about you, gorgeous?" He went to her and put the Colt under her chin, lifting her face until she couldn't help but look at him. "You want to love me?" Gil asked. The barrel traveled up, down, across her lips. "You want to suck on it?"

Betty started an allover tremble. Her eyes didn't blink. The pulse in her neck stuttered.

"Stop it." I didn't move, just let out two words. Not even strong words. I couldn't tell you where they came from, just that I'd had my fill of men bossing whores for the day.

Gil turned. He came to me. The barrel of the Colt was still warm from Betty's skin. "Why, darlin'? You want to suck it instead?"

He didn't have to force me to look up. I stared into his eyes. This close they were pale as driven snow, rimmed in red. Dead man's eyes, filmed over and days gone.

"How about it?" Gil pressed the barrel against my lips. My teeth scraped. I tasted blood.

I drew back. "Fuck you."

Gil grinned. "That's the idea." He backhanded me in the mouth, and the world went sideways.

His touch ignited something. It finished a circuit that I thought had died when I left the City. Like the big metal teeth that closed the circle on the electric chair up at Joliet. The cops who came in, the local boys from Eden, called it riding the lightning.

It was in me, under my skin. Making my muscles twitch, my

tongue swell. I was on the floor, staring up at Gil. My eyes were the eyes I'd possessed in the City. The switch had been flipped.

I saw what he was.

Here's the thing about demons—they were like us, once. The horns and the cloven feet of beasts, tails and claws, fire and brimstone... it's a bit of Church propaganda. Trust the Catholics to have that dramatic flair.

Real truth: demons look like you. They talk like you. They can steal into a dead body or a sinful one and make their hearts beat like yours.

But they aren't you. They're hollow, and inside is what crawls up out of Hell. They have black eyes and dead skin and teeth that can break your bones. And wings. Wings of smoke and hellfire, skeletons of what they lost in the City.

Gil jerked his head at Buzz. "Get her up."

I blinked as Buzz grabbed me. Gil and him both—the dead, mummified faces, the scent of smoke and the dry taste of ash in my mouth. Eddie, the quiet one, stayed the same.

I hadn't been able to see the demons among us since I fell, never mind mouth off to a pair of them. There wasn't time to celebrate now, either. Gil was pointing that Colt at each of us in turn.

"Anyone else feel like being chatty?"

Nobody did.

Gil came at me again. This time, he leaned down and put his lips against my ear. I smelled the heavy, almost floral scent of rotting skin and bone. Demon smell. All brimstone and death. "Now let's try this again. You know what I am?"

I nodded. Seemed stupid to do anything else.

"And I know what you are. You're a fly without wings." He turned away from me, to Eddie and Buzz. "Bring him in. Make it fast."

They disappeared, and Gil stuck close to me. "Haven't seen one of you in a while. Naples, 1893. You want to know what I did to her?"

Another fallen woman like me. I'd be surprised, except the night had pretty much killed my capacity to be shocked.

Hell, who was I kidding? My time on Earth had killed that, deader than Frankie's corpse in the hallway.

The door swung, letting in a little snow, and then Eddie and Buzz reappeared, holding a fourth man between them.

He was in a bad way, and from the noises the rest of the girls made I wasn't the only one who noticed. He wore a vest and a French linen shirt, a good-looking, square-jawed boy. The stain spreading across his midsection was black, shaped like a birthmark.

"Lay him down," Gil said. He leaned close again. "Now, little wingless girl . . . you're going to perform a laying on of hands. Fix up my boy here right as rain."

I met his eyes again, even though it hurt my head. I hadn't been able to see for so long that it was like a spotlight in my eyes. "I can't do that."

Gil pressed the Colt between my breasts. His other hand traveled up my thigh, thumb bearing down hard enough to bruise. "And why is that, little one?" His thumb brushed against the silk at the junction of my thigh.

I caught his wrist. "I'm not that kind of seraph." I couldn't heal and bring people into the light, even in the City. I was made for other things. Bloody things.

Gil *tsk*ed. "Too bad. You could have saved yourself."

I shook my head. "Nobody can. Not from something like you."

Gil winked at me. "A smart whore. Now I've seen everything." He turned his back on me. The gun was down. He had what he wanted—we were well and truly scared. Not liable to do anything rash, like save our lives.

Gil clapped his hands at May. "Bring us a bottle of something. We've had a long night."

He settled into a chair, as did Buzz. Eddie stayed against the wall, fingers tapping the faded paper in no particular rhythm.

I looked at the fourth man. He wasn't doing so hot. Pale, blue around the edges, and the blood at least a day old. Gut wounds bleed slowly, and give the bullet time to poison your insides. Even if I could do the trick Gil wanted, the wound wasn't his biggest problem. I'd seen the infection that raged like a fever through the trenches in France, and in every war before that. The fourth man was already dead, he just hadn't caught on yet.

If he died here, who knew what Gil would do?

It wasn't my place, I realized. Not my place at all. I didn't owe May and the girls anything. I should go before Gil decided to take me apart piece by piece, for fun.

Soon as I got the chance, I'd be gone.

And I wouldn't be feeling bad about it.

7.

After he'd drunk his way through two bottles of May's best whiskey, and grinned at us all the while, Gil parceled us out—he grabbed up Betty and Doris, and he shoved Eddie at me. Buzz got to watch the rest of us and the fourth man, who'd slipped into the kind of sleep that made his skin prickle with fever dreams.

Betty brushed the back of my hand while Gil herded us up the stairs. I caught her fingers in mine, twined them up and squeezed.

"Are we gonna be all right?" Betty whispered.

I couldn't lie to her, not right to her face, so I just made a nondescript noise.

"I'll fuck him," Betty whispered. "But I'm not gonna like it."

Eddie pulled me away and I went, even though my head was still swimmy from Gil's tap. I used to be a lot tougher. Time was, Gil would have burned up from touching me.

Eddie was hesitant, his hand barely circling my arm. I took him into my room. He stood with his arms loose, in the center of the carpet, staring at me. I sat on the bed, and didn't give him the luxury of turning my eyes toward my lap like a lady. "We might as well get this over with."

Eddie shoved a hand through his hair. "Christ," he said. "I don't want to force it." He was like me—dark hair and pale skin. Nothing like the big, barrel-chested, corn-fed body Gil was riding. Eddie wasn't from this flat frozen place. Just like me.

"You're not forcing it," I said. "You and your buddies have got guns. I don't."

"I don't kill women, miss," Eddie said, his brows drawing together, a narrow borderline of anger. "I don't hurt them, either."

I cocked an eyebrow. "Never?"

Eddie sighed, and sat down next to me. "Not unless I have to." The bed sagged under him. He was heavier than he looked.

"We'd better do something," I said. "Unless you want that ape Gil to beat the tar out of both of us."

"Fuck him," Eddie said darkly. "I told him I didn't want no part of this mess."

I shrugged out of my robe. "Where are you from? You sound... different."

"Chicago," Eddie said. "South side, born and raised."

"Irish boy?" I pushed out my chest a little. His eyes drifted down, and darkened. That was good. I needed him distracted. I tried not to think about downstairs, or next door, where Gil was with Betty. I needed to be gone by the time he finished.

Betty would be all right. I would be all right.

We were never meant to stay together. I didn't get friends and blood sisters. I got a gun shoved in my face and a quick rabbit before a demon ate me down to the bone.

"Eddie McHone." He stuck out his hand. I took it, and put it on my clavicle, over my heartbeat.

"Eddie, do you not like me?"

"It's not that..." Eddie said. Hand not moving, he leaned in. "I just signed on for one job, all right? I'm not a trigger man."

I put my hand on his cheek. "What are you, then?"

"I'm a wheelman," Eddie said. "I...there was trouble, back home. I came out to this backwater, and then Gil...it was only supposed to be one bank." His hand slipped down, squeezing my breast. He had rough hands, strong mechanic's hands. "You're really pretty," Eddie whispered.

"Tell me more," I whispered back, my hands finding his belt buckle while he sucked on my neck. "Tell me what a bad man you are."

Eddie drew back like I tasted rotten. "I didn't do nothing to those people. That was all Gil and Buzz. I told them that family wouldn't call the cops. I told them..." He drew back his lip. "You don't care, do you? You're just stringing me along so I won't try nothing."

"I'm trying not to get killed, Eddie," I said. "I imagine you're trying the same thing, and have been ever since things went south with your little crew."

He sighed and let go of me. "You seem like an all-right girl. I mean, I've fucked a lot of whores—no offense. Most of 'em are cold. But Gil ain't gonna leave no witnesses. We're headed for Texas, then Mexico. Until then..." He made his finger into a gun and pointed it at me. His mouth made a little puff of air when he pulled the trigger.

"We don't matter," I said, pulling him close again. Taking his mind away from the blood place, the death place. "We're just whores. Who'd believe us?"

"Right..." Eddie's hands drifted south of my tits, down my

waist and over my thighs. Stress and sleeplessness make some people crazy and some people horny. Some people both. Luckily, it was working on Eddie.

"You got anything to drink?" he mumbled, his lips and tongue grazing over the tops of my breasts.

"Sure, baby," I said. May didn't allow liquor in the rooms, but I had a bottle. We all had hidden things. Dope, booze, photographs of other lives. I reached into the bedside table, and handed it to him. Eddie took a long pull, another, and wiped his mouth with the back of his hand.

"Fucking farmer over in Lawrence shot Jake," he said. "The guy downstairs."

"I figured," I said.

"We weren't even doing anything. Just swapping out cars behind his barn. Unloaded buckshot all over creation. Jake..." Eddie sighed, drank again. "He ain't gonna make it. Gil won't find a doctor. Not even a vet to give him some dope for the pain."

"Don't think about that," I whispered. Eddie wasn't the kind of hard case Gil was—and human, besides, but he still wasn't going to let me waltz off. Not unless he got what he wanted.

I reached for the buttons on Eddie's fly. "What do you like?" I asked. He gave a little groan when my knuckles grazed him. He was hard already—Eddie might be all right. If he learned to keep his cool and give up feeling sorry for the folks that got in the way. He might live to be a real bastard, not just a pretend one.

"Just... your hand," he mumbled. His voice was thickening up from the cheap liquor. That was good. He closed his hand over mine, up and down, eyes closing and head falling back. I kept mine open.

After thirty seconds or so, Eddie gasped, and his eyes came open. "Your mouth," he slurred. "On your knees."

"Sure, baby," I said. I slid down to the floor, knobby old rug digging into my legs. Eddie grabbed me by the hair and put me where he wanted me. I started sucking him off, keeping my ears turned to the next room. Betty and Gil were in there. I could hear muffled cries, the steady, rhythmic thump of Betty's mattress. I tried not to imagine what was going on. What I couldn't do any more, but wanted to do very badly, to the demon in Gil's body. That would just get me shot and dying once had been enough.

Eddie pulled at my hair, shoving his cock deeper into my mouth. I worked at not gagging. It's a trade skill you develop. "Like that," he said hoarsely. I kept listening for Betty. Knowing she was alive when I left this goddamn deathtrap of a house would make it a lot easier.

She'd be all right. She was always all right, game for anything. The two of us was probably the only voluntary touch I'd given another person in the five years since I'd left the City. Her hair was soft and her mouth was softer, and I hadn't needed to pretend anything when we'd been together. "Quite an act," she said afterward, as we curled in her bed, still naked, counting the money a casino pit boss driving from Atlantic City to Las Vegas had tucked into her garter. "We should take it on the road."

Eddie came with a shout, yanking on my hair. Once he'd held me and made sure I'd swallowed him, eyes gleaming, I pulled my robe back around my shoulders. "I'm going to wash up." I could feel the dried blood on my lips, gathered at the corner of my mouth like a lipstick smudge.

I stood up, waiting for Eddie to stop me, but he didn't. His guard was down. I hadn't made trouble, and I'd been a good, generous little whore.

Out the door and down the hall. No noise. No one yelling to stop me. Just soft crying, from the room where Betty and Gil were behind closed doors.

In the bathroom, I pulled the chain and watched the single bulb swing back and forth. Light and shadow. Moonlight and night.

Outside the window, the snow had stopped. It was white, all around, far as I could see.

I tried the window. It was painted shut but it gave with some shoving. I was strong, as far as humans went.

Cold air sliced in, turning all my exposed skin to cooled marble. I looked down, past the slope of the porch to the ground.

Even if I could squeeze out the window, get down the roof without slipping and drop, it was too far. I'd end up in the snow with a broken leg and the demons would gather around me and laugh.

Why here? Demons hung around war zones and ghettos and plague pits. They didn't come to Eden, Kansas. Didn't ride in sleek black cars that looked like coffins.

Not that it mattered now. I fell. I was as good as human. And now it was time to listen to the man in black and walk away.

The door banged open, gouging a chunk of plaster from the wall, and bringing me back to Earth. Always back down to Earth.

Gil shoved Betty ahead of him. She stumbled and fell, leaving a streak of red across the white tile.

Grinning at me, Gil folded his arms. "You trying to fly away, little one?"

I took my hands off the sill. "Always. I never get very far."

Gil took a threadbare towel off the rack and threw it at Betty. "I like your friend. You get her cleaned up and ready for round two, and you just might get your wings after all."

He smiled at me. Not the body he was riding, just the demon. It was a smile full of howling nothingness, fired with bloodlust. Gil patted the Colt where it was shoved into his waistband. The top fly button was out of alignment.

"Then again, I always did like food on the wing," he said. "Five minutes. And stop her crying." He slammed the door and locked it from the outside with a skeleton key.

I knelt down next to Betty, folding my legs and putting her head in my lap. Her lip was cut. Her cheekbone was hamburger. Blood was all over her nightgown, trailing down her legs like stocking seams.

"Hey, doll," she slurred.

"Shit." I wet the towel and patted the blood off her face. "Shit, Betty. He did a number on you."

"He said I tasted like sin," she muttered. "What the fuck's he talking about, hon? What does he mean, you can fly?"

I felt Betty over, the instincts I didn't know I still had waking up. Her wrist was broken, and she was bleeding too much for me to stop. She needed Doc Pritchard. Battlefield wounds, I could dress and fix, but this was a beating, pure and simple.

The wind screamed against the glass and through the open window. The cold fell down all around us. I knew some things, things I'd been trying to tell myself weren't true, but I knew better. I'd been around too long not to know better.

Betty was going to die.

And Gil wasn't going to let any of us survive the night.

8.

Betty curled her chin down against her neck while I stroked her hair. She whimpered once, when I grazed a shallow cut at her temple. Gil must be wearing a ring.

"You never told me where you're from," she murmured. "You know everything about me. I know jack about you, honey."

"What's to know?" I said. "And I'll tell you, Betty. When this is over."

"My daddy was a preacher, did you know that?" Betty murmured. "He came out of the South. Way down near the delta. Had the thickest fire-and-brimstone accent you ever heard. Voice like thunderheads piling up over the Gulf. Said that the devil was in every man."

I brushed her hair back, and rolled the bloody towel to support her head. "He was probably right about that."

"Where are you going?" Betty said when I stood up and pulled one of the pins from my rolled-up hair. Eddie had yanked most of it down, and it hung in snarls at my neck. Like everything else in this little place I'd carved out in Eden. Tattered and used up.

"You stay put," I said, putting the pin in the lock. A purely human talent, like lying and pretending to think what johns said was funny.

"Don't leave me," Betty whimpered. I leaned down and touched her forehead.

"I'll be right back," I said, and opened the door.

In the hall, Betty's door was open. I could hear Gil humming to himself. He sounded happy. That was good. Happy was ignorant. He could keep on whistling Dixie right up until I snuffed him out and deported his skinny ass back to Hell.

Because that instinct was awake too. Once upon a time, I'd killed his kind.

And I'd been goddamn good at it.

I stayed away from the front stairs and went down the back, into the kitchen. Frankie's room was off the big drafty room, the old butler's pantry. I left the light off, finding the box under his cot by feel. It was wood, flat and long, covered in dust. I don't think Frankie had opened it since the day he came home from Europe after the war. He'd never needed to before.

Before, Eden had been a nice little town.

I fished a handful of shells out of the box, and pressed four into the Winchester's magazine. I shoved another handful into my brassiere. Then I opened the door.

I could say the demon had made me remember who I was, but I'd be lying. I hadn't forgotten. I just hadn't wanted to remember. Remembering it would make all of this—this house, the frozen world outside, my body, my trapped, aching self—all of it real. Fallen. Never going home. The shadow-body my real body, for however long something like me stayed alive.

That wouldn't be much longer if I didn't do something.

Buzz stood in the door of the living room, laughing as he brandished his pistol at Angie. Angie wasn't more than seventeen or eighteen. Running away from a father who messed with her and a mother who pretended Jesus would solve all of her problems.

I had to be fast. I wouldn't have more than thirty seconds or so to put down two demons.

Shit. I'd had worse odds in my time.

A few feet from Buzz, I stopped and racked the slide on the Winchester. I pulled it high and tight into my shoulder as Buzz turned around, needle-toothed mouth opening wordlessly. "You really thought I wouldn't?" I asked him, and squeezed the trigger before I got an answer.

The buckshot caught him high in the chest and threw him backwards, into the center of the carpet. Ruby red flowers on cheap white cotton, shredded and burnt at the edges of their petals.

Angie screamed. The guy on the settee opened his eyes.

The movements were second nature. Work the side. Watch the spent shell fall on the carpet with no sound. Press myself against the sliding doors of the front parlor, out of sight of the stairs. Wait. Wait for the demons to come to me.

My heart jackhammered and I could barely breathe. It wasn't fear, it was memory. I felt like I was picking up pieces of myself, gluing them back in place with every second Buzz inched closer to losing his grip on his borrowed sack of meat.

The wounded man watched me. His eyes were all white and shine. He was about the same color as the snow outside.

"You going to rat me out?" I asked.

He exhaled, and shut his eyes again. Humans know when Death is coming. We could learn a thing or two from them.

"Buzz!" A door slammed and Gil bellowed. "Buzz, what the hell is that noise..." His footsteps slowed. He saw the corpse.

Not that Buzz was dead. It takes more than a load of iron and black powder to get rid of a demon. But while they're riding a body, it'll give them something to think about.

"Fuck!" Gil shouted. "Which one of you did this? I'll put lead in every one of you fucking whores!"

I aimed for the small of his back, spine and kidneys drifting close to the surface under Gil's borrowed skin.

I didn't have anything to say to him.

The second shot seemed louder, and the parlor was starting to fill up with acrid blue smoke.

Gil went down in a tangle of legs, gristle and blood. I lowered the Winchester. Angie looked up at me, fist pressed to her mouth. Her eyes were wide and wet. I blinked. I was so fucking tired I could barely see. "Call the cops," I told Angie. "Do it now." For what May paid them, they'd be here in six heartbeats, even with the snow.

She bolted off the sofa, and I gestured to the rest of them. "Get out of here. Go lock yourselves in the office."

May stopped and gave Gil's body a kick in the crotch. "Fucking piece of hillbilly trash," she hissed.

Soon enough, it was just me and the demons and the dead man. Gil drew his lips back, black blood dribbling from his mouth. "You bitch," he slurred. "You're nothing now. You're nothing but a..."

I unloaded another shell into him, just to shut him up.

The demon in Gil was right. I couldn't kill him, not like I could in the City. I couldn't send him down through the spheres and back into Hell.

But I could hurt him, and it had been a long time since I'd made a demon hurt. My ears were roaring. My hand, though—my hand stayed steady. I was made to track and kill. It was in my blood. Even though I was just a human.

The Winchester in my hands wasn't heavy and my hard pulse wasn't from panic. I went over to Gil, bent down, and tugged the Colt out of his waistband. "This isn't yours any more."

He spat blood at me. "You got bigger problems now, little girl."

A small sound from the door, a click as a hammer dropped. "Put it down, baby," Eddie said. "You don't want to do that."

"Yeah," I said. "I think I do."

Eddie's pistol was a busted old .38 revolver, so little-used I could see rust. Humans put faith in the most broken things.

"I don't know what the hell you think you're doing," he said. "But you're not leaving me holding the bag for the bank job. Not for that family neither. I'm not a killer."

I lowered the shotgun and I took two more shells out of my bra. One, two, the vacuum-tube sound of buckshot slotting into its proper place. "Not yet," I said.

"Don't do it," Eddie warned me. "Don't you do it."

"Was any of that true?" I asked Eddie. "About Chicago and how you never killed anyone before?"

Eddie lifted one shoulder. "Some. Not all." He tilted his head, and gave me a smile and all at once, it wasn't a nice smile. Eddie hid his sin well, because it was so much a part of him it was woven right into his skin. I hadn't been wrong. He'd be all right.

"Are you going to be a good girl, doll?" he said. "Or do I have to teach you a lesson?"

I raised the Winchester again. "You know, I was good. For a long while." Eddie's fingers tightened around the pistol's grip.

"I think I'm through being good," I said, very quietly.

I pulled the trigger. Eddie was faster. The bullet caught me high in the chest, carving soft tissue and shattering bone. I fell, not gracefully, but in fragments. I wobbled, and my legs went, and then I was on my side. I could feel blood. The pain made me warm, my skin vibrate, except where blood touched.

Gil laughed at me. We were eye to eye, the demon and me, and he was smiling. "So much for salvation, little girl. Damnation's much more fun anyway."

Eddie came over and kicked the Winchester away from me. "You were really going to shoot me, weren't you?" He crouched down and smiled. "Imagine that." He turned his eyes on Gil. "Where's the take?"

Gil's lip drew back. "Go piss up a rope."

"You've got about five more minutes with that load of lead in you, fella," Eddie told him. "Five minutes you could spend comfortable..." He leaned down and put a finger in Gil's wounds. The demon screamed. Tethered to a body as it was, it could still feel pain. "Or, you know," Eddie said, wiping the blood on his pants leg. "That."

"Fuck you," Gil snarled. "I was gonna put one in your head when we got to Mexico, you little pissant. You're not getting shit."

Eddie shifted his weight. "Buzz? How's your chest there, buddy?"

Buzz coughed up a bit of what was left in his veins. "The wheel well. In the car. Wrapped in plastic."

Eddie tapped him on the nose with the revolver. "Smart, kid. And I'll think of you, when I'm sitting on the beach with sand in my trunks and a smile on my face."

He stuck the revolver in his waistband, took the car key from Buzz, and stood up. He nudged me with his foot. "And you, doll. If you don't die, look me up sometime."

I lifted the Colt I'd dropped when I took it from Gil. The Colt was heavy. "I died once already," I told him. "It's not as bad as you'd think."

I shot Eddie. I shot him three times, in the chest. And I didn't feel the least bit bad about it.

9.

I drifted. The old part of me, the part that had seen other seraphs bleed and die, knew that I wasn't going to last long. I was bleeding, and my shadow-body would die. Where would I go then? Down with Gil? Into the Nothingness, to be torn apart and remade for the rest of eternity? Neither possibility thrilled me.

Gil stood grinning over me. His body was falling apart, and his demon face was showing. "Looks like I'm walking away."

I watched him smile at me, and I couldn't do a damn thing about it.

"You know, I should have asked you how you fell," Gil said. "Always enjoy those stories." He grinned. "But seeing as how you're a whore, I guess it's not a mystery."

I returned the smile. "Tell the truth...I never really knew."

"Never?" Gil laughed, barked it. His chest made a sucking sound. He was old, and strong. He'd find another body before this one gave out. Keep going. More Bettys, on bathroom floors.

I thought of what I felt when he touched me. I thought of lying naked on the Earth, the night I fell.

I looked up, and thought of the stars.

Gil hissed at me. "The hell are you doing?"

I reached out, and up, and snatched him by the hand. "I'm not walking out of here," I said. "And neither are you."

There are doorways, if you know where to find them. Passage-
ways between the spheres, between the City and Hell and here,
where I lay bleeding to death on a threadbare rug, in a drafty
farmhouse, in a tiny pinpoint of light at the crossroads of two
highways. There are exits and entries, and you can find them
all sorts of ways. You find them by dying, or by living. Seraphs
know the way, know it from birth, to pass through the spheres
and send demons back to Hell.

I'd forgotten, but the demon had shown me. He'd shown me
that I wasn't really dead, not yet. That the blood that made me
human also made me something else, not seraph and not demon,
but not just meat either.

I held on to Gil and the feeling of the doorway. I was close,
standing on the edge of the whirlpool, but I didn't let go of the
demon. I peeled back the layers of its blood and bone, got down
to the core of the thing.

And I let go.

Gil got out one sound, just a half a scream, before he lost his
grip and Hell took him back. His stolen body had been dead for
a long time, old injuries running like railroad tracks across its
skin. Buzz was gone, not nearly as strong as his buddy. Eddie lay
with his eyes open, like he was waiting for someone to tell him
it was all right to go to sleep.

After a time, the man in black appeared. He looked at Buzz
and Gil, Eddie and the man on the sofa. "I did tell you to leave,"
he said.

"I've never been very good at taking advice," I told him. He
smiled, and knelt beside me.

"What I like about you."

"I guess this is where you make some big speech," I said. "About
how it's not so bad. Dying."

The man in black smoothed my hair back, and then he leaned
down and pressed his lips to my forehead. "I'm not here for you,"
he whispered. "Not tonight."

He lifted my hand to his cheek. I left a bloody fingerprint on
his jawline. "I do miss you," he said. "It's a lonely road. A dark
road, filled up with souls, but nobody like you."

My fingers were numb, or maybe it was just the man in black's
skin, cold as the dead of winter. "I'm here," I whispered. "I'm
here..."

"Yeah," the man in black said. He brushed his lips against mine, and then gently lowered me back to the floor and stood up. "I'll see you again," he said. "Not soon, but some day."

I raised my head a few inches. The bullet still hurt, but I could feel the whirlpool draining away. This sphere wasn't done with me, not yet. "You know," I said to the man in black. "You don't have to wait until then."

He nodded, the faintest ghost of a smile wrinkling that hard, perfect face. "I think I'd like that."

Breathing still hurt, but I tried to keep it slow and steady. "There's a girl upstairs. Betty. Are you..."

He shook his head. "Not tonight." He went into the hallway, and then raised one finger. "By the way," he said. "What's your name here?"

"Samantha," I said. "Call me Sam."

The man in black nodded. "See you around, Sam."

The door opened, the wind and the snow came in, and the man in black left with what he came for.

10.

Betty and I stood at the bus stop on the side of the highway, a little bend in the road carved out of the frozen fields. The cold cut through my thin coat and boots, and I smoked just to keep warm.

"Where are you headed?" Betty asked me. Her face was still blue and bruised across the cheek and jaw on one side, and her wrist was in a sling. Doc Pritchard got there in time to take care of her internal injuries. I'd let him work out his payment with May. I was already packing my things.

"I don't know," I said. I really didn't. I never had, and it had worked out with varying degrees. There was the body I'd left by the side of the highway outside Topeka. The bodies I'd left at May's.

Betty had cried at night for weeks afterward, long shuddering sobs, her whole body shaking with remembered pain. I'd crawl out of my own narrow cot in Doc Pritchard's back office and curl up next to her, petting her hair until she went back to sleep.

"I'm going home," she said, putting out her cigarette in the snowbank on the side of the highway. "No goddamn snow in Louisiana, that's a fact."

"Amen," I said.

"You know, I never thanked you," Betty said. "May and Angie told me it was you got that ape off of me. Glad every last one of 'em is roasting in Hell." She lit a fresh smoke with a crisp snap of a lighter. "Good riddance."

"Good," I agreed. "You don't have to thank me, Betty."

She reached out and squeezed my hand. "I know," she said. "I know you were my only friend in that place, Sam. I never thought you really gave a good damn about any of it, but you did a terrible thing for me. I ain't gonna just let that roll on by."

I looked down the road. The silvery hulk of the Greyhound bus was approaching, chrome glinting in the sun. I could go on and find another whorehouse, or another bar, another place to be anonymously human. But I'd never forget that night in May's farmhouse. Memories were indelible in my shadow-body's mind. The centuries no longer bled together like a ruined painting.

I pulled Betty close, by the nape of her neck, before the bus got any closer. I brushed her lips, just the slightest touch, light and dry like a summer wind. She smelled like gardenias and tobacco. She was blushing when I stepped away.

"I'd do it again," I said. "It's my nature." That much, I knew, was true. I wasn't a seraph. I wasn't a human. I was fallen, but I had plenty of time to figure out what that meant, if I could do things like I'd done to Gil again, if the man in black had passed me by because there was something else here in this mean, bloody, earthbound little place that I had to do.

The bus rolled to a stop, steam ripping a hole in the freezing air. The placard in the windscreen said LOS ANGELES.

Betty waved goodbye at me once I'd gotten a seat and the driver had started us rolling again. I waved back.

"Next stop, Junction City," the driver hollered. "Final destination, Los Angeles, California."

I leaned my head back against the vinyl seat, and let the rumble of the engine lift me out of Kansas, out of myself, and into a place where I could float and think.

Los Angeles.

The City of Angels.

That sounded all right for now.

CAITLIN KITTREDGE writes adult and young adult novels about such varied topics as werewolves, demons, British mages, superheroes, and steampunk. She collects comic books, does pinup modeling and photography in her copious spare time, has partially purple hair, and lives in a real-live crumbling Victorian manor. Find her blog and other eldritch horrors at www.caitlinkittredge.com.

When I asked her for a few words about this story, she provided the following:

I was raised a Unitarian, so the fire-and-brimstone version of Heaven and Hell was, in my youth, a story for other people. I've used all sorts of mythology in my novels: Irish, Russian, Japanese, and even the Lovecraft mythos have made appearances. But I never really forgot paging through my mother's theology textbooks when she was in grad school and marveling at the complex myth base of the Judeo-Christian faith. So when I had a chance to write something new, something unconnected to any of my series, I thought "fallen angels." And naturally, you can't have fallen angels without some demons, something I was accustomed to using in my fiction. As you can see in "Born Under a Bad Sign," Sam's version of Heaven and Hell isn't exactly like the Biblical stories, either. But all stories are interpretation, so for my purposes, Sam's version is the right one. As for putting my heroine in a brothel—postwar America was a very different place, and a single woman with no past had very few options. I'm a huge noir buff, and I wanted a fallen angel, who, let's face it, is the ultimate noir-style protagonist, in a situation that could easily have unfolded in a B picture, circa 1947. Falling from grace isn't just for crooked cops and nasty gangsters, and Sam's story fit perfectly into the noir mode.

ACKNOWLEDGMENTS

David Drake provided his usual invaluable guidance to this still-learning editor.

My business partner, Bill Catchings, has as always both done all he could to encourage and support my writing and been a great colleague for over twenty-five years—even though this book will almost certainly not be to his taste.

Elizabeth Barnes fought (and continues to fight) to tame the library portions of my home office, an effort that helps me calm myself for the work.

As always, I am grateful to my children, Sarah and Scott, who continue to be amazing and wonderful people despite having the Weird Dad and needing to put up with me regularly disappearing into my office for long periods of time. Thanks, kids.

Several extraordinary women—my wife, Rana Van Name; Allyn Vogel; Jennie Faries; and Gina Massel-Castater—as ever grace my life with their intelligence and support, and I remain surprised and thankful that they do.

Thank you, all.